Moon Over The Manukau

BOOK ONE OF

WIND FROM THE WEST

CLARK JAMES

Other publications by Clark James

Wind From The West series

Book Two — *Neap Tide*
Book Three — *Storm & Stress*
Book Four — *Waves On The Waitemata*
Book Five — *Spring Tide*
Book Six — *Setting of the Sun*

Fish Chips and Rachmaninoff

The political/environmental novel: *Plantation.*

Ebook version of Plantation: *Earth's Revenge*

Ebooks only: *The Consequence*
The Castaway Hat
How to Fix a Sick Planet

In collaboration with Rewa Walia:
Laxmi – The Odyssey of a Dancer

Cover design; Clark James

Moon Over The Manukau Copyright Clark James 2009

ISBN: 9781877245091

PREFACE

Moon Over The Manukau commences with the rural engagement of Ben Chester and Priscilla Caldwell on New Year's eve 1900. Simple as the engagement is it will lead to a saga of love and compassion, industry and pleasure and above all, generosity. As the story expands so the characters move from the valley into the wide world, yet they always return to the valley home of Kowhai, particularly for celebrations.

For those unfamiliar with Auckland: the original town was originally sited on an isthmus, with the Waitemata Harbour and main port to the north, and the shallow Manukau Harbour to the south. Between this harbour and the west coast is a strip of land known as the Awhitu Peninsula. Pollok is half way along the peninsula, and the valley farm with the fictional name of Kowhai — a native tree with bell-shaped flowers during September — between Pollok and the coast.

Imperial measurements are used until the date of change to metric, therefore there are conversion charts at the beginning of each book. Each Book has a character list.

While characters are fictional, many of the events are real: such as the opening of His Majesty's Theatre, the grounding of the *Reliance,* the strikes and Auckland Exhibition of 1913, and the Great War (WWI) goes without saying.

The novel was originally written in 1962-64, revised and expanded into six volumes, and the six novels published as paperbacks between 2006 and 2010. This condensed version for Createspace retains all the essential ingredients of the story.

Clark James

MOON OVER THE MANUKAU

CHARACTERS

Ages: Jan, 1900

Thomas and Louise Chester, 50s	Farmers at Pollok on the Awhitu Peninsula, west of the Manukau.
Jane, 23; Ben, 21; Alison, 17	Their children.
Maude Caldwell	Widow of Waiuku
Nigel, 25: Emily, 22; Priscilla, 20	Her children.
Jessica Caldwell, 22	Married to Nigel
William Todd; late 40s	Emily's philandering, well-to-do, business husband
Danny Carsen (24)	Local ne'r-do-well
Mrs Carsen	His acrimonious widowed mother
Alison Mackenzie	Young widow whom Ben and Danny buy sheep from
Annabelle	Maori friend of Alison
Sean Sullivan	Shipwrecked sailor

CONVERSION CHART

One guinea = one pound, one shilling = two dollars
ten cents

One sovereign = one pound = two dollars
One shilling   =   ten cents
Sixpence   =   five cents
Three pence (thrupence)two and a half cents
One penny   =   slightly less than a cent
Halfpenny   =   less than half a cent.
Farthing   =   less than quarter of
a cent

One mile   =   approx 1.6 kms.
One furlong   =   approx 200 m
One yard   =   approx 900mm
One foot   =   approx 300mm

One Gallon   =   four and a half litres
One Pint   =   over half a litre

CHAPTER ONE

Midnight, 1900

A zephyr ushered in the new century. It tussled Priscilla's hair as
Ben drew her from the celebrations: clomping down the front steps
of the valley homestead, and hurrying her along a shell path. From
the time of her arrival earlier that day Ben had humoured her. In
the festive spirit of the occasion she had gone along with his
humour: his little suggestions in her ear at the most inappropriate
times, making her blush, and playfully push him away. Now his hand
clasped hers tighter, he striding purposefully, she tripping gaily
beside him, wondering where he was leading her . . .

. . . Only as far as the wooden bridge, where he stopped, turned
to her, a glimmer of light reflecting on his serious face, lifted her on
to the railing as he would a fragile earthen vase, then, with the
accompaniment of the stream, he proposed reverently, "Prissy —
will you — will you — marry me?"

He may have been jesting and joking all day, however he was *not*
joking now. She leaned back, lightly biting her lip, he clasping her
tighter lest she fall. In response she first shook her head slowly,
unbelievingly, then nodded.

"Well?" he asked, confused.

Her mouth opened slightly in wonder and she asked herself, 'I
did hear right?' Ben had not given the slightest hint of this proposal.
'It isn't that we had discussed it. I was ever hopeful,' she admitted.
Accepting now she had heard right she slowly leaned forward
clasped him around the neck, slid from the railing and while still in
his embrace, choking with emotion, replied, "Yes, Ben. — Yes. — Of
course I will."

She *had* often thought of such a moment. 'I never pictured it
being in the middle of a New Year's party.' Turning her head to one
side, resting it on Ben's chest, she sought the boundaries of the

valley farm, however the night was black; made blacker by the many oil lanterns glowing behind them, some hanging in trees.

"Shall we go back and tell them?" Ben suggested, while still holding her.

"Tell them what?" Fanciful notions of the farm mingling with his proposal.

"Prissy, silly. That we are going to marry."

"Oh. — Oh." She shook her head to return to reality. "Of course."

They returned to the new century celebration.

Reluctantly, fearing a severe telling off for his lack of protocol, Ben took Priscilla's widowed mother aside and told her.

"I see," Maude Caldwell responded. "It's her life." Her mouth closed firmly, emphasising her ill-fitting false teeth. She fidgeted, then stated, "She could have done well for herself in town, you know." She expelled her breath with disgruntled sigh, and changing her tone to cautionary, she advised, "And don't you ever forget it, Ben Chester."

He grimaced. "No, I shan't." He had his thoughts on *that* subject, particularly concerning Priscilla's elder sister, Emily. She had apparently 'done well for herself in town'. There were two towns to be considered. The nearest to Kowhai was Waiuku: two hours ride away — on a fine day — where the Caldwells' lived. Town, real town, was the rapidly expanding city of Auckland. It was there Emily had supposedly 'done well for herself'.

Whatever Maude's view of her future son-in-law, the self-appointed band struck up with a disharmonious fanfare, drowning any noise she made about it, they having been informed by Ben's father of a pending announcement. They probably thought it concerned the discovery of another jar or two of beer. Priscilla watched for reaction as Thomas Chester put his weathered hands on the shoulders of his son and herself and broadcast the news in an authoritative voice, although by dress code he looked the least authoritative male present. His biggest chore of the day had *not* been farming, but having to change into his best clothes for the celebration.

However, it was his announcement that captured the gathering's attention. Few showed surprise. Those from Ben's two sisters were as divided now as they were on everything else. One clapped her hands with glee, and, before being enclosed in her embrace, Priscilla glimpsed the other daughter shrug and turn her head away, as if something more important had attracted her attention.

For the evening they had rearranged the large homestead; some of the lounge furniture evicted either to the central foyer, or to the veranda, leaving sufficient space for the band and several couples to negotiate a reel, or a few more to waltz. Food was spread on the large dining room table: this room on the opposite side of the foyer to the lounge. Most of the fifty or sixty family and guests had been herded into the lounge for the mid-night celebration, and as if the announcement was of no surprise the males wiggled their moustaches and returned to their assorted seats, or stood over their partners.

During the early hours the party unwound, many guests staying at Kowhai, some sleeping more or less where they fell. Priscilla shared a lantern-lit attic-styled bedroom with the sister who was so joyous over the announcement. She changed into an unflattering nightdress, hunched her shoulders, sat up in bed, and with expectant eyes, asked, "Tell me Ben's secrets?"

"Secrets?" Alison questioned, more cosily nestled between sheets, her head propped up by a hand. "You mean what he's been up to, and with whom?"

"On second thoughts, Ali, I'd rather not know."

"Actually, Prissy, he hasn't got any." She grimaced while weighing up what she knew about her brother. "To tell you the truth, Kowhai's been his life — until you came along."

"Oh!"

"You sound disappointed."

Priscilla hunched her shoulders again. "I suppose I expected him to — you know what."

"Prissy," Alison declared matter-of-factly, "I don't think my dearest brother has as much as kissed a girl behind the barn, let alone anything else." She watched embarrassment colour Priscilla's cheeks as she snuggled deeper into her bed. "I think I've got up to more than him," she admitted.

"Ali, you haven't?"

"I've been kissed behind the barn." She gave a chuckle, and thought Priscilla and her brother would make a great pair: each as naïve as the other.

Anyone prying into the bedroom could well imagine the two conspiring girls were indeed sisters: not so much by their looks, rather their nature and their obvious liking for each other as when they had earlier harmoniously baked together. On the other hand, Alison and her sister Jane were chalk and cheese in every respect, and Jane may well have passed for the daughter of Maude Caldwell.

Priscilla lay awake, imagining living in this large homestead. She assumed they would live there, since apart from the flat area of the valley farm most of the surrounding hills were in bush, and that would take time to clear, then presumably they would establish their own home. She had no doubts of sharing her new life with Alison, and privately admitted Ben's mother was easier to get along with than her own. However, Jane was another kettle of fish.

A mid-summer sun crept over the hills, cast its rays into the valley, filtered by haze within the homestead, and highlighted objects on the debris-strewn floor. It did not reach into the south-west-facing kitchen, where Louise Chester was pottering about, having gathered chopped tea-tree, sawn branches of puriri, and roused the range fire, ready for the first of many meals to be prepared this day. Her work came naturally, so her thoughts were on her son and the pretty little town girl he had chosen for a wife. The only surprise about the engagement was that Ben himself had not forewarned her. So she assumed, giving her son any benefit of doubt, he had proposed on the spur of the moment. Since he would be among the first to trudge into the kitchen, she could ask him, and if they were alone also ask him about other matters, particularly the farm.

Even before his mother had risen on New Year's morning, Ben had rolled out of bed, clomped down the stairs, probably hoping to rouse a mate or two, slung his working clothes on, and plodded drowsily into the shaded back yard. He coughed, spluttered, clearing the weeds from the night just gone, gulped in some fresh air, and his brain began to function. "Right, cows, you've got me today," he advised, glanced around again in case he did have some help, then strode across the glade, through the trees to the lower paddock.

Ben was not sure how Priscilla would take to swapping her town life for the country. Waiuku was only a small town, surrounded by farms, so hardly far removed from those surroundings. That is how it looked to Ben as he rounded up the seven cows he believed to be in milk, and their calves in case he needed to use them to start off a cow. He prodded one into a stall, clamped its head, fastened a rope to its leg, and, sitting on a stool, hand milked it, periodically glancing toward the yard gate to see if help was forthcoming. He slapped the rump of one now depleted cow and appealed to the next to come forth. So seldom did he milk them these days he left it to the animals to know their place in the small queue.

He had milked four cows when Jane arrived on the scene, saying, "Beat me to it, Brother." Expelling her breath ungratefully, her dark eyes drawing together with a frown, she shook her head to emphasise her annoyance.

"Thought I'd let you sleep in."

Jane again sighed, and complained, "My, just look at the mess."

Ben had slopped milk on the river-stone dairy floor. "Give me a chance." His turn to sigh: with exasperation. He knew it was impossible to please her.

"Now I have to clean it up." She let out another angry expulsion. "I just wish you had left it to me." Arms akimbo, she stamped her foot, and snatched a spare pail to wash the floor. 'This, on top of the ridiculous announcement last night,' she agitatedly thought, and very nearly expressed the thought to her brother.

Ben shook his head, and swore under his breath. He rose from the stool, plodded into the spic and span dairy set down the half-full pail, still shaking his head, deflated that his sister could have rejected what he thought was a decent gesture.

"Here, take this with you," she instructed, dropping one pail with a clang, and taking a covered billy of the previous evening's milk from the shelf. "It's for drinking," she told him.

So, with a shrug, he walked from the yard. No point in arguing. He dismissed his sister's acrimony, and thought of his much more agreeable fiancé. He now ventured a little further ahead than his proposal. Nothing definite had emerged by the time he trudged back into the kitchen, greeted his amiable mother, and he could only wonder how she could ever have had a daughter like Jane.

Jane meantime, arms still akimbo, pressing her thin waist, surveyed her dairy. She regretted sleeping in: wished Ben had also stayed in bed: wished that no one would set foot in her dairy to disturb its orderliness: wished people would mind their own business. It was *her* job — the milking — not his.

'What does that *child* know about farming?' she demanded to herself, loud enough for the cow to 'moo' back at her. 'Where does it leave *me*?' Her breathing sharp: despair verging on tears. 'I suppose little Miss Prissy will laud it over me. I wonder will Mother allow *that*?' She expelled a splutter through trembling lips.

Now, despite her annoyance, she sluiced the floor, then, milked the remainder of the herd. Being aware of the importance of pasteurisation, she first heated the milk, by lighting a fire beneath one vat, ladled the hot milk into another, set in a trough cooled by stream water, then separated the cream: some to be made into butter, or she added rennet to the milk for cheese making. She was aware her father, thanks to her efforts, got top price of a few pence per pound for her produce. All the time she raged within, sometimes her anger boiling over into words: unladylike expressions. She assumed Ben and his 'pretty little bride' would get ownership of Kowhai. No one interrupted her work, not even to say their goodbyes as they departed. By the time she strode back to the house carrying another billy partially filled with cream, there was little need for it.

"Ali's bound to drink it," she advised her mother, slamming the billy on the kitchen table. "You know how she loves the stuff."

Referring to her sister's liking for cream, and anything else sweet, including men.

"I'll put it to good use, dear," her mother assured, and continued with her baking, saying over her shoulder. "And by the way, Ben only thought he was doing you a good turn."

"He needn't have bothered, Mother."

"I'm sure he won't again, dear," the lady advised in her gentle voice, thinking there may well be a time when she *did* want help.

Early in the new year, Ben and his father decided they needed to get new equipment from the city. Ben, wishing to take Priscilla on a journey — and it *was* a journey in those days — decided to travel to Auckland by road. The weather having been prevalently fine gave them further excuse to use the roads. So, one morning a robust horse and a cart, Ben perched on top, plodded out of the valley, negotiating each bend with care, lest a wheel slip over the edge and all end up in a gully.

It may have been the height of summer, however a hundred yards along the peninsula's main road it was swallowed by trees, and became precariously greasy. A set of parallel ruts, that made no allowance for oncoming traffic, directed the cart. Time was not a factor, so Ben allowed the horse to rest periodically, graze on the roadside, while he sat on the ground, and gazed dreamily at the view: glimpses of the Tasman on one side, or of the long tidal estuary leading to Waiuku on the other. A small Onehunga-bound steamship was negotiating the numerous shoals and bends of the estuary.

When he encountered another cart on the eight-foot wide track, a case of one or the other backing up to where they could safely pass, and stopping for a chat during the process. Near noon he crossed the narrow wooden bridge at the north end of Waiuku. (A journey by car today takes twenty minutes.) The tide was falling, and the flat-bottomed scow *Elsie* was about to depart before the sea receded, stranding it until the next high tide.

The town itself consisted of two rows of wild-west wooden shops with verandas propped up by poles, convenient for tying horses to. The north end was dominated by the two-storey Kentish hotel. The unsealed thoroughfare between the shops sloped unevenly to the river side of the road, with two large trees — one a weeping willow — dominating the street. There was no definition between the footpath and the road except outside the Kentish where a drunk staggering from its portals would fall a couple of feet if he veered from the footpath.

A few horses and carts were parked in front of the shops: one or two being phaetons, and the rest of lesser apparent importance, although even the most rudimentary cart was important to someone. Nor did there appear to be a right and left side of the town street, and such was the lack of traffic drivers had it virtually all to themselves so took the less rutted route.

Priscilla had been ready and waiting for Ben since shortly after breakfast, several times had gone to the gate, and once the quarter-mile into town seeking him, and while she did not venture into the public bar of the Kentish Hotel, she did not think any of the various carts and gigs outside belonged to the Chesters.

If either Priscilla or Ben thought they were heading off into Auckland on their own Maude Caldwell had other plans. They were to be accompanied by Priscilla's brother Nigel and his wife Jessica. Ben did win one concession, since it would not be possible to use Nigel's new phaeton for machinery, or he and Priscilla, they would continue on the buggy. Priscilla eagerly agreed with her fiancé, only too glad to sit beside him, where they could discuss their future virtually alone.

Maude's final advice, ". . . And dear, use your parasol. You know how the sun burns you."

"Yes, Mother." With an embarrassed and exasperated sigh. As it was she had a broad-brimmed boater, held on by a scarf tied beneath her chin, her face free of obstruction, unlike her sister-in-law, who also wore a boater with a facial net to prevent dust from damaging her complexion. Priscilla's travelling costume was a full length pale green dress with a short bolero jacket side-buttoned and turned back cuffs; quite fetching, if Ben should notice such charm.

Maude Caldwell shook her head, withdrawn lips set in a thin line. She could not see the point of the couple travelling by road when it was much safer and quicker to go by boat, as she would do the next day. And as far as needing the cart for some machinery, she would believe that when she saw the machinery? She turned on her heel, without at least seeing them turn the corner, and strode inside, having to adjust her eyes from bright sunshine to the semi-darkness of the house, due to the holland blinds being half-down. The furnishings would fade if she allowed too much light.

At first Nigel's horse set off with a canter, and Ben, instead of giving his horse the gee-up, nodded wisely and said to Priscilla. "It'll soon tire."

"I don't mind, Ben. They can go on ahead as far as I am concerned." She chuckled, clutched her fiancé's arm, rested her head momentarily on his shoulder. The last thing she wanted was her brother and his horse literally breathing down their necks.

The leading couple did not get far ahead, because they suffered a break down, and as Ben approached a blacksmiths there they were.

"Just a shoe," Nigel shouted, his moustache twitching. "We'll catch you up."

Priscilla tugged Ben's arm again, with a glint in her eye. "So we don't have to stop." Her excitement of being with him had not diminished since setting out, and every so often she gave an involuntary shudder.

"Not if you don't want to."

"Not here," she murmured. "Perhaps if they haven't caught us up later."

The road was barely a cart-width wide, strewn with shell from Manukau beaches. About them pastures were losing their greenness, dry tinting the hills, the hottest days to come. The air quivered, and when Priscilla turned to see where her brother was the shimmering distorted her vision. She looked across the undulating land: that nearest the road fenced with grazing cows, while further away doomed scrub waited for the axeman. Smoke from two or three fires, driven by heat, rose quickly skyward, then drifted aimlessly in the light airs. "The trees up ahead, Ben, shall we stop there awhile?"

"Sure. The horse needs a rest."

Priscilla wondered what had happened to the romance on the night he proposed.

A quiet place: the only sign of other people, dust-covered roadside grass, indicating that horses and carts did disturb the tranquillity. A cold drink would have been welcome. All Ben and Priscilla had to quaff their thirst was now luke-warm lemonade. She thought, just thought, he might lay her back and kiss her passionately, yet dare not herself draw him into such an embrace. She did lie back, to look up at the sky, and watch the few clouds form and disperse. She recalled what Ben's sister Alison had said. 'I don't think he's as much as kissed a girl behind the barn'. Surely he must have kissed other girls, if not behind the barn. When she thought about it, she also recalled that he had asked her permission before giving her that first kiss — a mere peck — and thereafter she had to encourage him. She sighed, briefly closed her eyes, then heard the rattle of hoofs and wheels on the road, signifying, all too soon, Nigel and Jessica were catching them. They emerged from the heat haze, stopped while she and Ben climbed aboard the buggy and resumed their journey. This time instead of racing ahead the married couple plodded along behind. They met other travellers, most sauntering along: speed not essential. Priscilla knew one couple, eagerly introduced Ben, and for several minutes they chatted in the middle of the otherwise deserted road. Up and down dales the horses plodded: across basic bridges, fords, and for a few miles the couple had company, by way of two lads hitching a ride. Priscilla's time alone with Ben had been all too short.

While climbing out of a river ford they confronted trouble.

"I'll give them a hand," Ben immediately told Priscilla. "You just make sure the horse doesn't go off without me. Come on lads," he ordered the two youths.

They did not argue, and leapt from the cart.

"Darling, I hope I can." Priscilla held the reins, careful not to inadvertently flick them, and set their horse off on a trot. Not that they would get far going forward.

Ben and the lads joined other travellers and wagoners, and helped an unfortunate colleague: a log-laden dray with a broken wheel. The dray and its team of eight bullocks blocked the road.

"Nothing for it other than unhitch the bullocks," the wagoner decided.

"No chance of getting it off the road," considered another.

The men mumbled among themselves, some cupping their chins in hands as they contemplated the broken wheel. Nor was there any chance of offloading the logs. Offloading was not the problem, rather reloading after the wheel had been repaired.

Nigel appeared beside Ben and commented, "I say, you *have* to shift it. We can't wait here for the rest of the day."

Jessica adding, "We are being smothered by smoke."

Which was true: smoke from one of the piles of burning scrub settling in the depression.

One of the wagoners looked Nigel up and down, said nothing, and spat on the grass.

"You just see to our horses, Nigel. We'll sort this out," Ben advised.

The men tethered the docile bullocks to fence posts, then, using logs from the adjacent paddock, levered the dray so the wheel could be removed. They lashed the cross-bar to a sturdy log to keep the whole show propped up. Just when Ben thought he would be making a detour to Pukekohe and the nearest wheelwright, another traveller volunteered. With a one of Ben's hitch hikers holding the reins, Ben edged his horse and cart round the dray, while the other youth coaxed Nigel's horse round the obstacle, a third Drury-bound traveller following.

"If he's lucky the wheelwright might have a spare," Ben advised Priscilla, and to the youths said, "Thanks for the hand."

"Who's the hobnob?" one asked, indicating Nigel.

"My brother," Priscilla replied, with an apologetic smile.

"Sorry, Ma'am."

To Ben she said a few minutes later, "Let's hope *he* doesn't break a wheel," and glanced over her shoulder back at Nigel's phaeton, now fifty yards back.

With the haze-shrouded sun dipping to the west, they reached Drury, consisting of an inn, and few other buildings in sight. Ben handed his horse confidently to an ostler, while Nigel issued precise instructions. Two needs for Priscilla: a toilet, and to loosen her stays, so she could relax a little. One need for Ben: a comparatively cool beer. Nigel joined him. Jessica and Priscilla cast themselves at an axe-hewn table beneath a spreading oak, their cool lemon squashes poured from a stone jar. It was here Priscilla silently surveyed her situation: compared the two men who had now abandoned the smoky bar and sat at a table, barely a word spoken between them. They had little in common. Even now Ben looked of farming stock, and Priscilla reflected how she often saw him: dressed in a vest and tattered trousers rolled up to his knees, swinging a slasher, or cleaving sawn logs with one precise blow. His face tanned, lines at the corners of his eyes, his chin, after only twelve hours, a little rough, since he neither sported a beard nor a moustache. For Priscilla he was the epitome of a man, and she could only lovingly admire him.

Nigel on the other hand was so refined, so dignified, that since Emily had left home, their mother purchased split and kindled wood from the local merchant. She did not condemn her son for his lack of labour, only praised him for his business acumen. They could afford the extra cost. Even now he wore a cravat, which he fidgeted with, obviously uncomfortable, but too much of a gentleman to remove it. If in the past Nigel had got his hands dirty, it was when boys were boys, before their characters were shaped, and they went their individual ways. Certainly, Priscilla thought, every man should pursue the occupation best suited to him, although the natural environment must influence that decision. Nigel, having lived in a town, and being a son of a businessman had been drawn to that life. Unlike Ben, who could dress for the occasion, Nigel was only to be seen at his best.

The evening meal consisted of roast beef, potatoes and kumara, with mushy peas. They did have a choice of desserts: apricot tart with cream, or plum pudding. Priscilla longed for an apple dish, however she would have to wait a month or two until their home-grown produce was ripe. They did not miss having a wider selection, because exotic foods were not on their menu, nor many others, and would not be common for many years.

Night fell.

A new day dawned.

Between Drury and Auckland there were twenty-five miles of unsealed road: some of it bare clay, other stretches having a smattering of gravel, or sand and shell. With no rain to bog them down, they did have another problem: a hard and unrelenting road surface. A general store, blacksmiths, saddler, bootmaker, livery and bait, a stock and station agent, a baker, and maybe a fruiterer and confectioner marked the localities of Papakura, Manurewa, Papatoetoe and Otahuhu. Great South Rd was grossly misnamed. South Track would have been more appropriate, since it twisted and turned around the smallest of humps, dropped into gullies, with creeks spanned by narrow wooden bridges, as it linked communities where people lived and died seldom leaving them.

The road took its toll on the horses' hooves, so by the time they had trudged up the long drunkenly directed hill from the lava-strewn paddocks of Penrose to the Harp o' Erin, the horses needed some attention: a blacksmith being at the road junction. The foursome took lunch with ales and lemon squashes at the verandaed hotel that gave the locality in the lee of One Tree Hill its name. After the fresh air of their morning journey Priscilla found the atmosphere within the dining room claustrophobic, mainly caused by pipes men insisted on smoking before, during and after meals, her brother included. It was not race day, however she did notice out of the sash window horses and trainers coming and going from the nearby Ellerslie Racecourse: several stables being in the vicinity.

Back on the road again: a busier road now, all the traffic either pedestrian or horse-drawn. Farmers Hill was a hurdle: short and steep, named not because the local people were farmers, rather the original purchaser of the land was called Farmer. He had since sold out to John Logan Campbell, now an old man, with grand plans for the district: plans the people of Auckland would be forever grateful. From there the horses were the able to canter past Buckland's Saleyards and into Newmarket.

Rather than subject them to a long slog up Khyber Pass Road, with a few market gardens surviving beside the Captain Cook Brewery, the foursome merged with the traffic along Manukau Road (now Parnell Rd), cautiously descended to Beach Rd, beneath the triple-arched railway bridge, and the recently reclaimed Mechanics Bay. Some Maori children noisily chased after Ben, he returning their banter, with a few words in their own language. Customs St was bustling by comparison to Waiuku, yet such was their pace as they plodded round the corner into Queen Street, Ben was able to look up at a telegraph pole, tap Priscilla on the arm, pointing to the cross arms.

"Look how many telephone lines there are."

"Mm." She glanced upward: the one hundred and twenty lines not holding her attention. The busy thoroughfare did though, as they manoeuvred their way up Queen Street, avoiding haphazardly driven horses and carts, yapping dogs, pedestrians stopping to chat in the middle of the road, to the timbered Albert Hotel. Ostlers lifted themselves off upturned crates, took a couple of puffs of the cigarettes, stubbed them out, then took the horses along a lane to the back of the hotel, where they were stabled.

Maude Caldwell, who had travelled by steamer to Onehunga, and then horse-drawn bus to Auckland earlier, was waiting with obvious impatience in the foyer. She was not there to keep an eye on her children, not Priscilla or Nigel anyway, rather to locate her 'lost' child, Emily. Little did they know, Ben and co had passed within a stone's throw of her home in Parnell, not that she was there at the time.

The newly betrothed couple unpacked their bags, naturally in separate rooms, Ben being with Nigel, and Priscilla sharing with Jessica, re-met in the foyer, then stepped out into the hustle and bustle of Queen Street. While Ben gazed the melee of traffic, at least compared to Waiuku, Priscilla was drawn to the display in the adjacent Smith and Caughey's window.

Having surveyed the scene, thinking of Emily, he suggested, "I don't see how your mother can ever . . ."

"*Prissy! — Prissy!*"

They both turned, seeking the voice: familiar to Priscilla.

"*Emily!*" Priscilla squealed, considerably louder than usual.

That is how Emily *found* them as she emerged from the store. The sisters swept towards each other, a barefooted boy narrowly escaping the jaws of their embrace. Ben looked on, relieved they were thrilled to see each other. He somehow did not think Emily would react the same way towards her mother and brother when she sighted them.

There and then Priscilla grabbed Ben's hand and announced excitedly, "We're engaged!" To Emily's frown of not recognising him, she claimed, "You've met Ben." She clutched his arm and drew him to her side. "Aren't I lucky."

"That's nice," Emily responded with a half-smile; a smile that never reached its full extent, when replaced by a 'you have told me your news, now I shall tell you mine' look. Unlike Priscilla's proud announcement, Emily murmured, lest anyone other than these two hear, "I'm married."

"You're *what?* — When? — Who to?"

"Shsh. Don't tell the world."

"Why?"

"Ah — Just because." She suspected if her sister was in town then her mother was also bound to be. Maude Caldwell, having heard her younger daughter's cry on sighting her sister, ventured into the street, with Nigel and Jessica at her side. Her appearance confirmed Emily's suspicions. "Good afternoon, Mother," she acknowledged disdainfully. "Good afternoon, Nigel." Even less amicably. Jessica received only a nod of acquaintance.

"So, we've found you, even before . . ." Maude Caldwell confirmed sourly.

"Oh dear, surely, Mother, you did not think I was lost." Emily's expression was of mock dismay. "I am indeed sorry to have put you to so . . ."

"Of course you have not put us to trouble," Priscilla assured. "Ben and I were coming to town, and Mother, Emily, you know how she worries ."

They returned to the hotel's lantern-lit although gloomy lounge, Emily condescending to join them, only for a few minutes, she advised, since she had another 'appointment'.

They had barely arranged themselves, Ben sitting on the arm of a leather armchair, having dismissed the improperness of his position, when a debonair moustached character swung into the room, cast one inebriated eye on the group, opened the other and focussed on Emily.

"Ah, th-there yoush are, my p-pretty." He gave those about her another cursory glance, intent only on the object of his interest. "I th-thought yoush sshaid . . ."

Emily uttered a little cough, her eyes flicking to her relations, indicating the obviousness of the company.

"Emily — yoush did . . ."

"Not now, Karl," she stated firmly and expelled the rest of her breath with embarrassment.

Affronted by the refusal, the man, whose dress may have been businesslike, his behaviour anything but, swayed back, then forward, reaching unsteadily toward Emily. "C'mon-on, m' darling, letsh go to my r-room." He hovered. "Our bishness w-won't take long, and — and you . . ."

Emily's brother, Nigel, did not intervene. Ben did. Already on his feet and having discarded his coat, he challenged the intruder by warning, "Listen here, whatever business you might have, I can assure you this lady has no business with you."

The other did have business with her. He trembled like a thin plank, trying to maintain his balance as he rose to his full height in a vain attempt to match Ben's, now poised menacingly, his fists clenched. "S-She — has – lotsh of bishness — with me." Thrusting a hand accusingly at Emily, then tottering as he reached to grab her arm.

"Go away, Karl. Go — *away!*" Thinking, in his present state he may as well .not bother her, family or not family present.

"C'mon-on — Em-ily."

Nigel ushered his wife and mother to one side.

Ben Chester had learned chivalry: to defend women against unwanted — unwanted whatever. Towering over the obnoxious pest, he commanded, "Get out y' shagroon!" An expression he thought applicable, although not sure of its meaning.

The cocky sprite made a clumsy snatch at Emily, was grabbed by Ben, turned to shape up to him, despite being several inches shorter, and ineffectively flicked his chest. Ben took offence, leaned back, then let fly: an upper cut that sent the drunk hurtling across the lounge, slamming against a bar and slumping into oblivion, blood oozing from his rearranged mouth.

Belatedly Emily appealed, "*Ben!* — Don't! — I . . ." She clasped her hand to her mouth in guilt of what she had caused, grimaced at the inert Karl and murmured apologetically to him, "Oh dear."

Maude cried out in horror, and fainted.

While Nigel and Jessica fussed over her, Priscilla, so proud of her husband-to-be, drew him to one side, as others assessed the victim's injuries, and whispered, "I think, dearest, all is not what it seems. I don't think Em . . ."

There was another commotion behind them: in the form of a stentorian voice.

Heavily bearded cane-carrying William Todd prodded his way through the babbling throng to Emily, still peering open-mouthed down at Karl, and, assuming she was the cause of the disturbance, he accosted her. "Now, *woman*, what the devil have you been up to?"

She turned to confront him, raised her eyes to the ceiling, grabbed his arm to usher him out of earshot, which was difficult, and denied, "Nothing, Will." Her brain snapped into action, as it often had to with William. "This creature here got in Brother Ben's way." She preferred to think of Ben as her brother, not Nigel, cowering in a corner, fussing over his now vaguely stirring mother, her consciousness awakened by brandy and smelling salts.

Ben had heard his name mentioned, saw Emily being manhandled away, and made another attempt to defend her, arms outstretched, fists balling. Emily patted William's arm defensively, and smiled embarrassingly, Ben not catching on, and demanding, "Who the heck are you?"

William Todd released the lady and squared up to Ben Chester. Everyone knew who *he* was. Obviously this unknown country bumpkin did *not*. "I . . ." A dramatic pause as he clasped his beard, ". . . am — Mister — William — Todd." And nodding to Emily, announced matter-of-factly as if she was chattel, "This — is my wife."

Ben took a pace back, wondering if he had heard right, while chuckles were uttered over the shoulders of now dispersing onlookers, two of whom were dragging the felled Karl further from the scene.

Then, having resettled, minus Maude and Nigel, Emily told her story. It transpired she had been at a party where the well-known businessman William Todd was in focus. Apparently, during the wild night he had proposed to her, probably far from his full senses at the time. Emily, in the same state, had accepted. Or, had she used the opportunity to further her station in life? Anyway, they had married within weeks, neither giving up their hobbies: William's being philandering and gambling, and Emily's being men, generally. The Karl Ben had k-o'd was one of those admirers.

Yes, William was a gambler. Fortunately for his welfare he was better at business than at picking horses. When the starting rope dropped for the Auckland Cup during the New Year's Carnival at Ellerslie, his outsider, paying well, was behind the field and facing the wrong way, so had little show of catching the second-time winner *Blue Jacket*. Emily, resplendent in a full-length beige cotton gauze dress, and wide-brimmed hat with its mandatory feather, took a conservative approach, and with left-over housekeeping money backed the winner. (There was no dividend for coming second until the following year.) That dalliance aside, Will more than made up for in his many and varied businesses: some above board, others at street level. Nor was Emily his first wife. He had an eight-year-old son, who despised Emily's intrusion, and made sure his governess received what little affection he imparted. Most of it was reserved for himself.

Emily meantime, spent more of William's wealth. She had gathered a little weight with her new designation: her blonded hair piled above a naturally flawless face. There were few cottons in her wardrobe: mostly silks and satins, and velvet gowns for cooler nights; all the creation of a fussy designer, who did not appreciate the figure he regularly viewed stripped to her underwear, a sight most other male acquaintances only dreamed of. Fantastic hats for every occasion by Miss Harkness, an 'acquaintance' of her husband. Emily had also acquired a haughty stance, her pride having extinguished the twinkle in her eyes when living at Waiuku. Even there she had attracted admirers: a star with many moons.

As she entered her stately home Emily noted its similarity with Kowhai: hers poised on a hill, the other snug in a valley. Their grandeur might have been similar. That was where any comparison ended: the atmosphere within the two houses decidedly different. Emily had not previously had such thoughts about her home, and preferred to imagine the avenue outside was Kowhai's rustic drive. She may have had reservations, however there was no turning back. With a sigh she trudged up the grand staircase, entered her sumptuous bedroom, barely glanced at the Waitemata Harbour, before drawing the violet velvet drapes, and cast herself on her wide bed: one seldom used in its full capacity.

She rolled on her back, stared at the ceiling, thinking of the differences between her and her sister. Did Priscilla wish she had some of the lust for life as she had, especially when she clutched so lovingly on to Ben's arm? 'No Prissy, you are bound by rules, despite what your heart might desire. At least you have man — a real man.' Another remorseful sigh. 'Why could not I have met one like Ben — a *rich* one, with Ben's physique?' She thought — she knew — she got some pleasure out of her own liaisons: even if only superficial, momentary pleasure, often thought nothing more of. She did not yearn for any of them particularly, not like her sister must yearn for Ben. She only assumed Priscilla had the same desires as herself. Did not every woman? — Maybe not. With a chuckle, she recalled the incident at the Albert Hotel. 'Poor Karl. I shall have to apologise to him.' Certainly not for Ben's solitary punch. Again she chuckled, even though her eyes glistened with regret. 'Silly Ben, defending my character,' she mused, with a sense of honour. 'Even if his actions were misplaced, they were the actions of a *man*!'

She slept, and imagined Ben in dungarees coming into this very bedroom, hesitating, until she beckoned him to her. He knelt with one knee on the bed, reached out and gently stroked her face, and she purred . . .

. . . She woke abruptly to her cat licking her face, and the dream dissipated.

After leaving Emily, Priscilla, taking Ben's arm again, said, "Darling, I know you think Em is very beautiful — and she is — I think so too . . ."

"I don't think she's any prettier than you," he interrupted, defending his guilt, and honestly so, because he had admired Emily, and did harbour guilt.

Priscilla patted his arm, wondering how she could get through to him without being direct. Now, if she had been talking to his sister Alison, girl to girl, she would have been more forthright, not unladylike, in her choice of words. "I know you don't. Let me explain. Ah — Emily has — a — a fondness for men. And men — as you have seen — have a certain fondness for her."

"Mm."

"I think the man you — ah — hit was her — ah — lover."

Ben stared at her in amazement, shaking his head. "Nah?"

"Oh yes, my darling." she reddened with embarrassment, talking so intimately with her fiancé. "I could be telling tales out of school, but I rather think the reason my darling sister left Waiuku, ah — was to save an awkward situation."

Ben shook his head. It wasn't that he disbelieved Priscilla, rather he could not accept Emily was anything except a righteous woman. And as for the 'awkward situation' he was too naïve to imagine what it could be.

Priscilla nodded. "I *do* love her, for all of that." She chuckled. "So, I'm sure Em can look after herself — in any situation."

"I hope you are right — then." Even so he could not see himself being a spectator should there be a repeat performance of the hotel incident.

The sixty-year-old city of Auckland was, at the beginning of the twentieth century, rebuilding its main thoroughfare, Queen Street. A new array of brick and concrete structures were replacing pioneers' wooden shanties. Buildings of four storeys were thrusting their floors above the dusty street. Elegant places: ornate facades, with bay windows and balconies; buildings intended to last a hundred years. Almost complete was the Strand Theatre, and only yards down the road the site was being cleared for another theatre, later opened as His Majesty's, although no doubt its original drawings carried the name Her Majesty's. Long before completion, in fact a further year into the century, the most notable link with century, Queen Victoria, gone would die. This was the future.

With personal business over, Ben turned his attention to purchasing the gear he required for Kowhai, while Priscilla and Jessica fussed over materials, on occasions hoisting themselves on to bar-type stools, as shop assistants spread the offered cloths on worn wooden counters. There was no rush. Time to chat with a complete stranger perched on another stool. For Priscilla, one of the few occasions she and Jessica would spend harmoniously.

As the travellers set out for home billowing heat clouds gathered. Priscilla, fearing she was going to get awfully wet, kept one eye on the troubled sky, and the other on the road ahead, seeking places of shelter. Meantime the dust settled on her clothes, in her hair, even her parched mouth. Perhaps crossing the Manukau Harbour by boat was a better way. Then she glanced over her shoulder at the machinery Ben had purchased, and accepted his decision. She did not hear the popping of gorse pods above the clatter of hooves. Nor did she envisage that during this new century the villages scattered along the Great South Road would expand and merge.

They trundled all the way to Drury before the first full drops cascaded to ground. Priscilla shared a room with her sister-in-law, although shared a beer with Ben in the lounge: hers a shandy. With a sigh she laid her head on his shoulder, sought words to express her satisfaction, instead settled for the solitude of the otherwise deserted room: its silence broken by the hubbub from the public bar beyond.

*   *   *   *   *   *

Louise and Thomas Chester relaxed in wicker chairs on the veranda, another summer's day at an end. In the shadow of the sun's departure, always long before sunset, due to the eight hundred foot hill between the homestead and the ocean, Kowhai lay tranquil. Louise, was darning, and sewing on buttons.

Alison astride her horse galloped across the wooden bridge and along the driveway with racing determination only momentarily out-voiced the bitterns and tui. So swiftly did Louise's daughter ride away the noise soon dwindled, and she returned to her observations: watching the shadow ascend hills, and cling to a summit at the valley's junction.

Observance of nature was not her sole reason for spending time like this. The evening allayed the day's disturbances, particularly the trivial disputes between her two daughters: so heated at the time, often over and done with minutes later, or their parting with the argument unsolved.

Neither had much of their mother in them. Louise herself had placid determination to do a job and do it well. She had come to Kowhai as a pioneer young mother, and her open heart had turned the place into a refuge for many, particularly during the winter months. No creed, no colour had been barred from its boundaries, and that for religiously divided Pollok was a feat in itself. A person was as good as their behaviour in her opinion. Louise: a dominant factor, although not domineering, to her husband left the responsibility of managing the farm itself, while she took care of the household. They were a comparatively small family, with just three children. The homestead's situation, mid-way between the Manukau Heads and Waiuku, turned it into a stopping-off place. As often as not there were more than the family for dinner, and if the visitors happened to be males then they were made all the more welcome: not by Louise, rather by her younger daughter, Alison. Therein lay the basic problem between the two girls: one freely gave her friendship, the other guarding herself against intrusion.

Nor were they alike in appearance: Jane being of darker complexion, with deep-set hazel eyes, at times looking as if both had been blackened in a fight: which could be likely, since she and Alison often scrapped: shaking and shoving each other with anger. Alison was fairer: her face lightly freckled, since she insisted in going out in the sun hatless: as were her arms, sleeves often drawn to her elbows. Rather rebellious when it came to dress. It may have been customary to wear unrevealing dresses by day, however when Alison was on the end of the axe, she soon wiggled her stays loose, if she was wearing them at all, and untied her bodice. After all, who was there to see her? Only her brother, and he did not count. She was cheeky enough to think if it were Priscilla loosening her clothes that would be a different story. Or would it — being Ben?

As for Thomas Chester: far from being the less dominant figure at Kowhai, his presence highlighted by the fact they were living in comparative comfort. Now, as he sat alongside his wife on the veranda, he remained silent, knowing Louise was deliberating some matter. He was considering the inevitable announcement his son had made, and how he could accommodate Ben and Priscilla as a couple. They would want to establish themselves aside from the present household. He knew the ultimate answer. How soon could it be practically brought about?

On that particular evening his thoughts were interrupted by Alison's return. She galloped across a paddock, and at a narrow point of the stream lifted the horse across it, running on, then reining it in. Thomas frequently disputed her beliefs and pleas, however watching her then he had to admire her skill. She was just too self-confident. Horse with rider trotted back to the house, the horse's forelegs clawing the air, Alison staying on its back, leaning forward to pat its head, then caressing him to the veranda.

Thomas shook his head, and warned, "He'll throw you one day."

"Not at all, Father. He loves it." All the while she patted him, whispered kind words, for much as she loved every young man within miles of her home, she loved her horse best of all. As well she did look after it, for although horses were the dominant means of transport, there was actually a shortage of them, due to the Boer War.

As Alison approached the stable, her sister passed by, a round cheese tucked under one arm, and carrying a billy of milk.

"You'll not come for a stroll with me?" Alison asked negatively, knowing the answer.

"No, I haven't time for *that*. If you're going down to the beach, could you look for Russet. — She's wandered off."

"Has she her bell on?"

"I can't remember. — Probably"

The conversation was politely formal, although Alison would make an effort to locate the stray cow: a task made a lot easier when they were wearing bells. Farmers were only beginning to fence their farms, so not all the land was in paddocks. She continued into the stable with the thought that searching for the missing cow would give her an excuse to linger in the encroaching twilight. She gathered a handful of hay and rubbed the stallion down, and, since she had not ridden far, threw blanket over him, led him to a pail of water and with a final pat bolted the stable door. "Goodnight, Handsome," she wished, and received a snort in return.

The stable, barn and the cottage nearby were older than the homestead: obviously so. Thomas himself had been born in the cottage: a solitary unlined room, divided by hessian, so one area could be used for kitchen and living, the other as a bedroom. During their short lives Thomas' parents bunked on the lower level, while their two children slept in a loft. Made of pit-sawn timber neither the inside nor out had seen a coat of paint or whitewash. Thomas, unexpectedly inheriting the property at a young age, had the present homestead built, also of pit-sawn timber, although a far cry from the original. In style as grand a home as any on the peninsula or beyond. A river-stone-floored kitchen entered to from the back veranda, from where the bathroom and a separate toilet were also reached, all of which had stone floors. A single door connected the kitchen with a dining room. A wide foyer divided those southwest-facing rooms from the large northeast-facing lounge. It contained a clutter of dark-stained furnishings, with three sets of french doors opening on to the veranda on two sides. At the back was a small library, used also as a study. A triple-flight staircase, with the top flight at right-angles, led to the upper floor, with eight bedrooms: three large high-ceiling rooms at the front, smaller attic-styled rooms along each side, and single bedrooms at the back. The house was spacious, with cosy corners, and could accommodate several more than its resident family. This was the homestead Thomas was not about to vacate for his son and daughter-in-law to be.

After the flurry of Christmas and New Year life resettled into rural regularity, especially with dairying. Ben got himself offside with his father when he joined the year-long debate over whether New Zealand should become an Australian State: the Australians themselves were undecided on the issue of federation, rather than being individually governed from England.

"Son, it's bad enough being told what to do by Wellington, let alone from Sydney, or wherever they set up . . ." He was not sure of his ground, so changed the subject, and since New Zealanders were never put to the test on whether they wanted to throw their lot in with Australia, the family could carry on minding their own business.

CHAPTER TWO

Kowhai's social attraction did not result from Ben Chester's presence, or necessarily from his mother's hospitality. Jane and Alison were as much the attraction. Thomas could have had Alison's many suitors act out *The Taming Of The Shrew:* ordering one of them must win the hand of the elder Jane before the others could court Alison. Before any of them achieved that they would have to persuade either girl they could provide them with a better life than Kowhai offered.

Father and daughter worked together, at least Jane did the work, while her father pottered about: this day tending the herd, then gathering chopped manuka ready for Jane to heat the milk for pasteurisation and to begin cheese making. Thomas wondered if indeed Jane's temper was only a façade, and she had no wish to leave Kowhai, or to get married. Then she need only take that attitude with young men, not the entire household, except for rare occasions when they were alone like this, and she abandoned her defences. How he and his wife could produce two such different daughters was ever a mystery to him.

Alison was not idle: the otherwise quiet valley resounding to her axe blows. The sharp crack as she cleaved sawn tea-tree: enough for firing the copper for tomorrow's wash. Since marriage was in Kowhai's air her thoughts on the subject were quite resolved: not for a long time for her. After all, she was just eighteen, and while some girls were silly enough to get married and have families so young, she wanted to first explore the world beyond the peninsula, and stay several nights in Auckland. She knew of a place where she could stay, although feared her father would firmly disallow her setting foot in Emily's home. 'Fancy Emily being like *that,'* she surmised, as the blade sliced into the wood barely half an inch from her fingers, and she gave a mischievous snigger.

Of horses: although both girls rode astride, Jane sat like the daughter of a country squire, whereas Alison appeared more of a jockey, leaning over the mane when riding fast. She *had* been thrown on a few occasions, not that her father knew: once into the valley stream, and after cursing both her horse and her own stupidity, sagged back into the muddied water as if content to bathe in it. She was not wearing much more than when she *did* bathe in the stream. Then she chuckled because there had been times, when she was sure no one was within miles of her, she stripped to her barest underclothes, which many years later she would reflect was more than girls wore about town when she grew old enough to have those memories.

Contrary to what her father often said, Alison was not idle. Virtually barred from the dairy by her sister, she had plenty of work both around and within the house. Constant little jobs: like refilling kerosene lamps, cleaning their glass chimneys, trimming wicks. Scraping wax from candleholders, including bottles for re-use, and endless kitchen tasks, particularly preserving fruit and vegetables, kept her and her mother almost fully occupied. There was certainly no chance of 'the devil making work for idle hands'.

Nor was Alison's work confined to household chores. As a young girl she had often ventured into the barn: there to watch intrigued first her father and lately her brother work the forge. 'Being so far away from town, Alison, means we have to do a lot of repairs ourselves,' her father had instructed. Ben had said admiringly, 'Ali, whoever marries you is going to get a housewife and a blackie.' Although she did not know it, he did admire her, and hoped whomever she married would appreciate her.

Now in the present Alison, in a body length leather apron, pumped the hand bellows, saying to Ben, "You're supposed to do this." With tongs she adjusted the steel wheel rim, and when it was glowing red, almost white, she withdrew it, Ben holding it while she hammered the kink out of it. She studied its shape and asked, "Is it round enough?"

"Does it look round to you?"

"Almost!"

Then he condescended. "It's getting there. You'll watch where you're driving in future."

"I didn't say I minded," Alison accepted. "I'd much rather being doing this than sewing on buttons." Then she thought of turning the tables. "Next time you rip your clothes I'll make you sew them up. See how you like doing that." She placed the bent section of the rim back in the brazier, and drew back laying her head on his shoulder as Ben instinctively put his arm about her. "Prissy's so lucky," she praised, turned her head and looked admiringly up at him. "I don't think you'll have her doing this."

She lifted the rim from the brazier, placed it on an anvil, and again beat it: this time succeeding in making it rounder. "How's that?" and looked at him with satisfaction.

"Mm. Cool it, and see how it fits."

Alison dipped the rim in an old vat filled with water, backing off as it sizzled. Ben then placed it around on the repaired wooden wheel. "Right, Sis. All you have to do is nail it back on."

"Easy." And it was for her. She hammered the nails home without missing the mark. When she had finished she turned to Ben with a flushed face and tears in her eyes, and murmured, "I'm going to miss you — so much."

"I'm not going away — once I'm married."

"I hope not." Alison had not been told where Ben and his bride would be living, although she assumed at first they would stay at Kowhai. She could hardly imagine Ben moving in with Priscilla's mother. That day Alison did have doubts about Ben's choice of a wife. Not that she disliked Priscilla in any way, however wondered if she cut out to be a farmer's wife?

Ben had noticed during the trip to Auckland the old horse had laboured, so decided it was time to accustom two colts into drawing a cart. He found Alison curled on her bed reading, and said, "Do you want to help train the colts to harness?"

She nodded, eyes brightening. "Oh, yes, please." Anything, to escape the boredom.

They led a colt and a filly from the stable into the yard. Alison watched her brother a fit bridle with its long reins to her charge, then the saddle and collar, and breeching round the rump.

"Now, we'll walk them."

Ben allowed his horse to move off, and with longe (sic) lines attached to the reins, while Alison did the same to hers. Both horses had been ridden, so at least were accustomed to saddles.

"Which one first, Ali?"

"My one, I think." She hunched her shoulders with excitement, the breeze ruffling her loose hair.

While she held the horse steady, Ben carefully edged an old cart up to it: the horse poring the ground and neighing, but being calmed by Alison's tender talking. The shafts were fitted, the horse lifting its forelegs in mild protest, almost as if to say, 'I'm not going to make it easy for you.'

"Steady, Ladykiller," Alison whispered.

"You do it, Ali."

Alison moved behind the cart, using the longe lines to guide it, and round the yard they went, with Ben walking his colt behind. He opened the gate, and Alison steered the horse towards the house, and round it until returning to the yard.

"Seems all right," Ben opined.

"He knows he's in good hands."

"Try sitting in the cart."

"Do you think so — so soon?" she questioned, not so confident.

"I'm here."

All the while Alison crooned to the horse, and Ladykiller (sired by Handsome) a little reluctantly allowed her to climb on to the two-wheeled cart.

"Off you go. I'm right behind."

Gingerly Alison edged the horse ahead, again passed the homestead, then across the bridge and slowly along the rugged drive: the horse occasionally objecting. At the foot of the steep incline to the ridge road, she turned about, having to back the colt up, discovered to her horror Ben was nowhere in sight, and horse and driver retraced their steps: the horse's steps, and her guidance.

On reaching the yard again she sighed with relief, and boasted, "Easy, eh! I think that's enough for the day, though."

"Mm. I'll see how I go with this one." Ben changed the harness over, and trialled the filly. Alison groomed Ladykiller, washing him down, checking his feet for stones, giving him a drink of water and stabling him.

Jane walked past, and said sourly, "Having fun?"

Alison was having fun, at the same time doing something worthwhile. Jane would be the first to kick up a stink if the old horses broke down and she couldn't take her cheese and butter to the wharf.

The next day they repeated the exercise: and each time thereafter doing a little more, including taking a horse on to the ridge road, then back down, which was the more harrowing part, until both horses were ready to draw heavier carts, and the two old stallions could be retired.

Ben Chester was not the lay-about-son of a landlord. His father owned more land than some of the family knew, including apparently Jane. Either that or her continued anger over the coming intrusion of Priscilla into their lives made her blind to reality. Two or three days a week, while Jane was occupied in the dairy, Ben saddled his horse, strapped tools to a saddle bag, and with a cut lunch and a bottle of water, he would ride out of the valley, along the partially formed ridge road, and on the other side of it, clear the scrub, saving two-inch diameter straight sections of tea-tree for future fence posts. He usually worked alone, occasionally pausing to chat to a passing traveller or a mate. He would be home before dark, and since Jane never bothered to ask him how he spent his days she was none the wiser, and therefore her fiery thoughts over her future went un-quelled.

He was heading home late one afternoon when he passed a swagman with a young boy obviously making their way to Kowhai for the night. "Hello, there." He sized up the man before making an offer. Although unkempt, then man did not look dishonest. "Looking for a bed for the night?"

"Sure am. And a few days work."

"We could help there too. Scrub cutting, but."

"Suits me." He looked at his son. "How's that eh, Boy." With the flick of his head, indicated, "They told us back there this was a place for a square meal."

"I'm real hungry, Pa."

"I reckon you would be, Boy. Not eaten all day, he hasn't."

Whether that influenced Ben, or not, they got their feed, although sat at the kitchen table, and a bed for the night.

When Jane came through the kitchen, she paused looked down at the two, scowled and passed on.

Next day true to his word the swagman gave Ben a hand clearing the scrub, while the boy chopped the smaller branches into pieces suitable for the range.

The swag said to Ben as they worked, "So, why are you working this side?"

"This is my place. Getting married in the spring."

"You'll need an army to get a farm cleared, and a house built by then."

"We'll live with my parents."

The swagger nodded thoughtfully. "You ma's a fine woman."

"She is at that."

"I can't believe the girls are sisters. They're . . ."

"Different. Hard to believe, but they are."

The swagger nodded. He imagined if Jane could be tamed she might replace his late wife as a mother for his boy. However, that thought came to an abrupt end later when they were returning to the homestead with a tea tree laden cart, and met Jane driving cows along Kowhai's drive.

"Give her a hand, lad," the swag ordered his son, who obediently dropped from the back of the dray, and in doing so, caused the leading two cows to baulk, sending a chain reaction along the small herd.

Jane's, "Damn you! Just leave them alone," deterred the swagger from making a tentative approach to the spinster.

"He was only trying to help," Ben advised his sister, while the dispirited boy slouched along the drive towards the homestead.

The swagman had second thoughts about 'courting' Jane. He was not tempted to stay beyond a week, and moved on to wherever his feet took him: his son obediently following.

In the midst of the football season preparations for Ben and Priscilla's wedding gathered momentum: invitations being sent out.

"I bet you would not deliver Emily's personally?" Alison teased her brother.

He looked at her, thought about it for a moment, seeking a reason to visit the city, then answered, "Bet I would." With his cheek resting in the palm of his hand he nodded at her across the kitchen table, knowing what her next suggestion would be.

Her eyes widened. "Can I come too?" she appealed, rising from the chair, walking round the table, running her hand across the back of her brother's neck teasingly, and asking him, "Another helping?"

He shook his head, apparently at the second question, and such was the communication between them answered the first with, "Guess so." He did not accept with reluctance, largely because he enjoyed his younger sister's company.

"Prissy won't mind me tagging along, I'm sure."

"Of course not." Had it been Jane, then it would have been a different story. Alison and Priscilla got on just fine. When he thought about it, his fiancé in character fitted between his two sisters. Then, giving it further thought, he realised out of courtesy he should then ask Jane along for the ride . . .

. . . And later offered, "I suppose you're too busy with the cheese and . . ." Then he thought of something more seasonal. ". . . And calving to come into the city with us?" It was a deliberately put negative request, especially since calving was not in those days generally seasonal.

"As you say, Ben, I'm too busy. No doubt Ali has plenty of time on her hands."

Ben was equal to that remark. "Would you let her help you, eh?"

Jane shrugged and turned away.

The truth was: having time on her hands, meant somewhere between dawn and dusk, Alison had an hour or two to call her own.

Just as Jane spent three or four hours to round-up and milk the cows, make the cheese or butter every morning, then repeated the same tasks during the afternoon, Alison also had tasks that took hours, such as washing and ironing, and the less domestic jobs around the farm which she preferred doing.

Maude relented, and Priscilla went with Ben and Alison into the city. Jane took her siblings to the boat, at the same time making a delivery of butter and cheese to the local store, and cream to the wharf for despatch first to Onehunga, then by horse and cart to the butter factory at Mt Eden. At least Ben could watch over it during the boat trip. They collected more passengers and produce at Awhitu wharf and Graham's Beach before heading across the mist-shrouded Manukau to Onehunga against an ebbing tide. With four small steamers alongside the shed-less wharf, and only derricks to unload cargo, it was bustling. They walked round railway wagons, avoided the fish and produce sellers, only Alison pausing to purchase a solitary grannysmith apple for a half-penny, while Ben saw the cream safely on to a cart. Several offloaded baconers were grazing beside the path leading to the Manukau Hotel, where the third mode of transport was waiting: a horse-drawn bus. After changing teams they eventually drove past Emily's street: their intended stop. With their cases they trudged down St Stephens Avenue.

"Are you sure this is the place?" Alison questioned, viewing Emily's mansion.

"That's what she told me," Priscilla assured. "I didn't believe her, but . . ." She shrugged. ". . . We can only find out."

Ben rapped commandingly on the front door, a mis-matched coloured pane rattling in response. No answer, and the three callers grimaced at each other. He rapped again, took a step back, although the house appeared unoccupied.

A minute specimen with *pince nez* glasses answered, and with a mouse like squeak, enquired, "Yes?"

"Is Mrs Emily Todd at home — please?"

The squeak became a grind. "Come in." Without offering further hospitality she hustled away. She did not call her mistress, instead grabbed a hand-bell, rang it twice and passed on, disappearing into an obscure corner.

They stood abandoned for fully a minute, or it seemed that way. Ben's vision focussed on the room where the maid had vanished, expecting Emily to appear from there. Priscilla's eyes rose up the flight of stairs, and confronted her sister's defiant gaze: the gaze of a queen looking down on her subjects.

Unsmiling, she descended, not so haughtily, rather as if wary as to why Priscilla, with Ben, and Alison she believed, had called. "So, what do I owe this visit to?" she questioned sharply.

Priscilla, taken aback, fossicked in her handbag and produced the invitation, hesitantly handing it to her.

"Personal delivery," Ben offered, also puzzled by Emily's attitude. She certainly wasn't pleased to see them.

Emily looked at Ben, then the envelope, and finally her sister. She sighed, then reached out and embraced Priscilla. "I thought . . ."

"No, Emily. We just . . ."

"It *is* lovely to see you — and you two," welcoming Ben and Alison: pleasure rising on her face. "Truly it is." She looked over their shoulders as she embraced all three individually. "Is Mother not coming in?"

"*Mother*, is not with us," Priscilla assured.

"Then, this *is* a lovely surprise. How are you? You all look positively wonderful." Perhaps after all they were not here to fetch her back to Waiuku. She turned and called, "Tea for four, Hilda. — On the terrace," Then, combining two thoughts. "It is such a beautiful day, and in the middle of winter. — Or Ben, would you like an ale?"

He shook his head. "No, Emily, tea will be great."

"Ah — ha, Prissy, you have him trained already."

The accused shook her head. "On the contrary, Ben is training me — when dear Mother is not about."

Emily led the way through a sumptuously furnished lounge, Alison pausing admiringly, and on to the terrace. She had not opened the envelope, so asked, "When is the big day?"

"Why we have come to town . . ."

"What, a secret wedding?"

"No. — No. We're getting married next month, and since we were coming to town, we thought we'd ..."

"That is positively sweet of you."

"Both you — and your husband ..."

Even before Priscilla had finished her sister was shaking her head. "Not him. He would not be seen dead at ..."

"Kowhai's as good as this," Ben defended, assuming she was about to say something derogatory about his home.

"*Kowhai!* That is absolutely wonderful!" She clapped her hands, swayed back, eyes opening wide. "Do not let us trouble ourselves over William. Besides, it might be more fun without him." She giggled, her youth overriding her present womanly status.

"Emily!"

"Prissy, darling, you are too much of a prude."

Hilda must have assumed her mistress would be ordering tea, because she arrived with the tea trolley. Emily, a gracious hostess, did the honours, all very formal.

A horse and cab drew up outside the house.

Only Emily heard the arrival, crossed to the french door and gently closed it. If she intended to block out the sound of her husband's entry the crash of his cane against the front door, and his intoxicated voice rumbling round the corner announced it. "Damn — rowdy — beggar! — Cheeky in-insol ..." He failed to articulate the word, so slashed the pane with his cane.

Ben started: ready to protect the ladies.

Emily expelled her breath. "That is *two* I have to replace."

"Does he often do that?" Priscilla asked, concerned at the drunken entry of her future brother-in-law. The thought of him being a relation, if only by marriage, horrified her.

"My darling, windows are so regularly broken around here, I keep a stock of them."

Ben chuckled. He recalled observing the mis-matched front door pane. His mirth short-lived. William Todd was either advised, or had determined, Emily was on the terrace. Unfortunately the intervening door was shut. Not for long. William smashed his way through it, and stood swaying before his wife and her guests. "My — my, enter-shaining I — I shee."

Unfazed, Emily with a gesture said, "Yes, my dear. Now you know Ben, and Prissy, and Alison, so off you go like a good man," and under her breath muttered, "and sleep it off."

His eyes brightened at the sight of the delightful Alison, whom he was sure he had never met. Surely he could not forget such an exquisite jewel: a jewel to sober him. "S-sleep what off, mmm?"

"You stupid fool!" She stood up, her height pronounced by her hair-do. "God, you are an embarrassment." Any humour had drained from her.

He pointed to himself. "I — I em-ba-rish my w-wife." To Ben, he defended his state. "I shay, isn't it every man's — ah — good fortune to get a — a little tipshy — once in awhile."

"Every — *damn* — day!" Emily accused.

With that William staggered towards her, arms outstretched. Emily sidestepped, and her husband somersaulted over the railing, a shrub cradling his fall. The cat sprang out from under with a screech, fled across the lawn, stopped dead and turned to see what had rudely awakened it. The guests peered anxiously over the railing at the inert bundle, Emily then ushering them back to the table, suggesting, "He may as well sleep it off there. It will not be the first time." Although humiliated by his behaviour, she had no intention of allowing it to disturb her hospitality. "So, are you staying in town?"

Ben, ever protective of the ladies, would himself stay with Emily, drunken husband or not. To have Priscilla and Alison subjected to such incidents dampened his enthusiasm, so he answered, "Ah, yes — just for a day or two — at a friend's place."

Priscilla's quick glance at him gave the show away, and ever-astute Emily silently nodded. She was not offended: disappointed he had rejected her offer, even before she had given it, although she did not blame him under the circumstances. She concealed her disappointment with smiles. Later when she gave all three a parting embrace there were tears in her eyes, and Emily was not one for that sort of emotion. She waved them goodbye as they boarded a horse-drawn cab, and she despondently returned to the terrace, where she contemplated her situation.

Both angry and hurt, because she knew they had intended to drop in on her out of the blue: the sort of surprise she welcomed. Ben had then dismissed the idea. Why, they had barely drunk their tea. Slumped uncomfortably in the wrought iron chair, Emily was conscious of her breast rising and falling with exasperated breaths. Again she envied her sister. The couple may never have the financial wealth she was now accustomed to, however they would have matrimonial wealth. She knew Ben would never humiliate Priscilla. She rose from the seat, gathered the still warm cups, placed them on the trolley, then with a sigh glanced over the railing at her inebriated husband, and wheeled the trolley through to the kitchen.

*   *   *   *   *   *

Three days before the wedding the first guests arrived at Kowhai. These came from the south: Wellington and the South Island. They travelled by steamer up the west coast, buffeted by a southerly storm, tumbled across the Manukau Bar, negotiated the choppy ebb-tide to Onehunga, spent the night there, and the next day ploughed their way across the harbour, calling at several bays until arriving at Pollok wharf.

"Anyone for Kowhai," greeted Ben, having never seen some of his relatives. When he observed their grey-green faces he assured obligingly, "Just a short ride, and you'll be there." He did not have the heart to tell them the truth: rain and surface water had ruffled the shell and mud roads making their passage tortuously slow.

For those travelling cross-country, winter rains had played a rutting game with many miles of unpaved roads. Some guests stayed at Waiuku, then had to journey to Kowhai by road or harbour: either way subjecting them to a rough ride. Louise was grateful they had brought more than one change of clothing, because up until the day of the wedding, various garments were hung out to dry — between showers, or even pegged to the rack over the kitchen range.

Emily arrived two days before the wedding. Having declined an invitation to stay with her mother at Waiuku, she was not so far removed from domestication to believe she could be more help than a hindrance. At the wharf she lingered in Ben's embrace: his of greeting, hers of wishful thinking. At the homestead she paused as his mother approached, waited for her arms to reach out first, before responding gratefully, "Thank you for having me." Then assured her, "I really do not mind where I sleep."

Louise nodded. "I have put you in the little back room. Leave your things. Ben will bring them up."

Emily purposely carried one of her bags upstairs, and as she entered the so-called back room she blinked at the glare: late afternoon sun streaming into it. "It is lovely. Oh, Mrs Chester — it is just wonderful." She frowned, because she was undeserving of such hospitality, especially since she knew her own home could not provide similar kindness. She looked out the window, observing two cows and their offspring, chooks at their heels, a horse grazing in the enclosure and the steep, grassed hill rising immediately beyond. With a sigh she turned to Louise, and offered, "I shall be down shortly."

"You have a rest first, my girl," Louise insisted.

Emily could not rest. Besides being young and fit, travelling from Parnell to Pollok was hardly wearying. She surveyed her travel-soiled clothes, grimaced, and minutes later followed Louise down the stairs, although went out the front door then round to the back, paused to watch a hen round up her brood, a puppy tie itself into knots chasing its tail. Immediately she recognised the triple-chorded song of the tui, and the descending trill of the tiny warbler. A lovely foal was tethered to a rail, holding its head steady as Emily patted it. Here and there were pockets of daffodils, tulips, freesias and jonquils: purposely planted, yet natural in location. Spring at its splendour. So what was a shower or two: a little mud? She had intended to give a hand in the kitchen, although for the moment observed Ben and his father were in need of help to erect a large marquee: accommodation for some of Ben's friends, for whom sleeping under canvas was second nature. And for those who would arrive at the wedding without invitations: an oversight on the family's part.

Emily, glad her dress was only ankle length. Even so, its hem was soon soiled with mud: mud that flicked up as far as her waist, along her arms to her elbows. She tried not to laugh too much as wind gusts caught the canvas and entangled her, then crouched to hold an edge in place while Ben belted in a peg. She had the ghastly thought some might take her activity with Ben the wrong way, believing she should have been in the kitchen if she wanted to help. Why, even Alison was in *there*. Much as she admired Ben, she would not stoop to misbehave with him.

Alison gave her another excuse to be dirty as Emily eventually made her way towards the back entrance. Laughing she said, "Emily, would you grab some of that wood. You're grubbier than I."

"They needed a hand," Emily defended, indicating Ben and his father.

"I'm sure they did." She gave Emily a disbelieving grimace. "Come on, we need a hand too."

Emily negotiated the mud to the lean-to, piled the cut tea-tree on one arm until it almost reached her chin, then staggered through the back door.

"We need *that*," Louise assured. "Emily . . ." She shook her head. ". . . You are mud from head to foot."

"She's no lady, Mother — just . . ." Alison hesitated when she saw the hurt on Emily's face. ". . . a mud lark." With rearguard action she snatched some wood from Emily. "Here, give me some before your arm breaks." Desperately seeking an apology, because Emily had misinterpreted her 'no lady.' utterance, she said, "I'd love to have a photo of you like that."

"You, Alison Chester, aren't the only girl who can chop wood," Emily reminded her. "Anyway, Mrs Chester, I shall keep the fire stoked." Nor was her deviation from her formal life an act. Long before she had to put on airs and graces she had been a tomboy, so was already enjoying being there: mud included.

All hustle and bustle in the kitchen. Blustery conditions outside might have kept the temperatures cool, although inside the room was an oven: cakes and pastries surely cooking while they waited their turn in the range itself.

"Who's for a cuppa?" came an offer from another helper.

"That's wonderful," Louise replied. "We'll have to get some more flour." While in the pantry she had observed that the flour bag hanging from a hook, as was the sugar, to be safe from rodents, was almost empty.

"Who's still to arrive?" Not a question of phoning the local store, because that communication was still more than a decade away for Kowhai. "Ben can fetch it when he meets them."

"It would be nice to have mussel *vol-au-vents*," Emily suggested while stooping to re-fire the range, wondering if they knew what they were.

"Well, my dear," Louise in turn suggested, "when Ben next goes to fetch someone from the boat, you can go with him and collect the mussels, while I make some flaky pastry. I'm sure this lot wouldn't know how," she asserted, casting her eyes at the cooks.

Flour was not the only extra. By the time they had taken stock of what was needed, they had almost filled a cart, so Ben was ordered to fetch it early the following morning, and take several of Jane's branded cheeses: some for the local store, and the rest to be sent on to Onehunga, where Jane had dealings with two provision stores.

In the meantime baking was suspended, and tea preparations begun.

While Alison was here, there and everywhere, Jane lingered longer in her dairy. On one hand she did really want to be in the thick of it up at the house. On the other she knew even if she did try and be light-hearted, she would only be acting. So she kept to herself, saddened that no one ventured into her domain, even to say hello. She checked her curing cheeses, shrugged, and decided to begin making another batch. By the time this was done, the cows were due for their afternoon milking. As darkness closed in Jane washed, changed out of her work clothes into a high-necked evening dress, and took her place at the dining room table: the meal held back until her arrival.

Emily sensed her distress, and during the meal suggested, "Jane, how about we go into the library and have a game of crib, or something?"

"I'd like that," she answered softly. This was not the arrogant ill-tempered Jane they all knew so well, instead a subdued sister of the groom.

Later when Jane closed the door, shutting out most of the bustling activity, Emily looked into those older so sad eyes, held out her arms for a hug, and said, "Your father is so proud of you." She held her tighter. "However you *do* work too hard."

"How about that game," Jane responded, unable to accept such praise.

Although Jane was the elder by a few years she knew Emily was both more mature and worldly. As they played she often stared at Emily, unable to believe what was said of her was true. There was certainly no roughness about her: Jane assuming a woman of her character would be crude. On the contrary, she discovered a gentle, compassionate woman, and although conversation did not flow smoothly between them, what did was pleasant and correct. Jane's opinion of her rose, however she did not advise her family of the change of heart. That was Jane's nature.

Ben was about to leave for the store next morning when Emily said quietly to Louise, "Would it be a waste of time me getting some mussels. The tide will be down now?"

"I'm sure we can cope here, my dear." She assessed the activity in the kitchen. "They would be such a treat. Off you go with Ben."

"I shall just put my grubby dress on. I shall not be a minute, Ben."

Ben found himself a little in awe of Emily. She was so worldly: first praising the beauty of the valley, then starting a discussion on the future of the Manukau Harbour as the principal means of travel between communities: a discussion decades ahead of its time.

"Ben, darling, I do believe it will be only a matter of time before the horseless carriage drives the horse from our highways."

Ben hunched one shoulder, and suggested, "They're so limited. They might be good for town . . ."

"Do you think their drivers will be satisfied with being confined to towns?" Emily argued.

"At the moment they have no choice, unless they rapidly improve the state of the roads." Ben pulled the cart to one side to allow another driver to pass. "Gidd'ay Arthur," he greeted.

"All the best for the future, Ben," the other wished.

Emily smiled, half expecting to be introduced, however neither driver paused. She continued with her reasoning. "It is progress, Ben. It seems to me progress is accelerating."

"In town possibly, but . . ."

"Take steamships, Ben. After centuries of sail, who would have thought just a lifetime ago even, steamships would take over?"

"There were still a lot of clippers when we were last in town."

"There are, Ben, although fewer than even a few years ago."

In years to come Ben would recall that drive down to the Pollok wharf with Emily, and how prophetic her vision was.

In reversed roles, while Ben was obtaining produce from the store, Emily did scour the rocks for mussels and oysters, able to fill a bucket, with no concern of depleting the abundant stocks. Not only was the harbour a means of transport, it was also an almost limitless source of seafood. While crouching over a mussel bed she realised that she was actually alone: a state she seldom found herself in. She knew Ben would be ages at the store, so was able to pause and gaze across the harbour, at least the mud banks that filled most of the space while the tide was out. When she disturbed a loose rock several crabs scurried away, seeking shelter beneath another rock. She poked her finger into a sea anemone and chuckled girlishly when it closed about her finger.

"Your hands!" Ben exclaimed, when he sought her after loading the produce on to the cart, and she showed him her catch.

"Just a few scratches," she dismissed, and swished them in a rock pool. "There, all better," she displayed, offering the most angelic smile. "I hope your mother has made enough pastry."

The wind had dropped, the sun shone, and in grand homestead Nigel Caldwell gave his sister away. Priscilla wore a fussy two-piece ivory coloured silk dress, overlaid with chiffon and lace. It had three-quarter length sleeves, although long gloves with frilly cuffs concealed her lower arms. The whole outfit was very elaborate: very Priscilla. She stood beside Ben, had a fear her mother might oppose the marriage when the minister asked, then huskily repeated her vows. Ben clasped her hands when he said his.

Next: the register, before it was forgotten. Then the photo session, wedding party and guests arraigning themselves in various poses, including swinging from pillars and hanging from windows, while the particular photographer gave instructions for each shot from beneath a black cloth covering the tri-pod held camera.

Before the breakfast Thomas guided the married couple to a small hole, and with guests crowding around, they planted a kowhai, each shovelling what little earth had to be replaced, and over the sapling they kissed amid cheers and whistles. Maude Caldwell thought the episode silly, while Louise Chester had tears in her eyes. She would appoint herself guardian of the tree, and trusted within a few years others would be added, assuming of course both her daughters were married from Kowhai. No alternative entered her head. (Although there was a church at Pollok, weddings would not be held there until 1928.)

Not trusting the weather to stay fine, the breakfast was held indoors — sort of, spilling into most rooms of the lower floor, on to the verandas, and front and back yards. Guests filed around makeshift tables set up in the lounge, and informally helped themselves, then sat wherever there was space. Only the wedding party managed to be seated in the dining room, its table extended to full length with the two inserts.

For Priscilla, the occasion was a dream, and she said to Alison, "Pinch me, then I'll . . ."

"Of course it's real." She squeezed her. "Sister." No 'in-law' about it as far as she was concerned. She had grown to love Priscilla more than her own sister.

On this day there were other exciting objects for Alison: Ben's friends to entertain. Having obtained a claret cup, her third she thought, and about the last of the *vol-au-vents,* she was momentarily alone, wistful looking, when one of Ben's friends spoke to her.

"You are miles away, I think, Miss Alison."

"Oh, am I? Sorry. Did you say something?"

Which was a golden opportunity to start a conversation, although not what he would prefer to say to this adorable girl. "What do you think of the union of Chesters and Caldwells?"

"Prissy? Why I've never thought of her as being a Caldwell. I suppose she is — was — really." She shrugged, swirled her drink, then after a grimace added, "I think she's more one of us — she is now anyway, don't you think?"

"I don't think her mother is too pleased, not by the looks of her."

"The old battleaxe. I'm glad she's at Waiuku, and Prissy's here. At least . . ."

Alan had another angle to add. ". . . Mrs Caldwell must be very disappointed — one daughter goes off — doesn't Emily look gorgeous — I haven't seen her husband about . . ."

"He's not here. — Anyway," she complained, offended, "you haven't said *I* look gorgeous."

Alan swallowed. "Oh, you do, Miss Alison, you do, so much. I think you're the prettiest lady here."

"You are flirting with me, Alan, I know you are, and you don't mean a word of it." Even so it was nice to be referred to as a lady, rather than a girl.

Before he got into deeper water, although he believed she was as pretty as anyone, he returned to his original subject. "I think Mrs Caldwell is disappointed Priscilla married a farmer's son."

"So let her be."

"Still, Nigel is bound to live up to her expectations."

"Have you read it?" Alison asked sharply, not wanting to talk of the Caldwells.

"Read what?"

"Great Expectations," she elucidated, leaving Alan bewildered as to what it had to do with the present conversation. He shook his head. "Then let me introduce you to the great Mr Dickens," and she led him by the hand to the library, the young farmer actually expecting to meet this fellow guest by the name of Dickens.

"There's no one here."

"What?"

"There's no one here, except us."

"Of course not." Still holding his hand she took him across to one of the bookshelves. "This is Dickens." She ran her free hand along the titles. "Ah, here it is," and drawing it out announced, because by now she realised Alan did not have a clue who the author was, *"Great Expectations,* by Charles Dickens," and offered it, looking up at him. Surely at such an intimate moment he would kiss her — just a little kiss.

While festivities were at their height Jane began her twice-daily duty. In a calculated pre-wedding decision, she had taken her work clothes to the dairy, and also deliberately allowed her cows to graze in the adjacent lower paddock. Unobserved, she made her way to the dairy, slipped out of her full gown — the floor being so clean there was little chance of it being soiled — and also some petticoats, allowing her to wear her working dress, and over it a full-length apron. She rounded up the herd, without her dogs to give the show away, and then milked the beasts in their stalls, all the time hearing the continuous gaiety filtering through the trees. Holding back tears she bit her lower lip, every so often choking with despair, knowing no one would miss her: would care whether she was present or not.

She thought her wedding breakfast exit was unobserved, however one guest did notice her, and although he only knew her slightly, and he not being really part of the celebration, hesitantly edged towards the dairy, paused by a gate, fearing a rebuff, then asked, "Miss Jane .. ?"

She started. "Oh! — Oh!" She wiped her sleeve across her eyes, frowning, unsure who he was, then in a subdued tone, determined, "Daniel — isn't it?"

"I'm sorry." He backed off.

Quickly she begged, "Don't go." She shook her head, and repeated, "Don't go."

"Miss Jane, I — I just thought you might like help." He shrugged, solemnly staring at her, because he believed his offer silly, like he was.

Jane had paused, hands still clasping the cow's teats. "That — that is very kind of you, Daniel." Gone was any harshness in her voice. She did wonder what he knew about milking. She certainly knew of Danny — everyone did — though she had never heard of him being linked with farming. Then, she supposed, in this pioneering locality, rural people could turn their hands to most tasks.

She fetched a second stool, and as effortlessly as if he had been doing it all his life, he milked whatever cow she suggested. The milk may have flowed: conversation did not. For a start, Danny was in awe of her. She knew he was a partially educated ne'r-do-well, who had no fixed job, and seemed to mainly mess about with boats. No one had a serious criticism of him. In fact, Jane thought, conversation might spoil the occasion; she might say something to hurt his feelings. So, other than courteous instructions, she said little, although smiled a lot: smiled more in appreciation than she had done for ages. It did not matter if the cows were let out into their 'correct' paddock, and anyone at the house could see them strolling in ones and twos on the opposite bank.

Thomas Chester noticed, although was too wise to interfere. He later observed his again immaculately gowned daughter and a not so well-groomed Danny Carsen returning to the homestead together, and grimaced. 'That is one for the books,' he thought. He caught Jane as she came out of the bathroom. "All well, my dear?"

"Yes, thank you, Father." Then she admitted, "Mr Carsen kindly helped me."

"That was very good of him."

They parted: Jane intending to at least acknowledge Danny during the remaining festivities. However, on seeing him standing silently with a group of well-weathered friends of her brother, refrained from putting him in an embarrassing position. She learned that the bridal couple had left, so ventured into the kitchen, and without so much as a word picked up a tea towel. Her thoughts lingered with Danny, wondering why, of all people, he had sought to help her.

Earlier next day Jane had taken two guests and some cheese to the wharf. Who should be there? Danny Carsen. Despite having alighted from carts on her own for aeons, Danny first offered a hand to her, then her two guests. If it had been anyone else she would have rebuffed the courtesy. Now, as in the dairy, she knew while some people would be unoffended, or indifferent at least, Danny might be hurt.

Other intending passengers were assembling at the end of the wharf: a short timber structure, its piles waist deep in receding water. Two clinker-built dinghies lay on the beach.

"Should be here b' now," mentioned Danny, as the group grew silent in expectation.

"You did say eleven o'clock," someone said to him.

"That's what you told me yesterday, Danny," Jane agreed.

Danny looked puzzled. The truth had dawned on him, however he was too self-conscious to admit it.

Jane took him aside, and said quietly, "Danny, if Emily arrived with the tide —high tide or thereabouts — four days ago, and it was early afternoon, then Danny . . . I'm sorry, I should have checked. It always pays to check these things."

Danny was crestfallen. "I'm sorry, Miss Jane. I must have got mixed up."

She momentarily clasped his wrist. "Never mind, Danny, we all make mistakes." Indicating the three other intending passengers, she said, "They must have got it wrong also."

Danny had to admit another error. "I told them the time."

Jane debated the problem inwardly. By the time they wended their way back to Pollok, then down to Kowhai, they would barely have time for a cup of tea, before having to return. Not that they need to go so far for a cup of tea. On the other hand, for her to stay with her guests meant not being at the farm for the afternoon milking.

During her deliberations she heard one little brat say aloud to another, "Danny, Danny's a bit uncanny." Not the first time she had heard the rhyme, and she thought it mean of them to poke fun at less fortunate people.

A further thirty minutes passed without decision: the one consolation being it was fine. The tide reached the bottom of the piles, then slithered across the mud. Finally, assistance was sighted: the shallow draught scow *Elsie* chugging down the channel, barely having to use its engine, its sails limp. Danny hailed it, and the skipper drew the vessel into the bank.

"You'll have to slide them across the mud," he called to Danny.

Danny gave no second thought to obliging. Fetching one of the dinghies he made three trips: piling one or two intending passengers, depending on their weight and their luggage, into his dinghy, then sliding the lot across the mud, although almost up to his knees in it.

Jane waited on the wharf, in a way admiring his actions, and when he had finished, she asked him, "Have you far to go home?"

"Just across the gully, Miss Jane."

"All the same, I shall take you there." She beckoned him to climb aboard, beside her, not on the back, where he made for, and once settled, dollops of mud sliding to the foot well, she said sincerely to him, "That was very good of you, Danny. I'm sure they'll all arrive home none the worse for wear."

For someone who took such pride in *her* dairy, quite amazing that she should allow a passenger to soil the cart. However the vehicle was not hers, rather the family's, so was not kept in the same immaculate condition as the dairy.

Try as she might she could get very little conversation out of him, and although she did not know just where he lived, she knew by his insistence he could walk the rest of the way, his home was still a long way. And that was down a treacherous hill, Jane knowing she should not be taking the cart down it, across an unfenced log bridge and into territory she had seldom ventured, since it was beyond the boundary of the Scottish Pollok people. Her brother Ben had befriended Danny because prejudices such as religion, or background in Danny's case, did not interfere with his friendships.

"You live with your mother, don't you?" she interrogated, due to his reluctance to part with information.

"Yes, Miss Jane, with me ma."

As the horse heaved itself and the cart up the opposite side of the gully, Jane recalled someone having said of Danny, he had rowed a dinghy all the way to Onehunga in the teeth of a gale. That made her think, had the unscheduled boat not arrived, he might well have offered on this day. With an inspiration she suggested, "You know, Danny, with your experience, you could be captain of one of those boats."

"Aw, Miss Jane, I don't know the charts."

"I'm sure you could learn, if you put your mind to it," she advised without thinking, because gaining knowledge to her was second nature.

"I'm not much good at reading, Miss Jane," he admitted.

"Ah, I see." She was not sure what to say. She had the inexplicable urge to offer to teach him. Only a passing urge, and although it lingered at the back of her mind, reality arrived.

"This is where Ma and me live, Miss Jane." He indicated a rough cottage, surrounded by a junkyard of broken-down equipment.

"Is it! So it *was* a long way for you to walk." She concealed her shock perfectly. Admittedly road conditions, particularly the one they had just travelled, took toll on carts and equipment. As a result Danny's place was probably a forerunner of a used parts yard. As he alighted, wiping the mud from the foot well with his hand, she again said, "Thank you very much, Danny for doing that today. It was very good of you."

"It was my fault, Miss Jane."

"No, Danny. We all should have checked." She splayed her hands. "I for one should have known, because of Em — Mrs Todd's arrival." She watched him scamper along the overgrown driveway, like a small boy running home because he was late. A strange feeling of compassion overwhelmed her as she turned the buggy and headed home, trusting she would get there without an accident. In all she believed she had done right.

Danny washed himself down the best he could from the tap on the water tank. At least his mother could not accuse him of wasting water; the tank was overflowing after winter rains.

It would have been easy for Jane to blame Danny for her delay in returning home; she blamed others for things that went wrong, even if the fault was hers. She simply said the boat was late, unconcerned whether they themselves knew the timetables. Not that regular boats left at the same time each day: the Manukau's nature, its shallowness, meant when the tide was out the great expanse of water was reduced to several channels separated by vast mud banks. Later, while Jane milked her cows, she imagined Danny squatting with her, helping. Not a chance in all the wide world of that happening again. And for the life of her, she could not fathom why she even wanted him there.

During the couple's honeymoon, staying at the beach resort of Takapuna, on Auckland's North Shore, Ben plucked up the courage to tell his wife of the decision he and his father had come to weeks before the wedding. "Prissy, I know you love Kowhai, but . . ." He looked at her solemnly.

"We won't be living there," she confirmed, before he said it. His earlier silence on the matter had caused her doubt. "No, my dearest, I don't expect we can, really. So . . ."

"Just wait on." He put his finger to her lips. "We will for a little while. You see, we have another property . . ."

"You never told me."

"Because, Prissy . . ." He shrugged. ". . . It will mean roughing it. The land over the ridge, on the harbour side of the road, is also ours. I've begun to clear it," he said, as if he had only felled a few trees.

Priscilla frowned, trying to picture the landscape. All she could visualise was very rugged terrain. 'Surely we are *not* going to try and farm that?' she mused.

They were! The land was there, and in those pioneering days, regardless how rugged and steep, farmers set to and stripped it of native bush, then sowed grass. The unwiseness of their actions would arise in later years. Ben's property had already been stripped of most of its kauri, and the re-growth was scrub and tea-tree. Gum diggers had also squatted there, and no doubt concealed in the scrub were still there: living in thatched huts, eking out an existence by prising kauri gum from the ground, its value largely dependent on its clarity. They would probably pack up and move elsewhere when Ben's planned development got too close for their comfort.

Ben himself drew up plans by night, and hacked his way deeper into the bush to clear the home's site by day: with axe and slasher. He knew of some almost inaccessible kauri logs in a gully. Undeterred, he thought, 'I'll have those.' He gathered together some mates, a couple of gum diggers, a team of bullocks, and hauled the logs out of the mire. 'That's the easy bit,' he surmised. He then sawed the logs into manageable lengths, while thinking about the next operation. That required digging a pit, rolling the logs crosswise on to other logs, and when his father slid down to the set, Ben said admiringly, "Pretty good, eh, Father."

"You can go below," Thomas conditioned.

So Ben, willingly at first, stood in the pit, the log above him, his father on top, and they began the laborious task of pit-sawing the timber into planks: each length taking several hours to cut. Ben knew while his father had to put in the greater effort, dragging the large double-handled saw upward, he below was continually showered with sawdust — great chunks of it. When he tired of the effort, he thought ahead to when this hard-won timber would be fashioned into a house.

Had he purchased the timber, it would have been milled by steam-driven saws. The kauri on his property was free for the taking, and since his own time was not at no cost, then it was the pit saw.

Using his father's tools he began building the house: every job he completed giving him a sense of satisfaction, of achievement. Remarks from Priscilla, like, "It will have such a lovely view," and,

"I'm going to be so proud," spurred him on, and rather than do a rough job, he did take time over details, ensuring the home was both sturdy and neat in appearance.

"This will be my kitchen?" Priscilla determined, as she gingerly stepped from floor joist to floor joist, and gazed out where the window would be. "It will be sunny in the morning."

"Hmm," Ben agreed. "I thought — the one at Kowhai never gets any sun — much."

"Yes, I think it will be lovely." She did not mind that the bedrooms would be on the cold side of the house, because she did not think they would be spending much time in bed. For both, their days would be long, and she would spend most time in the kitchen, so to have it sunny and warm was a good plan. Their corner lounge would face north and east, so when they did rest, they could look down one of the valleys and at the distant harbour. 'That will be lovely too,' Priscilla thought.

Ben did make one temporary building: a wood store for all the tea-tree he had axed while clearing the site. Later he would add a barn and a washhouse off to one side of the home, and even erect a roof over the space between the two. Ever thoughtful was Ben, ensuring the comfort of his Priscilla.

Priscilla did not wile away hours at Kowhai while Ben built the home. Content at first to fetch and carry for him, she gradually did little jobs on her own, more than just holding a weatherboard while he nailed it. She had secretly practiced nailing, so as he nailed one end, she nailed the other, if not so speedily, or without bending them, then still saving him having to move from one end of the scaffold to the other. Maybe also she wished to in some ways emulate Ben's sisters, particularly Alison, who was as familiar with carpenter's tools as baking utensils. Alison certainly had retained her femininity, so Priscilla thought why should not she also.

"As soon as the walls are up, we should move in," she suggested to Ben. "It will save us traipsing back and forth."

"Do you think so?" He knew it was a practical idea, although one he had deferred suggesting himself, because of the hardship it would impose on Priscilla. Although he could rough it, he did not want to subject her to such crudeness. Ben, ever-mindful of her background and blind to her own intentions of overcoming that upbringing.

This they did, staying for a few days at their home, going down to Kowhai for a decent meal and a clean up, before repeating the performance. Probably because of this Ben began to clear the farmland when the house was still far from complete. He looked at it this way. "Prissy, when the weather's fine, I should work outdoors, and when it is wet, I'll work indoors."

Priscilla nodded thoughtfully. Being summer, she imagined the house would go unfinished until the next winter. Ss long as there was just the two of them, she could cope. Much as she wanted to do so many little jobs within the home herself, she knew that with Ben outside they could accomplish a lot more where it counted.

Although Ben worked from dawn to dusk outside, he did have a couple of hours after supper, when he could work inside, and room-by-room matchboard planks concealed the studs. Priscilla managed to tack scrim over the completed walls, which they would later wallpaper.

"This time next year we could be grazing sheep," he advised her. "Even a few sheep."

The mention of sheep at first surprised her. Then, when she thought about it, Ben was being practical, given the nature of their land. He would have to clear a lot of land to make sheep grazing viable. As for having a few cows, there was no suitable land near the house. Maybe they should clear some land in their valley, such as it was, while the land nearest the house could be turned into a vegetable garden. She made that her priority, believing she could grow sufficient for them, and have ample left over to give to her mother-in-law, who had her own vegetable garden anyway. She could grow things Louise did not grow? She simply wanted to be helpful.

Despite the hardships, Priscilla was never more content than that first summer with Ben. She did not envy Emily in the city, or her sister-in-law Jessica living the high life at Waiuku, or what Jessica thought was the high life. So, with gardening, pottering about in the house, plus the usual feminine duties, running back and forth to Kowhai, she was not only content, also very busy; never a dull moment, in fact.

For Emily her honeymoon was over: long over. When she thought about it, it had been over almost before it began. She had imagined waltzing down Queen St on William Todd's arm, sneering haughtily at ladies who must surely desire to be in her position. Now, not only did she never waltz anywhere much with him, she discovered other ladies did not envy her at all. She was sure some she knew actually felt sorry for her as she went to town on her own, shopped on her own, lunched on her own, most embarrassing, and made her own entertainment.

She could not say truthfully that she often slept on her own. "Could I, puss?" she said, stroking her cat's chin: the animal lavishing the attention. Emily had taken to leaving the bedroom door ajar, and each morning Kit would climb the stairs, meowing several times, rub her face against the door, at the same time assessing who was in bed. If Will was absent she would enter, and with a satisfied growl spring on to the bed, and muzzle up to Emily. "Good morning, Kit," Emily greeted, usually sleepily. "Do you want to be tickled? So do I." Emily could meet the cat's wish. However Kit, being a cat, considered the affection no more than she deserved, and after a few minutes nestled into the quilt and went to sleep.

One attribute Emily did possess was a sound education. Her mother had seen to that, not that mother and daughter always agreed: in reality, rarely agreed: one of the reasons Emily had left home at an age when young women should be chaperoned. So, while she might appear scatty, and often acted it, she did have that education up her sleeve, able to hold an intelligent conversation, often with the very people who thought her scatty. She furthered her knowledge by being seen regularly at the local library perusing technical and commercial books, and borrowing them.

'William dear,' she murmured to herself, 'I shall one day take charge of your affairs.' She meant his business affairs: he could handle his personal affairs without her involvement.

She also allowed herself to be snared by masculine acquaintances, going by the adage, what was good for the goose was good for the gander. She craved to be loved, and if William would not oblige as often as she required it, then other men filled the gaps. And, she did not have to be too secretive about it. Unfortunately, like the ill-fated Karl — whom she had not seen since the day he had fallen victim to Ben's fist — she often chose liaisons unwisely. While she had no intention of making herself available to Ben, she did in fact envy her sister. Not only was Ben the rugged epitome of a farmer, he was also a gentleman; whom she would gladly be seen with at the theatre, not that Ben was artistically inclined. So, she sought an urban 'Ben'.

In a way she envied Alison, knowing the girl was not always bound by codes of dress. She had told her so. While Emily loved her clothes, she also thought they were unrevealingly restrictive. Before leaving the home she paraded before an elaborately framed full-length mirror, her tight eighteen whale-boned corset drawing her waist into twenty-two inches, thrusting her bottom out so it swayed, and her bust in the opposite direction, its fullness emphasised to show how great it was. Everything as tightly swaddled as a new born babe. She wondered what this women's franchise movement had in mind for fashions? Definitely a case of allowing men to ogle her, without seeing any flesh except her face, and ankles when she was seated. In the evening she could flash her cleavage off to all and sundry: usually the sundry, since her husband was rarely around to admire it, and when he was, demon drink blurred his vision.

Some would say she was an enigma: flaunting herself in public, studying business practices in private. She soon learned her husband's knowledge of how much money it took to run the household was considerably more than reality. So she let him continue to think so, while she invested the difference, in her own name of course.

Her love for clothes graduated to fabrics, and believing, quite rightly, that as the city grew in population so more women would require fabrics to make those clothes. Therefore by investing in a drapery she could not go wrong. Young as she was she began to acquire a sound knowledge of the industry. Emily thus turned otherwise idle days into educating herself for the future. She had the audacity to believe William would not make old bones, so rather than rely on him providing for her in his will, she would have her own nest egg, and by then have acquired the knowledge to make her nest egg provide for her. It still did not solve the problem of having little love in her life, and her affairs did nothing to compensate for what her sister Priscilla must be experiencing.

CHAPTER THREE

Jane overtook Danny Carsen on the road from Pollok Wharf. Her heart lifted as she offered him a ride, then she was annoyed with herself over such impossible feelings.

"Where would you be going, Daniel Carson?" she asked him in mock earnestness.

He paused in his stride, studied the shelly road, and replied almost inaudibly, "Just home, Miss Jane."

"Then, would you allow me to take you?"

"It's no trouble, Miss Jane."

She tut-tutted, and patted the seat beside her, as if commanding a dog to scramble aboard.

He reluctantly obeyed, and sat silently, in shyness and in awe of this superior woman: so much more intelligent than he. So used to being treated as an oaf, he was worried Jane's reputation might be damaged if someone should see them riding together. Fortunately the rough road along the peninsula's spine was almost deserted: most people travelling between communities preferring to use the Manukau's shipping service.

Jane could not understand her own feelings while riding beside Danny. She well knew he *was* only an idiot to most people. She had met so many eligible young men; believed they were untrustworthy, no matter how gentlemanly they appeared. She felt in charge of the situation with Danny, and could not bring herself to spurn him. Instead she asked, "Did you give further thought about becoming a ship's master?" She assumed he had not.

"Yes, Miss Jane . . ." He paused, wishing only to be worthy of her. ". . . I — I thought I'd sign on one of them coastal boats, and . . ."

"So, that's a good start, Danny." Quick encouragement.

"Do you really think so, Miss Jane?" Desperately in need of reassurance.

She turned to face him. "Yes, I do." Then she imagined how she could further help him. Facing the track again, she frowned, shaking her head, puzzled over her attitude. Why on earth did she want to further help him?

She did not have a chance that day, because they arrived at the bottom of the gully, where Jane knew Danny would only have a mile or so to walk home, and she would not have to cross, then re-cross, the precarious bridge. So she suggested perhaps he could walk the rest of the way, and he was only too pleased to oblige, since to get a ride any distance was a treat, and even more so with Jane. Besides, if she took him all the way home, she would see his place was as much of a junkyard as ever.

Also at the bottom of the gully they came across a typical sight: a bullock floundering in the mire.

"I'll get someone to get it out," Danny said to Jane.

"We could do it ourselves, don't you think?" was Jane's response to the animal's predicament.

Danny looked at her, and despite her stature he knew she would have hauled her cows out of bogs. The cart carried 'spares' such as a length of rope, and a few tools. Danny waded into the mud, while Jane knotted the rope, then tossed the noose to Danny.

"You push, and I'll pull," she commanded.

The beast was a reluctant participant, despite their efforts being for its own good.

"Come on, you stupid animal," Jane abused it, tugged harder, and slipped, only her outstretched hand preventing her from sitting completely on her backside. "Damn creature!"

Danny glanced at her, his attention though taken with shoving rather than her language. "It's moving."

"I should think so, if it knows what's good for it."

"Ma will say I've been wallowing in the mud again like a boy," Danny said, resigned to the prospect of again facing his mother in such a state.

"That's life in the country, Danny. Tell her so." She surveyed her own condition as the beast snorted and plodded up the hill. She splayed her hands, and said, "It looks as if I've been wallowing in it too."

Jane re-boarded the cart and without a backward glance headed homeward, while Danny walked slowly up the hill, putting off confronting his mother for as long as possible.

Danny did sign on, although did not think Jane would want to know, and told his mother the day before he left, then ducked for cover as she abused him for deserting her. The problem of the house was not his. He did not consider it so. His father had left the grounds in that state, and he, Danny, had no inclination to clean them up. After all, who would want it all? He did think if they were tidier it might impress Jane. That was before he decided to go to sea.

Thomas Chester soon discovered how important Ben had been: a youth who had pitted his strength against the odds, and had done so much to expand the farm. He could not now expect him to make further progress at Kowhai, so hired youths to further clear and grass his side of the property, adding to his stock of cattle. He expected a good day's work, and gave a comparatively good wage. An added bonus for these young men: two ladies to choose from, although they only fell for Alison's charms.

"I trust, dear, you did not distract Mr Benson from his task," Louise cautioned, as her daughter returned to the kitchen after a long absence: having taken a fresh cut lunch to the scrub cutter, whose work was considerably more than cutting scrub.

"Mother, I did not. I just talked to him while he ate. He *is* entitled to a break, you know." As her sister appeared she added tauntingly, "I think he enjoyed the few minutes I spent with him."

"I bet he did!" Jane snapped, face snarling with contempt, as she handed her mother a hotplate-heated iron, and placed the now cool one to reheat.

"I knew you'd say that," Alison retaliated, inflicting injury by adding, "I can't help it if they prefer me to you — sour puss."

"They just take what's offering . . ."

"Girls! — Girls!" Louise intervened, brandishing the iron. "That —
will — be — enough."

"She does not really mean it, Mother," Alison contended

"Oh, don't I just."

"She's just jealous because no one likes her." And grimacing
spitefully, she accused, "Why, Sister, not even Danny bothered to
tell you he was going to sea."

"He did." Said while her back was turned to Alison as she fiddled
with a condiment holder on the dresser.

"Ha! Ha! — So, you *do* care for him." Alison sniggered, then
poked out her tongue.

Jane swung round, as Alison's tongue retreated. "I don't!" Her
flushed face said otherwise.

Louise Chester frowned. "Daniel Carsen? — Surely . . ."

"Surely what?" Jane demanded, not giving either any room for
tittle-tattle.

"Nothing, dear, nothing," Louise relented, puzzled that Jane
could have the slightest interest in the roustabout.

Her behaviour made it obvious she *did* have an interest in him.
The stamp of her foot, swirl of her dress as she whirled about and
stormed from the room, leaving Alison chuckling: her own activities
pushed aside by this new revelation.

Jane turned, and re-entered the fray, arguing, "If you weren't
flirting with the scrub cutter, then you were hiding round the corner
until Mother finished the ironing."

Before she had finished the tirade, Alison was laughing at her.
"Oh, Sister, you are so — so — jealous." She shook her head in
disbelief. Unfortunately Jane's accusation was partially true. Alison
hated the ironing. A whole day wasted. She was sure she would
have a maid to do the chores.

Louise *did* have a maid: two, in fact — her daughters.

Undaunted, the following day Alison again took Peter's lunch to
him. This time she did linger a little longer. The cool west wind
sifted through the bracken and pohutukawa covered seaward
slopes, although permitted the sun to shine unchecked into gullies.
She sat with Peter, regretting she had not brought her own lunch,

so said little to him while he devoured his sandwiches and eyed the freshly baked scones. Alison gave him something else to watch — her.

He watched her hunch, clasp her hands around legs, only slender ankles showing, since she was wearing dress shoes, not her farm boots. When she rose his thought, 'She's going already,' dulled the moment. Instead, leaving her seldom-worn hat on the ground, she walked towards the fire, and his heart lightened again. He took another bite of a sandwich, mesmerised.

Alison knew she was being watched, and as graciously as she had risen she bent her knees, back straight, gathered a few slashed twigs and tossed them dart-like on to the fire, turning to smile at him, as the dry leaves crackled into flame, sending sparks scurrying into the air. She knew Priscilla did this often with Ben. Hardly an excuse to assist Peter. She was not wearing her old clothes, not wanting Peter see her in anything other than her best. With a sigh she returned to her hat, swooped down, and with a, "I'd better get back," gathered and flicked it on, hitched up her skirt, and imagined him watching her exquisite ankles tripping across the stumpy ground.

Alison thought of how she could on help Peter. 'Maybe I could use the sledge,' she considered, and having considered it, immediately put the thought into practice, changing into old clothes, locating the sledge, hitching it to a horse, and returning to where Peter was working. Collecting branches and some quite large logs — to show she was no weakling — she stacked them on the sledge, then nudged the horse into action. No sooner had she got it going, than she called, "Whoa!" clambered off and ran back to collect the fallen branches. Her next attempt was disastrous: the sledge capsizing, sending her and the load tumbling down the steep slope. Gathering her wits, her first thought being, 'I'm glad I'm out of sight of him,' she picked herself up, reloaded, and this time succeeded in the reaching her back yard. Thinking she would get another load the next day, she then sawed the logs and cut the branches, ready for the numerous home fires that consumed a large quantity of wood.

Alas, she could not use the sledge next day — Jane had it.

"Do you have to have it — today?" Alison protested.

"Yes, Sister, I certainly do," Jane assured her. "You shall have to find other ways to entertain the scrub cutter."

"I am only helping."

"Yes, of course." As Alison walked petulantly away, Jane flung at her, "I suggest you help Mother today and the scrub cutter tomorrow." She smiled as she saddled her horse, because she knew by looking at the mare's tails clawing across the western sky, before the day was out rain would set in.

Since the buggy had gone, no doubt Thomas having taken it to Waiuku, Jane secured her cheeses to the sledge, hitched it to her horse, and more wisely than her sister, rode the horse out of the valley via the old track: even less suited to carts than the new track, then down to the wharf, taking care not to let the sledge run into the horse's legs down hills, as well as ensuring she did not to spill her hard-earned load. Jane's cheeses at the time were considered of superior quality because she had pasteurised the milk, unlike many dairy farmers.

Regaining the ridge road: a silvery Manukau on one side, and the grey Tasman beneath a brooding sky on the other, she knew her demand to have the sledge was justified. 'I'll be lucky to make it home,' she calculated, also observing a heavily leaden cloud colliding with the eight hundred foot high hill between Kowhai and the coast, knowing within minutes rain would envelop the valley.

Alison kicked herself for not acting sooner. If she could cleave logs for firewood, then she could use and axe or slasher to cut down the scrub. However, not a case of turning up one morning on the job, rather, edging herself into it. Next time she took Peter his lunch, suitably dressed, she lingered, not only to talk, but to experimentally swing the axe at a three-inch manuka trunk. The blade buried deep, so the tree might have been pushed over. With the next blow she felled the tree, turned and smiled. "How's that?" she skited in a more masculine manner.

Peter had his thoughts. While he admired her skill, he wondered just how long and how often she could cut down a tree with two well-aimed blows.

"You finish your lunch. I'll do a bit."

She did not repeat her debut performance, nevertheless had felled several small trees before Peter was prompted back to work sooner than intended. Alison handed him the axe, then panting slightly with exertion, carried the fallen trees over to the burning pile. She looked at one of the trunks, evaluating its size. "You know, Peter it's a shame to waste a lot of these."

"Plenty of it."

"Maybe now, but not for always."

Peter gave her a sideways glance, then looked at the bush, as if seeking its end, being several hundred rugged yards to Kowhai's boundary.

"Even so," Alison also assessed, following his imaginary gaze.

Not to be deterred, next day at lunchtime she rolled up by horse towing the sledge, and tied to it a wooden sawing frame and a saw.

Peter looked at her astonished.

Alison shrugged. "We can never have too much wood for the range. Besides, if we've a lot it'll dry out, and be good for winter."

"I guess so."

"I know so. We've scratched around for dry wood often enough, what with the range, fires in the lounge and bedrooms."

That prompted Peter to ask. "Do they all have fires — the bedrooms, I mean?"

"Just some of them."

The innocent comment and reply that led to intermittent conversation between the two as they worked.

A blustery December did not promise good weather for Christmas, and only the week before a severe storm swept the land. Lightning cut the air, sliced a hilltop pohutukawa. Thunder bounced about the valley, shook the homestead. The rain relentless, ground saturated, valley streams climbing their banks, swirling across paddocks, and sending Jane racing to move her cows.

She was battling forces of nature on three sides, when she noticed two strays being rounded up by a weather-protected person. 'Danny,' she murmured to herself. 'It's just what he would do.' Her heart lifted. 'No, it will be Father.' She sighed, and continued with her task, pushing and prodding three beasts to higher ground, at the same time hoping the water would drop before they were due to be milked. 'Well, it'll be your own fault,' she accused.

"Get over there," came a demand.

Jane turned and through water-filled eyes peered at whoever was making the demand. "Oh, It's you!"

"Of course. Who did you expect?" Alison answered, with a pout. She might have known Jane would be ungracious. "Now move!" she ordered a reluctant cow.

"Thanks, Ali," her sister condescended. "It's good of you."

"If it's like this later, Sis, I'll give you a hand."

"I hope it won't be." Was Jane's way of saying, 'No need to.'

Although the weather had abated by mid-afternoon, Alison reapplied her wet-weather gear, soggy as it was, and assisted her sister, their conversation restricted to the task in hand: milking.

When all was spent, the last of showers had vanished over the eastern horizon, Christmas day dawned cloudless, the kindest of breezes crisping the air. Thomas milked the cows that morning, allowing the Jane to go to an early church service with her mother and sister.

After breakfast the smaller family gathered round their traditional tree to open presents. Alison did spare a thought for someone else: Peter, alone in his quarters, neither friends nor presents. Slipping from the festive scene, she first went to her room, sought a handkerchief she had put away for her father – as a future bribe — wrapped it in so recently used paper, and trotted over to the cottage, knocked and called, "Peter, it's me, Ali."

She stepped back and waited, was about to knock again thinking he may have gone for a walk, or even be working somewhere on the farm, when he appeared, wearing longs and a singlet.

"Oh, hello," he said, as if embarrassed by his dress.

Alison took a step forward, reached up and handed him the parcel. "Merry Christmas." As Peter accepted the gift, she excused, "It's not much, but I suppose it's the thought that counts."

"Ah, thank you."

"Mother did tell you to come across for Christmas dinner."

Peter nodded.

"Earlier if you want to. You don't want to be alone on Christmas Morning. I wouldn't want to be."

Peter nodded again.

"The weather seems to be holding," Alison added, lingering, "so we'll be having it outside. Much less stuffy, don't you think." Peter raised his eyes to look at her more admiringly than he dared to verbally discloser. "Oh, well, I had better get back and help." She turned away, and as Peter began to retreat into his sanctuary, she confirmed, "We will see you later." She walked across the yard, talking as if Peter was beside her. "Yes, it's going to be a lovely day; it will be like having a picnic." To the dog which trotted up to her, she said, "You like picnics don't you; eating all the scraps."

Having done everything that needed to be done, so they believed, the sisters were in wicker chairs on the front veranda when Danny Carsen and his mother drove up. The girls exchanged looks: one arrogant, the other perplexed. Danny tethered the horse — not his own, nor was the gig — and helped his aging mother alight. Alison's attention was drawn to the fact that both gig and horse were her father's, so somewhere along the line her sneaky sister had got them both to Danny's place, without her knowing. She watched her sister, and was disappointed that Jane simply acknowledged Danny, and gave the slightest of curtsies to his mother. He even looked respectable. Uncharacteristically he was out to impress someone. When Alison broached the subject, Jane simply raised her eyebrows and gave a slight supercilious nod. Jane knew exactly what her sister was thinking, would not give her the satisfaction of witnessing any affection toward Danny, despite what was filling her heart.

There were no such reservations later when Ben and Priscilla arrived, Peter getting a handshake and a slap on the back from Ben.

Other relatives and friends rolled up, the front yard filling with various horse-drawn conveyances — the horses sent to graze, while out the back family and guests assembled at one of three trestle tables: this one serving drinks. There being no ice to cool the beer and lemon squash, they had the night before lowered crates of jars into the stream, the jars now glistening with drops.

Peter watched Alison — could not take his eyes off her — and wondered if her drinking would take full effect before she got to eat. Louise Chester and two domestics from a nearby family called all for dinner. Alison thought either one of these girls would be better suited to Danny. She had to chuckle, sniggering to herself as he, completely ill at ease, tried to fill a plate for himself and one for his mother simultaneously.

Jane came to the rescue. "Here, Danny, I'll get something for your mother."

Alison did beckon Peter to the table, and by way of trite conversation, said, "Aren't we lucky with the weather." Then she recalled she had said something like that to him earlier in the day.

Peter politely gathered smallish amounts from the selection, noticed Alison piling her plate high, and wondered where she would put it.

"That won't feed you," she said to him. "You can always come back for seconds." Then further assured, "Eat up. It will only go to the pigs — if you don't."

Making the remark as she brushed shoulders with her mother and receiving an admonishment, "Peter is quite capable of looking after himself, my dear."

Alison's corselet was loose round her waist, so she could eat plenty. She detested the things anyway, and believed she was slight enough to do without them altogether. Since her mother was discouraging her familiarity, she also thought, 'She's not discouraging Jane and Danny.' So with a pout inwardly observed, 'Maybe she knows no one else will have her.'

Nothing ever happens as wished for. When Alison did encourage Peter to the front veranda, she discovered Ben and their father in earnest conversation. 'No doubt business,' she moaned to herself.

When she sought another less-populated place, her mother spied her and beckoned, "Alison, dear, you might give a hand in the house."

"Yes, Mother." Her shoulders sagged, and she said to Peter. "Don't go far away. Cleaning up won't take long. Many hands make light work, and all that."

Peter responded, quite out of masculine character, "Maybe I could help?"

"Peter, it's not your place."

"I used to at home." And by way of a reason told her, "There was just us four boys, so we had to help Ma in the house." He was next seen clearing tables.

Jane, having left Danny's side, nudged her sister while they were at work, and murmured, "Trying to get him into the good books, eh?" Adding, "It won't do you any good."

Alison had composed her answer before the last remark. "No, he offered, like the gentleman he is." She checked out those present, ensuring her reply reached the right ears, adding, "I don't see Danny doing anything."

"He's going to help me with the milking," Jane retorted.

"How positively intimate. Do you want Peter and me to help also?"

"No, thank you very much."

The earlier rain had left peninsula roads muddy and rutted. The thought of negotiating the tracks out of Kowhai, then the ridge road deterred many guests. Most would have to allow two hours or more to get home, so, despite the long evening, they declined to have left-overs for tea, gathered reins, hitched up the horses, and plodded out of the valley: some heading north, others south.

As before, little conversation passed between Jane and Danny while they milked her cows; Danny still in awe of her: knowing that his vocabulary, his very speech, was not in the same league as hers. Jane knowing there was nothing crude about the way he controlled and milked the cows, and until he opened his mouth he could have been Ben, or any of her brother's mates. When he did speak his lack of education showed, and Jane had to wrestle with what she felt for him, and what was right for her.

One operation he was not familiar with: cheese-making. Although he thought that his mother might want to get home, he lingered with Jane as she began the process.

In the meantime Ben was required to go considerably out of his way to take Mrs Carsen home.

Declining all alternatives Danny set out to walk home. He never believed himself worthy of the lowliest bred girl, let alone someone of Jane's stature. Did she felt so sorry for him she befriended him out of sympathy? Was she now rollicking with laughter with the family, having some joke at his expense?

Jane was not laughing at his expense.

"You seem very keen on Daniel?" Louise Chester challenged, completely perplexed as to why, except out of courtesy, Jane even bothered with the fellow.

Jane lifted her chin, and eyebrows. "Danny is very nice, when you get to know him."

Alison overheard the defence, and chortled, "He never says two words, so how could you possibly . . ."

"Some people say a lot, yet have nothing to say," Jane retorted

"Oh my, we are very defensive." Alison pouted teasingly, suppressing a chuckle.

Her sister did not snap back in her customary manner, instead said knowingly, while nodding her head in response to Alison shaking hers, "I could say the same to you. You seem very attracted to the scrub cutter."

Jane's lighter mood lasted only days. She had no idea Danny had gone back to sea, and each time she took cream and cheese to the wharf looked out for him. Eventually she learned the truth, and her disappointment turned to misery. Was she *that* bad, not even Danny could be honest with her?

Peter continued to fell the bush and do other jobs about the property. Being so remote from a town of any size he never went far from the farm, only on rare occasions to fetch a guest from the Pollok wharf. He grew fond of Alison, although in his heart knew he could never expect approval from her parents. Keeping his distance emotionally did not mean keeping his distance socially. One day the conversation between them drifted to fishing, and without giving the time of day a thought, with rods they trotted off to the valley gap, and cast lines from the spur that jutted out into the turbulent sea. Separated by yards they had to talk loudly to hear each other: breakers tumbling on to beach north of them, and into the gap on the south.

"I can never work out how fish survive in that," Alison yelled, a gust whipping the words from her mouth, so although Peter snatched the gist of what she said, anyone a hundred yards away would have heard her clearly. His shake of the head was taken as agreeing with her. Fish *did* survive in the agitated sea.

Never had Peter more wanted to take her in his arms, believing she would respond. To take their eyes off the sea would be fatal: rogue waves every so often sending the fishers scampering higher up the rocks.

Never had Alison more wanted to be embraced. All past so-called suitors paled to insignificance alongside her feelings for Peter. Every so often she looked at him, gave a pleasant smile, and desired to say, 'Let's forget about fishing.'

They may as well have done, because the fish certainly were not biting.

Alison remarked, "There's not much out there today," and raised her eyes to where she knew there was a grassed ledge twenty feet above them. She imagines herself scrambling across the rocks towards the cliff with Peter chasing her, swiftly climbing and calling down to Peter, 'Come on slow coach.' Just as she reaches the ledge her foot slips, and he catches her, and as she flops on to the ground he clasps her shoulders and kisses her passionately.

Peter was also imagining being with Alison other than fishing: walking hand-in-hand along the beach with spent waves swirling around their bare feet.

With a sigh, Alison decided, as she wound in her line, "This is no use at all. I think we may as well call it a day."

They strolled home. For Peter the desire became ever stronger, while Alison wondered if she was contaminated. They parted with emotions unfulfilled.

"I thought you were going to do the ironing?" her mother admonished, as her daughter ambled dreamily in the door.

"Mm. Oh, so I was." What a dreary chore to face up to when she had just spent . . . She must have been gone longer than she thought. If the fish had been plentiful they would have been home much earlier, so it was not entirely her fault. "I'll get right on to it now." And with a sigh she sought the iron.

"No you won't, my girl, because Jane has done it." Not quite true: rather Jane had done some of it, and herself much of the remainder.

"Oh, poor Jane." And in a moment of revenge she announced, "She'll have to get used to working from dawn to dusk if she's going to marry Danny Carsen."

She already worked from dawn to dusk.

"What? — What, are you going on about, Girl?"

"Mother, can't you see . . ."

"Danny hasn't been here — for goodness knows how long."

"That doesn't mean our Janey hasn't . . ."

"Surely she has not been meeting him elsewhere?" Terrible thoughts raced through Louise Chester's head: such as when her daughter went to the wharf, did she meet Danny, and . . ? No, never: not Jane.

"You had better ask her," Alison challenged, and slithered from her mother's interception, because she knew Jane had not seen hide or hair of Danny for — several weeks. Jane had made enough accusations about her, so it was time to get one back. Alison 'amused' herself by sewing mother-of-pearl buttons back on, they having been removed before being washed: the wooden rollers of the mangle designed to crush such fragile fasteners.

The trouble for Alison, the matter was raised over tea, and in the presence of Peter. Thomas Chester had something to say on the issue, beginning with: "Well, my girl, I hear you've been shirking your duties again."

He did not get an immediate response from the accused: firstly, because she had her mouth full, and secondly, because Peter leapt into the fray. "I'm sorry, Mr Chester, but I — I encouraged Alison to go fishing . . ."

"So, you are the culprit. I thought you were employed here as a farm hand, not a fish . . ."

Mouth now only half fill, Alison blurted, "The *hell* he is!"

Jane shrieked. Their mother sat back rigidly, mouth agape.

Ignoring them, and unrepentant over her language, Alison defended Peter with her life. "He is entitled to have time off just like anyone else." The fact that it was a Tuesday was irrelevant, since farming generally was a day-in day-out life, without weekends. She reminded her father, "You've said yourself you owe him at least a week's holiday."

All eyes, except Peter's, turned to Thomas Chester, Louise dropping hers to choose with her knife and fork something she could hurriedly eat. Even before she raised it to her mouth, she had decided what to say. "I'm afraid, my dear, Alison, on this occasion, is right. Peter was quite within his rights. I'm sure the matter would not have arisen had Alison returned in time to do her duties."

"I did not know what the time was! If it is *that* important, buy me a watch," Her cheeks reddened with rage. "Then I can come running home like a naughty child."

"It's because you act like one, we treat you as one," Jane accused, having done some of the ironing before attending her cows' demanding needs.

That gave Alison another weapon. "At least I don't weep and wail because my lover has . . ."

"He is not! He is just a friend." Jane glared defiantly at her sister.

"Well, you act . . ."

"Girls! — Girls!" their mother intervened, wishing she had kept her mouth shut, having some consideration for Peter, who sat uncomfortably, not daring to eat his rapidly cooling meal. She turned the conversation back to the subject in hand. "So, Peter, did you catch anything?"

"Of course we did not, Mother," Alison snapped. If they had done so, for sure it would be fish they would be eating now.

"I am sorry then." Louise had thought they might have been hanging in a tree waiting to be gutted for breakfast next day.

Peter was sidelined, hesitant to continue eating. Not the first time he believed he had caused a disruption, so decided best for him to retire. Next morning he solemnly packed his kit bag, and would have slipped away unnoticed, had not Louise come out the back door with a basket of washing.

"Peter?" She laid the basket on the ground, and reached out for the young man. "Peter, where on earth are you going?"

"It is for the best, Mrs Chester."

"You can't just leave. I mean . . ."

"I've caused trouble."

Louise clasped his wrist. "Of course . . ."

"Mr Chester does not like me." With that he gently tried to break free.

Louise shook her head. "If you must, but first come into the kitchen." There she led him, reluctant as he was, believing the good lady would encourage him to stay. She sat him at the table and insisted, "You shall not leave here empty handed." She crossed to the cupboard and withdrew a loaf of bread, cut of a thick slice, then from the safe took a block of cheese, cut off a segment and wrapped both in a tea towel. "Just one more moment, Peter." She left him fidgeting in the chair, fearing her husband would enter, or worse still, Alison.

Alison on walking across the yard from the hen house had spotted the abandoned clothes basket, and had dutifully begun hanging the washing.

Louise returned to the kitchen, and from her pocket took two sovereigns, placed them in Peter's hand and closed his fingers over them. "I'm sure we owe you at least that much."

Grateful for the wages, Peter murmured, "Thank you, Mrs Chester."

She solemnly shook her head, and allowed the young man to leave.

As Peter walked down the back steps he sighted Alison hanging the clothes. However her back was to him, so he was able, he believed, to sneak away.

Later from the kitchen window Louise sighted her daughter standing against a tree with a pebble in her hand. Her head dropped, then snapped back again, and she wiped her eyes with her sleeve. Louise was tempted to go to her, but let Alison mourn her loss on her own, believing the period would not last long.

Several days later Alison was chopping wood, when her father rounded the corner of the house with another young man: this one having a shock of red hair. Alison barely paused in her work.

To the prospective employee Thomas stated, "As you can see there is a lot of work to be done here."

Vernon looked across at Alison, and agreed.

Louise appeared on the back porch, and called, "Thomas, could you give me a hand in here for a moment."

Thomas nodded, looked at his wife, then at Alison, who seemed more concerned with her chore. To Vernon, he suggested, "Take a look around."

As Vernon approached her Alison looked up, shielding her eyes from the
sun.

"You've got that down to a fine art," he complimented.

"I suppose I have. I've been doing it for donkeys"

"So, you don't need a hand?"

Alison looked critically at the well-dressed man, assessing he was probably a townie out of work and prepared to take on labouring. "No, not at all," she rejected, gathered the chopped wood, crossed the yard, totally ignoring her father as he strode towards her. However she did lift her long dress to expose her trim ankles as she walked up the steps.

Thomas observed Vernon's gaze, and said, "Sorry about that. I gather you have already met my daughter."

There was a look of incredulity on Vernon's face.

"Yes, young man, out here, women can handle most jobs. Alison is a great help to me in many ways."

Vernon's mouth remained agape.

Many men lived almost nomadic lives in the early years of the twentieth century, carrying their possessions from one place to another. So Vernon dumped his swag in the cottage, and the very next day picked up the tools previously used by Peter and hacked away at the bush. On cue Alison brought him lunch and returned home with a sled of logs: that's when Jane wasn't using it.

From the outset he was attracted to Alison, farmer's daughter or not. He also soon learned the lie of the land: from the rugged farm to the situation between the daughters. However, unlike Peter, he was more deviant in his quest for Alison's attention, and possibly hand. He would flirt with Jane. As he was passing the dairy — as it was called in those days — early evening, tools slung over his shoulder, he paused to watch a dishevelled and agitated Jane. "Are you just about done, Miss Chester?" he enquired, as if about to help her.

"Does it look like it," Jane retorted, as she endeavoured to coax a stubborn cow into its stall.

Swallowing, Vernon walked on. So much for that overture.

Jane for once felt apologetic. "I'm sorry, Mr Smart," she replied without turning, but when she sought the bushman, he had gone. She shrugged and continued milking.

Later, when both Vernon and Jane had dressed for dinner, and were seated at the table Jane was intent on making amends. She was seated beside him. Alison entered the dining room from the kitchen with a dish of potatoes, her mother following with peas. Mother and daughter took their places.

"Would you kindly say grace, Alison," Louise ordered.

Alison sighed, then quickly recited, "Lord, we thank you for this food. Amen." She ignored her mother's sharp look.

Vernon and Jane both reached to spoon potatoes on to their plates.

"After you, Ma'am," Vernon offered.

Thomas gave his opinion of Vernon publicly. "I must say, Vernon, you are clearing the land a lot faster than I expected."

The new bushman half-smiled. Jane chose then to make amends of her earlier behaviour. "Don't they say, Father, you cannot tell a book by its cover."

Her mother was appalled by the comment, and said, "Jane, I'm sure Mr Smart must be offended by that insinuation."

"Not at all, Mrs Chester."

Jane then slid the dish of potatoes closer to Vernon, although the gesture was unnecessary. "I was only remarking, Mr Vernon on first appearance did not look like a scrub cutter. Indeed while he might labour tirelessly, he, I am sure, could show the same diligence in any profession."

By now Alison's mouth had dropped in astonishment of such a compliment coming from Jane.

Vernon, playing along, replied, "That is very kind of you, Miss Chester."

"I'm sure it is true."

Vernon decided that was enough play for the moment, so ate his meal with little further contribution to the table talk.

While taking a breather, the late afternoon sun intense enough for him to be sweating profusely, he watched a stray cow trying to make a meal of what little grass available in the clearing. Jane came striding out of the bush, and accosted the cow. "There you are, Russet."

Vernon ran his fingers through his red hair, and determined, "Are you referring to me, Miss Chester?"

"No, the cow." The animal, sensing trouble, moved away. "Come back, you stupid animal. Can't you see there's no grass here."

Vernon rose to head the cow off. "It certainly isn't a case of the grass being greener . . ."

"She's always doing this. I spend half my life looking for her."

They prevented the cow straying further into the bush, only for the animal to evade capture and plunge across the clearing.

"At least she's going back in the right direction," Jane accepted, with an exasperated sigh.

They stood facing each other.

Vernon spied Alison emerging from another quarter, so said distinctly, "Glad to be of service, Miss Chester."

Jane looked over her shoulder to also sighted Alison. "Please call me Jane," she requested, and observing Alison's frown, added, "Thank you again, Mr . . . Vernon."

"My pleasure." With that he gave Jane a slight bow, picked up his axe and resumed work.

Alison was left bemused. To counter his rejection of her presence, she advised, "You know my sister is to be married in a few months."

Vernon continued slashing.

Alison pouted, then proceeded to load the logs on to the sled, and without saying another word led her horse from the clearing.

A hot day, so having chopped wood, Alison decided to cool herself down in the stream pool. She looked about, then slipped off her shoes, dress and petticoat and, only in her underwear, cautiously slid into the cold stream, crossing her arms across her chest as she shivered.

Being the end of the day Vernon was walking up the track beside the stream with the axe and slasher slung over his shoulder when he sighted the maiden, and paused, unsure whether to proceed or retrace his steps.

Carrying a billy of milk and a cheese Jane materialised beside him. "Spying on my sister, are you?"

Vernon shook his head. "Ah, I'm not sure which way to go."

"Just carry on the way you were going. I'm sure my sister will not mind a bit." She brushed past him and led the way, although paused as she was abreast of Alison, who, unaware of their presence, was dreamily skimming the water with her hands. "It is a lovely day for bathing, Sister."

Alison turned and quickly crossed her arms over her well-covered chest.

"Vernon was just admiring you." With that Jane tucked the cheese under the arm carrying the billy, and with her now free hand drew him away. "Come Vernon, we shan't embarrass my sister further."

Alison stared after them, her reverie at an end.

She to some extent got her own back over the evening meal, when her bathing was brought to her parents' attention. Jane insinuated that Alison had been in the pool with Vernon.

"No, Mother, only I was in the pool, being such a hot day, and me having chopped a load of wood, as you might notice when next you go to the barn." When that explanation failed to get a response, she added, "Anyway, Vernon and my sister happened to pass by."

"It all seems most improper."

"Not on my account, Mother. However, I did notice Jane's hand was in Vernon's, and my sister about to get married." She gave her sister a smarmy pout.

"That is a lie," Jane retorted.

"So my eyes were deceiving me."

"I — I was . . ."

Their mother looked from one to the other astonished at such goings on.

Their father added fuel to the fire, unintentionally it might be said, when a few days later he and Vernon surveyed the old partially tree-enclosed track leading from the farm. Barely a cart-width wide it wound round hills, was steep in places and generally hazardous to negotiate, summer and winter.

"Jane has often said how precarious driving round this corner is." The bend had a bank with overhanging trees on one side, and a drop on the other. Thomas rubbed his chin and pointed with his pipe to the upper slope. "I suggest you clear the trees from up there. It will allow sunlight to dry out the track."

"If it is for Jane' safety, Mr Chester, I shall clear it immediately."

Looking surprised, Thomas assured, "Not only for Jane's safety."

"Right you are."

He did so, since he had brought his tools with him. He had not long started when Jane on her horse towing the sled with two cream cans plodded by. She halted the horse with a, "Whoa!"

"Your father thinks it should be cleared to let the track dry out," Vernon explained.

Giving Vernon the credit, Jane complimented, "That is very thoughtful of you, Vernon." With a flick of the reins she urged the horse on up the hill.

"I'll have it done by your return."

That assertion prompted a rare laugh from Jane.

True to his word Vernon attacked the scrub with renewed vigour.

So intent on his work he did not hear Jane returning fully an hour later. Admittedly she was not in sight when she halted the agitated horse to reposition the sled with now empty cans. She hesitated whether to walk the horse round the bend or ride, but since she had negotiated the track many times decided to remount her horse. Vernon, with his back to her, gave the large tea-tree a final blow of the axe, slipped, so he was trying to regain his balance when the tree toppled down the slope and across the path.

The horse reared, sending Jane over the edge, the two cream cans barrelling after her. It then bolted, crashing through the upper branches of the fallen tree, the sled bouncing along behind.

Vernon slithered on to the track, witnessed only the horse's flight and began to chase it, before realising Jane was not on it. He looked about, ran back up the track, thinking she must have fallen before reaching the bend, then came to his senses.

"Jane! — Jane!"

From the kitchen Louise first heard the horse's frantic gallop, then watched wide-eyed as it thundered past the window. She hurried out the back door as the agitated horse came to a standstill in the yard, mouth frothing. "Oh, my goodness." She looked back to the house expecting to see Jane chasing after her horse. "Jane, where are you?"

Alison appeared from the barn. "Mother, what has happened?"

"Isn't it obvious. The horse has come home without Jane."

"It isn't the first time," Alison dismissed.

"But look at the sled. A wheel is missing."

"Oops!" Alison held the horse by the reins and patted its head. "It's all right, old boy, all right."

"She must be up the hill somewhere."

"She's probably sitting on the trackside cursing this creature — and me for overloading the sled with logs."

"Go and find her — now! And don't be so . . ."

"If I must."

Dazed, and dishevelled, Jane sat among the felled scrub Vernon had tossed over the bank. Beside her was a battered cream can, its dents the result of several wayward excursions from the sled.

"Jane!"

The voice at first seemed from afar.

"Jane!"

Someone was calling her. They must be concerned for her whereabouts. In that case she must give them something to be concerned over. She felt her shoulder, then her knee, however settled for her ankle being injured.

Vernon plunged through the scrub. "Jane, are you all right?"

Bending low over her 'injured' ankle Jane retorted, "No, of course I'm not."

"What have you done?"

"Just about broken every bone in my body."

"Oh, no. — Surely."

"It feels like it."

"Can you get up?"

Their cheeks were close, although Jane actually wished for them to be closer: a feeling she did not experience with Danny. She looked at the tangle of branches. "I think so. But I will need a hand."

"Of course." Wondering just how to lift her without offence, he hesitated.

"Just get on with it."

He clutched her around the waist and began to haul her upright.

"Do you know what happened to the blasted horse?"

"Bolting, the last I saw of him."

"Ouch!"

"Sorry. Almost there." As they reached the track, Vernon suggested, "You wait here, and I'll fetch the buggy."

"I think I can manage — with your help." She glanced provocatively at him. "If you don't mind helping an old crock?"

"Hardly old."

So, with his arm securely about her, he edged Jane down the slippery track, and when on the flat he began to slide it from her waist she placed her hand on it and looked at him appealingly. She had sighted Alison before Vernon had, her sister strolling along the track towards them, as if in no hurry at all.

Alison certainly sighted the cosy arrangement. "Humph!" With that she turned on her heel.

"Alison! — Alison, come and give Vernon a hand."

"Oh, I'm sure he is doing fine," she suggested over her shoulder. As their mother hurried to the scene, Alison recommended, "Mother, let them be. They are enjoying every moment of it."

"Oh, dear me, Jane. What happened?"

"Don't ask. I'm sure Vernon didn't mean to." Vernon looked sideways at her, catching a glimpse of an impish grin. "He chopped a tree down just as I was passing."

"I'm sure he didn't mean to, dear."

Vernon decided the act had proceeded far enough so released Jane into her mother's care, and began walking back along the track. He looked over his shoulder to see Jane walking without a limp beside her mother, and chuckled.

A day later Danny arrived on the scene, his boat having docked about the time Jane was careering down the hillside. Thomas was having none of his loitering around the place, so set him to work beside Vernon.

Noon, and Jane, carrying the same wicker basket Alison used to convey lunches to the bushmen, strolled purposely along the track. She sighted the men before they sighted her, and for a few moments watched the comparative rate of the work: Vernon again belying his appearance, and Danny making a great effort of it. When she called, "Lunch time, men," Danny dropped his slasher so fast it almost sliced his foot, while Vernon continued to fell a tree, then dragged it across the track and tossed it among the fallen scrub below the road.

Alison at the time was busy cleaving logs. She stretched, wiped her brow, and with a puzzled expression walked briskly towards the house, just as her mother appeared on the back porch. "Lunch time, Alison."

"Already. I'll just take the men theirs first."

"Oh, Jane has done that."

The look on Alison's face was of dismay and hurt. "Since when has she taken it upon herself to do that?"

Further injury came late that summer's day when Alison was gazing out of her attic window. Below her on the track Vernon and Jane appeared to be in earnest discussion. What she imagined they were saying and what they were actually saying were two different dialogues. In disappointment she withdrew from the window.

"I do believe, Jane, I have got it wrong."

"How so, Vernon?"

"I must confess I was using you to win Alison's favour."

"Do you not think I knew that."

Vernon's mouth dropped.

Jane informed him, "It has been the case for some years. You men always seek my younger and fairer sister."

"I admit I did. However . . ."

"However what?"

"I do believe you are the worthier woman."

He reached for her hands, but Jane kept them at her side.

"Oh, do you now," she murmured, and turned her head aside. "The pity is, Vernon I am betrothed to Danny."

"Betrothed, but not yet married."

"I'm sorry, Vernon, so sorry." With a look of despair she began to walk away.

Instinct caused Vernon to look to Alison's window, however she was not in sight, so he walked thoughtfully towards his cottage.

Not totally rejected, next day Vernon, as he was leaving his cottage, spied Alison walking across the yard. He hastened to intercept her, however she also increased her pace, and hurried up the back steps to the sanctuary of the kitchen, where her mother was bound to be.

*   *   *   *   *   *

The second year of the twentieth century was dragging for Jane, waiting for word from Danny. For other people, however, it was flying by. Thomas advised his daughter she would soon have calving on her hands, to which Jane's, "Don't remind me," was out of character. More by accident than design three of her herd were in calf, although spring was a few months off.

She admitted lately her heart was not fully on the job. She continually thought of Danny out there on the high seas. Why, he might be on one of the many ships that passed their gap *en route* to New Plymouth and further south. When she thought of him, their social gap also continually nagged her. She feared not being there when he did return, so declined invitations more than an hour's ride away, on the pretext she had the cows to attend to — morning and night, and in between.

The family did not join the throng heading for Auckland for the May visit of the Duke and Duchess of Cornwall and York. Disastrously, only days before arrival, their accommodation was gutted. Among highlights were 2500 children forming a Union Jack in Wellesley Street, and mayor for the occasion, Sir John Logan Campbell, giving the skirt of One Tree Hill to the city, naming it Cornwall Park after the Royal couple: a gift that would endure. The former Maori pa offered a rugged playground for the expanding city. It would not be long before public transport, by way of electric trams, would convey people to the foot of the hill. New tracks were being laid, replacing those used by horse drawn trams, and when only a few years later they extended across the isthmus, people living round the Manukau found the journey by boat and tram just that little more comfortable. So, who would want to drive along rough roads via Papakura? In fact, over fifty years would pass before the last of the Manukau's launches was withdrawn from service. In the meantime they and the harbour would play an important part in the Chesters' lives.

When Priscilla learned she was expecting, her main concern was it would stop her helping her husband clear the land. For that reason she kept the news under her belt, although was careful not to do anything too strenuous.

When Jessica, her sister-in-law, discovered she was in the same state, she promptly blamed her husband, and would not let him near her. She might have accepted the damage was done, and been thankful they were having a family.

When Alison prised it out of Priscilla, she being first to know, she saw it as an opportunity to escape Kowhai's restrictive bounds and help Ben.

"Prissy," she offered, while the two women were alone at Ben's place, affectionately called after a widely-spread tree with little white flowers, Kanuka, although less appealing names described the rugged land. "You wouldn't mind me helping my big brother," adding unnecessarily, "I shall take your place." The unwisely stating, "I'm fitter and stronger than you, so I'd be a great help."

"You are not!"

"Not what?"

"Fitter and stronger than me."

"So, I aren't." Not to be deterred, she agreed to differ. "Let's say, I am in better condition for physical work." She gave Priscilla a superior pout, and rested her cheek against hers, because the difference of opinion was only superficial, unlike the differences she had with Jane. "Honestly, Prissy, please don't do anything silly."

Even so, Priscilla was suspicious as to why she suddenly wanted to help, and narrowing her eyes, accused, "Have you had an argument with Jane?"

"No! — No more than usual — in fact, less." Then, confiding in her sister-in-law, she mentioned, "Jane's been acting funny. She can't even be bothered arguing most times."

So the subject switched to Jane, and naturally Danny. They exchanged opinions, and the opinions of others. Then abruptly Alison returned the conversation to Priscilla, and demanded, "You still haven't accepted my offer?"

"It's a lovely offer, Ali. And I love you so for making it." She sighed with gratitude. "Yes, of course you can help Ben. And I'm sure you really *are* fitter and stronger than me." She crossed to her range to remove the scones from the hot plate.

"Mm, they smell lovely." Alison complimented, taking a sniff.

Priscilla, placed the griddle on an already scorched wooden table, and pleaded, "I won't tell Ben just now. I'm feeling fine, honestly, so let's wait a little longer."

"I don't know, Prissy," Alison argued, reaching over to feel the texture of the scones. "I'm sure if I were you I could not keep it a secret for a minute."

Had Alison been suitably attired, she would have gone off to help Ben there and then; after a cup of tea and two scones. The very next morning however she advised her mother she was going back to Ben's for the day.

"Two days in a row?" Louise questioned. "Has Ben got a helper up there?"

With a stamp of her foot Alison, knowing what her mother was inferring, retorted, "Yes, me and Prissy," and expelled her breath in disgust, because for once a male was not the attraction.

"Prissy and I," Her mother corrected.

"Eh? — Prissy and I then. — What's the difference?"

Louise pondered, 'If Ben has *not* have a helper — a male helper — then what is the sudden attraction?' She went off on that tangent, and in doing so she completely overlooked her daughter-in-law may have been the reason why Alison was helping out: soon spending two or three days at a time away.

Eventually the truth emerged. It did not actually emerge, rather was arrived at, when Louise took herself out of her valley across the ridge road and dropped in on the couple, intending only to call at the house, presuming them to be down the gully. "I didn't expect you to be here?" she challenged her daughter-in-law. "No one else about?"

"Ah no. — Um, Ali and Ben are way down the valley," Priscilla indicated. "I'm about to take some lunch and a fresh brew down to them."

"So, that is why you're up here?" And Louise looked directly at her daughter-in-law, with raised eyebrows.

Priscilla could not restrain herself any longer, dropped her eyes, bit her lip. "Mrs Chester, I have not told Ben. — Ah, I just was not feeling too well this — today." She had twice changed her mind about confessing during the short explanation.

"And it would not be something Ben should know about?" Again the lady raised her eyebrows.

"It would, Mrs Chester. Although I do so much want to be all the help I can."

"You'll be a better help telling him, and taking care of yourself." She took Priscilla's hand, squeezing it. "So how far are you?"

"Almost four months."

"Prissy!"

"I know. I feel so mean."

"You aught to — not telling any of us — except . . ."

"Ali. That is why she is here."

"And here's me thinking she had a secret admirer, or something."

"No such luck — for Ali." They both laughed, and embraced, tears flowing freely from the mother-to-be, while Louise's tears slipped from closed eyelids.

"So, dear, let's go down and tell him now."

"Oh, I thought . . ."

"My dear, if I don't prompt you, I do not believe you shall tell him, until he works it out for himself." She shook her head. "I don't know . . ." She did not complete the sentence, because she was sure Priscilla would not be putting Ben through the same rejection as Jessica was doing to Nigel — this far out.

Confronted with his mother, wife and sister, Ben was not sure how to react to the news. He had been so obsessed with clearing the land, he had not given having children at this time much thought, so replied, "I wondered why Ali had suddenly turned up." Nor was he put out by the fact his sister and mother learned first. He assumed it was one of those feminine confidences.

With smoke from the fire swirling about the clearing, so that wherever they sat it wafted across them, they had their picnic, Ben digesting that he was about to be a father — just when, they had not told him — and also digesting the hearty lunch.

Jane had a cold.
It made her even more miserable.
Sloshing water over the dairy floor did not help. Her nose a beacon on her pallid face: hair all over the place. Her only consolation, she was alone. Her mother and Alison were at Ben's, and her father and the farmhand up the valley somewhere. She assumed the maid was in the house, although she did not count.
Jane's thoughts, when not on her misery, did lift themselves from her almost sea-level location to the new house high on a hill, and she wondered what was going on. Something was amiss? For a start, Alison would not normally volunteer to do manual labour for her brother, or would she? And why had her mother suddenly gone there? It did not take her long to work out the truth. What a fuss. Anyone would think Priscilla was Lady Muck. She could not imagine them running after her if she was having a baby. She could not imagine ever having a baby. 'I'll be the spinster aunt to them all,' she murmured, and was further saddened at the prospect. That she only had herself to blame if she ended up unclaimed did not occur to her. Surely someone must want a woman of her nature, although not one with a cold as well.
The one man in the world who did want her — warts and all, including a cold if he had known — was riding hell for leather, on a borrowed horse, along the drive at that very moment. As he crossed the bridge he slowed, his dull mind having been fixed on the homestead being its customary mecca, now wondering why the front door was shut. Having tethered the horse, he plodded up the back steps, paused then knocked.
He did not enter the house, instead turned away, looked up at the sky as if seeking guidance, then walked across the yard, his gait gathering momentum as he approached the dairy. When he reached it he paused, stood hesitantly in case he was not welcome,

watching Jane hang up two ladles. Watching silently, until she turned.

With eyes wide, she gaped at him, then hurried to him. "Danny! — Danny!" She forgot her appearance, even if momentarily. "Danny, you're home again." Without hesitation she reached for him, arms about his neck and fervently kissed him. "Danny, and here's me only now thinking you had gone for good."

So dumbfounded at her fervency he could not respond.

"Danny?" she queried. "Everything is . . ." She could not bring herself to learn the truth. "You do . . ."

He nodded, and offered meekly, "Hello. — Are you not well?"

That reminded her of her condition, and she grimaced, pleasure dissipating. "As you can see, Danny, I have a deuce of a cold. I had better not give it to you."

Danny could only think for the first time in his life a woman — not an aunt, or anyone like that — had kissed him. He was stunned, bewildered.

She backed off, looked him up and down, and appraised, "You have new clothes."

"Mm." His mind still fixed on his reception, then awakening to the fact she *had* noticed his appearance. "I got them last week. I get good money now, so I thought . . ."

"You *do* look smart." The maid may have seen through his clothes. Jane knew what was behind those clothes — a sweet caring, if not very intelligent, man. "And here's me all a mess."

To Danny Jane looked regal. "I thought I could help you."

"Oh Danny, you have not come here to work." Then she thought, 'How long is he here for? Here today and gone again tomorrow.' She sighed, arms akimbo, not at all inviting to look at she considered, so altered her stance, head to one side.

Looks did not mean much to Danny. He would have worshipped her had she been the ugliest woman on earth. At least that is what he told himself. Lost for words, because she was actually pleased he was here.

"So, how long are you in home for?"

He paused, as if calculating the question. "A whole week — almost."

"I expect your mother will have lots of things for you to do?" she stated, hoping to the contrary.

He nodded. "But I wanted to see you first, Miss Jane."

That was something anyway, and Jane told him so. "Since you have put me first, then we should just have time for a walk before lunch. You will stay for lunch won't you?"

He nodded again.

She had so much to tell him, and had been gathering news for months: some almost ancient. Now he was here, and it all seemed irrelevant. "So, where did you go this time?" she asked, believing his adventures were far better conversation than her domestic news.

"All over."

"All over where?" She tugged at his arm, something she had never done to any man; which would not have been hard, since Danny was about the first man to get this close to her.

As if he had been wayward, he owned up, "We went to Sydney . . ."

"To Sydney! How wonderful." Sydney conjured up all sorts of exciting things. "I bet you went out on the town?" She hoped he had not, because being a sailor going out on the town, meant — she cared not to think he was like that. He must be. All men were. No, not true. Ben had not been, nor had some of his friends, she believed, although was not sure. So engrossed in her analysis she actually missed most of his answer.

". . . For my new clothes."

"Sorry Danny, I was thinking — ah — I missed what you said. A noisy tui."

"I didn't, Miss Jane, because I was saving for my new clothes."

Oh well, one reason was as good as another, she supposed. "That was wise of you." They had crossed the lower paddock, and were negotiating the streamside track leading to the gap, where the valley stream tasted the salt of the sea moments before being absorbed into it. Standing on a ledge, the stiff sou-westerly moulded Jane's dress against her, accentuating her stature; a queen seeking her fleet returning from plundering far off lands.

Danny stood to one side and a little behind, admiring her, not believing the moment was true. A fleet did not appear, only a small steamer, wallowing as it was lifted from aft by waves, being jockeyed along so it might reach the Manukau just that much earlier. Its size was about the same as Danny's ship, although he did not tell Jane.

"So, that will be you in a few days time; out there without a thought for me."

"I do, Miss Jane, I think of you — all the time," he blurted.

She turned slightly toward him, looking over her shoulder. "Do you, really?" And when he assured her he did, she suggested, "So why don't you put your thoughts to paper and post them to me?"

His face clouded, and when she read its anguish she immediately realised her error, bit her lip, and clasped his arm. "Danny, please forgive me. I am so selfish." She so much wanted to reach for him, reach into his soul and fill it with knowledge. He had knowledge. He just did not have the ability to convey his knowledge to paper. Would he allow her to teach him? Would he be too humbled: too embarrassed by such a suggestion? She held his arms, gazed into his sullen eyes: eyes lowered in shame. She believed then she *was* in love with him. How could she, the well-educated daughter of a prominent farmer, fall in love with a ne'r-do-well? Unlike her sister who had fallen in and out of love a dozen times, Jane had no former loves to compare her feelings for Danny with. She humbly offered, "Danny, my dear, I'm terribly sorry for what I said. Please forgive me." Drawing him to her she begged, "Please allow me to make good my mistake." Even as she spoke, she wondered just how many of her words or phrases Danny fully understood.

And when she kissed him while standing on that rock, surging sea below, was she merely a mother kissing her child? She was unsure, although appealed to him, "Danny, please come over every morning until you go, and let me teach you?"

He shrugged, and she tugged gently on his arm. "Why, we could start this very day. There's no one up at the house. And Ali's over at

Ben's. No one need ever know." Was that the right thing to say, to have him conceal his ignorance to everyone else? Then she thought with dismay he did not have to conceal it; it was painfully evident. She knew people were already sniggering behind their backs at such a mismatch. 'Very well,' she decided, 'I will change that. I'll have him as educated as the best of them, then see what they say? As a gentleman he is already up there with them — higher than many of them. He is polite, thoughtful, caring. Who else came to help her with the cows on Christmas Day?' She knew very well why no one else had dared to approach the dairy, Christmas Day or not.

Jane drew him from the beach — the tide too high to walk along it anyway — and literally dragged him back to the house, made him some sandwiches, and coaxed him into the library. For three solid hours she had him under her tutorial spell: first assessing what he could and could not do, then sitting beside him teaching him to write rather than scribble a few letters.

The only interruption was her mother's arrival: the lady having opened the library door, standing there surveying the educationally intimate scene for half a minute before Jane turned, started, and said, with her hand resting on Danny's, "Just a moment," and ushered her mother out of the room, looked solemnly into her mother's puzzled eyes, and admitted, as if she was guilty, "Mother, I am giving Danny some lessons."

Louse nodded slowly, thoughtfully. "That is very good of you. Don't forget, it's almost time to milk the cows."

"Oh yes, so it is." She thought quickly. 'Danny will want to help.' Then thought again. 'No, it will make him too late getting home. It will be dark.' She rested her hand on her mother's arm. "He is so deserving of what I am doing."

"I'm sure he is, my dear," the lady responded wisely. "And why would you be so intent on teaching Danny?"

Without hesitation, she confessed, "Because I'm — I'm very fond of him, Mother."

Her mother nodded, sighed resignedly, and replied, "I knew *that*." She shook her head, believing it to be more than fondness.

"You know best, my dear — I suppose." The rider was intended to cause doubt in her daughter's mind.

Jane bit her lip, looked at the floor, then with pride returning said, "I'll just finish, send him on his way. I — ah — suggested he came over every day until he sails again . . ."

"And when will that be, dear?"

Jane pouted. "In less than a week."

"I'm sure his mother will be disappointed, him at home, yet not at home."

"She can be disappointed. He can't be tied to her apron strings for the rest of his life."

"No, my dear." Louise Chester now had secondary thoughts, as to whose apron strings he might instead become tied to? She did not relish that thought. If Jane had had other suitors in her life, not that Danny was a suitor in Louise's mind, then she would compare those with Danny.

So Danny came under Jane's spell. Whether he wanted to be educated or not did not come into it. That caused conflict, on all sides. Conflict with his mother: who promptly told him he need not bother to come home at all. Conflict within himself: not accepting Jane was doing this for him out of kindness. She just pitied him. He was like a younger brother. He might in fact have been younger than her for all he knew.

On one such day, by prearrangement Jane, having taken cheeses down to Pollok wharf, met Danny at Pollok itself where four tracks converged. Less hesitantly than before Danny scrambled on to the cart beside Jane, although conscious that his hurried climb from the gully made him sweaty.

"Do you admire nature, Danny?" she asked him bluntly.

"I suppose, I've never taken much notice of it."

"You should."

"It's just there."

"That does not mean we should not enjoy it, Danny."

Danny did not know what to say to that. However, as they rode in silence, except for the clip-clop of the horse's hooves and the crackle of the cart's wheels as it trundled over the recently laid shell from a Manukau beach, he tried to take in the 'nature' about him. To him it was simply bush; mist-shrouded trees taking advantage of the roadway to spread their branches into the gap, and in places embracing those from the other side.

There was no such intimacy between Danny and Jane along the winding track, hills falling away on alternate sides, nor as Jane negotiated the drop into the valley: the cart often skidding alarmingly.

He did learn a lot in those few days. And he learned a lot more once he had gone back to sea, laden with books Jane had loaned him.

CHAPTER FOUR

Priscilla presented her husband with a son: taking the whole episode in her stride.

Louise moved in with her for the last few days, and moved out again only days after the birth of her first grandchild — George Chester. Breaking with an already teetering custom, the first male child was named after the maternal grandfather, not paternal one.

Thomas was least offended. That mother and baby were well, and he had a grandson was sufficient. Naturally Alison was at her brother's, leaving the Kowhai veiled in peace.

They received news from Waiuku that Jessica Caldwell had also given birth to a son, whom she and Nigel named Stanley. Born only days apart the cousins would develop in vastly different climates: at least for their first ten years. A piece of tittle-tattle arriving with the announcement was Jessica had vowed to have no more.

When Alison did return home four days after becoming an aunt, Jane pleaded sourly, "Perhaps I could go and see them now."

To which Alison assumed she was being reproached, so genuinely offered, "I'd be only too pleased to do the milking for you . . ."

"I'll be back again long before then," she assured.

With a shrug, Alison went to see if their maid needed the copper, was advised curtly that all the washing had been done, so she filled it, set a fire beneath, then went to her room to gather a complete change of clothes. Kindling heated the copper surprisingly quickly, so she bucketed the steaming water from the copper into the conveniently placed bathroom, tested it with her finger, ran a little cold from the solitary tap, the water drawn from large tanks of roof and stream water, undressed, and slid gently into the soothing bath, sighing dreamily. Wise enough to leave a full bucket of hot water beside the bath, because she intended to have a long soak. She checked her ankles and wrists for any bite marks, satisfied only scratches flawed her fair, slightly freckled skin. So relaxing was the soak that she very nearly went to sleep. The scare forced her from the bath, dry herself, dress only lightly — one petticoat beneath a cotton dress — pile all her soiled clothes into the copper, re-stoke the fire, grate some homemade soap into it, and allow it to simmer away, while she retired to her room, lay on her bed, sighed, and drifted into a well-earned sleep. Well that Jane did not take up her offer to milk the cows, because she slept until being called for tea, remained awake long enough to eat it, then returned to her bed.

Another year went by.

Alison still assisted her brother: although now considered the days monotonous, through which she ambled without direction.

Priscilla did not conceal her second expectancy from Ben, and Ben in turn toiled harder to develop the rugged land given to him.

Jane could count the occasions she saw Danny on one hand: not including the four or five days in a row, so on this late winter's day, she said to him, "If your horse hasn't rested, borrow one of ours."

"Why?"

"Because I want to go riding with you."

The suggestion seemed innocuous enough, so he agreed, with a, "Yes, my love." The words of affection did not come naturally to him.

Sharp gusts threatened to dismount Jane as she rode along the cliff top. "I just love it when it's wild, Danny."

"It's blowing me to pieces." Apart from that, the cliffs were unstable: sections frequently sliding into the sea.

"Come on, Danny, you've had far worse than this at sea," she challenged.

The cliff track detoured behind some wind-shaped pohutukawa, and in calmer conditions Danny felt more at ease. Jane was not at ease. Something within her was tearing her heart and soul apart: one yielding, the other sheltering behind this wall of idealism. Out on a bluff they again faced the wind, gazed down at the restless ocean, sea whipping the shore with a thousand lashes.

After courting a girl for almost two years, Danny had gained some self-confidence, at least to accept that Jane must like him. He again wrestled with the words he wanted to say, could not pluck up the courage to say them. The fear of utter rejection deterred him. They had dismounted, Jane's hand clasping his, squeezing it from time to time, as gusts buffeted them. "Jane," he said cautiously, "I have known you for a long time . . ."

"Yes, you have," giving her mare a pat to steady her.

The interruption deterred him. He tried to put his thoughts into words, then said to test his ground, "You won't think me — ah — you won't laugh at me — if — if I ask you to — to — marry me?" He had said it. Yet hardly knew the significance of the proposal.

After a quick and decisive mental battle, Jane replied softly, "Yes, Danny, I will marry you."

Numb struck, he did not know what to say next. Jane drew him towards her, kissed him first on the cheek, then his lips, and repeated. "Yes, Danny, I will be yours."

Would her head ever forgive her heart for its treason?

He had no ring to give her, and she did not expect him to have one. That formality could wait, although hopefully she could coax him into Waiuku before he went to sea again. They walked their horses down to the valley, rode them across the lower paddocks, Jane urging him indoors for another lesson, although neither could concentrate. She then sent him on his way, without advising her father of their betrothal.

"I'm marrying Danny," she mentioned to her mother, while kneading dough for bread.

"Oh, that's nice." Then Louise Chester's mind clicked. "You're *what?*"

Jane continued to knead: dusting the mixture with flour, before affirming what she had said, although rewording it. "Danny and I — we are going to be married."

The tears were coursing down Jane's cheeks, when her mother first clasped her arms, then embraced her daughter. After a minute: a minute when the maid entered only to be given the please go away toss of Louise Chester's head, she said solemnly to her daughter, "I am sure, my dear, Danny will make a very fine husband." Sliding her hands down her daughter's arms she held her hands. "Jane, he may not be your dream husband," then confessed, "Your father was not my dream husband either, although, as you know, I have never had a day's regret — never." She knew the analogy was not appropriate, although added, "I wonder if any of us ever find them. As you know, your father and I came from very different families."

"Thank you," Jane whispered, tears turning to sobs. "I — I just love him so, Mother."

"I know, dear." She wondered if her daughter knew what love was.

"Mother, you always know. You've always known what I feel."

"My dear, Bess and I will do this. You run along, have a lie down."

Jane, fighting back more tears, strode from the kitchen, hands to her face, ashamed should anyone see her in such a state, and fled to her room. Face down on her bed, slapping the quilt with her hands, she repeated, "I do love him. — I do! — I do!" Would she be in this state of she did not love him?

What should have been a joyous occasion at Kowhai, was instead as solemn as death.

Nor would Jane believe that Danny had no time to study. If he really loved her, he would make the time. The ships passing their gap seemed to sail themselves, so sailors aboard must be an idle lot. Then Jane only saw those ships on relatively calm days. New Zealand's coasts were not always calm: in fact were notoriously turbulent.

Danny did try. However two things irked him. First: there was little privacy aboard cargo ships. Second: the rest of the crew tended to scoff at him, to the extent one smart alec tossed his textbook to another sailor, who tossed it to another, who missed and it went sailing over the side. Danny fought back tears, because grown men did not cry. It was mean, very mean. He reported it to the captain, who promptly told him being brainy was not a shipboard need. Had he told the captain his intentions, then he would probably have been paid off at the next port.

Worse still: having to tell Jane what had happened. He would have bought an identical textbook, except he did not have a clue where to get it, and could not remember the title anyway. He did try. He did use time in Wellington to go to a bookstore, and search through hundreds of titles, hoping to find the one he had lost. Of no avail. He spent some hard earned money on one that looked about the same. Hopefully this would appease Jane.

Frankly Jane, that spring, did not care a damn whether he lost a textbook or not; as long as he came home. There was the bizarre shipwreck off the Northland coast, where the steamer *Ventnor*, carrying the remains of almost five hundred Chinese — victims of the cold on Otago's gold fields — was wrecked, and although the crew cleared the ship, sixteen died trying to reach shore. Worse was to follow less than two weeks later, when the *Elingamite* was wrecked on Three Kings Islands, with the loss of forty-five crew and passengers.

"Danny's not going to sea again," Jane declared, when those at Kowhai learned of the second disaster, while the family were in the lounge: the three women with needlework.

"My dear," her father assured, turning the page of the newspaper. "It is only coincidence two ships should . . ."

"It is not coincidence, Father," Jane insisted. "Do you know how many ships have been wrecked off our coasts?"

"Ah . . ." He laid the paper on his lap, and looked across at the daughter challenging him..

"You don't. — No! — It is hundreds."

"I'm sure it's not."

Jane was right. Every year, several times a year, ships were wrecked around New Zealand. Not all cost lives. The fact was, the worst tragedy of all had occurred within sight of Kowhai: the loss of the *Orpheus* on a sand bank off the Manukau Heads. That was almost forty years earlier, when communications were less sophisticated.

These days Jane knew when Danny was due home. However, when he was due, and when he arrived were usually different times. He did write to her, and the day his letter arrived at the gate, an invitation also arrived. Jane devoured the letter first. It was not a very long letter, although it took time to decipher both Danny's writing and his grammar.

Alison had also received an invitation, and leapt from the dining room chair. "I've got an invite to His Majesty's."

To which Thomas Chester promptly argued, "I did not know the King was coming."

"Father, not the King, silly." She shook her head at him. "His Majesty's! — His Majesty's! — It's the new theatre." She waved the letter about for them to see.

Louise chuckled. "And dear, who would have sent you that?"

"Emily, of course," She announced. "You've got one too, Jane, I bet." As if eager for her sister to also attend.

By now Jane had opened her invitation, and muttered. "Oh, blow!"

"So, what's wrong?" Alison asked with a pout: now a gleeful pout.

"Danny's coming home then."

"What a terrible shame," Alison lamented mockingly. She was free to go, and Jane would have been a bore anyway. "I wonder if Ben and Prissy have got one?"

"Priscilla cannot go for a start. Not in her condition," Louise advised.

"I bet Prissy wouldn't say so."

The event was weeks away. Christmas had to be got through first. *Got through* for Alison, although celebrated by the rest of the family.

This time Alison packed two dresses — her entire social wardrobe — petticoats, hats and bonnets, gloves, capes, and more personal items. Emily had said in a letter she had a suitable gown for her for the actual occasion. Again Jane trundled her to the wharf: the summer morning bright and cherry about them, the season's offspring gambolling in paddocks, in the days when lambs arrived in spring, and not mid-winter. As she boarded the *Weka* she noticed Maude Caldwell in the ladies cabin, and inwardly pleaded, 'I hope you're not going too?' She again made her way to the top deck, and begged the very same captain as last time to allow her to stand with him. The weather was breezy, the sea fairly calm, so she was able to chat.

"My future brother-in-law is studying to be a captain," she proudly announced.

"And who might that be?"

"Why, Danny Carsen."

The sailor swallowed, although good manners in the company of a lady prevented him from being rude. "So, that's what Danny boy is up to. I heard he is at sea."

"Yes. He's due back . . ." Alison did not know exactly when. Besides, she had tired already of talking about Danny. Much more exciting events were waiting for her. At Grahams Beach, she held the wheel steady while the captain moored the vessel. She was thrilled, and made sure bucking waves did not toss the ship away from the wharf. She was relieved to notice Maude Caldwell getting off, obviously not travelling to her daughter, Emily's. Alison thought impishly should the boat suddenly swing the old crow would tumble into the sea.

Then came the long run up the harbour.

Quite unexpectedly the captain said, "Here, Miss Alison, you take her."

And Alison did. Her, a farmer's daughter, steering this little steamer across the harbour, her feet apart, eyes keenly ahead, not that there was much on the surface to avoid. Any threats lay beneath the keel, as the deep-draught *Weka* chugged against the ebb tide, hints of sand banks beginning to show, and what appeared to be a broad harbour was rapidly draining into a series of narrow channels. "Oh, this is wonderfully exciting," she said with a shiver, expecting to be relieved of her duties. Instead, the captain stepped away from the wheel and lit his pipe, so she was in sole charge, ensuring she steered a centre course along the unmarked channel, only the water colouring telling her its depth.

"Keep a little to the right," he advised her as another boat approached them.

Even though she knew right was really starboard, rather than claim her knowledge, she concentrated on getting through the — oh — so narrow gap without hearing horrid crunching sound if they grounded.

Alison was still at the wheel as they neared Onehunga, and only then did the captain take over. So excited she reached up and pecked his bearded cheek, gathered her baggage, and was gone. She did not linger, because even more exciting things awaited her. She had no dread of arriving to find Emily away, and having to play cribbage with the maids. First she had to lug her case to the bus stop, heave it aboard, since there was no kind gentleman to help, then sit patiently while for the second time that year she was horse-drawn across the isthmus.

Emily greeted her with open arms, Alison falling into them, and then giving both Isabella and Hilda a hug.

"So, my darling, you are here all on your own?"

"Yes. Janey is so sorry. She is so disappointed. And so are Prissy and Ben."

"Never mind, pet. You and I are going to have the most marvellous time."

"Emily, I'm ready for it. Life has been such a horrible bore," she lamented, giving a sorrowful pout.

"Surely not. And did you have a good trip across?"

"Guess what? I steered the boat for ages, all the way across the harbour." Alison grimaced excitedly at the recollection.

"So, you are all ready for tonight?"

"I most certainly am."

Emily suggested she might like to rest. Alison could not contemplate wasting a moment of this day. They had a late lunch, and Emily agreed to take her sister-in-law into town, albeit reluctantly, since she had business there.

She could only window-shop, because it was Boxing Day and all the shops were closed. However, lower Queen Street, now paved, and with new electric tramcars jostling for position, was a hive of activity. Late afternoon: people thronging the ferries. Those who had been in Auckland for the day scrambling to get back to the North Shore, or to St Heliers and Mission Bays. While those who had picnicked on the shore and eastern beaches were beginning to crowd back into the city. Caught up in the melee Alison was swept on to Queens Wharf, and avoiding those queuing for ferries at the nearby terminal, she strolled along this broad pier, admiring the many and varied craft moored alongside. There was large steamer from overseas, and beautiful sailing ships, some with partially furled sails hanging to dry. There were laden colliers, waiting for the wharfies to return to work the next day. Numerous dinghies tugged at their moorings, and from a canoe Maori were unloading vegetables to sell.

She gazed down at a wicker basket brimming with dwarf beans. Whimsically she asked the tattooed Maori woman, "Can I have a few?"

The lady thrust her hand into the basket and drew out a clutch, silently handing them to Alison. Astutely Alison did not ask her how much, just dug into her pocket and fetched out some coppers. "Here," she offered. "Is tuppence enough?"

"Have them, my dear. For you, nothing."

"I must pay for them," Alison insisted, and firmly placed two pennies into the woman's hand. "Thank you. They look so fresh."

The Maori splayed her hand with a nod. "Picked today."

With an appreciative smile Alison walked away, then turned back to the woman, who was gazing after her. Only then she realised she must look quite odd chewing a raw bean. Being raised on home-grown vegetables she was accustomed to eating them raw, allowing the taste to linger in her mouth.

She stood at the wharf's end, gazed out at the breeze-caressed harbour, admiring the keel yachts gliding through the waves. A paddle ferry approached, its knife-like bow slicing the sea, curling it beneath the whipping blades, leaving it churned in its wake. In that entire crowd, not a soul she knew, so unlike the Pollok wharf. Barefoot children sitting on the edge dangling lines into the green water was closer to her scene.

Alison now had a watch — her present the day before — and she knew it was time to meet Emily again, so she swept back along the wharf, her full length dress lifting with the breeze. Certain she was in the right place. Of Emily there was no sign. Surely she would have waited a few minutes. 'Oh well,' Alison thought, 'I can always get a tram to her place.'

Alison caught the slight whiff of tobacco on Emily's clothes when she emerged from the crowd, although thought it was her husband's. Emily did not offer an explanation as to where she had been, and even if she had, she would have found it hard to get a word in edgeways, since Alison did most of the talking during their short ride back to the Todd home in Parnell.

"Why won't you show me what I'm wearing tonight?" Alison pleaded. "It might have to be altered."

"I can assure you, dear Sister, it will not." Ten minutes later she relented, just in case they did have to make last minute alterations, and by then it was *the* last minute.

The gown: a two-piece damson coloured creation of silk velvet, with a fitted bodice, leg-of-mutton sleeves, puffed out at the elbows, then tapering to her wrists. It shrank to a twenty-one inch waist. The skirt blossomed mainly to the sides and back, until its hem perimeter was over eighteen feet. Alison stared wide-eyed. "Oh, Em, it is gorgeous." Her eyes misted. She was ecstatic, hugging Emily lovingly.

"It is for a gorgeous girl."

It did fit, perfectly.

Around her neck she wore a white silk scarf that fell in frills to her waist.

A fine summer's night allowed Alison to become the first Chester to be transported in a new era — an automobile: one of the few in Auckland. She was excited, awed, and a little afraid as Will Todd manhandled the roofless contraption down the ever-steeper Manukau Rd, (Parnell Rise) and relieved when they chugged along the now mis-named Beach Rd, since the beach had been buried beneath reclamation.

They putted their way up Queen St, amid carts and carriages and strolling pedestrians. Alison's lips were permanently parted in awe, gazing dreamingly at the flickering street lamps, at the buildings, and most of all at the people: gracious ladies swaying along the footpath, with a bobbing array of hats on both men and women.

Lingering daylight when they arrogantly parked the vehicle almost outside the new theatre. The great building was a blaze of electric light, another new invention being used to mark this glorious opening. They swept along the arcade — shops being fitted out — and paused for introductions to Emily's friends, customarily dressed in extravagant, bosom showing creations. When William bowed to the ladies, doffing his bowler hat, Alison asked herself, 'Should I curtsy?' She was a little envious of them, although believed she was as beautifully attired as any lady there, thanks to Emily. She adjusted Emily's dress, as if her maid, and smiled demurely at another noble lady.

A young man sidled up to the group, and Emily gushed over him. "Mr Styles, what a pleasant surprise." It should not have been a surprise because she had earlier personally — very personally — invited him to join their party.

"Frederick," she swooned, "may I introduce you to my sister . . ." She did not get the rest out.

"My, what a charming piece." Freddy immediately clasped Alison's gloved hand and raised it to his lips. "Delighted, I'm sure."

Alison was unsure whether she or her dress was the 'piece'.

"Are we all present and correct?" William called, looking about, and raising his eyes in exasperation at Styles' performance.

To Alison's amazement they were ushered into a box. Above them the frescoed roof was festooned with electric chandeliers. Below: the richly guilt proscenium. The curtain swayed ever so gently in response to the rising tempo: the hum of praise being blown towards it, as if the curtain alone adorned the theatre.

Shivers of excitement spiralled down Alison's back, a smile on her lips. She turned slightly to say something: discovered not Emily sitting beside her, instead the young man, whose name had escaped at the moment of introduction. She tried to think of it. Anyway, he was engrossed in conversation with Emily.

The overture set a comical theme: the rush of the lifting curtain, and the stage was ready. A brilliant new musical comedy to inaugurate a brilliant new theatre: one of the largest in Australasia. *A Runaway Girl* was, 'contemporary, gorgeous, radiant, musical and humorous.' A well-versed cast and harmonious orchestra performed this comical tale of a schoolgirl intent on escaping the humiliation of an arranged marriage.

Alas, the cast may have performed faultlessly: regrettably the electricity did not, and amid hisses and groans from the audience, it did its best to disrupt proceedings. By interval gaslight had been reverted to: not as dazzling as the new method of illumination, although more reliable. Alison was not embarrassed by her tears of excitement as the feature song marched forth: *Soldiers of the Park:* first a soloist, then backing from an emphatic chorus. She sought Emily's hand to squeeze, however this family friend was sitting between them.

Almost too soon the musical swept to its finale, the grand curtain dropping as the last chorus reverberated through this enchanting theatre. The curtain calls, sweeping players back and forth across the stage: bowing and curtsying, presenting another chorus, allowing the curtain to fall again, waiting hand-in-hand for it to rise yet again, for audience to shower the shining faces with acclamation. Previously reticent to boo over the electric light failure, Alison now sat on the edge of her seat, and cheered and clapped, savouring this most wonderful moment.

She glimpsed Emily smiling at her, thrilled that she was so overwhelmed. On and on, egos heightened by continuous ovation, hands now bared on this summer's night, until thirty minutes before midnight, when the elated audience spilled into Queen St: some to walk to their nearby homes, others seeking cabs, and a few, like Emily's contingent, cranking their automobiles into life.

Late as it was for Alison, their celebration was far from an end. Back to the Todds' place, for supper and a few drinkies — and a few more drinkies, she biting her lip, and pleading, "I ought not to," although accepting a teensy-weensy little one, with a teensy-weensy little cuddle to go with it. "I'm quite tipsy," she burbled, and smacked a wayward hand — ever so lightly . . .

. . . Alison lay drowsily in bed, eyes partially open. Shafts of sunlight cut through gaps in the curtains. Even that glare was too intense for her, so she squinted. It took her fully a minute to recall where she was, and feared she had company in the room with a double bed Emily had inexplicably allocated her the previous day. She established she was alone, and the pillow next to hers was not ruffled — not very much. She might have rolled over on to it during the night: what little was left when she retired.

So, what had happened? — 'Oh, we went to the theatre. Mmm. And we came back here — and I was drinking, I think, some funny thing Will had made us.' She called him Will now, like an old buddy. 'Did he get silly with me?' She frowned, then remembered the sobering incident. 'No, he got silly with some young thing — gorgeous she was,' Alison further recalled. 'And Emily was flirting openly with that chap — the one who had sat between her and me at the show. Then what happened? Oh, yes, Emily got mad, and upended the girl — over the balcony. Another lady and me rushed outside to see the poor girl struggling to get out of the same bush — I think — he had gone into during my first visit here.' Alison vaguely recalled other people arrived, and a young man — 'Fred — that's who he was — Freddy Styles. He was so awfully nice, because I was in such a state, seeing her in such a mess . . .' And, there is about where her memory faded completely.

It was also when her bedroom door creaked open, and Emily poked her head round it, with a, "You *are* awake," and entered bearing a breakfast tray.

"I don't think I could eat a thing."

"Now you must, darling. You must get something into you, to regain your strength."

Alison frowned. She did not recall doing anything strenuous. Reluctantly she heaved herself into a sitting position and accepted the tray, while Emily wickedly flung open the curtains.

"Em — close them."

Emily turned, raised her eyebrows enquiringly, then closed them partially. "Now you have that, then go back to sleep, so you are right as rain for tonight."

"Tonight?"

"Yes." She smiled devilishly, and reminded Alison, "Did I not tell you, we are having a little get together."

Alison looked at her sideways. "I've the feeling your little get togethers are more than they sound."

"Not at all, my dear. Last night was a little unfortunate." Emily left the room before she could be interrogated about the previous night, because she was not sure what had happened to Alison either, or even when Freddy had left, *if* he had at all!

Late morning when Alison drew her curtains fully, gazed out at the placid harbour, watching yachts and ferries mingle, as they negotiated steamers and sailing ships anchored in the haven's neck, its head broadening out, unruly tresses merging with both haze and the distant hills. She sighed, 'It would be lovely to go sailing. I could say I know how to steer.' It did not occur to her there was a difference between steering the little steamer, and keeping a heeling yacht in the right direction. Stretching her arms far above her head, and sighing again, she gradually returned to reality. Slipping on a dressing gown, loaned by Emily, and heavily scented, she gathered an armful of fresh clothes, her toilet bag, and stealthily crept downstairs, hoping not to meet anyone she did not want to meet — just then. All was quiet, except for sounds issuing from the kitchen. To Alison's relief she did not have to ladle water from a copper. Emily had both hot and cold running water: hot, courtesy of gas. Cold: directly from Western Springs, not that she knew that. Anyway, where they came from was beside the point. She thought she was still a virgin, initially because she had not fully undressed, or *been* fully undressed, before being put to bed. The knowledge allowed her to enjoy a good soak, since no one else rapped on the door seeking a bath.

Emily seemed to be busy, so, after a snack from the side-board for lunch, Alison, in an ankle length dress to clear the dusty pavements, strolled first to the corner of St Stephens Ave, undecided whether to walk down through Parnell, with its mixture of roadside homes — how anyone could live so close to the road with the noise and dust — and shops, or to stroll back towards Newmarket and venture into the Domain: a large rugged area between the city and its eastern suburbs. To escape the dust swirling from carriage wheels was the wisest direction, so she strolled into the Domain, hitched up her dress so it flowed over the long grass. She reached a mound, from which she looked out at the city on all sides. She could not see the Waitakere Ranges, or the Awhitu Peninsula due to the Symonds St ridge, so was a little disappointed.

The previous night's escapade — after that fabulous musical — still concerned her. All her previous flirtations had been conducted in and around Kowhai with men and a terrain she was familiar with. Here at Emily's she was on unfamiliar ground, and should really step cautiously. But what adventure would there be in that? Oh, dear, city life was so complicated. Emily's behaviour was quite bewildering, as if she and her husband had some sort of arrangement. She could not recall anything like that at Kowhai: certainly not of her parents', or Ben and Priscilla.

With that comparison she wondered what those at home were doing right now: certainly not killing time between parties. On one side Mt Eden beckoned her. She thought it was further than it looked, so she declined the invitation, and adjusted her wide-brimmed hat, so it sat askew on her head to protect her left shoulder, although not exposed, and sauntered dreamily back to Emily's. She did peer over the roadside railing, where the eastern portal of the Parnell railway tunnel abutted the road, and looked down at the few houses perched atop a steep gully flanking Ayr Street as it plunged into Hobson Bay

The silent home she had left, was now bustling with activity.

"Ah, there you are, darling," Emily hailed as she entered.

"Yes. — I've been . . ."

"It does not matter where you have been. You have a visitor."

"Oh." Apprehension. Who from Pollok could have possibly turned up?

"Freddy."

That again reawakened Alison to events she did not want to be reawakened to, because she could still not recall how she got from the lounge to her bedroom.

The man himself appeared, swooped on her, hands outstretched, Alison in a dither whether to raise hers, or keep them safely at her side. "Miss Alison, you look radiant. — Your hat, it's gorgeous — positively enchanting."

"My hat?" Alison had forgotten that it was still slanted, almost covering one eye. She would hardly describe her appearance as being enchanting: her last desire now that this Freddy was back on the scene.

Before he could ask her, Emily did the honours. "Frederick thought you might like to dine with him . . ."

"At the best hotel of course?" was Freddy's contribution.

"I'm not — I'd have . . ." She did not know whether she wanted to dine with him. Yes she did. It would be a lovely experience. ". . . Certainly, Mr Styles," she accepted, becoming formal. "However, you must allow me time to change."

"All the time in the world, for you dear, sweet lady." He was gushing again, and Alison wasn't used to such attention: not such effusiveness.

"Do you want to bathe first?" was Emily's suggestion.

"I had a long soak before lunch, thank you, Emily."

Being taken out for a meal was a new experience for Alison: so different from sharing food at Kowhai's dining table with a beau, and she did take time to make herself look even more beautiful, absolutely divine in Freddy's eyes, when she presented her elbow for him to clasp as they descended the front steps and climbed on to Freddy's carriage. The horse trotted obediently down Manukau Rd, then traversed a hill, St Andrews Church on one side, a park on the other, its trees already obscuring the view. The near new four-storey hotel overlooked the reclamation of Mechanics Bay, with now almost lifeless harbour beyond. Freddy had secured a window table, and in the gathering dusk, Alison gazed wondrously at the mauve and indigo eastern sky, sun frilling the edges of barely discernible clouds. She quite missed what Freddy was saying.

"Ah, the menu. It all looks so divine." She cast her eyes up and down the page, some of the offerings of French origin, or were they quiet ordinary dishes with fancy names? They sounded exotic anyway.

"The *Coq au Vin* looks most appetising," Freddy suggested.

"I was just thinking about that myself," Alison lied, and searched the menu for something that looked like what Freddy had suggested, only able to decipher the first word. 'Ah,' she murmured very much to herself, 'they've told us what it is in English.' "Yes, I think I'll have that," she agreed.

Alison casually picked up a silver knife, and was glad she had the strength to hold it. For once she was at a loss for words. Should she talk about domestic matters, the farm? No, that would bore this city person. They had already discussed the weather. Was there something out the window to point out? She knew the dark looking island shaped like a broad-brimmed hat was Rangitoto, so used her knowledge, to mention. "I believe Rangitoto blew up only a few hundred years ago."

"Did it? I believe it did."

The end of that subject. There was no lengthy discussion on the volcanic island dominating Auckland's harbour entrance. Nor would there be intellectual discussion between them, and it did not really matter, because Alison was thrilled just to dine in such a lavish atmosphere, and Freddy was beguiled by the Alison's beauty. He was wildly in love with her already.

So the meal progressed with only sporadic conversation: nothing like that which flowed between Alison and a scrub cutter, or any local young man.

In the dark, with only gas lamplights to guide them, they returned to Emily's place, to be immediately flung into the party: a far cry from the hotel's formality. The party itself was neither as eventful nor exciting as the impromptu affair of the previous night.

Alison was not concerned over this, because she had enough to keep her entertained: Freddy Styles. Conversation now flowed freely, except when they strolled in almost silence through Emily's garden. Freddy plucked an apricot rose, and fastened it to Alison's bodice, fiddling a little too long, she allowing his hand to linger; it made her heart beat faster. The action ended with a fervent kiss, which crushed the rose, although Alison was too enchanted to care.

On the terrace he talked of exotic places, and Alison wondered if ever she would see just one of them. 'Certainly not while stuck on a farm,' she lamented. Other than Emily, she did not know anyone, so was less reserved, and in the half-light they could not see much, so when Freddy again fiddled with her crushed rose, she looked into his eyes, her arms wrapped round his neck, allowing him just a little freedom.

Emily saved Alison's day, so very indiscreetly. Not then, rather later, while Alison was sitting dreamily on a couch, Freddy off somewhere, her hostess offered, "If you are so infatuated with him darling, he is welcome to stay . . ." She did not complete the offer.

That immediately reminded Alison of what she had suspected about Emily the previous day. She knew Emily had lovers: one at least. The knowledge flashed a warning to her heart.

Wouldn't it be wonderful with Freddy. No one at home need ever know. She looked up at Emily with glassy eyes, reached out for her drink, as if it might give her courage. "I don't know," she answered undecided. "He's so awfully nice, and I'm quite in love with him." She made a sweeping gesture, spilled her drink, upsetting her trance. "No! — Never, Emily!" She put the glass firmly down. "How could you suggest such a thing?"

Emily gestured with her hands. "I am sorry, my dear." She puckered her lips. "You are not too annoyed with me, are you?" she appealed, with a pout.

Alison, rapidly sobering, believed her sister-in-law was actually contrite, so took her hand and forgave her, with, "How could I possibly be. But, Em . . ."

"Ah, there you are my little chicken." Freddy had returned.

Alison gave a half-smile. "Emily here is telling me I'm looking weary and it's time I went to bed." Then she thought Freddy might take *that* the wrong way.

"Must you?"

"It has been a wonderful night, and I have to thank you for making it so wonderful." As she rose Freddy clutched her into his arms, and it took a lot of will power to resist his charms.

"Will I see you tomorrow — ah, later today?" he corrected.

"Maybe. — Perhaps." And Alison, with Freddy tagging along as she wound through the remaining guests, was herself undecided whether she wanted to see him again, or wanted to stay another night. She was afraid next time she might not be so unyielding, because in her heart she desired so much to be loved: properly loved.

Ironically when she did reawaken her thoughts did not go back to the night gone, instead she wondered which steamer would take her back to Pollok, and whether her friendly captain would be on board. She shook her head, because how could she more wish to steer a boat than stay at Emily's and see Freddy again?

She decided to return home, and Emily suggested they first drive into the city, and for another new experience, she could catch a train to Onehunga, and instead of being covered in dust, she would arrive home covered in soot. They both laughed, and Alison very nearly changed her mind, and stayed on another day.

The trams at the time met the trains at the foot of Queen St, and Alison, having done some shopping with Emily, gave her a final hug and a wordy thank you for the wonderful time, boarded her train, initially travelling back through Parnell, into the tunnel, which contributed most of the soot on her clothes, through Newmarket and beyond where the fields they skirted were the eastern flanks of One Tree Hill where its lava flows tumbled down to Penrose, Te Papapa and Onehunga. A different steamer awaited her. She heaved herself on to the top deck, and on this crossing chatting to some neighbours, completely oblivious to the craft's wallowing as it first chugged down the choppy harbour, gave shallow bays a wide berth, rounded rocky headlands with their precariously perched pohutukawa, crossed to the Awhitu side, then, with flowing tide, hopped round the peninsula's coast, Alison and her neighbours disembarking at Pollok wharf.

She then had to rack her brain to recall whether she had pre-arranged for someone to meet her. Not to worry. Such was the traffic to and from the wharf with its store sooner or later someone was bound to be heading her way.

Thomas Chester was at the wharf to meet her, and Alison was unsure who would be worse to confront: her father or sister? She had not done anything wrong, although felt guilty about wanting to.

"Oh, Father, thank goodness you are here," she exclaimed, wisely deciding to show appreciation rather than misgivings.

"So, how was it, my dear?"

With a shrug she admitted, "Absolutely wonderful." He did not quiz her, and Alison did not enquire as to why he just happened to be at the wharf, she asked, "Did Danny get back?"

"Oh yes, Danny has spent most of his time with us."

And that was the end of that conversation.

With the late afternoon sun shimmering on the hills, casting shadows into valleys, Alison decided for all Auckland's attractions there was something stable, something safe and secure about the peninsula. On looking back over her shoulder, far across the harbour, there was nothing to show Auckland even existed. Nevertheless it did! Bustling by day, and soon surely to be all lit up with elect — elect something; with theatres and concert halls, galleries and so many shops. She sighed, and thought, 'Oh my, what to do?'

The next few days were absolutely, inexorably boring. 'I mean,' she thought, 'it's the festive season, and what is everyone doing? — Working as if that is all there is to life.' If Freddy could see her now, back bent kindling wood, stoking the copper, catching her nails while grating the soap, plunging sheets and dresses up and down, winding them through the mangle, soggy cotton sheets flapping about her face as she pegged them out. Then having to gather them all in because of a stupid rain shower. Hang them back out again. Bring them in, and iron everything — absolutely everything. Emily did not do anything like that. Nor would she have to, if she flew back to Freddy. He would take her away to one of those exotic places, or take her out for meals, and have a maid do the washing and ironing, and cooking, and just about everything. Certainly she would not be chopping wood. She would not have to do that here either, if her miserly father employed a new farm hand. He would be a bore. How could she possibly derive pleasure from watching a scrub cutter cut scrub, and she get all smoky because she condescended to take lunch to him?

At other times it was pleasant to sit on the front lawn, listen to the gurgle of the stream, and bird song, the lowing of cows, not a care in the world. No dust, or traffic noise. Just dream the afternoon away. Not having to worry about money to buy this or that, because there was nowhere out here to buy anything. Everything was for free.

"Alison!"

'Ho-hum, is that my sister calling?' From reverie to reality.

"Alison! — Where are you?"

'Here, dear Sister, if you'd care to look,' Alison silently replied.

"There you are; lying about as usual."

Drearily Alison turned to confront Jane. Emily did not accuse her of lying about. On the contrary, Emily had encouraged her to lie about, and . . . Alison very briefly reflected on one interpretation of Emily's lying about. With a sigh, she acknowledged, "Yes, Sister, what is it you want?"

"Mother needs a hand in the kitchen."

"Oh yes, I suppose she does." So Alison heaved herself up, gathered the book she had begun to read, then discarded it after a few pages, and obediently went indoors, into that stifling kitchen where her mother was rolling out pastry, preparing all sorts of unappetising food for New Year's Eve. Not the dainty pastries presented to her at Freddy's hotel. The hotel definitely belonged to Freddy — why else would waiters hover about so attentively?

Alison became immersed in baking, daydreams evicted from her fanciful head. Every now and then she sighed, wiped her brow, and continued to with the monotonous chore: baking and more baking.

When, the following day, the usual guests turned up, all familiar, and utterly boring, Alison wondered why her mother went to so much trouble, because half of it would not be eaten, and a lot would be thrown out to the birds in a day or two's time. It was, by Kowhai's customary occasion, a subdued New Year celebration.

Thomas Chester rose as the grandfather clock rang out midnight, said, "Happy New Year, everyone." With his wife gathered them around to sing *Auld Lang Syne*, and everyone promptly resettled, chatter became more sporadic, and within thirty minutes the lounge, indeed the whole house, was in darkness.

A veil of mist shrouded the hills. Grass freshly painted with dew. Alison begged Jane to let her help, and together they milked the cows, with no sign of Danny, who with his mother had stayed overnight. Belatedly and apologetically, Danny did appear, and Alison, on Jane's instructions led the cows across short-cropped paddocks, opened rough-hewn gates for them, and herded them into a more palatable paddock. She lingered with them, smelling both beasts and farm, then strolled with two dogs nipping at her heels along the driveway, paused to look over the bridge, see how low the stream was, then went indoors to the familiar aroma of bacon and eggs and tomatoes, all home grown, so to speak.

Emily was curious. Her curiosity arose the night after the opening of His Majesty's Theatre. The woman Will was openly flirting with: her small fair face familiar. Try as she might, she could not place it. Not until she strolled up Queen St on a calm summer's day: one eye window shopping, the other always looking at the footpath. The trouble was, more than pedestrians used the path, leaving their trademarks: dogs being the worst offenders. Her dress lifter was handy, and if some gentleman happened to see more than he should, lucky him, she thought.

Then she had it. As she passed her favourite millinery on the frontage of the Albert Hotel she paused. That is where the face belonged. She could at least pop in and say hello. As she entered, not the scent of women and hats that wafted in the air, instead the aroma of a familiar brand of tobacco. She decided to feign pretence.

"Good afternoon, Mrs Todd. Ah — this is — a pleasure." The lady's greeting loud for a face so petite.

"Good afternoon, Miss Harkness." Wiggling her nose, Emily astutely suggested, "You are not about to close early are you?"

The lady recoiled. "Why ever for, Mrs Todd?"

"Emily, dear — Emily." Although younger than Miss Harkness she spoke in a more mature and patronising manner.

The milliner quickly offered, "So, you are seeking a new hat?"

"Ah, thinking about it. I shall just browse." And while she was browsing Emily tried to listen above the clatter of street noise for the rear door closing — if the shop had a rear door — as whoever was out the back discretely retired. She knew some men had a habit of setting up their fancy women in such premises as millinery shops. At least Will was not having an affair with someone even younger than herself, for Miss Harkness was all of five years older. Even so, she was a quaint thing: a little fussy, prim and proper. Although, apparently not so proper. Then, nor was she for that matter. She deliberately lingered: for several minutes, while other potential customers came and went, one lady collecting a hat altered before purchasing.

"No, I think I shall leave it for today. However I *do* like that piece over there." And she again walked to the rear of the shop, where only a curtain separated her and the concealed person, whose 'fragrance' filtered through the curtain. How she dared to impudently draw the drape aside.

Instead, she swanned out of the shop with a smirk, walked a little further up Queen St, and stepped into Smith and Caughey's recessed entry, with one eye peeping back down the street. And, as she expected her dear husband emerged, checked that the coast was clear, and began walking towards her. Emily slid into the store: fortunately a store where she was entitled to be, unlike her husband at the milliners.

Oh well, she thought, she could tuck the information away for future reference. She still liked that particular hat. She would return and buy it. She maybe could get it at, would it be 'mate's rates?' They were hardly mates, although did have a common interest.

CHAPTER FIVE

Ben had nothing personal against Danny, and in fact considered that side of the affair a great joke. What he believed unjust: his father had given them the north-eastern reaches of the main valley: land far more suitable for farming than his own 'mountainous' region.

The Chesters were pioneers: none more so than Ben. His father had been proud of him when at his own volition during the years before he was married he took up a slasher and beat back the scrub, actually establishing some of the farm to be given over to Danny and Jane. Unlike most pioneers Ben did not entirely clear the land, instead here and there left pockets of native bush, spared large puriri or kauri, to provide shelter for animals to graze on the new-won land, and pockets of ferns, where the winter sun rarely reached into clefts.

Ben married, and his father watched the progress at Kanuka: much more difficult terrain to convert to farmland. Ben's enthusiasm had not waned: slowed a little during the winter, and steadily hard-won acres became productive. Much of the kauri had gone from Ben's property, although puriri had to be felled, and scrub cleared. He adopted a method of felling stand of big trees on steep hills by chopping a lower tree part way through, then methodically doing the same to those above and each side of it in a rising triangular formation, until reaching the apex. This tree he chopped all the way through, amused by the domino effect of the falling trees.

However, he was far from amused about the new state of affairs sprung on him. He did not begrudge his sister, for she had done her fair share of work, yet felt cheated and envious that this inexperienced plod had been given such a head start. He knew he would be expected to help the lumbering oaf.

Ben brooded, and his wife caught the brunt of his ill-temper. What would his son have to inherit? Nothing! Not if another oaf married Alison and was likewise rewarded. He did not tell his wife why he was so frustrated. She had to prise it out of him, although her first attempts did not get the desired answer.

"Nothing!" A reply that could neither be believed nor reasoned with.

With a reluctant sigh, Priscilla advised him, "All I can say, is the house is more peaceful with you outdoors."

That accusation provoked a bull-like snort, slam of the door, and Ben's disappearance for the day. Priscilla could only ensure when he did eventually return there would be nothing to vent his disapproval. George was put to bed early on this occasion, something Priscilla had never done, because no matter how tired, Ben always wanted to have a play with his son. He clomped up the back steps, kicked off his boots, his hands caked in blood and dirt, face grazed by a falling tree and slumped into a kitchen chair, too tired to enjoy his meal, gulped it down, fell on to the couch, mumbled a few words, then slept.

Choking back tears, not hiding them when they did overwhelm her, Priscilla placed a blanket over her husband, peeped in on George, whispered, "You stay asleep, little one," and sneaked from the house. She felt furtive going behind Ben's back. She wanted to hurry, however her expectancy made that dangerous. The sun had set, however a near full moon reflected light into their valley. In this twilight she witnessed the day's work: observed puriri logs, and hundreds of bleeding tea-tree stumps, logs piled nearby for home fuel. Also piled nearby were smaller branches. No doubt the next day Ben would fire them, still green enough to burn slowly, and not raise sparks. By dusk only ashes would remain. At this rate Priscilla knew nearby there would be new piles from tomorrow's work. Horse and sled would drag the logs home for Ben to laboriously saw into lengths for the range and lounge fire.

"Why are you doing this, husband?" she cried aloud. "Why are you being driven to the limit? What has made a slave of you?" She sighed, and having seen enough to wonder why he was toiling without rest until his weary body tumbled through the door, too exhausted to appreciate a meal so lovingly prepared. Her tears flowed freely as she cautiously made her way home, careful not to stumble in the gloom. She stared down at her husband, her mouth quivering, dared not even kiss his forehead should it wake him, checked George, quietly prepared for bed, and lay alone in the darkness, trying to fathom why.

She did not sleep well, except apparently during the hour or two before dawn. Ben had not come to bed, so she stealthily arose, intent on two things: to be cheerful, and to prepare her husband a hearty breakfast. Expecting to find Ben still asleep on the couch, she crept through the room, saw the blanket on the floor, was annoyed that he was up already, and hoped to find him in the kitchen. He had been! All that remained was an empty bowl. He certainly had not cooked a meal, just eaten some cereal, and hunks of bread, as if he wanted to be out of the place without having to confront his wife. Priscilla's heart sagged as she went to the back door. Of Ben there was no sign, nor of his tools. Slumping into a kitchen chair, ignoring George's cries, she buried her face in her hands and wept bitterly.

Louise Chester chose to drive over the hill that morning: horse and gig wending their way out of the valley, clip-clopping along the dusty ridge track, and down to Kanuka. She had the satisfaction of knowing her visits to this farm were always welcome.

Coincidentally Priscilla, after crying until she could cry no longer, had sadly taken up her duties: her thoughts transferring from Ben to his mother. Did she have the strength to carry George all the way to Kowhai in her condition, and on a hot day, there to seek her mother-in-law's advice? It was gratifying, even if embarrassing, to be able to confide in her mother-in-law, rather than her own mother. Admittedly Louise Chester lived across the road, so to speak, even if a rugged mile between doors.

While contemplating the prospect of walking to Kowhai, Priscilla hung the washing on her line. Even that made her realise how fortunate she was. On the shortest winter days, so long as it did not rain for a few hours, she managed to get it dry: a constant breeze, often a gale, gusting up the valley. Seldom did they have to contend with washing hanging above the kitchen range, or with a clotheshorse taking prime place in the lounge before an open fire.

She heard a horse snort, turned to see Louise agilely stepping from the gig.

"Good morning, dear," the older woman hailed, with a loving smile.

Priscilla could not conceal her depression. "Hello," She turned back to the line. "I'll just finish hanging these out, and make a cup of tea."

"You do that, and I shall make the tea," Louise suggested, and without too much concern, went into the house. When Priscilla trudged in the door, she enquired, "George asleep?"

"Yes — thankfully."

Her expression did not sound right at all: Priscilla grateful her child was not bothering her. Louise searched her daughter-in-law's face as she placed cups and saucers on the kitchen table, and witnessed the sadness.

With tears again rising to her eyes, Priscilla begged, "Mother, where have I failed your son?" She shook her head, and added to her appeal, "Do you know why I've made him so unhappy?"

Louise's head shook slowly, then nodded in wisdom. "I think I do, my dear, if you say he is depressed." She frowned. "It is not you, dear, who has made him unhappy." She removed the steaming kettle from the range, selected a jar of scotch shortbread, being almost as familiar with this kitchen as her own, then advised, "I can only assume that my son has taken umbrage at our gift to Jane — and — and Danny . . ."

Priscilla's waning aspiration of one day living at Kowhai fell across the wooden table. "I don't blame him!"

Louise shook her head. "No, Priscilla, surely it is not how you think?"

"But — but Ben has worked so hard."

The lady nodded. "And so has Jane, dear, so has Jane." That truth checked Priscilla. Louise could see this young mother did not accept that. "In a different way Jane — as you well know, my dear — has done a lot around the farm." Then she added by way of practical reasoning, "Who has supplied you with milk, and cream, and cheese?"

"Jane," came the admittance.

"Yes," Louise reached across the table and clasped Priscilla's trembling hand. "Jane is very much deserving of a share of the farm. Father knows his son. He gave him the challenge of this place: one we all know Ben is rapidly conquering. Aren't you so proud of him?"

Priscilla's nod gave way to a soft, "Yes."

"There is no real challenge for Danny. He even has a head start, with some land already cleared. Nor does he have to think before clearing any land. He doesn't face the same problems as Ben. One false move, and Ben will lose much that he has gained."

Priscilla cupped her wet chin in her hands.

"I'll tell you what," Louise offered, "you make lunch for Ben . . . Has he made himself something?"

"I'm sure he hasn't."

". . . And I shall take it to him. After all, what is unusual about a mother seeing what her son is up to?"

Stifling her sorrow, Priscilla obeyed. Louise had not unhitched the horse, so tended its needs, returned to the kitchen, collected what Priscilla had prepared, including a cold beer poured from a jar — that Ben had placed beneath a shaded bank where water from the hillside dribbled over it — into a clip-topped bottle.

On this hot day Louise thought Ben *must* appreciate that gesture from his wife. Although her thoughts were more with the problem than his lunch as she strode purposefully down the valley. While she had no intention of interfering with her son's life, she had her own ideas about this subject. She agreed with her husband that Kowhai's tumbling acres could economically be sub-divided into four, not just three, separate farms, knowing there was another unconquered valley. 'Why, everyone is cutting them up,' she thought, as she opened a gate, and passed from a paddock to uncut scrub. 'Ben knows that.' She made a sucking sound. 'He's being silly, and I shall tell him so.' Emerging from the scrub and on to some flat land cleared of bush, the hot sun cast its burning rays on her bare head, scolding her for journeying so unprotected.

Ben was sitting on a stump, apparently peering at an object on the ground. Louise assumed an insect had captured his attention. As a boy nature had not escaped his notice, and seemingly it did not escape it now.

Louise's hand rested on his shoulder at the same moment as she sighted his bloodied hands. "Ben!"

"Got a rag?" he stammered: a maimed lion.

Her petticoat was the only suitable 'rag', Not Ben's hand injured, but his left leg: the victim of a glancing axe, the severe looking gash allowing blood to flow unchecked. Ben's attempts to stop it were futile. His mother's garment made a tourniquet, with a twig applying the pressure. Before she wrapped the wound, she told him, "It's not as bad as it looks, Son."

"Thank God for that!"

Louise looked severely at him. "What do you mean by *that*?" She began to bandage the wound. "I think this is an excuse for you to lay down those tools, and put your feet up for a few days." She was hoping for an easy victory.

"What? With all I have to do!"

"Yes, Son, with *all* you have to do." Then she reminded him, "After all, Rome wasn't built in a day."

"This isn't Rome," he flung back at her. "This is my life, my family's livelihood."

Now on a different subject than what she had proposed to say, she enquired, "Have you not put a little aside for a rainy day?" She did not wait for an answer. "Ben, I could give you ten sovereigns, and tell you and Prissy to have a holiday. I know you could well afford to have some time off. Then you don't want my hand-outs." She checked the bandage, released the tourniquet just a half twist. Could she now broach the reason why she was here?

Ben certainly believed he could not spare a minute, so why was his mother suggesting it? What did she know that he did not? He knew only too well his mother would not enter into an argument unless she was sure of winning it: by reason.

"You *have* worked well this morning," she acknowledged. "In fact you've done a day's work already." A barbed compliment . . .

. . . That Ben swallowed. "I was getting through it — until this happened."

She had an answer. "Son, maybe this was a result of too much haste." She laid a maternal hand on his shoulder. "Let's get you into the shade." She helped him up, secured his waist with her strong arm, and edged him into uncut scrub. "Lay back now, Son." As he complied, she advised, "You are just too pig-headed. This is what happens when you go at a thing like a bull at a gate." She did not allow him the chance to contradict her. "So, without raising your voice, tell me what has got into you lately?"

Ben looked away, laying his head on the dry ground.

If he would not tell her, then she would tell him. So, after a false start, she set her son straight. "So, you want Kowhai. One day, it will be yours no doubt."

"What's left of it!"

"That is up to you. If you are *that* selfish, maybe all Father will leave you is the homestead."

That snapped his head round, which made him a little dizzy, and it fell back again. "It's not that, Mother. It's just Danny's so — so inexperienced, and I know it will be Janey who'll do everything. Even clear the land."

Louise nodded. "Yes, I'm sure you are right, Son." Now for the crux. "As for Danny's inexperience — ah — that is where you come in." She raised her eyebrows, knowing his opinion.

"And let this place go back to bush. Leave it a day and y' can see the weeds grow."

"I don't think they grow quite as fast as that, Son." She shook her head, rested her hand on his brow, and hoped the dampness was perspiration, not a fever. "No, Ben. You have heard of the word compromise? You give Danny a hand — say a day a week, it would be invaluable to him . . ."

"I bet it would."

She sighed. "I think we'd better get you home."

"No, I'll be all right."

"Don't argue with your mother. Just have a rest — even for today." When he tried to rise, his body was heavy, head dizzy, and he meekly submitted to his mother's helping hand. As they stumbled across the uneven ground, lunch left behind, Louise re-composed her thoughts, and in the cool of a copse, she advised, "You see, Ben, you give Danny a day of your time, and it is only reasonable to expect him to return the gesture." She paused in her stride to gather her breath. "When he does, be sure to find tasks that need two pairs of hands. Do you understand me?"

They staggered on in silence for a few yards, and like the child he still was in his mother's eyes he declared, "So, I won't lose anything at all."

"No, not really. You know yourself you can struggle for hours on a job — like fencing, although with two of you, it takes no time at all." A slight understatement.

Ben reluctantly agreed. Danny's inheritance still irked him.

They were all smiles on reaching the house; entered like buddies after a round of the pubs, Louise's sober arm about her sagging son.

The summer lingered, and Priscilla had another boy, whom they named James.

Danny made a final trip to sea, returning only days before his marriage.

A late May wedding. The weather held. The bride did not emit the radiance her sister-in-law had done. She seemed happy enough, all smiles, though some thought those smiles were a little forced. Radiance stems from the heart, and the heart is supposed to be controlled by the head. Jane's heart had betrayed her head, and a little acidity filtered through.

Again Alison played the role of bridesmaid: her third occasion, having also been bridesmaid to a friend, as well as Priscilla. She dearly hoped one day she would get the leading role. Kowhai hosted the occasion, where little feminine groups weighed the chances of a successful union, and doubted whether this couple would see their silver wedding, let alone a golden occasion. A long way off, and the chances were most of those spiteful little mouths would have long since shut for good. Their speculation was not without reason. A second kowhai was planted near the first. Would this tree flourish as the one Ben and Priscilla had planted?

Danny had few close friends: none actually. Everyone knew him by sight, although that was about all. Nevertheless after racking his brain he did come up with three to invite, two of whom were in the same category as Danny before Jane's influence, and another of quite dapper character. Contrary to Danny this young man thought he was God's gift to women. His eyes feasted on the bridesmaid. 'You are lovely, my gorgeous,' he drooled to himself, and waited until he spied her momentarily alone. "I don't think I have had the pleasure," he breathed, and held out his hand. "Andrew Buck at your service."

"Ah — um — Alison — ah — sister of the bride."

"Most adorable sister of the bride," he complimented in a soft secretive voice, obviously not wanting his approach to be noticed by others, possibly because one or two of them knew him — only too well. "And unwed herself," he observed.

"Mm," she sighed. "I'm just too busy on the farm to . . ."

"I cannot believe it. Surely there is many-a-man who would willingly assist you — with the most laborious task."

"No, I am afraid not. I do the milking, make the butter and cheese, take cream to the creamery, mend the roof . . ."

"Stop! — Stop! — You flay me with your talent. Surely someone must wish to remove you from such slavery," he pleaded, then added, "as I wish to do myself."

"I think not, kind Sir," Alison refused. "I am quite sure a man of your worldliness would find me a bore — a simple country girl."

"How could one so beautiful be a bore?"

So the charm and responding banter went on. By now they were walking side-by-side, edging away from the house, across the yard towards the barn. Andrew tried to be casual about his intentions, and Alison was most obliging, being well aware of where they were going. She held out her hand for him to steady her as they crossed a muddy patch: not that she needed any steadying, having walked the ground a thousand times.

Alison was not naïve. 'He'll get me behind the barn, tell me I'm the most beautiful girl in the world — how many times have I been told that? — and then want to kiss me.' She wiggled her mouth. 'Will I let him?' She leapt lightly over a puddled wheel rut, changed direction and walked beyond the barn to the stable door, where just inside her horse was tethered. "Hello Whisper. You don't like it in here do you?" The horse neighed and flicked her head, voicing her disapproval. Pausing to pat her neck, she said to Andrew, "She is so trustful." She smiled, and thought of something witty thing to say. "She never leads me down the wrong track."

"I'm sure she is," he agreed, impatient to get Alison out of sight of the homestead. All he had to do was take a few steps back into the adjacent the barn to achieve that. Except the barn smelled exactly like a barn: hardly a romantic setting; nor was behind it for that matter.

Of her own accord Alison moved from the stable, took Andrew's hand again and drew him where he wanted to take her. "If you wish to kiss me, Mr Buck, you need not be so secretive about it." Her manner was hardly encouraging.

"Oh, I — I . . ."

"We could have gone into the library, and saved you getting your shoes muddy."

A cart partially blocked the barn entrance, so Alison drew Andrew around it, paused and frowned. She canted her head towards some hay bales, and leaned forward, then facing Andrew she put her finger to her lips. "Shsh, I think the kittens are here." She gently drew a hay bale aside, but of the kittens only that they had been there was evident.

"Oh, Miranda has taken them elsewhere." Taking a step back she stumbled, into Andrew's arms. "Thank you, kind sir," she accepted, then twisted from him, and with a frown, asked herself, "I wonder where she is?" She called, "Miranda! — Miranda!"

There being no answering meow, she stated emphatically, "It was a silly place to have them, anyway." With a sigh, she looked at her watch, recoiled, and blurted, "Gosh, is that the time. I have to milk the cows."

Without a backward glance she rushed from the barn, leaving the suave Andrew Buck agog.

Afterwards she sighed often, debating with herself whether she should have been more disposed towards him. She did not get a second chance, because he soon made his excuses and left the wedding feast.

Danny and his bride departed a short time later, spending a few days in Auckland, although not with Emily. In fact Emily was away.

Since the couple did not have a home, they made use of the vacant farm hand's quarters. It was convenient for Jane, who continued to milk and tend Kowhai's cows, and Danny who only had to walk across the fields to work on his own property.

Seemingly forever in the past, summer and winter, rain, hail or shine — the shine coming from the moon — she, without a second thought, had risen by five, made herself a cup of tea, and sometimes toasted bread before the open door of the range. She donned wet weather gear over her breeches, which were tucked into knee-high gumboots, fetched the dogs, shshed them so not to wake the household, and sought the cows. Her usual murmur was, 'Ah, there you are,' hearing those with bells plodding towards the yard. Quite likely they sighted the kitchen lamp, and knew it was milking time. In the depths of winter, with fewer cows to milk, she would have the dairy washed down as the sun cleared the hills.

This winter was so much different. In the dark she stealthily dressed, not seeing Danny, although knowing he was asleep, so a little peeved he did not offer to help, having earlier said he had a day's work to do without tending the cows. So did a lot of other pioneer farmers. Jane now felt lonely out in the dark, and wondered if this was it: her life from now on. That she might have children was unlikely. They had not consummated their marriage. There was no eagerness on her part, and she knew Danny would make no demands on her.

When Jane did return to the cottage, the chances were Danny would just be up. "How did you ever do a night watch?" she chided him, with a prod, about as amorous as if it were Ben she was coaxing. 'Is that it?' she revealed to herself. 'He's not a husband at all. I do love him — I suppose — as a brother.' The thought appalled her. 'How could I have made such a mistake: not knowing the difference between romantic love and platonic love?'

Danny tried. However it was hard to get out of bed on frigid mornings. Once up, he did plod across to his farm, slowly slashed away at the bush and chopped down larger trees. Some foundation studs for their home arrived and he set them in the ground according to a plan Thomas had prepared. They were not even, although that could be rectified later when the floor joists were laid. When Jane brought him some lunch, he would eagerly advise her of his progress. On the days Ben helped, he was more subdued, because even he could see more than twice the work had been done. It was either too cold, or too dark to work safely, according to Danny, so before five o'clock he stowed away his tools in a shed, and ambled back to Kowhai; taking his time, so it appeared he had spent longer on the actual job.

Jane was milking, so he would wash and sit alone in the cottage. That she was still very much part of the household was evident, because Louise held tea back until her daughter was ready, no matter how hungry the others were.

"How many have lost their milk, my dear?" her father asked.

"Three or four, Father."

Alison suggested, "You'll be able to lie in when they all do."

"You know I can never lie in. Besides, what will we do for milk if they all do?"

"Try it, Sister." She could have again offered to milk them, so Jane could have an early morning frolic with Danny rather than her dogs. Alison thought her sister was more at ease with the dogs.

Her father asked Alison, "So, how did you fill in the day?" Then almost demanded, "How *do* you fill in your days?"

"If you don't know now, Father, you never will."

To which the girls' mother, and his wife, advised, "Dear, you are not very observant. Alison has been very busy lately . . ."

"Mother!" Alison did not want her father to know, since he had not seen.

"You have, dear, and it deserves to be said."

Thomas Chester frowned. His wife continued, "Since we no longer employ a farm hand, and you spend as much time in town, who do you think has been working on the fences, the gates, even cleaning the leaves out of the spouting?"

Thomas raised his eyes to the ceiling. Alison waited for the reprimand. "You could have fallen," was his unrelenting comment.

Softly she said, "I didn't." She had been very careful: up to twenty feet off the ground, and had one or two scares. She did not add it was she who had repaired the spouting: perched up a ladder: first cutting out a rusty section, then soldering a new section into place: all without the aid of electricity, having to make use of the farm's forge: Ben having taught her its rudiments. While up there she climbed on to the roof and cleaned out the spouting. She also knew Kowhai's library was a fountain of knowledge, including technical knowledge, and do-it-yourself books for farmers. They did not specifically include farmers' daughters, although Alison took that for granted, so combined practical experience with theory to maintain the farm.

As for Thomas' whereabouts when Alison was on the roof or up a ladder, on the mentioned occasion he was at Waiuku, staying overnight at the Kentish, while he and other locals pressed the Roads Board for improvements. Well then, he had two capable daughters.

When Danny thought he could have a holiday over the Christmas period, Ben had other ideas. "We're going to the fair." That sounded great to Danny, and even Jane frowned, because she had not heard of any fairs — the sort that had merry-go-rounds, donkeys and toffee apples. Ben shook his head. "Wrong sort of fair. We're going to get some stock for your place. — Sheep."

"Now, at this time of year?"

"The fair's on now," Ben advised. "They're not going to postpone it, because Danny wants to lie about over. . ."

"It's our first Christmas together," Jane objected.

"Sorry, Sis. We'll only be away a day or two." Ben knew that they would be away longer than that. There were few sheep on the

Awhitu Peninsula, and none for sale. Nor were there any to be had from Penrose to Pukekohe. The livestock on these farms were cattle. However, there were mobs up for sale at Newmarket.

"So, how do we get them home?" Danny asked as the two men boarded a train at Onehunga, after a wet and windy crossing of the Manukau.

"The best way we can, Danny," Ben answered, because he was not sure how to accomplish the deed himself. "We'll need to get a couple of dogs," he advised, and wondered if the dogs would be useful from the moment they got the sheep.

As the train skirted One Tree Hill, puffing through a lava strewn region called Te Papapa, Ben pointed to one answer of getting them home to Danny, where a few cattle were being coaxed along a track width road. "Like that, Danny. We'll drive them."

"All the way?"

Ben shook his head. "No . . ." He was going to add 'stupid.' That was too close to the truth. They joined the main line at Penrose: the landscape dominated by One Tree Hill's lava flow, and a few farm houses where people tried to make a living from this rugged terrain. It did get better as they neared their stop at Market Rd, running between two of Auckland's volcanic hills. They jumped from the train, and joined the throng at the saleyards: a long row of pens with a covered aisle held small groups of cattle — although no sheep. Ben looked beyond the yards, and said, "See, others are driving stock along the streets, so we'll do the same — if there's any about." Also evident that the sale had been in full swing for several hours, and he thought they would have been wiser to have travelled to the city the day before, stayed at the Junction Inn at Newmarket, and been on hand first thing that morning.

"It's on for two days, Ben . . ."

"There won't be anything left for tomorrow. There's not much left now."

"They might bring other sheep in for tomorrow."

Ben grimaced. "Good thinking, Danny. Let's ask." They jostled their way through the crowd and animals, searched for someone who looked important. Before finding him Ben was advised that there were a mob of sheep in a nearby paddock to be auctioned next day. Ben slapped Danny's back, and with a flick of his head, suggested, "Let's look them over, eh."

There were three paddocks of sheep. All Ben had to learn was which had already been sold, and which were the next day's lots. They clambered over railings, trod in muck, at times overpowered by the smell, got separated, Ben re-locating Danny yarning to some codger he knew from his days around the Manukau, and eventually perched themselves on a rail and looked over the animals destined to be sold next day.

"Them? You don't want to buy them," advised some passer-by. "Only good for the knackers."

Ben disagreed, and said to Danny, "He wouldn't know whether they broken-mouthed or not. They look pretty good to me." He did not consider himself good enough to judge their condition on his own, so sought help.

"There's a bit of everything here, Mr Chester. A few two-tooths, but mostly four, and some full-mouthed ones. They'll be a bargain. The way things are, you'll probably be the only buyer."

Ben nodded. "Hmm." He would hate to pay a high price and discover he had bought both himself and Danny a rum lot.

"You'd best do a deal with the seller," suggested the stranger.

"And where will I find him?" Ben instinctively reached down and patted an inquisitive collie.

"You won't. See the lady over there — the sad looking one. They're hers."

Recovering from the surprise information of a woman being at the sales, and apparently charged with selling her husband's stock, he cautiously asked, "Why's she selling them?"

"Widowed — just recently." He grimaced. "Selling up, I hear. — Everything."

"Thanks, chum." Ben nodded, still perplexed that the lady was selling her stock, rather than having an agent represent her. He made his way through the melee to the owner, waited until she had finished talking to someone else, and almost shyly approached her. He first sought in her a likeness to a rough-hewn character who could pit her strength and brazenness with men, instead viewed a lady not unlike Priscilla. He greeted politely, "Good afternoon." Also saddened that a lady no older than he should be a widow.

"Hello," she responded softly.

"Ah — hello. I'm — ah — Ben Chester, and this is my — ah — Danny Carsen."

"Hello. — Are you interested in my sheep?" she appealed. "Ah, I'm Mrs Mackenzie — Alison."

Ben smiled. "The same name as my sister."

That put them both on a more personal footing, although Mrs Mackenzie was not comparable to Ben's sister, except for naturally red cheeks. Ben did feel more compassionate toward her over her loss, while Alison hoped the minor connection between them might be to her advantage. Surely something had to go better for her. It was true she had recently lost her husband in a farming accident, and with two young children she was neither in the position to continue farming, nor wanted to remain at their farm: having to daily pass the site of his death.

Ben explained his and Danny's mission, and they made their way back to the paddock were the flock was held. Danny tagged along, wanting really to take a greater part, because some of the sheep could be his in future, however Ben dominated the proceedings. Two small muck-splattered children tugged at their mother's skirt, and Ben imagined Prissy being in the same situation if he died. If so, Prissy would not be on her own. He still wondered why this lady was doing everything herself. It was hardly the place for a lady: not one as gentle as this woman.

"There's more here than we intended to buy," he calculated, "although, we're buying for two properties." That sounded contradictory.

"Maybe they can be divided." She was anxious to make a sale, any sort of sale.

"No, we'll take the lot, if the price is right. We can run some on m' dad's place." And Ben could hear the wails from Jane: mixing sheep and cows on Kowhai. Ben believed some of Kowhai's land was better suited to sheep anyway.

Other buyers and sellers intervened: their opinions as diverse as to be expected. Ben was soft-hearted, sympathetic, and after checking prices, mulling it over, bringing Danny into the decision, they both agreed to make an offer.

"I'd be lucky if I got more for them," the lady said. "Thank you, Mr Chester. You too, Mr Carsen." Whether the auctioneers were impressed that a sale had been made before the sheep went on the block was another matter.

Alison Mackenzie's farm close to Auckland was being sold, and broken up into smaller sections: housing for this rapidly expanding city. She had two sheep dogs, and, although reluctant to part from them, at least knew they were going with the sheep to the life they were used to.

Due to the sales Ben and Danny finally found accommodation at the other end of Newmarket: at the Carlton Club. While dining in a spartan room, Ben's thoughts often returned to the widow. She seemed so utterly deflated: her whole world collapsing with the death of her husband. It did not really register with him, for it was the first time he had felt something for a woman, apart from his wife and his sister Alison. After a restless and noise-interrupted night, he and Danny went to her place to collect the dogs. The sorrowful lady and her children had a last frolic with them. Ben looked directly into her glistening eyes, and assured, "They'll be well cared for." He continued to look at her as she put her arm about her son.

"I'm sure they will, Mr Chester. I told my children that, didn't I, Son?" The boy nodded, his mother wiping away her tears. "Say goodbye to Mr Chester and Mr Carsen."

Ben at a loss how to say goodbye. The woman's circumstances moved him more than any other event in his life. He did not understand why. He did not fully know those circumstances, although believed she was now alone in the world, having to fend for herself, and raise her children unassisted.

In a few years time the government would provide her with a widow's benefit, although she was not to know this was in the wind.

Just how rapidly the city was expanding — thirty percent in ten years — Ben and Danny were soon to learn, when they attempted to drive their sheep to Onehunga. Only a few years earlier they could have driven them almost directly from the saleyards to the port. With the advent of electric trams, houses and shops had sprung up almost overnight along that same route. Nevertheless they did, with the help of the dogs, coax the animals around the western flanks of One Tree Hill, the grazing animals helping to mow newly subdivided sections recently part of Sir John Logan Campbell's estate.

The park, now known as Cornwall Park, was given to the city for recreational purposes, including football, cricket and most recently golf, while the adjacent Potters Paddock (now Alexandra Raceway) was for horse racing.

Someone coarsely advised them, "Y' don't bring sheep this way no more."

To which Ben replied. "No one told us."

"You can see for yourself. It's all built up."

"It wasn't last time I came this way," Ben protested, not that he had previously driven any livestock along the route.

"Lad, take Symonds St, if y' going to Onehunga Beach."

"Right." Ben did not know Symonds St from a bar of soap, so assumed somewhere along the line they would see it, probably after all the sheep had continued along Epsom Rd. Which is precisely what happened, so Ben, Danny, the dogs and the sheep continued to skirt One Tree Hill, and where five so-called roads met they wisely drove the sheep along what was in name only Symonds St. It was little more than a track drunkenly weaving between stone walls, with cattle grazing each side of the undefined road. Fortunately there were no sheep for Ben and Danny's flock to mingle with, and only a few of their sheep sought greener pastures through open gates, and had to be re-directed. At the foot of Onehunga's Symonds St they herded the flock into a reserve bordering Onehunga Beach.

"That's the hard part," Ben told Danny. "All we have to do is get them on to a punt, or something." Not the sort of task that could be pre-arranged, since Ben had little idea before setting out of what they would buy, if anything, and how long it would take them to reach Onehunga. So, after spending the night in the Manukau Hotel where Onehunga's Queen St met the wharf, Ben ensuring Danny did not get too carried away by mates he bumped into, the next day they set about finding transport for the sheep across the Manukau.

"I reckon I might know someone," Danny suggested.

To which Ben replied, "You ought to."

And Danny did. However it took all day. It meant another night at the hotel: Danny having run out of money entirely, and Ben being down to his last few shillings.

They beached two barges, Danny in his element, mid-tide being early morning, coaxed the sheep aboard — one hundred and sixty of them — and as the incoming tide lapped the craft, along came Danny's boat owner friend, and making sure the hawsers were strong, the long tow to Pollok began. They took a chance and cut directly across the harbour, rather than follow the twisting channels. The chance paid off: the barges grounding where the tiny Pollok beach met the mud. With the dogs, Ben and Danny set out on the last stage of their journey: driving the flock from the beach, along little used roads, and as dusk settled across the peninsula, Ben suggested, "Let's just put them into this paddock, and sort them out tomorrow, eh?"

That suited Danny just fine.

The barking dogs had their last fling at the sheep, jostling them into Ben's roadside paddock: one he had earlier cleared of cattle for just such an event, and while he went one way with the dogs, Danny scurried home, all smiles and chatter, eager to tell Jane of his experiences.

Jane smiled, and replied almost enthusiastically, "Our first flock." Then she added, "It must have put us into a great deal of debt?"

"No, not much." He swallowed, waiting for a rebuke. "Ah, I do owe Ben some money — having to stay . . ." And his voice trailed off.

"How much?"

"A sovereign — or two — maybe less — no more." He hadn't a clue how much.

She nodded. "I suppose I can find that."

"No, you don't have to," he assured her, although did not know where he was going to get the money himself.

In a couple of months the sheep would be shorn, and that would give them some income, providing Danny learned how to shear them himself to minimize costs. He hated having to get money from his wife: it was not the right thing to do.

Jane, on the other hand, accepted her portion of the cream and cheese income should go into their farm. It was just that she thought Danny may have got in with his mates at Onehunga and drank those profits away, even with Ben on hand. She would not be in debt to her brother, so extracted the money from her hiding place, actually in the dairy, and paid back her brother.

Those savings had other things to buy, although she had not nearly enough to pay a local chippy to help with the house.

Where Thomas Chester intervened. "I'll not have you owe a penny to the bank," he advised her. "One or two bad years, my dear, and you could lose your farm."

"It wouldn't come to that. Besides Nigel wouldn't do that to us."

"Jane, I trust that Nigel Caldwell fellow least of all. He'd bankrupt his own sister, if he thought there was something in it for himself." He nodded to emphasise his opinion.

"It would be a mean thing to do." Jane was horrified at the thought.

Thomas remained insistent. "I know you only too well, Jane. You have gained one thing from me, if nothing else, wisdom when it comes to money matters. I don't see you frittering your money away on trifles."

"Because, Father, I know how hard it is to earn," she said, agreeing with him.

"You do at that, my dear." Thomas dreaded the thought the time would come when Jane could not milk the cows night and morning, and unless Alison took over the role, he would have to go back to milking them himself.

Rather than have the flock wander off into the scrub where apart from getting lost their coats would become matted with tea tree leaves and bits of bracken, Thomas joined the gang extending Kowhai's fence line. The gang consisted also of Danny, Ben, a farm hand and Alison. Yes, Alison — if nothing else to prove a point to her father — neatly stapled wire to posts while one of the men pulled it taught. At first, when her father inspected her work, she gestured impudently, and hoped her would be satisfied and mind his own business.

The mention of Nigel at the time of the flock's purchase raised the subject of his wife, Jessica. She was insistent couples were having smaller families these days, and a solitary son was sufficient to continue the Caldwell name. Nature had other ideas, and so Penelope was born into the world. From her first moment Penelope made her presence known, and to the distress of the blessed parents, both she and her older brother Stanley may have borne the name Caldwell, however were Chesters in character: a problem which would arise as they grew older.

CHAPTER SIX

Now Jane and Danny had something to show for their efforts Jane became more content, her tongue less sharp, and when she admonished Danny she did so without shouting. She began to accept fate had destined her life, and there was no point in fighting it. She had once seen herself as taking on a more scholarly or academic role in life, and perhaps she could still achieve this. Being so close to Pollok, she thought, 'When they next require a teacher, I will apply.' She believed their sheep did not take up a lot of time, Alison could look after the cows, and she could earn extra money teaching. That was her plan. Unfortunately, nature also had plans.

One evening, after milking the cows, preparing a meal for Danny and herself, washing up, darning some socks, she sagged into bed beside her husband, and murmured, "Are you still awake?" Rather hoping she could defer her news.

"Yes, my love."

She rarely called him 'my love,' and paused while reflecting. "I — I think I am expecting a child."

"Oh. — Ah."

"I am having a baby." There was no doubt about it. The only doubt being in her mind: whether she wanted it, because those other plans did not include children. Then, she supposed having children was why she got married, or one of the reasons. If she did not want children, then she should not have got married. Being a mother was her expected role: not a schoolteacher.

She had one consolation, she was not alone: not alone in having a baby. Wives all over the peninsula were having babies. Much closer to home her sister-in-law Priscilla was having her third child. So, at least Jane could go through with it with Prissy at her side, and Jane accepted Priscilla as being more experienced. The whole episode further subdued Jane. Her temper may have been quelled. In its place arose another mood: frequent periods of depression, and tears. Unlike Priscilla, Jane did not have a comfortable time. Sickness, despair, disappointment dogged her.

Dutifully she rose long before dawn, despite her now evident condition, tramped lantern in hand across frosty fields, herded the now nearby cows into the dairy yard, and began to milk them. So cold were her hands on occasions she wept: short sharp bursts of temper doing little to relieve her misery. When Danny did wake early enough, and offered to help, she always rejected his intrusion with, 'Let me get started first.' Was it, despite the cold, she could spend time alone with the dogs: able to command them? Once the cows were rounded up their job was virtually over, as was the morning bond between her and those dogs. Danny invariably arrived, as she was about to release the drained cows into another paddock.

Desperately in need of a shoulder to cry on, she could never allow Danny to see how weak she really was. So, with barely a word between them, he would open the gates, and with the dogs drive the small herd into what Jane termed 'day paddocks'.

One morning Alison appeared. The sisters stared at each other in silence, until Alison offered, "I suppose it's time for me to take over — if you want?"

Red-rimmed eyes, her lower lip quivering, Jane relinquished her task, and Alison finally took charge of the dairy: temporarily of course. Thomas was on hand for the afternoon milking.

The time came when Louise was called for, then a mid-wife, and to the concern of those lingering, Ben rode to Waiuku for the doctor, both returning by way of the beach, since the tide was low. Thomas Chester — Jane was *his* daughter — lingered near Danny's place. He got as close as seeing his wife through the kitchen window, and softly hailed her. "How is she, Mother?"

"She shall be fine," Louise assured, although was far from sure herself. "Now dear, you just keep everyone away — including Danny. — Go on."

Thomas strolled from the scene, rounded up the cows: on his own, since Alison was also tending her sister. Jane: so strong, so vigorous. How could anything possibly go wrong? He dined alone that evening: for the first time he could remember. And he did remember. It seemed all so recent, he and his wife and their three squabbling brats, and later two argumentative daughters. Now, tonight, he alone. It would only be temporary. In a day or two both Louise and Alison would be back. Even then it would not be the same, he reflected: the atmosphere would be subdued with only one offspring flitting about, settling momentarily at the table, long enough to peck at her food, and fly away again: to another branch, another room within the home, or outdoors. Tonight was cold enough for a fire, even so he did not think it worth the effort for one, so he sat and shivered in the spacious lounge, perusing a journal, not taking in a word.

He must have dozed. Aroused by the clomp of shoes being discarded at the front door, its opening, and then Alison's sobs as she stumbled up the stairs. Thomas' strength lapsed. He knew something must we terribly wrong for Alison to be weeping over Jane. 'I have to know,' he insisted, heaved himself from the arm chair and followed his daughter to her room, laid a paternal hand on her heaving shoulders, and begged, "Jane, is she . . ."

"God, please help her."

At least that was some assurance. She must be alive. "And the baby?"

"Brute of a thing."

Thomas gently rubbed her bared shoulder. "Janey's no craven. She'll pull through." The trouble was: they were so far from a hospital, should Jane need intensive care. Why though? There had been no sign things could go wrong. He did not ask, instead himself went into the kitchen, as he had done earlier that night to prepare something for himself, and boiled some milk, toasted two slices of bread, and returned to Alison's room, insisting she got it into her.

"If that's what it's like, Father, I'm never going to have children," she informed him, sitting on the bed, hands about the mug to warm them.

Thomas had no immediate answer for, because although he knew his wife had had four children without trouble, and Priscilla two, with a third due shortly, the reassurance would be unconvincing to Alison at this time. "Now, don't you go bothering with the cows . . ."

"I shan't, Father." The last thing on her mind: having to get up in a few hours to milk the cursed things.

Since it was only a few hours, Thomas resettled in the lounge, dozed on and off, made himself some porridge — he was not entirely helpless in the kitchen — and as a squall cascaded from the black sky, he rounded up the few cows in milk, and subservient to their unrelenting demands, got little for his effort. It took as much effort whether they released a flood, or a dribble. He would separate it later. When he returned to the cold homestead — the range fire reduced to embers — of Alison there no sign. He sighed wearily, plodded along the veranda, and saw his wife, head down, thrusting herself against another squall as she crossed the saturated paddocks. Small consolation for her, he was on hand to help her remove her coat and boots, take her arm as she wearily climbed to their room. "How are they?" he dared to ask.

"Let's trust her strength will pull her through," Louise believed. Of her daughter-in-law she opined, "At least it will be Prissy's third, and it won't be as bad."

"No." Strange, he thought, for Priscilla did not appear to be anywhere near as strong as Jane, however she encountered no problems. "What are they calling it?" He realised he had not even got the sex of the child out of Alison.

"Douglas."

So, Daniel Carsen had a son. With Jane's tuition there would be little chance of him being a chip off the old block.

For the moment what her son turned out like was the last thing on Jane's mind. In fact there was very little on it at all. The ordeal had all but broken her spirit. She asked for Danny, her voice gentle and undemanding. Baby Douglas, though, was demanding: screaming every time he was hungry, and Jane had no option other than to feed him. So, one protested when he wanted to be fed, and the other protested over having to so frequently feed him. Their relationship did not begin on an auspicious note.

                    *   *   *   *   *   *

Life moved on for everyone, except Alison. She stayed put: the
handsome debonair good catch she had thrown back was hooked
by someone else, and Alison hated her. She did not know her, but
hated her all the same. She also hated the farm. No longer did
animal talk entertain her. Fine when she was a girl. Now an adult,
she wanted more than the drudgery and isolation of farm life. Her
thoughts crossed the Manukau, and when at night she finally
flopped into her bed, during the moments before sleep overtook
her, she sometimes imagined flopping on to a bed with a man. She
wondered whatever had happened to Freddy Styles, and she
combined the memory — the occasion of the opening of His
Majesty's — with flinging herself at Emily and imploring her to find
her a man to worship her, as Freddy had done: albeit briefly.

    Responsibility had robbed Ben of youthful pleasures. Since
marriage his entire character had been rebuilt on new grounds. The
easy-going youth, who invited a bunch of mates to Kowhai at a drop
of a hat, had metamorphosed into a mature father. He still had
many friends, still had a swig of beer, although for both he had little
time to spare. Priscilla often only saw him in the grey light of dawn,
or lantern light of night, unless an exceptionally foul day drove him
indoors. With summer around the corner — the days were longer,
even if the weather remained wintry — Ben simply increased the
length of his workday. When Priscilla heard someone comment,
'He'll wear himself out before he's thirty,' and another make an
even more devastating remark, 'I don't know why she married him.
I doubt if he knows she exists,' she decided it was time to beg her
husband to slow down.
    Not for herself: at least that is the way she put it to him.
"Darling, the children will be all grown-up, and you won't know
them."
    "Of course I know them." Inappropriately George tumbled in on
what was supposed to be an intimate conversation. "I know you,
don't I, Son?"

The almost four-year-old had no idea what his father was on about, snuggled into his lap and murmured something affirmative.

"There, Prissy, see."

His wife shook her head, because he had missed the point altogether. She would just have to take another tack later.

Apparently Ben had more important things on his mind. "Why don't you invite your sister — ah — Jessica and Nigel out for the — um — I guess they could stay the night?"

Priscilla frowned. In five years Jessica had visited six times, and Nigel just twice. So, why the sudden urge to have them out? A whole weekend with them. 'Mind,' she thought, scheming, 'it will make Ben take the time off.' Because she knew Nigel would not be there to pitch in. "I suppose so," she then agreed.

"I'll leave you to ask them." He confirmed, "Just think, Prissy, you will — and the children — see me for two whole days."

Priscilla shook her head. She would love to have him for two whole days, as a single family.

Ben had an ulterior motive for being so hospitable to his banker brother-in-law. He wanted money to sink into a useless swamp adjoining his property. There were woeful tales how this — the present owners — were the third family to go bust trying to farm it. He thought he knew how to make it a worthwhile part of his property.

Nigel only saw the controversial land from afar, spending some hours with Ben strolling among the ridges and valleys of Kanuka, surveying what he had accomplished. Nigel had nothing to lose, so they struck a deal, Ben later going into town to sign the papers, and for what he considered small monthly payments Ben purchased the property from very grateful half-starved tenants, who by the time they had paid their creditors had barely enough for a square meal. That would not happen to Ben?

Thomas Chester belatedly heard of the plot, when they were gathered at Kowhai. The colour rose over his entire face, and he exploded, "You young fool!" Then he thunderously abused his son. "I give you a farm freehold, not a penny of debt hanging over it, and what do you do? Mortgage the damnable thing. Why?"

Despite the expected opposition, which is why Ben kept it quiet from his father in the first place, he held his ground, literally and figuratively. "I can pay it off sooner. Even if I don't farm it now, it will be there for my boys — like you . . ."

"I'm sure it will, Son. A magnificent duck pond. I suppose they'll make a living shooting the damned things, or dredge it and start a crayfish farm." Which was probably the first time anyone ever suggested such an occupation in New Zealand. Thomas was being sarcastic, since freshwater crayfish were caught by leaving the head of a tea-tree branch in the stream, among which they would gather. "I'll see if I can get the deal revoked. I'll tell them you made a mistake."

When Louise intervened, placing her knitting on her lap. "Now, Thomas, can you honestly say Ben has — ah — over-extended himself, his ability to repay . . ?"

"What do you know about finance, woman?"

Louise nodded. Priscilla wide-eyed. Never before had she heard Thomas speak like that to his wife, whom she herself worshipped.

Quietly Louise responded, "Not a lot, dear, but enough."

Ben could only reaffirm. "Look, Father, I *can* pay it off sooner. It was a bargain."

"I'm sure it was. How do you expect to farm it? No one else has."

"Drain it. Like you could do to your own swamp."

Louise chuckled. She knew Kowhai's swamp was a thorn in the side for Thomas. His refusal to meddle with nature, believing their swamp served a purpose, although Louise could never determine what purpose.

Thomas nodded, glared at his son, and warned, "All the same, don't expect me to sink a penny into your blasted swamp . . ." He was going to also warn, 'Or any other part of your farm if the swamp sinks you.' Jane and Danny arrived, and attention immediately turned to the still recovering mother.

Louise changed the subject, asking her elder daughter, "Do you think you can manage the picnic?"

"Of course we can, Mother." She snapped her mouth shut, her lips a thin determined line, then complained, "I don't know why people keep fussing."

"That will be lovely," Louise said, without reminding Jane she had not tried to stop her fussing during her convalescence.

"And don't you make up an excuse not to go either, Ben Chester," Priscilla advised her husband.

Ben's mind was still on his swamp, and the deal with Nigel. He mumbled something, and sat brooding while the conversation settled on the forthcoming district picnic. Something as simple as a day's outing took detailed organising, even to the extent of checking carts for roadworthiness and horses hooves for wear.

In their separate kitchens Louise, Jane and Priscilla spent the day before baking, preparing hampers, so, on the picnic morning, all they had to do was get themselves ready, hitch up the horses and trundle up their respective driveways, joining other families as they drove several miles to Te Toro wharf, where there was a shelly beach of sorts, and nearby a grassy area. Whoever had chosen the day, had for some reason opted for one when the tide was out, although there was sufficient water for the children and some adults to wade.

Already a dozen craft were clinging to the wharf, those nearest the shore settling in the mud. Although children leapt off anchored boats and waded ashore, their parents either waited until the bows touched, or women were manfully carried to the beach.

"Here, Mother — over here," Priscilla called, having secured a grassy spot beneath a spreading pohutukawa.

Louise momentarily confused the two voices, and thought Alison had called. She looked about, although did not see her daughter. There were so many people: so many ladies in white, with broad-brimmed hats, it was hard to identify individuals from any distance. And for the life of her she could not think of anyone who actually had planned to have Alison aboard their cart. The truth hit her. All the family, including herself, had thought Alison was with someone else. In the meantime the children were hungry, rugs had to be laid, hampers opened, food spread out on tablecloths. Jane settled beside her mother, looking a little sickly after the cart ride, while her husband was off yarning to his mates. Ben had taken George's hand, and wandered up a creek, where he located a sand dump. He needed some for his driveway. So, they busied themselves, including the children who wallowed or fell into the muddy estuary.

Alison shooed the cows into a lower paddock, paused to check some fencing, although new, that had been damaged. The last thing she wanted was to retrieve the cows from the beach. Then she sauntered homeward: to a silent house. She surveyed the kitchen like a police inspector, to ensure not only was the house silent, but apparently empty, since although there were washed dishes on the bench, there was not a filled hamper on the table.

'They've gone — without me.' She sighed despondently. 'That's all they care for me.' Tears came to her eyes, her lips trembled. They had gone to the picnic, and not bothered to check that she had a ride. For a brief moment she contemplated staying at home, having it all to herself. She was always staying at home, and often virtually to herself when her father was at Waiuku and her mother either at Jane's or Prissy's. She sniffed back those tears and pledged, 'I'll show them. They'll never forget me again.'

With temper-coloured cheeks she strode from the house, noted that the buggy was indeed missing from the barn, saddled a horse, spurred her friend into action, galloped along the drive, plodded out of the valley, unsure which route to take: along the main road, or via the gully. She opted for the more familiar main road, wound through the hills, then cantered to Te Toro, let her horse free in a paddock, and sauntered into the gathering.

"Oh, there is Alison," her mother advised those about her. "I knew she would be here somewhere." Relieved, Louise returned to fussing over the family, not that many of them were nearby at the time: only Jane and Douglas, and Priscilla's youngest, Kathy.

Priscilla defied her husband and entered the ladies race. So did Alison. Really only two in the fifty-yard sprint: Alison and Priscilla. With the fleetest feet — bared — and the fewest petticoats — one — Alison flew across the rough grass, although Priscilla surprisingly was not far behind. Alison smiled graciously at the man who presented her with a prize, glanced contemptuously at her family, then returned sullenly to her horse: not to ride back home, rather because the mare was her companion.

Being the last race before lunch, everyone made a dive for the hampers. Priscilla, still puffing, commented, "What on earth do you feed Ali on?"

"She's always been a fast one," Louise said. "Lick the hide off the boys, eh, Ben."

"I didn't see you enter anything, Son," Thomas said.

"No, I'm past it."

So small talk mingled with sandwiches, and cakes and various drinks.

"Now where's Alison got to?" her mother eventually observed.

"Probably peeved. — She usually is," Jane suggested.

"Now that is not a nice thing to say at all. Alison has been working very hard . . ."

"Making up for lost time."

The girls' mother decided the only consolation to Jane's unwarranted criticism was she must be getting stronger if she had the strength to be bitter.

Alison did not join her family for lunch, hungry as she was, instead, still bare-foot, strolled towards Maori canoes. One was aground, the other tugging at a mooring, the stream flowing about it. She searched for the owners, and located them cooking pipi over a fire. "Ah. — Hey, you," she called, splashed across the stream and ran up to them. Some turned to flee. So Alison called them again. "Hey, don't run away." She sagged on to the sand beside them. "If I give you my prize, will you take me for a row?"

Even before that offer was accepted, a girl, probably about her own age, offered Alison a pipi. Alison juggled the hot shellfish in her hand, blew on it, prised it fully open, and swallowed the only just dead shellfish.

"I'm Alison," she said to the girl her own age.

"I'm Annabelle. I've been to your place with my father."

"Have you? I don't remember you."

"It was quite a long time ago."

Minutes later Alison had joined them digging where the shelly beach met the mud: her hands deep into the grey mire searching for more pipi, carrying a handful back to the fire, and sharing them with the group. "This is better than dry old sandwiches," she said, although knew very well her mother's sandwiches would not be dry.

Suddenly they all leapt up, Alison tagging along, and made a dash for the canoes. At first she trod delicately through the mud, then, after being laughed at for her reluctance to get wet, splashed the last few yards, and with another girl's help tumbled into the canoe. "Let's go!" she demanded.

And they did: weaving through the picnic armada, and out into the channel. "This is such fun," she giggled at the same girl who had first offered her a pipi.

"You shall have to come again, and we shall take you fishing," the olive-skinned girl said in most precise English.

Alison had noticed her skin, because, although modestly dressed, her arms and legs were bare. Now she also noticed her grammar: her whole manner.

The girl smiled shyly at her. "What are you looking at?"

"Ah! — I'm just thinking — ah — how healthy you look; much more than I."

The other girl laughed. "You wear too much. You wear so much, you smell."

That set Alison back. "Oh. Do I?"

The girl nodded. "A little. But your perfume disguises it."

"I haven't got any on." Alison could not remember the last time she had worn perfume. "Anyway, if I went round half-naked, I'd be laughed at, or put in jail."

The Maori girl laughed, leaned forward, and touched Alison's arm in friendship. "You come with us, and go round half-naked, as you put it. We won't laugh at you."

"Yes you will. Because I am so white — look." She lifted her dress to expose her only slightly tanned legs.

"See, you're not white at all."

Another girl joined in the jesting. "In this sun — you would frizzle up, eh."

"Thank you." They all laughed, and in spontaneous gesture the three young women embraced, much to the concern of the rowers: the movement upsetting the equilibrium of the canoe. "Whoa!" Alison yelled, fearing she was about to be flung overboard. For her concern they rocked it again. Alison's fear was only superficial, because she could actually swim — sort of, with her feet on the bottom, which was more than many of her family. This was much more fun than having to be all-polite at the picnic. Before she could think much about that, the canoes headed for shore, all the children leapt out, and much as Alison tried to keep up, she was left far behind, and sagged on to the small beach nestled between two rocky outcrops.

After several minutes she shrugged with a pout, murmured, 'So much for them,' and walked to the far rocks, noting the tide sliding forward across the mudflat. She decided she had better take one of the canoes, and try and paddle back to the picnic. She only had a vague idea how to get there across the paddocks, and it was a long way on foot. The trouble was, she had never paddled any craft, let alone a canoe. She mastered the technique enough to slowly but surely manoeuvre the boat in the correct general direction, with the help of the flowing tide.

She had gone a hundred yards when she spied the Maori surging out of the bush, brown arms waving at her. She waved back with the paddle, noticing them sling two laden sacks into the second canoe, shove it off the mud and paddle fast after her. Meanwhile the remainder ran along the beach, scrambled across rocks in a bid to intercept her. Only now did Alison get the message; they wanted to stop her. So, obligingly, she turned her canoe, more or less, towards the shore.

Within seconds slippery hands were grasping at the frail craft. "Hey, don't do that!" Alison begged, her heart racing, fear rising to her throat.

"Don't tip — her — out," called the girl Alison had so recently laughed with, as she swam towards the canoe.

Too late! The boys *did* tip Alison out, sending her plunging to the bottom, shallow enough to touch, but too deep for Alison. Surfacing, gasping, panic-stricken, she grasped at the girl coming to her aid, then went under again, was dragged along until her feet touched the bottom, and she stood up. She staggered to keep her balance, then burst into tears, still up to her knees in the water.

"Why did you do that?" the girl demanded.

Alison placed her hands to her face, sniffing and swallowing, even if being cowardly.

"Why did you take the canoe?"

"Because you ran off."

The girl clutched her waist, helped her ashore, where Alison flopped.

"You stupid boys!" Annabelle scolded. "Now see what you have done. You could have drowned her." She shook her head sharply at them, and repeated her tongue-lashing in Maori, until most scampered away in fear.

"She should swim," retorted one, and joined the others to rescue the canoe and tip the water out of it.

The Maori girl lifted Alison to her feet. "We will take you back to the picnic now."

"I'm sorry. I panicked."

The girl shook her head. "We only went to get you some kumara."

Still shivering, thoroughly soaked, Alison smiled wanly at the girl, and apologised. Unconcerned about her appearance, she sighed, waded back out to the canoe, climbed aboard, and was rowed back to the picnic. However before the Te Toro wharf was in sight Alison said to the girl, "I'm such a mess, I think I'll get out here, and go home without . . ."

The girl was smiling. "We don't mind you looking a mess."

"Look at you," Alison said. "You're like a beautiful mermaid." And she did: her slender figure, clothes clinging to her body, plaited hair draped each side of her shoulders. Alison envied her. Even so, she sensed the girl's life was not what it ought to be. True, she was educated. For what? She could be a schoolteacher, a nurse, or take up a good job in the city. When she thought about it during those few minutes, she herself also was educated. A fat lot of good it was doing her.

Over the side she went as soon as she could see the sandy bottom, and leaning back inboard, she kissed the girl's cheek, the Maori responding with a rub of their noses.

"Hey, your kumara," yelled one of the boys.

"What happened to my prize?" They laughed. "Maybe you'll find it in the mud. It will probably be all right. I'll only be able to carry one sack."

Slinging the sodden sack over her sodden shoulder Alison waded ashore, turned to wave and throw the canoe a kiss, then stealthily crept round the rocks. She took a bush track on the near side of the stream, crossed it, muddy water oozing well up her legs, and like a rustler captured her horse and laid the bag of kumara in front of the saddle. She was about to climb on, when she sneaked a look to see if anyone was watching her, slipped off her single petticoat, being so horridly wet, mounted the horse, and edged it away from the picnickers.

Since all and sundry were at Te Toro Beach, then the rough roads home were deserted. Almost dry by the time she reached an equally deserted Kowhai, which pleased her, because she did not want to confront anyone in her condition. Re-stoking the copper, she stripped off in the wash house, ran with only a towel around her through the house, amused at the thought that she knew some men would like to see her such — she could tell by the way they had looked at her in the past — quickly threw on some old clothes, and almost jauntily fetched the cows, a little late, however since the sun did not set until seven, she could get the milking done long before dark. Anything else could wait until the morning.

"I saw Miss Alison go off with some Maoris . . ."

"In a canoe," advised two children, excited over the news no one had seen the lady for hours, and she was lost.

"I don't even know how she got here," Louise Chester admitted. "She did not say two words to any of us."

"Fool of a girl," Jane spat.

"She's a blasted nuisance . . ."

"Ben, mind your tongue."

"Sorry, Mother, but she is. Look, you go on. Someone leave me a horse."

Gradually the picnickers gathered up their hampers, discarded shoes, togs, towels and other possessions, the children arguing as to who should take what, all the way from the grassy bank to the beach — a distance of twenty yards at the most — and clambered aboard the various craft. Others, including the Chesters, hitched up their carts and began to wend their way back to peninsula homes. True, Maori had been nearby: some had joined the picnic, including Tom, an old friend of Thomas'. There was not a sign of them now.

Ben watched their departure, and sat despondently on the beach, as the setting sun lengthened the shadows, and the day gradually died. A Maori waka with twenty or more paddlers came down the channel. Ben leapt to his feet, hailed it, and immediately the sleek vessel swung toward shore, slicing into the shelly beach. Greetings all round. Ben only wanted to know one thing.

"Have you seen my sister — Alison?"

"Alison? No Ben." Tom turned and called to some children in the canoe, then in precise English, asked, "Annabelle, have you seen Miss Chester — Alison?"

"Sure we have, Father." The girl scrambled forward, and Ben despite his anxiety observed her litheness and remembered that he knew her. "We were with Alison. She came with us. But she came back here hours ago, Mr Chester."

"Eh. Y' sure?"

The girl giggled. She actually blushed, her olive cheeks reddening noticeably. "I don't think, Mr Chester, she wanted to see you — any of you . . ."

"Why?"

She giggled again, followed by giggles from the other children. "Mr Chester, she fell out of the canoe, and was so wet, I think she sneaked home, so no one would see her."

"How — ah . . ." He had forgotten her name, although knew it sounded pretty.

"I think she had her horse. She told me she did. She is a good rider."

"She's good at everything," piped up one of the other girls.

"Damn her. I wished she had told someone." Ben kicked at a footprint, sand skidding away.

"Look at it this way, Ben, you know she's safe," Tom assured.

"Thanks, Mr Waikari."

Annabelle called from the departing waka, "Tell Alison, she is welcome to come with us anytime."

Alison had finished the milking, turned the cows out, and was cleaning up, when the family arrived home. Thomas immediately investigated, striding down to the dairy, his anger rising with each footfall, and confronted his daughter. "Do you know, Child, they've got a search party out for you."

Alison, equally as infuriated, snapped back without pausing in her sweeping, "I don't know why."

"Girl, have you no sense of responsibility?"

The accusation was fended off with the same curtness. "I thought I was acting very responsibly. Milking the cows before I went out, returning home to milk them again; missing half the fun."

"You know very well what I mean. They're *all* out there this minute searching."

Alison briefly considered her thought, 'At least they cared enough to search.' "As soon as I've finished, I shall ride back, and tell them I'm alive."

"You will do no such thing."

The standoff continued, each sparring.

"So, who is searching then?" Alison demanded.

Her father paused, and had to admit, "Your brother stayed behind; only because someone had seen you with the Waikari lot."

Alison reddened. "So, just Ben. Not a whole search party then? Anyway, I don't know whose lot I was with, although I had a most interesting time. And, there's a sack of kumara for you — a bit wet, but . . ." She sniffed, lips quivering. ". . . very edible." Her bravado sagged, and she turned away, continued sweeping, tears streaming down her cheeks.

Her father was about to relent, when his wife entered. "So, she's here."

Thomas nodded, while Alison whipped round, ready to do battle with her mother, however her spirit was broken, and she flung the broom to the floor, attempted to brush past her parents, Louise arresting her flight.

Bewildered by his daughter's fluctuating behaviour, her defiance and tears mingling, Thomas suggested, "I'll clear up. You two go."

"I'm — I'm sorry — Father." And with eyes and face flushed, she allowed her mother to take her from her duty.

Thomas gave the dairy a cursory sweep, went to the stable, saddled up, detoured to Danny's place, paused long enough to hail them from their yard, with, "She's home," and for Jane's benefit added, "She came home early to do the milking."

He heard Jane's remark, "She might have told us," as he rode on.

In the cottage Jane jostled Danny, "You had better go with him. He's going to fetch Ben no doubt."

"The old man will be all right," Danny assured her.

"I'll go myself then."

"You can't, and you . . ."

"Please, Danny, for my sake."

With a sigh Danny heaved himself from the comfortable old armchair: one of the second-hand pieces of furniture they had acquired, saddled up a horse, and trotted after Thomas, fortunately a half-moon assisted them. They met Ben on the gully road, and what Ben thought of his sister was not complimentary. Only Thomas offered any excuse. "She was peeved at being left behind — this morning."

They urged the horses on, and as Ben reached his boundary fence he said over his shoulder, "She owes me something for this."

Thomas nodded. Defending his daughter he murmured to himself, 'I think, Son, you are still in her debt — by a long way,' The same thought could be extended to Danny: the number of times

Alison had put herself out for both men. If Danny, for one, had given her a hand that very morning, then none of this would have happened. Of course, on further reflection, he could have given her a hand himself. So, as he rode silently beside Danny — there was never much conversation between them — he came to the conclusion Alison was the least guilty of all, and he would tell her so, when he got home.

Alison recalled that she had seen the Maori girl before, although like so many people she had not taken specific notice of her. Only days later, while delivering cream to the new butter factory, there she was, also delivering cream. "Hello there," she greeted with a wave. The girl smiled, and Alison ran up to her. "How are you? Do you often come here?" Bursting with questions, because the canoe episode was still vivid: especially meeting this girl.

"Only when we have a lot of cream," the girl said, because it was hardly worth the trouble of carting it when they managed to crudely separate a little from their milk. She also had her questions. "They found you?"

"Oh, that — a storm in a tea cup."

Annabelle still wanted to know more about Alison being lost. "Your bother was terribly worried," she lamented.

"Ah — Annabelle — it's over and done with. A storm in a teacup. — All over and done with." She dismissed the subject, and eagerly asked, "Tell me about yourself? Your life is much more exciting than mine."

The girl shook her head as she replied, "I wish it *was* exciting."

"You go rowing and fishing and swimming, and all sorts of things I never do; I'm not even allowed to do, and it's mean." When Alison thought about it then, why her brother knew 'the Waikari lot.' He had played with them as a boy, and she realised they were still his mates, as much as other young men in the district. That was not the question. Her question was, why was she never 'allowed out to play?' Almost all her adventures being confined to the valley, and when she did take herself off to the picnic alone, all hell broke loose. Now she wondered how meeting Annabelle could change all that. She tended to forget she had been to Auckland — twice, on her own.

What promised so much in wishful thinking did not eventuate. Their meetings instead were coincidental and infrequent, and always pleasant encounters. After completing their business, they sat on the back of one cart or another, and chatted away, oblivious of the time, or, whether they were supposed to be doing something else.

During the height of the summer, while Alison was actually moaning about the heat, Annabelle suggested, "Why don't you come for a swim with me?"

"Now?"

"Yes, why not?"

"I haven't anything with me — to wear."

"I know a place. Come on."

The tide was in, and the cove dead quiet, overhung by ancient pohutukawa trees. They might have been the only two people in the world. Without hesitation or modesty Annabelle stripped to her underpants, Alison admiring her litheness, not realising she was as slim. "I can't."

"There's only the two of us."

"Someone might come."

Self-consciously Alison discarded her dress and petticoats, and the two slid into the cool sea, Annabelle immediately striking out, while Alison managed to dog-paddle, with her feet still touching the bottom. Swirling about, the Maori girl said, "Here, give me your hands?"

Alison reached out, and Annabelle towed her: one fearing she would drown, the other instructing, "Now, kick your legs." Trusting her not to let go, Alison allowed her legs to float upward, floundered for a moment, and thrashed with her legs. She laughed, took in a mouthful of seawater and spluttered. "You okay?"

"I think so." She was still a little panicky, at the same time excited over the prospect.

Her tutor let go one hand and said, "Now paddle."

"I can't."

"You can."

"Don't let me go."

"I won't."

Alison looked into the other's brown eyes, and in that moment felt she was beginning a new venture. If she could swim, then being tipped out of a boat would never concern her again. She knew then she was both very fond of and admired Annabelle. She began only now to understand her own mother's hospitable character: her acceptance of people regardless of their colour or creed, and although her mother apparently had not met Annabelle, she knew the two would get on famously.

Alison did not learn to swim that day, however secretly practised swimming rather than bathing in what space there was at Kowhai's water hole. She even leapt from the ledge into the deeper water, and later discovered the ledge actually went behind the waterfall.

Never would she dare to venture further than her knees in the Tasman. It was to be the Tasman where she first put her newfound skill to practice.

For a few brief months learning to swim put on hold her ardent desire to leave the valley for good and cast herself at Emily's feet. It had during those months occurred to her in Auckland she would have to work for a living: and certainly not have idle moments during the day to chat or swim with Annabelle. Such occasions now could be fitted in almost at leisure: their timing dependent on the tides and weather, not on the demands of paid employment.

On one occasion when Annabelle stayed at Kowhai for a few days, and they went swimming in the pool, Annabelle had the courage to dive through the waterfall. Alison's eyes opened in amazement. "Come on try it," Annabelle urged.

After much hesitation she did: her plunge lacking the grace of Annabelle's dive. Alison, determined to achieve something, practiced the dive: braving both the uncertainty of whether she would resurface, and the chill of the water. In doing so, she in that small way became the first of the family's sporting achievers, although unlike future generations, her efforts remained known only to herself and Annabelle.

For Alison there were days, weeks, when her social life was non-existent.

While on her own in the dairy, an idea — not a new one — came to mind, and after mulling it over while checking some curing cheeses, and tasting a small one, she took it up to the homestead, catching her mother on her own actually almost idle, with a cup of tea.

"Mother, try this." She cut of a slice of cheese and hand it to her.

Louise tasted it like a professional, and murmured, "Very nice."

Alison cut off a second slice, breaking it in two, giving apiece to her mother and eating the other herself.

"Mother, can Annabelle and I go up to Auckland and stay with Emily for a bit?" She chose to ask on this occasion rather than tell her mother she was going to Auckland.

Louise raised her eyebrows, surprised Alison had asked. "So, you were using the cheese to butter me up?'

"Certainly not, Mother."

"Do you think she wants you there?"

"I suppose so. I'll write."

"You have discussed this with Annabelle?"

"No. Although I know she would love to go." She did not say half the reason for Annabelle would be to get away from her family for a few days. She loved her siblings. She would love them even more after a break. It would be simpler for the two young ladies to arrive unannounced on Emily's doorstep. Alison had made that mistake before, and ended up playing crib with the maids in Emily's absence. She thought of Freddy Styles, and wondered what sort of lifestyle she would now be living if she had responded to his overtures.

So Alison first arranged it with Annabelle, and that meant riding to her home, where she learned first-hand what it was like for her: no privacy of her own room like Alison. The farmhouse had a permanent communal character, compared to Kowhai's occasional madhouse. Originally built to accommodate a family of four or five it had been crudely added to, and had two ponga-walled out houses, where Annabelle's brothers slept. She shared with two

younger sisters, while her grandmother had a room to herself —
sometimes — and her parents also had their own room. The house
was surrounded by potholed paths and puddles. It did have a
flourishing vegetable garden, and needed to with so many mouths
to feed, and a dairy Jane would have been appalled at. She was
more appreciative of her own home after the visit, although still
wanted to escape its 'confines'.

Then she wrote to Emily, and several days later got a gushing
affirmative reply, and again made the horseback ride to
Annabelle's. All that took over *three weeks* to confirm.

Annabelle caught the Onehunga bound steamer at Te Toro, and
downstream at Pollok where it broadened into the Manukau
Harbour Alison was eagerly waiting, with a not so full suitcase, and
a couple of cheeses to drop off at Onehunga. For some inexplicable
reason, although both had made the journey to Onehunga and
Auckland before, there was something more exciting and
adventurous about this excursion: a sort of anticipation Emily had
something up her sleeve.

The weather obliging, and during the morning trip across the
placid harbour the two ladies chatted like schoolgirls. Alison
wondered if the fabulous damson gown she had worn at His
Majesty's would still be at Emily's, and she could wear it again.

"Father has given me a few shillings spending money," Annabelle
mentioned, and although it was said enthusiastically, she knew in
the city it would not go far.

Alison responded by assuring her, "My father has finally
admitted that I am worth paying for my efforts. I mean, Janey
always got an allowance, so he decided I should." Then she clasped
Annabelle's hands. "I don't think we have to worry about money.
I'm sure Emily will be so pleased to see us, we won't have us pay for
a thing."

"I can't expect her to pay for me?"

"You don't know Emily. So don't feel bad about it."

They effortlessly sprang from ship to shore at Onehunga, and
jostled their way through crates of produce destined for west coast
ports such as Raglan, New Plymouth and Wanganui.

Annabelle crouched and patted one of several wandering baconers, who seemed to have escaped the attention of their owner.

They duly arrived at Emily's, to her effusive greeting. "My sweet things, you are so, so welcome. Life has been a positive bore. I don't think I have done a thing since you were last here, darlings."

Which Alison believed to the letter! "We are two young ladies in desperate need of a good time."

Emily raised her eyebrows.

Annabelle was less outgoing. "Not too good-a-time."

Emily looked at Alison and pouted. "First of all, lunch — or have you had it?'

"Um, Em, we had to deliver a cheese to the Sans Souci, so we had something there."

"Never mind. I'm sure you shall need to settle in today. Now tell me, how long are you here for? Do we have to cram everything into a few days, or can we spread ourselves out a little?"

"More than a few days, Em, if we are no . . ."

"Do not mention it being a bother," she dismissed. "Now there are two stage productions on over the next week. You know how much I like going to them. The magnificent entrepreneur, Mister Fred Rivenhall — you must have heard of him . . .?"

Neither lady from the country had heard of Mister Fred Rivenhall.

"Never mind. Fred has produced two delightful pieces, *Are You Asleep,* which brings to mind all sorts of delightful scenarios. Imagine," she gestured with wide eyes, "a lover kissing your cheek and whispering, as he slides his hand across your naked shoulder to explore your hidden talents, 'are you asleep'?"

"Emily, you are wicked," Alison protested: only mildly. The nearest she had come to experiencing that sensation was — come to think of it — when Freddy Styles in Emily's garden pinned a rose on to her bodice, his hand lingering lusciously. She gave a little sigh at the memory, snapped out of it, and almost demanded, "And what else?"

"Something of quite different theme, although said to be the military drama of the century."

"Em," Alison now contested, "has anyone told the producer we're only into the seventh year of the century?"

"Must you be so pedantic?" Emily expelled her breath. "Anyway, it is called, *Human Nature.* And we might be lucky to get tickets, since it is bound to be popular." She had already in anticipation secured tickets for the following Wednesday night's performance.

"I'm sure we shall enjoy it." Then Alison lamented, "Em, we hate to impose on you, however being poor wretches from the wilds of the country, we do not have suitable clothing for such illustrious occasions."

Emily looked at Alison, shook her head, and sighed despairingly at Annabelle. "You shall just have to wear some rags from the barrowman."

Matching her sarcasm, Alison responded, "I am sure you don't want us to embarrass you. I hope to wear the gown I wore to His Majesty's. I suppose you have put it out with the rags?"

"I have saved it for just such an occasion as now. So, all we have to do is fit out Annabelle. And *that* we shall do tomorrow." The way Emily said it, left no room for argument from Annabelle. "I am afraid I have nothing in my wardrobe that would fit such a petite figure?"

Alison pointed at her friend, mouthing the word 'petite' questionably, although in envy.

Annabelle knew the difference between courtesy and genuine friendship. Emily was not being nice to her out of politeness, and any reservations she had about staying with her soon dissipated.

For the remainder of the afternoon the three talked: sometimes jovially, sometimes seriously, and for the guests Emily displayed, without bragging, how worldly she was.

They also caught up on world news. There were two tragedies reported in that week's *New Zealand Herald*: the French mining disaster, which entombed nine hundred workers, prompting relatives to demand the murderers should be downed, and a famine in Japan.

"Now, what does your father think of this *Free Trade* proposal with Britain Balfour is proposing?" Emily asked Alison, referring to the British Prime Minister's reported 'airy graces'.

And to show she also wasn't entirely ignorant of world affairs, Alison responded, "Father's all for it, except he wants to know what the catch is?"

"That would be typical of your father," Emily assessed.

So engrossed in conversation they failed to notice a change in the weather: the sun slowly enshrouded by gathering clouds.

Sharing a room with Alison, Annabelle felt a little uncomfortable over its plushness: a step or two higher than when she had shared a room with Alison at Kowhai. Sleep eluded her, and she was sure she heard rain on the roof.

Accordingly the following day Emily bundled herself and the two girls into a horse-drawn cab — although motorised versions were available — and were deposited in a slushy Queen St: it having certainly rained overnight. She fussed over Annabelle, embarrassingly so. The young lady was smitten by an Astrakan cape and jacket, with a flaring ankle-length skirt, and insisted it was just perfect. However, Emily had her try on a multitude of garments, including as advertised, various furs sought after by women (in those years).

"Now, ladies, a must see is the display in Hallenstein's window."

The display was of the famous almost unbeaten All Black's return, although a throng of admirers kept them away from the window: in fact they were in danger of being run down while standing on the roadway.

"Never mind," excused Emily. "It certainly proves what heroes they are."

What amazed Alison in this 'teeming' city was the number of people who acknowledged Emily, particularly men: and by the looks of them she would not mind one or two of her cast offs, if indeed they were.

The three ladies were forced to interrupt their progress when they were almost 'abducted' by two of Emily's admirers. One turned to Annabelle, and declared, "Emily, where did you find such an exquisite Italian piece?"

Annabelle wasn't sure if it was a compliment or not, thinking a 'piece' might also be a chattel.

"Just some waif I gathered on my travels. Isn't she a gem?"

By now Alison was trying to swallow her laughter, with her gloved hand hiding her chuckle, and when the ladies had broken free of the pair, she said, "Wait 'til I tell her dad. Italian, my foot!"

"Oui!" Annabelle acknowledged.

"That's French."

For a few minutes Annabelle reflected on being referred to as Italian by Emily, wondering whether she had said it in preference to admitting she was Maori — even if not full-blooded, and having facial features more akin to her European heritage. No, she decided, Emily was just being her mischievous self, with no prejudices: not of that nature anyway.

By the hour Annabelle more enjoyed her stay in Auckland. Alison was almost envious. While both she and Alison would have happily been clothed in any one of several dresses they viewed, Emily passed them over, "Lovely, but let us look a little further. We can always keep them in mind, Girls."

"But what if someone buys it in the meantime," Annabelle protested.

"I am sure at the end of the day we shall have both of you dressed to satisfaction."

Annabelle smiled, but behind Emily's back grimaced at Alison, who responded with a shrug.

For Emily, no excursion would be complete until visiting Smith and Caughey's. Annabelle did not know which way to look first, such was the wondrous dress display. They were immediately all but set upon by an enthusiastic attendant.

"We require a dress to show off Annabelle's olive complexion," Emily insisted, speaking as if she was a fifty-year-old outfitting her daughter, rather than a lady not yet thirty.

"A pastel shade, Mrs Todd, don't you think?"

"Indeed."

The attendant looked Annabelle up and down almost as if she were about to purchase the girl rather than clothe her. She nodded, then crossed to a display dummy, on which was a pale cream dress with a modest rounded neck line, three-quarter length mutton chop sleeves and a drawn waist fanning out to a wide hemline.

Emily looked at Annabelle, and Annabelle stared agape, began to shake her head, but Emily pre-empted her refusal by saying, "All you have to do, darling, is try it on. But I can see now it should be a perfect fit."

"We can have it altered, Mrs Todd," the attendant assured, removed the dress, and as she handed it to Annabelle she caught a whiff of a fragrance she was sure originated from the store.

Emily turned to Alison. "So, that is Annabelle attired, now what about you?"

Alison had been admiring the same garment, so turned her attention to another display. Her viewing was interrupted when Annabelle reappeared in the dress. Such was the effect several attendants and indeed customers edged their way towards the buyers.

"Turn around," the attendant ordered, and with her hand admiringly on her chin viewed the garment for all angles.

"As I said," Emily decided, a perfect fit for a perfect lady.

Annabelle had while donning the dress looked at the price, and now raised her eyebrows silently asking Emily to make a decision based on that.

Emily simply settled the deal by saying, "If you are satisfied with it, darling, we shall have it parcelled."

Annabelle's eyes were glistening as she returned to the fitting room, and changed back into her simple day dress.

By then Alison had also chosen a garment, although no less attractive than Annabelle's purchase, she felt she could not do it the same justice as her friend had done.

There was always something to do in the city. The girls had only intended to stay a few days: a week at the most, however their host encouraged them to stay on for something else.

The something else this time was the highlight of the social year: the Citizens Ball, to be held in the Drill Hall in Wellesley St. (Years later where eighteen-years-olds were recruited for compulsory military training.)

"We haven't anything to wear for *that*," Alison advised Emily, although such an excuse was a waste of words.

"So, we shall get you something."

Even Will Todd was enchanted by the thought of having three lovely ladies on his arm, despite having to pay an extra three guineas as guarantor — for their behaviour presumably. Since the charge also included two additional men, Emily came up trumps with a couple of suitable escorts.

"You must look your very best," Emily insisted. "I do believe Sir John will be there." The Father of Auckland, Sir John Logan Campbell, now in his mid-eighties, was the organisation's vice-president.

Looking absolutely resplendent the three ladies joined a hundred or more of their sex also looking absolutely resplendent, in the shed, converted for the occasion into a palm-fringed hall, with streamers and flags. Emily was in a more traditional deep blue gown with crocheted white trimmings. Alison apricot dress displayed a hint of fashions to come, with 'v' shaped white trimmings on the skirt. As for Annabelle: her loose fitting flowing pink gown with the train caught on one wrist, was years ahead of its time. As if they were belatedly being presented to Auckland's society the two girls were a new attraction, despite there being many equally beautiful young ladies at the ball. They waltzed, reeled and curtsied after exotic movements. Of the two Annabelle attracted more attention. It left Alison a little envious of her friend: 'the Italian piece,' even though Annabelle insisted she did not have a trace of continental blood in her, unless some distant relative on her mother's side was of Mediterranean descent. And she could dance. Despite her crowded home environment someone had taught her not only to grace the ballroom with presence, but to grace it with her steps: something not lost on Emily.

Alison was surprised how beautifully Annabelle waltzed, rhythmically turning, her body swaying back, head to one side, then being drawn close prior to commencing the next movement. Had she observed herself in a mirror, she would viewed the same grace.

"Absolutely charming, Emily," Annabelle's partner gushed on returning the girl to her place at the end of the bracket. "Where have you been hiding her?"

"Where *have* we been hiding you, dear?" Emily agreed. To Annabelle's admirer she advised, "Like my sister-in-law here," indicating Alison, "she has been so busy with domestic duties she has not had time to circulate."

Annabelle blushed with pleasure. "I don't think I have ever enjoyed myself so much," she confided to her host.

"Not even swimming?"

Annabelle reddened further. "Who told you about that?"

"A birdie." Emily was in this instance envious of Annabelle. While she had undressed covertly for lovers, Annabelle had undressed covertly for the sea: a sensation Emily had never experienced.

With only minutes to recover from one dance the girls were whirled into another: this time changing partners. Even while weaving and spinning both girls thought how far removed they were from their domestic duties. Surely, after this night, their rural lives would never be the same.

Alison, now in her mid-twenties, as was Annabelle, was not frantic for personal romance that night. The drill hill might not have been a castle ballroom, however it did not lack atmosphere, and Alison in her flared apricot gown felt like a princess rather than a spinster. She did check William when he was too complimentary, reminding him how fabulous Emily looked in her dark blue tired gown. With another partner for a waltz she briefly closed her eyes, giddy with delight as she was sensationally spun, then reopened them to observe her partner was looking at her with wonderment.

"Oh, don't mind me, Sir, it is so seldom I have danced like this."

"Surely you have attended many balls."

Alison took that not as a compliment but a comment on her single status. However she replied resignedly, "I live in the country,

Sir, and I fear our lounge, big as it is, does not allow a great deal of room for such manoeuvres." Said as they swept into another swirl, her dress careering out, hem turning back on itself as they reversed the spin.

Alas, all too soon the ball and their stay with Emily were over, and they swapped glamorous gowns for mud-splattered dungarees.

What did come out of her stay with Emily was a friendship destined to last for over fifty further years, even though time and distance often physically separated them. On parting they were all promises to each other they must do it again, however other events put those wishes into a box, not to be extracted until circumstances brought all three together again.

CHAPTER SEVEN

1907

(The following event and its sequel are partially factual, including the vessel's name, its cargo, and what happened to that cargo.)

Only the slightest breeze ruffled the dawn air. It blew from the nor-east: flowing down the main valley, fanning the grass, scurrying through the gap out to the restless Tasman. The brooding surf concealed a latent temper: its smooth surface heaved by long slow swells lazily lifting from the depths, curling and crashing ashore, swirling among the rocks, then reluctantly receding. To the south blueblack clouds accumulated, halted by unseen forces. The breeze whispered to the trees: advised them to dig in their roots into the soggy earth and brace themselves. Leaves quivered as excited birds flitted about branches.

Throughout the morning at Kowhai they moved their sheep to higher leeward paddocks, and cows closer to the dairy. Ben on the other hand plucked his sheep from the heights, and set them grazing in clefts. Twenty-five years of farming on the peninsula had made them wary of days like this. Thomas predicted that during the next twelve hours nature would disgrace itself: with a heavenly fanfare and earthly response, the rain, wind and sea would engage in a thunderous battle.

"I'll fetch the eggs, Mother," Alison offered, and scurried down the back steps, deciding to stable her horse. "Come on, old girl. — You know it's going to be stormy. — You just stay right in there," she advised, shutting only the lower section of the door. Then she sought eggs: as usual in the oddest of places. She shook her head at one chook. "You can't fool me." The clucky hen squawked and flapped away, and Alison wondered just how old that egg was. She added it to the others in her boat-shaped wicker basket, then sliced several leaves from bunches of silver beet, and returned to the kitchen.

At its zenith the sun wrangled with clouds, sought to fulfil its daily duty. The odds were stacked against it: subduing then banishing it. The restless wind blew this way and that, whirled, raised eddies of dust, skipped through trees, teased leaves. It whined about the house, rattled loose iron and windowpanes. In the Chester's yard a fire flared in response to the irritating forces. Then it stilled, as if to warn, 'I'll be back; brace yourselves.' Birds broke into urgent chatter: a lark ended its sky-high song and swooped back to earth.

Along the coast from Hokianga to Taranaki, ships ran for shelter. There were few havens on this coast. Harbour entrances foamed as violent seas, ebb tide and wind clashed, spume curling back over broken waves.

Captain Wisdom of the scow *Reliance* had earlier run down the Manukau under sail, cleared the bar, then, since this was the days before radio, decided on his own initiative to turn back and re-enter the Manukau. He was warned off by the signalman, and he had no option to take his heavily laden ship out to sea.

Clouds raised their voices in hostile rumblings.

Kowhai heard them and trembled.

By dusk tempest's fury was in full force. Wind thumped houses, whipped grass, snatched leaves from bent trees, swept them along in the dust. Roots took the strain, relaxed in a respite, then tensed for another tug of war. Farm animals plodded for shelter behind thorn hedges, beneath trees. Birds snuggled against boughs, or sought safe holes. Seabirds nestled against cliffs, closed their eyes and weathered the storm.

At sea were several coasters: with no way of knowing who was in trouble and who was not, with visibility contracting to a few hundred yards. The *Reliance* plunged up and over or through rising seas and headed into the lion's den. Rollers caught her starboard bow, wrenched it, forced the helmsman hang on, lest the wheel spin from his grasp. She was carrying a burdensome load of bricks and timber for a courthouse at Raglan. Her destination so near, yet now, so far.

Sean Sullivan was aboard. He was Irish: neither red-haired, nor sharp-tempered. An easygoing young man: a jack-of-all-trades. Although not a sailor by occupation, he had taken sailing ships and steamers across bars, tinkered with automobiles, crewed a fishing schooner, farmed the land, and auctioned cattle. The only thing he never seemed to do was get his hair cut. Now he stood facing the tempest, his eyes peering through angered crests, seeking what lay beyond.

Young as he was, his many adventures had taught him a thing or two, particularly about the sea. And although he was not officially on watch, he kept a sharp eye for trouble. New Zealand's coastal waters were treacherous. The wind swung to the nor-west, drove across waves. He watched a squall approach, braced himself as driving rain beat his heavy clothing: penetrated, trickles running down his chest and back. A little water never hurt anybody, least of all he.

Rain pressed the sea into submission, stamped up the beach, left sand pimpled with fury. It drove horizontally through the gap into the valley, washed over coastal hills, swirled round Kowhai, rapped window panes: a big bad wolf demanding to be let in, fell down the chimneys and splattered hearths. Within the homestead Louise baked, occasionally shuddering involuntarily when an extra vicious gust wrenched her home. Thomas had his wet-weather gear on, sometimes searching for trouble from the veranda: other times going upstairs for a better view. Alison pottered about in the dairy: tasks she had inherited from her sister.

Driving engines, racing screws, rising bow, then plunging. Sea-washed decks, storm-drenched sailors. All battled the elements, out beyond the coastal shelf, beyond the most frenzied waters: out in the open sea where waves strode like conquering warriors. Captain Wisdom had complete control of his vessel. He almost commanded the sea, and certainly commanded his ship. Now at the helm himself he anticipated every encounter: steered the ship straight through heaving waves, up and over as sea challenged ship, and ship defied sea.

Sean Sullivan came into the wheelhouse. "'Tis a wild day, Cap'in."

"No worse than I've known."

"To be sure, I've sailed in worse m'self."

"Be a good lad, and fetch me a hot drink."

"Aye, I shall." The door almost wrenched from his grasp, and rain drove into the wheelhouse as Sean obeyed, scrambled down to the galley, stirred the stove's embers, heated some water, made both himself and the captain a hot drink of cocoa.

At Kanuka the hostile weather drove Ben indoors, finally, and with nothing to do he squatted on the floor with his children and built castles from wooden blocks: blocks shaped and painted by his own father from off-cuts while building the home. When Ben and his sons had built a tower, complete with drawbridge, Kathy crawled across the floor, made a grab at it, and cried as a tumbling block slapped her hand.

"Serves you right," snarled an unsympathetic brother, while her mother snatched her up and whispered words of comfort.

"Never mind, Son," Ben consoled. "She is only a baby. It won't take us a minute to rebuild it."

"She's still mean." George was going through a stage when he did not like his baby sister one little bit.

The younger James lifted himself from the floor, sat on the couch beside his mother and reached out for year-old Kathy, the child snuggling into him, her whimpers subsiding as he lovingly cuddled her, more characteristic of his father than George.

Snug in its setting, the homestead was spared worst of the storm's fury. Even so Ben could not settle, wanting to do some work, knowing full well the moment he stepped outside, went a hundred yards from his home, he would be blown off his feet. The afternoon was short: leaden clouds drawing the blinds early.

On the other side of the hill his sister Jane was not so secure: fidgeting, uttering little gasps every time vicious gusts charged up their valley and assailed the cottage. In the lantern light she could see her husband was in his usual dreamy state, and she assumed he was recalling the times he had been at sea in such storms. Surely he felt safer ashore. Or did safety mean nothing to him, he preferring adventure and risk?

The roofing over their veranda began to rattle, and when Sean raised his eyes to the ceiling, guilty because it had needed a few extra nails for — since the home was built, his wife chided him. "Just one of the jobs you should have done . . ." As he heaved himself from the armchair, she said with the shake of her head. ". . . It's no use doing it now. You'll only get blown away." And as she stirred a pot on the range added, "Let's just hope it does not rip off tonight."

It did not rip off during the night, although its incessant rattling kept them awake. At first light Danny braved the storm, and secured the damaged iron, while Jane held the ladder, issued instructions as if her husband was incapable of hammering in a nail or two. Within the house their son Douglas had not slept well, and was now terribly moody: whimpered and wailed, refused to eat his breakfast, Jane later flung it to the birds.

"There, they'll appreciate it," she shouted, and Douglas hollered louder.

"He's just scared," Danny said. "It'll be over in a few hours."

"It's all very well for you, Daniel Carsen, you can get out of the house. I have to put up with him."

To which Danny suggested, "Would you look over the farm, while I mind him."

"Don't be so silly," she retorted, face colouring. "You say the most stupid of things." In truth, not so long ago Jane would have been doing just that.

Danny shrugged, and since he already had his wet-weather gear on, crossed to the barn-cum-stable-cum general shed and saddled his horse. He loaded his tools into the saddle bag, and rode from the yard, leaving Jane to pacify Douglas the best she could. Shredded branches lay piled against immovable objects. A large tree had been uprooted: its flaying branches having flattened a fence. There was little chance his sheep would go to the trouble of climbing through the fallen tree, so he repaired only the section where they might escape, and rode from the mess. Common sense made him look for more trouble on the higher reaches of his land.

Away from the house, despite the conditions, he was less tense. He could repair things without being nagged. If he was not doing it properly now, he would come back and do it right later. After all, these were just temporary repairs. He did not take into account that his temporary repairs tended to become permanent. So, despite the wind and rain, he was inwardly calm, at peace. He stopped to gaze from a high point. Visibility was severely reduced by clouds tumbling over the seaward hills and plunging into the main valley discarding their contents liberally.

"Hi there!" Barely audible words whipped from the caller's mouth. Through wet eyes Danny made out Ben approaching. "Everything all right?"

"Sure. Just a tree down."

"Must be bad over your side?"

"No, not really." Then Danny thought again of his in-laws. "I wonder how the others are?"

"Just where I was heading, Danny." Meeting his brother-in-law raised Ben's opinion of him, because not for one moment did he expect him to be out in such weather, and to have come this far meant he had been out for some time.

On the flat another rider approached, Ben first thinking it was a traveller who had spent the night at the homestead.

"Hi there, you two," came Alison's crisp voice.

As they met, Ben said, "I might have known you'd be out in it."

"This," Alison indicated with a toss of her head skyward. "Just a shower."

"Oh yeah, I bet you didn't want to milk the cows this morning?" Ben challenged.

She pointed to the herd ambling across a paddock. "There they are, Brothers, all content. How's everything at your place?" She could have told them she had already separated the cream, not risking taking it to the creamery on this day, and had some milk on its way to becoming cheese, storm or no storm.

"We've just come across to see how you are?"

"Sorry to disappoint you. We've had guests. Some have gone. I haven't checked behind the home." There was a small side valley parallel to the coast. "You'd better come in for a hot drink." She wheeled her horse edged it into a trot, then heedless of the slippery track urged it into a gallop — a slow gallop — and left the two men to follow her.

It had been a long night. The scow *Reliance* still offshore, bow into wind and sea. Although the storm's front had passed, a succession of sou-westerly squalls pursued each other, whipped up in the southern Tasman Sea, scythed across wave crests, New Zealand's west coast taking full brunt of their lashings. Captain Wisdom was forced by fatigue to relinquish command, and retire to his cabin.

At the helm McConnell gripped the wheel, fearful he might renege on his duty: to keep the ship into the wind, to ensure her cargo was safe and sound. When, after almost thirty minutes he had mastered the relentless rising and falling, corkscrewing, he began to relax. His relief was short lived.

The mate first saw the danger, as a huge wave heaved itself above mere minnows before it. "Bring her round, man!"

"I'm trying! — I'm trying!" The ship refused to respond, and she clawed askew up the advancing wall, balanced precariously, and as the force passed beneath her, tumbled side down into its wake.

The wheel spun wildly, wrenched from McConnell's grip. The mate dived for it, flung the helmsman aside, to discover the wheel ran free through his hands. "The rudder's gone, or somethin'!"

"I know." Before he could regain his balance the *Reliance* broached, a monstrous successor breaking over the wallowing hull. Agitated sea swirled among the cargo, gushed through wrenched open door, swept crew off their feet. The tyrannical sea snapped bonds: bricks and boards hurled about, planks shattered windows, flung overboard to tumble among waves, bricks jostling along the sea floor.

She did not founder, rather lived up to her name, sluggishly rose up the next wave, rolled through its crest and spiralled into the trough. A respite followed: a succession of lesser seas, each one lifting the helpless vessel, and carrying her shoreward.

Captain Wisdom, flung from his bunk, staggered into the wheelhouse, as the retreating sea burst out. "Get rid of that timber!" he ordered. "Cut it free."

Dangerous work. Long planks whipped as men attempted to free them. Brick stacks tumbled as the sea rolled her beam on, perilously close to overturning. The dead weight below brought her back before the next wave slammed her on beam's end again.

A thump: a thump that was not a wave, but the ship hitting bottom.

"How on earth did we get *here*?" Wisdom yelled. He could not believe it. They could not have motored ashore so fast even if the helmsman had turned her about and deliberately beached her. He had not done that; nevertheless the shore they had struck, not some uncharted sand bank.

Another stack of timber tumbled over the side, plunged into breaking waves, and subdued them — slightly. More thumps as bricks threatened to break through the steel hull. Wisdom made a decision, right or wrong. They were still too far offshore for the crew to reach it safely. He did not know how many of them could swim in a pool, let alone in this treacherous cauldron. "We've got to get rid of those bricks," he ordered.

The mate stared at him aghast. Such a task was suicide.

"Jump to it. Form a line. Do anything. — Just get rid of them."

Three leapt into the hold, stumbled among the fallen bricks, and began laboriously passing them up to those on deck. Wisdom himself pitched in, and Sean Sullivan tossed the cargo overboard, grasped the broken rail to keep himself from going over with them. Each time a wave swept over the ship, those below got drenched, while those up top hung on for dear life. Their rate of progress such, there was little chance of the ship surviving the onslaught before being relieved of her cargo.

Oblivious of the drama at the gap, Ben, Danny, Alison and a traveller tucked into some freshly baked scones. "Another cup," Louise offered them.

"No, I'd better be off," Danny said, "Thanks all the same, Mrs Chester." Difficult for him to call her Mother, since his own was still alive. This lady was like a mother, and no matter how hard a row he had to hoe, she was there to ease his pain. He never seemed to get it right.

Ben sensed his reluctance, and suggested, "How about coming with me, and see what's been damaged up there." He indicated with the flick of his head the hills between Kowhai and the sea. "I might need a hand."

"Ah — sure, Ben." Still, hesitant because he had been away from his home for hours, and the thought of confronting Jane daunted him. The chances were she had also baked scones, or had a pot of soup on the range, in expectation of him returning cold and wet, from wherever he had been.

"I may as well come too," Alison decided.

Her mother mentioned, "Father said he'd finish off the cheese." Unlike Jane, Alison did not object to people helping in the dairy. She found her workload tiring at times, with little social activity to lighten her life. Funny how after being his kid sister for so long, to go riding with Ben was one of her small pleasures. Her expedition to Auckland with Annabelle was already a distant memory.

Even before reaching the gap, carefully negotiating the stream bank, Ben sensed something was amiss. He halted. "Did you hear that?"

"Hear what?" Alison determined, drawing on the reins of her horse.

"I thought I heard voices." He pressed on, reached the gap, dismounted and led his horse up onto the rocks, with spindrift swirling about them. "There's a wreck!" he yelled to Danny and Alison. "A boat's aground!"

The *Reliance* was not yet solidly aground. Broadside to the waves she thumped the sand, wallowed then bounced again, until the next tumbling wave carried her just that much further from her habitat.

Ben became the communicator. "Hello there!" he hailed. Whether they heard him, or saw him, was answered with waving arms, and he yelled across the turbulent ocean, "We'll get help."

The boat fell back into another wave, its crew holding on as it broke over the ship. Then a sailor held up a harpoon-looking gun, and Ben got the message. So did Danny, with a, "I'll get up there." He indicated the cliff.

"Be careful," Alison warned, concerned that Danny was not sure-footed, and knowing the sandstone cliffs were unstable. Another squall flayed the coast: so intense, ship and shore were visually separated. A line did arc across, Alison having to leap aside, slither, regain her footing, scramble among rocks as the bolt tumbled seaward, a wave breaking over her as she grabbed it, emerged from the foam, and clawed back to the shelf.

"Ali!" Ben belatedly shouted. "You could have . . ."

"Here." She reached out, not for a helping hand, but for Ben to grab the line. Her actions were instinctive. As she momentarily sat on the rocks, she had no time to reflect of the danger to save the line. Her brother climbed the cliff, passed the line on to Danny, who secured it to a lone pohutukawa, its roots savagely undermined, yet able to cling to the unstable cliff.

"That's not going to hold it." Alison advised, referring to the thickness of the line compared with the ship's weight. "They'll need more than one rope."

"They're not going to. It's for the men to get ashore."

"They could just about wade," Alison assessed. "It's not *that* deep."

"You just about drowned."

"Rubbish." They had no time to argue. Alison indicated the taut line, from which a sailor was hanging precariously. "Rather him than me." She began to undo her oilskin in readiness.

Another awesome wave rose from the depths, overtook it predecessor: the combined forces thudding against the *Reliance* scouring decks, including a stack of bricks for'ard, hurling them into seething sea as it lifted the boat, uncannily tipping her seaward. The line slackened, then sprung taut. At that moment Sean Sullivan was dangling above the waves, crests spitting venomously at his feet. In an instant, the second he took one hand off to reach forward, the line catapulted him high, tumbled him over and slammed him backward into the surf, his leg snapping against a rock. He went under, gasping as another wave broke over him, the next lifting him on its foaming crest and dashing him on to rocks.

Ben and Danny watched the drowning sailor.

Alison discarded her oilskin, boots, dress and petticoat with surprising alacrity and leapt into that seething sea, half wading, half swimming as tumbling waves lifted her, drove her shoreward, then dragged her out. She snatched the sailor as another sea broke over them, and wrenched him from her. Spluttering, she let the receding wave take her out, fleetingly remembered what Annabelle had taught her about the surf. 'Don't fight it,' were her words. She could not help but fight it, as a wave punched her, barrelling her backwards, her backside thumping a wave-smoothed rock. Saturated she might have been, but a flame within fired her. She lunged for the sailor. "Got cha!" She heaved him more-or-less upright, and during the lull dragged him toward shore, as fully-clothed Ben waded to their aid.

"Ali! — Ali! — What . . ."

"Here, take him." She glanced over her bared shoulder to see another breaker climb over a smaller forerunner, and braced herself. The force was too great, and all three were flung against rounded rocks. Oblivious to her semi-nakedness, intent only in saving the sailor, she fought the torrent, stood her ground against an ebbing wave. Panting, spluttering, wiping the water from her eyes, she then helped her brother heave the limp form on to a ledge, scrambled on to it herself, and with Danny, dragged the sailor out of harm's way.

Ben crouched on the rocks, turned to confront his sister. "You could have drowned."

"I can swim," she snapped, although knew her experience fell far short of being able to survive for long in that sea. She crouched on all fours, heedless of her appearance, regaining her breath, trusting she was high enough to be out of a rogue sea's reach.

Sean Sullivan opened one eye, and was sure he was in Davy Jones' locker with a mermaid bending over him. For surely no fair maiden would be out on a day like this, and certainly not coming to his rescue. With that wonderful vision, his water-filled eye closed and he lapsed back into unconsciousness.

"He's not dead," Danny assessed.

"Better not be either, after the trouble we went to save him," Ben stated. He again looked at the grounded ship, flung one arm in the air in a sort of 'he's alive' wave, and suggested. "You two stay here, I'll get help."

"Is the tide coming in or out?" Alison asked.

"It's just about high, whichever way," Danny noted. How high was high: spring or neap?

Alison shivered, reached for her clothes, and roughly flung them on. Her soggy dress clung to her body, making her wish it was summer, and the only person present was Annabelle, so she would not have to worry about her state of dress. Funny she should think of that and Annabelle at a moment like this. Her brother and Danny were too occupied to notice, and what did it matter anyway? They had saved the sailor.

Ben called his horse, walked it through the gap, rode across the rushing stream, and back to Kowhai. Alison and Danny tended the beached seaman. That he was alive, apparent by the groans he made. Alison observed, "His leg's broken. I hope Ben thinks to bring back a stretcher, or something to carry him."

"He's sure to, Ali.".

It was 'something to carry him', for there certainly was not a stretcher at Kowhai.

"Ben, you'll have to go for the doctor," his mother ordered, wishing for a telephone, although not realising that many of those closer to Auckland with phones, were now without them due to the storm.

Ben weighed up the alternatives. He could not ride to Waiuku via the coast, so he would have to risk the road, and that was as dangerous as wading into the surf to rescue the sailor. He changed only his trousers for a spare pair of his father's, then spurred his horse up out of the valley.

Thomas and a traveller rigged up a stretcher from poles, rope and a blanket, and rode back down the valley. By now the incoming tide and the sea had driven the stream back, and the track Ben had so recently used was deep in water: too deep and murky to safely use. So they had to leave the horses and traverse the hill on foot, the wind funnelling through the gap threatening to dislodge them.

"There's no other way?" queried the traveller.

"I'd have used it if there was," Thomas retorted, then, less annoyed considered, "Ben did not actually say what was wrong with him." And he thought the injured sailor might be up and about. No such luck, as Thomas edged round the cliff face, and discovered to his dismay Alison, Danny and the sailor on the opposite side of the stream. "Why didn't you tell me," he called back to Ben, who was far out of earshot, having gained the ridge road in his bid to get a doctor. "There's no way we can get through that," he determined. Ben must have got through it, because he had come up the valley on the homestead side of the stream, which was why he did not direct his father down the far side, the only crossing now back at the house itself.

He stood there assessing the situation. Could they wade across? How deep and dangerous was it really? What stage was the tide? Hard to tell. Alison scrambled towards him, and he yelled at her, "Ben didn't say you were on *that* side."

"It wasn't this high minutes ago, Father. I'm sure it wasn't." Another wave surged into the gap, clawed up rocks, washing over Alison's feet.

"What is wrong with him?"

"Knocked out, and a broken leg, at least."

"He won't be able to walk."

"Here, give me it," she called across the ten-yard gap. She waited for a wave to recede, slid from the ledge, splashed through knee-high water, snatched the stretcher, turned to see if she could make it back before the next surge, and risked it, confident having survived further out, she could survive in whatever force was flung into the gap. She heaved the stretcher on to the ledge, grabbed Danny's wrist as the sea snatched at her legs, surged to her waist before he dragged her clear, the rocks adding more grazes to her bleeding legs.

"Ali, why did you . . ."

"Let's just get him home."

Again she had acted so swiftly, her father and the traveller were left on the opposite side, agog. Only after the next surge receded did they attempt the crossing, then just made it to Alison's side, before the next eagre tumbled into the gap.

"You go first, Alison," Thomas ordered, so she would be nearest the opposite rocks should they be overtaken by the surge. The traveller also took the front end, and Sean Sullivan was unceremoniously swung between them, barely above the water as they carried him across the stream. Both Alison and the traveller slipped as they climbed from the rapidly flowing water. Sean's head thumped on the rocks, either stirring him, or knocking him further into stupor. They did not pause to determine as Danny and Thomas heaved and dragged the stretcher on to the rocks.

"What about them?" Alison queried, indicating those left aboard.

"They're safest there. If she hasn't broken up now . . . She looks pretty solid," Danny determined, and the others assumed he must know something of the boat's soundness.

"So why did he . . ?" Thomas questioned, cut short by Alison's:

"They didn't know we were here." Then she realised they did know. Irrelevant now, and there were more important things to think about, like holding on for dear life.

They humped the injured Sean Sullivan to Kowhai.

Louise, with Alison's help, bathed and rubbed him down, put him to bed, then turned her attention to her bedraggled daughter. "You'd better get out of those things."

Alison had decided that for herself. "Bags the first bath." As an afterthought, because unlike at Emily's Parnell home, hot water was not on tap, she appealed, "I hope the copper's going?"

"It is, dear," her mother assured. "However leave some for the others."

"They can use mine. — I'm not all that dirty." She had the cheek to assess whether the previously unknown traveller would want to have a bath after she had been in it. She was not going to scent it, or do anything like that. She had, come to think of it, got thoroughly mucked up milking the cows, gone off on her horse to survey the valley, plodded through mud, then been plunged into not the cleanest of sea water and a stream so silted it was brown. So, when she did lift herself from the bath, the water was as dirty as when she had bathed her two nephews, and she doubted if anyone would want to use it after her, so she let the water go.

"Sorry," she said to her mother. "I was filthy."

"You look more ladylike now," her mother accepted. "Never mind, I filled the copper again just in case."

"Any sign of life?"

"No, and no sign of Ben either."

"He'll be ages, Mother. Besides, the doctor might be out somewhere else."

"Of course. — Of course he is likely to be." She again looked at her daughter, seeing her in a new light, never believing she would have been so brave, having been enlightened of Alison's heroism. "You had better lie down."

"I'm fine, Mum, honestly." And changing the subject, she said as she gazed out the window, "I think it is easing."

"And, about time."

"Where's Danny?"

"Gone home."

"He'll get it."

Louise reprimanded her. "Now don't be like that. I'm sure when he explains to Jane, she will fuss over him."

Alison chuckled. She could imagine Danny being made to strip off outdoors, gather some firewood, heat and fetch his own water to the bath, while her sister berated him for getting in such a state.

Which is pretty much what happened; not because Jane was so vexed with Danny, rather their son Douglas continued to be irritable, and Jane had her hands full tending his demands.

Ben and the doctor reached his home at the same time, and as expected the part time practitioner *had* been out on a call: several calls that morning. He also had to eat, and Ben too needed nourishment. At least the wind had dropped. Was the storm over, or just a lull, before a series of pursuing squalls lashed the land? After eating, the two men rode cautiously along the mud-churned and foliage-strewn peninsula road, mist shrouding the hills, gloom gathering early on this afternoon.

For Sean Sullivan, once he regained his senses, the wait for medical assistance was made almost pleasant: as pleasant as it could be with a broken leg and a multitude of grazes where shell covered rocks had sliced through his clothing. Fresh after her bath, Alison became his nurse, helped him to sit up so he could eat. Sean was momentarily captivated by the closeness of her body: the neckline of a dress Emily had encouraged her to buy not throttling her, exposing enough for Sean, despite his condition, to whet his imagination. His memory of the mermaid had been obliterated, and he did have the desire to kiss the cheek so close to his, yet shied away from tempting fate.

"There, now," Alison said gently, oblivious of his thoughts. "Is that better?"

Should he get her to adjust the pillow a little more: just a little? Again his better judgment overcame wishful thinking. "Ah, it'll be fine, so it will."

She shook her head, tut-tutting, "You men will do silly things."

"'Tis sorry, I am. And would I be right in a-thinking t'was you yourself who saved me?" Or did another admirable lass save him?

"Yes, you would, with my brothers. It took all three of us to drag you ashore."

"And here's me a-thinking I floated on a magic carpet, right into this room."

"Sir, I can assure you it took four of us to carry you here, you're such a lump of a thing."

"All twelve stone of me. Tell me, m' colleen, where're m' mates?"

"They used their brains and stayed aboard."

"Aye, you're a hard girl. I remember now, so I do. I swear we, none of us knew where we were, nor that you good people were waiting for us."

"I can assure you Mr . . ." She did not know his name.

"'Tis Sullivan, my dear angel, Sean Sullivan, and should I die now, tell them I departed this world in good company."

"Mr Sullivan, you are a lot more alive than you were an hour or so ago. (She had lost all track of time.) My father is down there, and I should say they'll be able to walk off soon without getting so much as their feet wet."

"Ah, but you are still scolding me, m' colleen." His interest turned back to the charming, if severe young lady. "Now, I have disclosed my name, what would yours be?"

Being Alison she readily obliged. "It is Alison — Alison Chester."

"Now that would be a good English name. No Irish in you m' lovely."

He was already flirting with her. Well, she could give as good as she got, and corrected him, "It is Scottish, actually. Now, you just rest up there, and not ask so many questions, otherwise you won't recover, and if you die on me how could I possibly . . ." Her advice was long-winded, so she settled for, ". . . I'll go downstairs and see what is happening. The doctor will be here shortly."

"I don't need a doctor."

"Oh, yes you do. That leg of yours needs to be set." And adding insult to injury, "No one wants an old crock limping about the place."

"Ah, you would be right." Disappointed he watched her flit from the room, as if she had been a mirage, and the conversation had not taken place. He imagined the crew and passengers, all six of them, tramping up the valley, barging their way through the house and jostling into this quaint room. He hoped they would not, because he could not see the family tolerating it, not if they were all as stern as this fair daughter. He said a little prayer, trusting it would be transmitted discouragingly to the crew.

By mid-afternoon the *Reliance* was high, although not exactly dry, only spent waves surging about her keel. Captain Wisdom finally allowed his storm-tossed crew to leave the ship, slosh through the surf, and mill about Thomas Chester on the now exposed beach.

"Nothing more than a broken leg," he assured them.

Wisdom was relieved. They may have been grounded, however no crewman had been lost. His first mate was far from relieved. He had been on duty at the time, and it weighed heavily on him that the ship had grounded while under his command. Several times he had attempted to express his apologies to the captain, however the master only seemed concerned about his crew, not at the time knowing the actual fate of Sullivan.

Now the crew stumbled through the gap and made a beeline for Kowhai, while Wisdom, and Thomas Chester discussed the possibility of re-floating the vessel. Thomas had ascertained despite the apparent height of full tide, largely caused by the storm, over the next few days each high tide would be lower, or certainly no higher than today's, depending on the phase of the moon. He would check the moment he got indoors, so the feasibility of re-floating the ship could be decided then. During the night another tide with pounding waves could crush her, or dash her on to the rocks.

Ignoring Louise Chester's plea to be quiet, the crew charged through the house, up the stairs, and crowded Sean Sullivan, whose doze was rudely awakened long before they packed through the bedroom door. Their voices and manners did nothing to comfort Sean, especially when he spied Alison, the fair maiden, in the thick of them. "Would you be quiet, boys," he appealed. "You're bursting m' ears." Unable to put any strength into his command.

"Gentlemen, if you can't be quiet, and give Mr Sullivan some peace, you had

. . ." Alison warned, her order also lacking authority.

"Aye, what does he want peace for? Lyin' there like the king."

"There, wee lass, don't disturb yourself. He's fine."

"Sean revels in hoo-ha."

"Ah, he'll think he's back in the bar."

Tanner, the only quiet one, bent over Sean, his low voice barely audible to the injured sailor. From the corner of his eye, Sean saw a burly shipmate bodily lift Alison off her feet, and carry her through the door.

"Put me down!" Her legs kicked wildly, hand beating his back.

Sean tried to rise: his condition painfully obvious.

"Let go — you monster!" Alison bit his bare arm.

"Jesus! You — bloody — little — vixen . . ." He threw her to the floor . . .

. . . Precisely when Thomas Chester and the captain entered the fray: the girl's father flaring ferociously. "My God!" He grabbed his daughter, who was already back on her feet, hand raised to beat her assailant, thrust her aside, squared up to the sailor, and, with clenched fist, caught him on the chin, his beard failing to soften the blow, and he catapulted along the landing, barrelled down the stairs.

"That's another the doctor will have . . ." Alison snarled at her father.

"The rest of you — *get out!*"

Sean grabbed Tanner. "Not you."

Thomas Chester glared at the less-violent looking sailor, because at the moment they all were violent to him, and allowed the concession. He also glared at his daughter, and warned, "I'll deal with *you,* later!" He charged down the stairs, chased the lot out of the house, and stood on the back porch until the last of them had shuffled from the yard.

Alison watched her father's actions from the landing, quivered, her struggle with the sailor telling, fled to her room, flopped on her bed, and shook: trembled with both anger and fear. Her despair resulted from such brutish behaviour. Not the first time she had been picked up and threatened with one punishment or another. Ben's mates — in days gone by — had delighted in carrying her off, and always released her unharmed. Now her pout became a tremble: her tremble sobs.

Anticipating the crew's arrival Louise had prepared sandwiches, baked a selection of delicacies, some of which were snatched up as the lads entered, the rest left untouched as they were evicted. The captain was still there, so she bundled them up in tea towels for him to distribute later, not knowing what had caused the disturbance, although guessed Alison had something to do with it.

Thomas, still raging, thundered through the house, barged into his daughter's room, and accused, "Can't you for once behave yourself. You deserve all you get."

She turned her head on the pillow, narrowed her eyes. "Father, I . . ."

"Don't give me any of your excuses." In those few minutes his admiration of her had been replaced by censure. They glared defiantly at each other.

Red-eyed, Alison retaliated, "Do the *damn* cows yourself then, if . . ."

"I intend to."

So, instead of she inflicting punishment on her father for his wrongful accusation, he punished *her* by not allowing her out of the house. Her tears returned in a gush, and although she considered asking sarcastically whether she was allowed at least to tend the sailor, she rolled face down and clasped her hands to her ears, refusing to listen to further admonishment.

It *had* been a long day for Alison, and a tiring one, so, whether she intended to or not, fatigue overtook her injured pride, her eyes closed and she slept.

The doctor arrived: he and Ben having parted company where Kowhai's long driveway wound down from the road.

In all this time no one had thought to let Priscilla know where her husband was. With three young children she had been confined to the house, beside herself with worry. On seeing him canter into their yard, she burst out the back door in a high state of anxiety, "Ben, where *have* you been?"

Far below in the main valley, Louise had overlooked the fact that her daughter-in-law had been stranded, or maybe she had assumed Danny would ride across from his place and tell Priscilla what had happened. Louise's thoughts were now centred on giving the 'doctor' they had known for many years a cup of tea and a snack.

"The patient's waited this long, another five minutes is not going to harm him further."

"Ah, you'd be right there, Louise." Then he added, "I suppose that fair daughter of yours is fussing over him?"

Louise shook her head, raised her eyes to the ceiling. "My fair daughter, as you call her, had a nasty experience . . ."

"A what? — Is she injured?"

"Yes, very much so, although not physically."

"I see." Then he realised Alison was not about. "So, let's see this sailor."

"What do you need?"

"That depends on what I have to do." He picked up his Gladstone case. "A broken leg, you say?"

"Mm. So Thomas says. For myself, I haven't been poking about under blankets to determine how bad, if you know what I mean."

The doctor did not poke under the sheets either. He flicked them off the sailor, allowing cold to rush in. There was a fire. With one thing and another, it had been ignored, and burned lowly in the grate. "Thankfully, a clean break, Lad."

"Aye, it doesn't feel too bad."

"Maybe so, however you shan't be walking on it for a good few weeks."

"To be sure I will, Doctor."

Sean was not to know the 'doctor' was also a farmer, although his medical practice was growing, so he thought it was time the district got a real doctor. He ignored Sean's courageous belief, because he knew well from experience while the sailor might be able to hobble about on crutches, nature would have to take its course, whether he liked it or not. He also knew getting the sailor to hospital, at least within the next few days, would be impossible, and once he had set the leg, the man would be better off in the care of the Chesters. He would not have to suggest that, rather allow the good woman beside him assume it, if she had not already. To emphasise his point, another squall lashed the valley, beat the iron roof directly above them.

The racket roused Alison, and after coming to her senses, first anxious because it was near dark, and she had not milked the cows, almost a wasted effort these days, then recalling her father was, and why. After lying on her bed, tears slipping from closed eyelids, miserable gasps rising within her, she decided to get up, as if she had been sent to her room for misbehaving at the table. Except *that* was when she was ten, not in her mid-twenties. She stealthily opened her door, half expecting her father having stationed a sentry outside, and still clutching her sodden handkerchief, crept along the landing. Hearing her mother's voice in the sailor's room, she hesitantly entered.

"Just in time, dear," her mother said. "Give a hand here, while I get dinner."

Silently Alison obeyed. The doctor wanted to ask her how she was. Alison wanted to ask the sailor how he was. And the sailor wanted to apologise from the bottom of his heart for the ruthless attack on her fair soul. Instead the doctor only issued curt instructions to Alison.

Downstairs Louise confronted her saturated husband, and accepting his condition, asked, "So, my dear, what happened to the crew? Have they gone off?"

"Humph! I've put them up in the barn for the night. I'll not have them set foot in this house."

"Oh, dear, surely they should come in for a meal."

"Where's *that* girl?"

"Now, dear, she is very sorry. I'm sure I don't yet know what happened. She has just woken up, and is helping the doctor."

"I saw his horse. She shouldn't get into further trouble while he's there."

To which Louise countered, "I think we had better hear Alison's side of it, dear, before we make any judgements." She had more important matters on her mind. Since the sailors were in the barn, and whether or not they were allowed indoors for a meal, someone would have to prepare their meal. It was no use suggesting Alison help out, not that she would refuse, rather her father would disallow her going anywhere near the men. The only thing for it: to fetch in the ship's cook, if there was such a person among them. Who she got was the equivalent of a kitchen hand.

Having tended the sailor, the doctor turned his attention to Alison. "Now are you sure you are all right, my dear?"

She silently nodded.

"You don't want me to give you anything to calm you."

"I am perfectly calm," she retorted, although in the softest of voices.

"Aye, let the doctor give you something," pleaded Sean. "I'm sure, Doctor, she has had a difficult day all round." And before Alison could object, he advised, "It was this good lass who fetched me from the sea. To be sure I'd have more than a busted leg if she had left me battered on the rocks."

The doctor turned and frowned at Alison. If she had been such a heroine, even in the probably exaggerated eyes of this Irishman, then why was she so distressed now?

The sailor's, "Be sure, wee lass, when I get m' hands on that brute I'll crush the life out of him, so I will," did not reassure her.

Then the doctor sort of realised what had happened.

"I'll just go and see if Mother has something for you," Alison murmured, left the room, peered over the landing rail to ensure there was not a bunch of sailors at the foot of the stairs ready to molest her, then descended, her step far less light than usual.

"I suppose he'll have to stay here," her mother suggested to her.

Alison shrugged. Whether he recuperated at Kowhai or not, did not matter to her: not at the moment.

"I've got help here, Alison. I'll get something ready soon for you to take up to him. And you'd better have a bed is made up for the good doctor. He cannot possibly go back tonight."

Only another storm in a teacup: not so bad when she thought about it. The result, and particularly her father's actions, and enforcements, made it far worse. So much so, while the crew crowded into the kitchen for a feed, and later the family with both the doctor and captain as guests ate in the dining room, Alison surreptitiously took a small plate of food to her room, despite its chill, covered herself in a quilt, and nibbled at what she would normally have relished.

Long before dawn the next morning she was up, and without breakfast, without even a hot drink, she crept from the house, and in the blackness of the dying storm she went first to the dairy, lit the lanterns, then fetched the few cows still in milk. Every so often she glanced at the yard gate in case a sailor was about to attack her. She shivered throughout task, sometimes wept, her numb hands agitated, the cows not nonchalant to this and pulling at their stalls. She turned them out into a nearby although soggy paddock, and with the awakening day crept back to the house, placed a billy of the previous night's milk on the table, gave her hands a cursory rinse over the kitchen sink and went to her room to change, rather than use the wash house. As she entered her bedroom, she heard her parents' door open.

Despite her anger towards her father, she poked her head back out her door, and said softly, "I've milked them." Before he could say anything, good or bad, she closed her door, discarded only her dress, and snuggled under the quilt, her breathing interspersed with sobs. She might have been a heroine: her father's treatment of her — at her age — reduced her to a miscreant child.

*　　*　　*　　*　　*　　*

The sea did not destroy the *Reliance,* and as soon as the weather permitted she was towed from the beach, bruised and battered, however with a bit of repair work able to continue plying the coast. As for her cargo: left where the storm had dumped it. Thomas, Ben, Danny and Alison fetched the boards, now strewn each side of the gap, loaded cart after cart with timber and bricks, and stored the lot at Kowhai. In the days long before economic feasibility was a catch cry, authorities decided it would be too much trouble to cart the jettisoned cargo from the valley, barge it from Pollok, transfer it to a coaster at Onehunga, and transport it to its original destination of Raglan. Besides, the good people of Raglan wanted their courthouse long before that could be accomplished. Thomas said to them, "I'm sure we can put it to good use." At the time even he did not envisage what use, or for whom, and if he did, he certainly kept the thought to himself, hoping *that* would not eventuate.

CHAPTER EIGHT

Alison did not know it then, nor would she have accepted, this was the beginning of a new chapter in her life, although the significance of Sean Sullivan's appearance took its time to further affect her: the first episode having deterred any informality on her part.

At one time or another during his convalescence Sean Sullivan encountered all the Chester clan. He and Danny got on just fine, there being a little Irish in Danny. The difference between the two seafarers lay in experience. Danny had messed about in boats, even gone to sea for a time. Sean on the other hand, was a sailor, tried and true. In Danny's mind that made Sean so much more superior, and he looked up to him as an elder brother, although in fact Danny was the older of the two. Needless to say Danny seemed to always be at Kowhai.

Then, when his time with Sean exceeded the hours he spent on his own farm, in his wife's opinion, she decided to intervene, personally, rather than harangue Danny at home. Her domination over the household returned with her strength. The days of a quiet appreciative wife had long gone, and love Jane as he still did, Danny was fearful every time he entered the back door. Only visitors, what few they had, entered through the front door.

Jane stormed across to Kowhai, flung open its *front* door, and unexpectedly encountered her mother.

"Why — hello — dear . . ." Her mother's greeting fading, as the daughter swept past, thrusting young Douglas into her arms.

She took the stairs two at a time, and burst in on the invalid and her husband. "Daniel Carsen! — *Home!*"

Her mother, still in the foyer, winced. She raised her eyes to the landing, and watched with shaking head the meek being driven from the bedroom, prodded down the stairs, and as the enraged shepherd drove by, Louise offered the infant, her daughter snatching Douglas as if were a bundle of clothes. Louise had cautiously warned Daniel. Even so, Jane could have been more tactful. Then, knowing her daughter so well, it was not Jane's character to show tact.

Louise climbed the stairs, knocked before entering Sean's room, and with an apologetic grimace, advised, "Sean, you and I had better do something about Daniel."

"I am sorry, my lady. Be sure to tell me to discourage him. I just hate to see him dragged home by the scruff of his neck, so I do."

Louise nodded. "Both of us will have to try, for Daniel's sake." She suggested, "I think, young man, we shall have to put you to work, so you will have little opportunity to talk to him."

"Aye, Mrs Chester, I think 'tis me you are reproaching, not your dark daughter. I do believe the man prefers my company than that of his own wife, so I do."

"That may well be so, Sean, although we both know it is his wife he has to please."

Louise had her thoughts. She waited until the following day, then set out to cross her daughter's path.

Unfortunately Jane was not in the most entertaining of moods. "Good afternoon, Mother," she acknowledged: hardly a loving greeting.

Louise nodded. "Your garden is looking nice."

"I tend it. That is why. I care for my crops."

"Yes, my dear. However do not be disappointed if some are not as prolific as you would wish," her mother advised, accepting that her mission was going to be even more difficult than she supposed.

Jane, fully aware of her mother's analogy, retorted, "There is little reason why they — why *he* — shouldn't . . ."

"If you say so, dear. All the same, I do think you sometimes expect a little too much of other people."

"Oh, do I?"

With that exchange of beliefs Jane offered her mother a cup of tea. While brewing they toyed with other topics, then at the table sat in counsel.

"Jane, my dear, I thought you had quelled your tongue."

"What do you mean, Mother? Be explicit!" Her telltale cheek colouring rose.

Louise nodded thoughtfully: a little hesitant in coming to the point. It was now or never, although she knew her timing was wrong. "Do you think any husband is going to stand by and be humiliated in front of his friends?"

"I suppose you mean that useless invalid you are harbouring?"

"I mean Sean Sullivan, a very pleasant young man, who is making a speedy recovery — and who — I am sure — means well." Then she drove in the wedge, and trusted the timber would not split. "Jane, had that been your brother, or your father, whom you decried — abused — I am quite sure either would have retaliated with such force, *you* would have been the one smitten."

"Mother, it was not Ben, or my father."

"No, it was not. — It was your husband. — The man *you* chose to marry."

"God knows why!"

A splayed hand lashed that vile mouth, its impact sending Jane reeling. Stunned, she lay on the floor, short breaths quaking her body, and gazed bewildered at the mother who had never before laid a violent hand on her. Louise thrust her chair back, gathered up Douglas, fearing her daughter might harm him in revenge, and strode from the house, slamming the back door — *tight!* Her actions wrenched her, and as she marched across the intervening paddocks she shook with wrath. For the remainder of the afternoon she busied herself in the kitchen, muttering under her breath, was short-tempered with Alison, and her own husband, although did not disclose why.

It took a courage, a great deal of courage, for Danny to cross to Kowhai, because he believed he had been locked out of his own home, and he was hungry after an honest day's work. Like a wayward child he came in through the back door. Alison was his first encounter. He stared silently at her, ashamed over begging her kindness.

"Sit down, Danny. You look all in."

"Is your father about?"

By the look on his face Alison judged that Danny hoped her father was *not* about. "He is in the lounge. He won't disturb us," she assured him. "What would you like? — I suppose you haven't eaten?"

"Anything, Alison; just the leftovers will do."

That was when Alison knew something really was amiss, not a simple row with his wife. "Danny, I'm sure we can do better."

Louise Chester entered. "You are here again, are you?"

"I've — I've just come to see if . . ."

"Your son has been fed, and I'm about to put him to bed. So, if you have not eaten, Alison get . . ."

"I was just going to, Mother." She splayed her hands, and pleaded, "Would someone please tell me what is going on?"

"This is between Daniel and I." Louise had not kept her voice lowered. Her husband heard the word 'Daniel' and decided to investigate, while Alison scooped a good helping from a pot of stew simmering on the range, discovered some leftover potatoes to go with it, and placed the meal before Danny, and wisely made herself scarce.

Thomas nodded, glared at his son-in-law, and although he knew his wife would contradict him, advised, "I am master of this house, and I suggest you act as master of your house." He also knew that was easier said than done as he left the kitchen again.

Danny placed the full fork on the plate, rose from the table to leave, his shoulders stooped with distress, eyes glassy. Louise stopped him by placing her motherly hand on his shoulder. "Daniel, have something to eat, and — then we shall find you somewhere to put your head down." She sat him back at the table, pulled out a chair for herself and sat silently opposite him, while he wolfed the food down.

Long after her mother had stormed from the house Jane remained on the kitchen floor. Most of her tears were from the shock of her mother's hand, only few from remorse. Slowly remorse overtook hurt, and she rose, first to her hands and knees, with head down, then, although feeling so low as wanting to crawl all the way to her bedroom, she did stand, shoulders stooped, walked wearily into the lounge, sagged into an armchair, head lolled to one side, listening for Danny's return, only hearing distant dogs. Eventually, still crying, she went to their bedroom, took off only her dress, and collapsed on to their bed, sobs slowing subsiding, until restless sleep overtook her. The night was long, and disturbed.

As the sun climbed into the sky, brushed aside morning mist, she listlessly pottered about in the kitchen, had porridge ready for Daniel should he enter, sniffed back more tears when she saw him on foot and without the dogs moving sheep from one paddock to the next. He was not going to come to her, so, wiping her hands, taking off her apron, deciding to make amends, she tugged open the *jammed* back door, walked across those paddocks, and for the first time since knowing him, buried her face in his chest, clutched his arms, and begged forgiveness. Bewildered, Danny could only see plain sailing ahead, and when this opportunity was suddenly upon him to be master of his wife and home, he was too slow to react, and it drifted by.

*　　*　　*　　*　　*　　*

There had been a succession of storms at the Todd mansion. Here, the master's high spirits had been dampened by recurring squalls of rheumatism. He found the ailment rendered him incapable of gadding about, and perhaps this made him realise how important Emily was, in fact, more than just a pretty face.

Emily was as attracted to men as they were to her, so mixed earthly pleasures with taking a responsible interest in the home: such as seeing Jonathan did his homework and passed his exams. So much so Jonathon, after several years, finally accepted her as a mother figure, and a far more intelligent mother than he first believed. Whatever school subject he studied, he found Emily sufficiently versed to assist. Emily, for her own education, was gaining knowledge of her husband's business affairs.

During these blighted spells William Todd was grateful for one thing; Emily rarely left his side, so to speak: possibly because such times were paralleled with inclement weather. Consequently gadding about on Auckland's roads was no fun, unless one delighted in wading through mud. 'Mr Macadam' had stepped ashore, although his tarry spread had not travelled widely. When the sun did shine, and Will lingered, Emily sometimes slipped from his grasp, to seek a change of scenery elsewhere. Her latest admirer happened to be an artist of no mean reputation, as far as art went anyway. So she had an excuse to visit him.

What dawned as a sunny day concealed in its course nasty squalls. Swinging her parasol gaily, Emily tripped from the house, wearing a gorgeous three piece outfit: a high-necked frilly ivory blouse, over which she had a midi royal blue jacket with a sailor collar. Her unadorned fishtailed skirt, also royal blue, cleared the ground. Around her waist she wore an uncomfortably tight silver plated belt, from which a silver purse hung. Knowing how good she looked, she strode proudly up the road, nodded to neighbours, including an elderly gentleman whom she believed wished he were a lot younger. And indeed even at his age he was handsome, and Emily supposed what he would like to do with her, and what he *could* do were two different things. She spied a cab, and was duly transported across the city to Herne Bay: the horse taking College Hill in its stride. Here she alighted, dusted herself down, and only when satisfied that she looked spic and span, did she pay the grumbling driver, holding out her gloved hand for the threepence change.

Emily turned, and encountered the impudent stare of three vagabonds, none exceeding five years of age, and one almost a girl; at least her unruly mop was slightly longer, and she wore a shabby dress and an equally shabby pinafore to protect it.

"Won't let you pass!" The challenge came from the grubbiest of the trio.

Emily raised her parasol, aimed at the urchin's stomach, and prodded him aside. She strutted by, intent on her business. Undaunted, the gang leader scooped muck from the gutter and fired a mud pie at her, the pack plastering her cheek, and dribbling on to her bodice.

A little stunned, Emily paused, whipped around, clipped the urchin's ear and warned, "You young demon! I have a good mind to call a policeman."

"He won't do nothin'!"

"Won't he just." When Emily looked about she observed an almost deserted street, with no chance of their being witnesses, so meted out her own punishment. She grabbed the boy, lifted him clean off his feet, and contemptuously thrust him against a picket fence, the boy's mud-covered hands grasping her lace-frilled wrists as he slid to the ground. She gazed unbelievingly at her soiled clothes, then demanded, "What is your name?"

He whimpered, "Shan't tell!"

"His name's Alec Mason," pimped the girl.

"So you are Alec Mason. I have heard a lot of nasty things about you, young brat." In truth Emily had never heard of him before, and had no desire to see his grubby face again. However, the remark served as a warning, and with his partners in crime he scampered off.

His oily black hair, olive complexion of undefined origin, raw feet, filth, runny nose, all lingered in Emily's mind, forming a rather nauseating picture: a vivid impression of the less fortunate members of society. 'Alec Mason,' she soliloquised. Nothing more than a trifling incident, annoying at the time, yet for some inexplicable reason Emily cemented it and the urchin's name in her mind.

Wiping the worst of the muck from her, she proceeded to her destination, and although not wishing to be fussed over encountered her artist-lover's dramatic performance. It took more to settle him, than herself, and the sitting was not particularly pleasant. Besides, the low fire in the grate did nothing to warm her. Maybe, they should forget about her portrait that day. Nor was she in the mood for his fondling, and after brushing his hand away, she partially redressed, sagged into an armchair, and berated him. "If you had not made such a fuss, I would have been fine. Now you have me . . . Oh, never mind." She expelled her breath in exasperation. "I had better go."

"My darling — my little cherub — I beg you to stay." He knelt at her feet and placed his hands prayer like before her.

"I cannot be bothered," she rejected in her precise manner, and thought, 'Surely I can do better than this wimp.'

"Please! — Please, my dearest darling. Don't leave me in such a distressed state."

"It is me — you fool — who should be in a distressed state." She very nearly lifted her foot to push him over.

With him still grovelling she rose and replaced the remainder of her clothes. In a moment of anger she moved to lift the easel and painting and fling it at him. On glancing at the portrait from the front raised her eyebrows and sighed. "It is nearly finished so you do not need me to come back."

"Just one more sitting," he beseeched. The thought that he would never see her again, let alone make love to her, appalled him.

"Oh, I don't know. Just get out of my way!" With that she stormed from the house . . .

. . . She stormed from the house at the precise moment a heavenly storm broke: the deluge thrashing her parasol, designed for the sun more than the rain, splattering her shoes, stockings, indeed muddied her almost to the knees. She took shelter beneath a shop veranda, having to thrust herself against the window, while passing horses and carts, and a blasted automobile sprayed the footpath with mud. She was so dirty when a motorist got stuck she considered helping him push the fangulation out of the mire, but went no further than her thoughts.

How would she explain her condition to Will when she arrived home? She hoped he was in the lounge, and she could creep up to her room, or get the maid to go, while she went straight to the bathroom, and fling herself into hot water: the sort to bathe in.

Her course of action was successful. She felt guilty on this occasion, when in fact nothing had happened, other than having a lovers' tiff. Her guilt, because the intent was there. At least, it had been there, until his pathetic performance. 'Why — oh — why do I need such miserable creatures? Surely I do not feel sorry for them?'

She had a fleeting thought of her brother-in-law. 'There has to be a Ben out there for me,' she wished. She had her bath, and smelling all clean and sweet ventured into the study.

"Ah, there you are, my dear. I was just saying to — um — thingamabob . . ."

"Grace."

"Grace. I knew it had religious connotations."

"So, what were you saying to Grace?"

"Um — ah, I can't for the life of me remember, my love." And he uttered an almost imbecilic laugh.

Emily wondered honestly if he was going senile. If so it would be at a relatively young age. Perhaps he had not told her the truth about his age. Surely he wasn't even older than she knew? She abruptly changed the subject. "Now, you did check through those accounts Mr Wilson gave you?"

"Ah — yes."

"You sound if something is wrong?" she quizzed him.

"I'd prefer you, my dear, to have a look yourself."

And, conveniently more important matters — as far as each was concerned — arose, and Emily perused the accounts. On this occasion everything seemed to be in order. That he had trusted her with such responsibility was endearing, and maybe, just maybe, she should forget about her portrait. She did not particularly like the fellow anyway. On the other hand she rather liked the portrait, although wondered where she would hang it?

A few days later she made her amends to her artist-lover, reclined on a *chaise longue,* chatted cheerily to him while he added a few more strokes to both the portrait, then her, until his passion overtook his artistry and he made love to her on the elegant item of furniture. Needless to say it took a longer than necessary to complete the painting. When it was done Emily possessed a portrait destined to be admired by herself and her own admirers, and relations, for many years.

*　　*　　*　　*　　*　　*

Thomas Chester had grown so accustomed to Alison falling in and out of love he did not see any future in her infatuation for Sean Sullivan. Indeed for religious reasons alone he trusted Alison would not encourage him.

Sean was no roustabout. As soon as he was able, he endeavoured to return the kindness the family had lavished upon him. Before his leg was out of plaster he managed to hobble about, attend to numerous jobs. The gig he stripped down, obtained new parts, which regretfully he could not pay for, and restored the vehicle to new.

To Thomas Chester he advised, "It'll do until you buy an automobile, so it will."

"Lad, the day I buy one of those — if for a moment I could ever afford one — will surely go down in history, so it will." He shook his head. He was beginning to sound like the Irish rover.

"Ah, Mr Chester, the rate they are sealing roads, surely your road will be as smooth as . . ."

Thomas roared. "Even you will be an old man by the time they reach here." And they both laughed, because it was true.

Anyway, to Louise Chester, he offered, when she inspected the shining gig, "There you are, my sweet lady, fit for a queen — which surely you are."

"Oh, get away with you, Sean. You *have* made a lovely job of it. I'm sure it is too clean for our roads. I will be so proud when I trot into Waiuku." She could imagine the scene, for surely it was the finest looking vehicle on the peninsula.

To Alison, Thomas admitted, "He certainly is a character. He has your mother round his little finger."

"Father, this is what I've been telling you; he is the most wonderful character in the world."

"I'm sure he is — if you say so, dear," her father agreed, although only in jest.

Alison thought, 'I've had dropped a hint.' Next would come the bombshell.

Unlike previously, Alison did not fall in love with the shipwrecked sailor on sight. On that fateful day with its sequel — her rough treatment from one of the sailors — romance was far from her thoughts. During the following weeks her ministration was, if not professional, certainly nurse-like, and she had no desire at all to be swept off her feet by him, figuratively in his case. Her tenderness gradually grew to fondness. She compared Sean with Danny: there was no comparison: only they had both been to sea. Danny was just a nice big boy. Sean was a charmer, and Alison eventually fell for his charms. As she succumbed she knew if Jane had caused a tremor over Danny, then she would cause an earthquake over Sean.

In the meantime life returned to normal at Kowhai.

The family generally caught up with the news when they met neighbours or when passing travellers informed them, or when they ventured into Waiuku, and obtained local papers. Occasionally a *Herald* came their way, and they digested news from the world, having to peruse each column, each page, since even the greatest events were not blazoned across the front page

As 1907 drew to a close the family did learn parliament had lost its great wooden house: the largest timber structure in the world: both buildings destroyed in what was described as *a volcanic eruption of flame and smoke*. At the fire's height a finger of flame stabbed a button, fused wires, and from the inferno the division bell clanged its last call, until like everything else it succumbed to the fire.

"It's been a good year," Thomas Chester announced as the family gathered for Christmas. He was still undecided what to do with his windfall of bricks and timber, and his assertion was based on farm profits had matched the nation's upward trend.

They re-gathered a week later for New Year, and apart from the immediate family, Nigel and Jessica condescended to join them. Alas, Jessica was expecting — again, although her two children received the most attention. This occurred later in their stay.

As New Year's celebrations went, Kowhai's was nothing out of the ordinary: most guests staying overnight. Unfortunately the rivalry between George and his cousin Stanley got a bit, perhaps, over-competitive.

"My dad says your dad's dumb," Stanley challenged.

George worshipped his father, and no one, but no one, was going to get away with calling him dumb. He leapt at Stanley, flung him to the ground near the stream and rubbed his nose in — actually, it might have been a cowpat. Then it was full on, fists, feet, teeth: anything to inflict mortal wounds on the other. Their cousins — all under six — goaded them on, until locked in combat they both tumbled into the stream: flowing abnormally high after rain two days before.

Penelope was first to vacate her ringside seat, the bridge railing to be exact, leaping from it and bounding into the house, tugging her mother's skirt. "Mummy! — Mummy! Stanley's fallen into the stream. He's *drownded!*" Jessica heaved herself from the couch, waddled from the room, all but fell down the front steps, barely hearing Penelope's, "George felled in too." This prompted Priscilla into action.

"Nigel!" Jessica screamed. "Nigel!"

Nigel, and indeed all the men, was preoccupied in the back yard.

Jessica dropped to her knees, and clawed at a mass of hair, Alison at her side, lifting one boy clinging to a vine from the torrent. "I'll get him," gurgled George, spluttering out excess water, while his rival was carried downstream.

"Nigel!"

Hobbling along with amazing ability, Sean was first man to respond, seeing the boy's body tossed in muddy waters, then plunge over the waterfall. Now shoeless, Sean leapt into the pool below the fall, gathered up the sodden bundle, and was swept toward the opposite shore. Alison was also in the stream — a familiar venue for her — able to help Sean heave the boy on to the bank. Slapping the child's back, freeing a jammed tongue, Sean laid Stanley face down, and applied pressure to his back.

Jessica, as everyone else, ran across the bridge, all but demolishing it in their stampede. Fate adhered her feet to another muddy patch and she fell flat on her face, while the mob jostled past, only Louise pausing to stoop over her.

Ben also waded across the stream, and held the horde back, allowing Sean and Alison to get on with reviving Stanley. Actually

Stanley did not need much reviving, already sitting, doubled over coughing out water, eyes brimming with tears, at the same time looking about for George to finish him off — good and proper.

Nigel belatedly answered his wife's call, lifted her out of the mud: the woman feeling her belly, although detested what was inside her anyway, and led her back to the house. Louise considered getting the doctor. That would take hours. By now George was sitting on the front steps, surrounded by his cousins, bragging over his win. Only Jessica was causing concern: the family fearing the upset might bring on her baby.

Priscilla cuffed her son, abruptly ending his big talk, dragged him to the bathroom, and stripped him. "You've got nothing else to wear, so you can go naked."

"I'll be a Maori."

"With your skin, they'll laugh at you."

Although local Maori had largely and needlessly been driven from the peninsula many years earlier, the children of those remaining thought nothing of swimming naked. Any indecency about it was purely in the minds of Europeans. Unknown to his parents, George had swum naked with them. Alison had often swum in the waterfall pool wearing only her undergarments, and similarly dressed down with Annabelle at their 'private bay,' being more naked than any decent lady should get.

No such adventure on this afternoon. George was wrapped in a towel and put to bed, while his mother hurried up drying the clothes he had messed up the day before. Stanley, the other contestant, decidedly worse for wear, was also stripped, bathed, rubbed vigorously down until he cried, and also put to bed. Penelope, his sister who raised the alarm, crept into the bedroom, gave him a lolly, and assured him his tea would not go to waste, because she would eat it, as well as her own of course.

Jessica recovered sufficiently to dismiss the idea of fetching the doctor.

Next day the two boys approached each other from opposite ends of the kitchen, and were made to shake hands by Louise who sat them at the large wooden table, and advised, "If you two must fight, then do it in the open — on the front lawn — not beside the stream."

She looked sternly at each of them, and received two silent nods.

From a jar she fetched a couple of sweets for each.

The sequel was: Sean emerged the hero. So did Jessica: for not flinging George back into the stream on discovering she had saved him almost at the expense of her own son. Alison's part in the rescue was overlooked — as usual.

Two months later Thomas Chester was relating the episode to a friend — not that he had seen much himself first hand — when he complimented, "That fellow Sullivan showed great essence, the way he saved Caldwell's boy."

Alison, across the room, overheard the remark, and said softly, to no one in particular. "He did. He was so brave. That is why I am going to marry him."

"Yes, he certainly is worth his keep," Thomas continued in his praise. "Of course, at the time he was still recu – pe – ra . . . What, did you say, my dear?"

"Nothing, Father. It can wait."

Thomas shook his head. "No, no, my girl. Why, Mr Hudson is a good friend of the family. I'm sure . . ."

Alison hoped by making the announcement while an outsider was present she might avoid the expected opposition. She had not told Sean her plans — having none until that moment. "Please excuse the — ah — inopportune moment, Mr Hudson, however you must agree such a brave — and handy — man would make an excellent husband?"

Thomas Chester did not give the guest the chance to reply, and taking the announcement as being nothing more than Alison asking for money for a new dress, he suggested, "Dear, perhaps we should discuss this later, ah — as you said."

Later, was sooner than expected: Thomas excusing himself as Alison slunk out the door and accosted her. "The *devil* you are!"

"Would you have me break my promise then?"

His eyes opened wide. "Mother, come here this instant!" he shouted towards the kitchen, the usual place for Louise to be. To his daughter, he demanded, "I trust you have informed your mother?"

Alison's defiant gaze lowered, and she shook her head.

"Yes, dear," came his wife's calm reply, from the top of the stairs.

"I thought not. You had *not* the courage even to tell your mother." He grasped his daughter's arm. "Because you know damn well how upsetting it would be to her . . ."

By now Louise had correctly assumed what her husband's latest ferocity was about. "Tell me what, dear?" she requested, looking at each in turn as she walked down the stairs. "Has our daughter decided that Sean Sullivan is her man?"

Her husband did not catch her placid acceptance. "She has, Mother." Angry also, because Sean had not gone through the formality of first asking him.

Softly, timidly, Alison said, "Sean and I have talked about getting married . . ."

"He has not asked you?" Thomas determined, giving him a way out.

"Sort of. We just — I love him . . ."

"You've loved every rat-bag who's stepped through that door."

"Thomas!" Louise berated. "That is neither a nice thing to say, nor true. And it could hardly be said of Sean Sullivan."

"He's a blo . . ."

"Don't you dare, dare say *that,* Thomas Chester!" his wife warned. "I'll not have such talk in my house, and you know it." She raised her hand first at him, then directed him back to the lounge. "You'd best go back to Mr Hudson."

Mr Hudson sat squirming in the chair, having heard every word of the argument, and had deliberately picked up a *Weekly News* rustling the pages, although unable to concentrate on its pictorial presentation.

Thomas Chester could not concentrate on what Hudson was saying — something to do with electric power supply to the area, although Thomas dismissed the idea as so far off any discussions were way ahead of time. Even the telephone was still several years away. For the moment he had more important things on his mind. He made his excuses to Hudson and pardoned himself.

Entering the kitchen, observing mother and daughter in discussion, he demanded, "So, what stage have we got to?"

Alison turned sharply, eyes red, mouth quivering. "Just what I was telling you, Mother, it's like war in this house." They were not quite the words she wanted to say. She had no time to change them.

"Perhaps she is right, dear. Perhaps we are only thinking of ourselves — trying to arrange her marriage for her."

"I just wish she would fall for someone who's right for her."

Alison brushed past her father, stumbled up the stairs, slammed her bedroom door, and instead of flinging herself on her bed, gazed solemnly out the window. She looked at the bush-clad valley to the south of Kowhai's drive, knowing it was reserved for her and — but would her father allow it. He had no qualms about giving her sister and Danny the other side of the large, forked valley, so why ——just because . . . Her thoughts trailed off, she flicked her sodden handkerchief to the floor, crossed to her dresser, grabbed another, and sat forlornly on her bed.

Weeks later Alison and Sean formally announced their engagement: Priscilla goading Alison into having a party, while Alison was making one of her now less regular visits to Kanuka, Ben's place.

"You've got to," Priscilla insisted.

"No one will come."

"Don't be silly. *I*, certainly will come."

"I bet Ben . . . What does he say?"

Priscilla shook her head. "You know Ben, Ali: he's only got time for the farm. I am sure he is quite used to the idea." She placed her hand on the side of her face, contemplating the outcome of her sister-in-law's choice of husband.

Alison was right. Only half — less than half — of the invited guests turned up, and that for Kowhai was not normal, when usually on such occasions more turned up than invited, but not unwelcome.

"Annabelle, thank you for coming," Alison greeted tearfully, as the Maori girl she had befriended at the picnic, and had shared adventures with since, arrived on horseback, wearing the most delightful of dresses. "You look positively gorgeous. You'll be belle of the ball," she promised. Alison did not mind one bit if Annabelle stole the show, although her reasons were a little ulterior. She had already experienced Annabelle stealing the show: the occasion of the Citizens Ball.

"Mother," Alison announced, with her arm linked in her friend's. "Annabelle's come."

"What did you expect? Of course she would come." Louise reached forward to kiss the girl.

Did the girl's father, believing his daughter would be the odd one out, ensure no one could possibly say anything derogatory about her? He was wrong for that reason, because Ben had a couple of Maori mates, and they turned up, although hardly outshone the few other men present.

In the event, Annabelle got talking to Ben: the two side-by-side on the couch, deeply engrossed in conversation, Ben's beers going flat, and neither paying much attention to anything else.

Jane had dreaded coming to the party. Now she was here, she decided she might as well make the most of it, and then the most of Sean's company. Unexpectedly during the evening when she entered through a french door, Sean was sitting on the arm of the armchair, while Alison in the chair was talking to someone else. Jane leaned on the doorpost, and said encouragingly to Sean, "So, something good has come out of you being shipwrecked."

"Do you think so?" He raised his eyebrows at her acceptance of him. "I'll try my best to make her a good husband, so I will."

Jane took a breath, trembled slightly, and agreed, "I'm sure you will." She offered him both a half-smile and, "Can I get you another drink?" She plucked the empty glass from his hand.

Priscilla began to wonder, dread the thought, her husband was so infatuated with Annabelle he was about to run off with her. She had never been jealous of anyone, although now a fear of losing Ben pained her. Her son James arrested her attention, and made her realise she was a mother of three while Annabelle was single woman, surely much more attractive to Ben.

Jane meantime was trembling with desire when she returned to Sean. She had never felt this way with Danny — with anyone.

Sean observed her agitation and innocently put it down to the temperature, although it was not cold. Then much to Jane's displeasure, Alison sidled up to Sean and kissed his cheek. Jane choked back her jealousy and went outside, perhaps to cool off.

Priscilla did catch a snip of Ben's answer to some discussion with Annabelle. ". . . Never thought of it like that."

"Your people are new to this land, Ben, and people like my dad do know a lot."

"I agree. Yet you must admit . . ."

Someone moved between Priscilla and her husband and she lost the conversation, although the gist of it gave her no cause to worry about the direction their talk was heading.

Annabelle placed her hand on Ben's arm, and the touch thrilled him. He honestly had not considered what other people must have thought, or realised how long he and Annabelle had been talking. "Where are the children?" he asked his wife, who had joined the group.

Looking at Annabelle, obviously a little jealous, she answered, "*Our* children, my dear, were put to bed hours ago."

Annabelle became all-apologetic, hoping she had not caused a rift between Ben and his wife, because she had not given the insinuation a thought either. Admittedly she had not become tired of Ben, or wishing him to talk someone else.

Ben did not dismiss his conversation with Annabelle. Not so much the subjects, rather the girl herself lingered in his memory. He could not help compare her with Priscilla, and he tried to recall what conversations they had had before their marriage. None were as serious as that with Annabelle, and since his marriage the farm and family dominated any conversations with his wife. He also recalled the hours spent with Alison. Then being so much younger their talk was usually teacher — pupil instruction. It did put him in a quandary, because despite the time he had spent with Annabelle they had left several topics incomplete, and Ben wondered if he would ever get the opportunity to finish them.

After only a few hours sleep Alison and Annabelle crept back down stairs, and although summer, only a hint of dawn outlined the rim of the eastern hills, so the girls had the cows milked before the sun cast its rays into the valley. It was while milking them Alison the idea of Annabelle as her bridesmaid was born. However, since she herself had been bridesmaid to both Jane and Priscilla, they might be put out not being asked? Or would they?

Also playing on her mind; her father had not mentioned the other valley, and even as the two girls urged the cows into a paddock bordering the undeveloped land, she thought the sooner he offered it to them the sooner they could begin clearing it.

"Oh, well, that's done. Thank you so much, Annabelle. We can go back to bed now."

Annabelle looked astounded. "Of course not! It's such a lovely morning, why waste it in bed?" Then her face saddened. "But, I suppose I had better go home."

"Don't make it sound so . . ." Alison did know what her home was like. She also knew it as a loving home, probably more so than her own. Whereas, she herself could escape to her own room, or to a quiet part of the farm, she doubted if Annabelle could do the same. Perhaps why when they met at the creamery or wharf, it was always she (Alison) who, admittedly reluctantly, said, 'I'd better be going.'

Conveniently, Sean, the family and overnight guests slept in. It gave the two girls an opportunity to further talk: not light-hearted girlie talk, rather more in line with the serious conversation Annabelle had with Ben the previous night. They snuck down to the waterfall while there was no one else about, and Annabelle again dived gracefully through it.

"Your turn now," she prompted Alison.

"Do I have to? I made an awful splash last time." She made an equally inelegant splash this time. Remarkably, by her third attempt she did manage to keep her legs out behind her, and with less water disturbance was encouraged to practise.

Alison looked upon Annabelle as a girl just like herself. Different upbringing, different culture, yet the same feelings, and certainly the same education, although having to achieve it in a less congenial environment: meaning Annabelle had no library to use. That is where the two girls spent the morning at Kowhai, even Sean getting the brush-off when he eventually poked his nose in.

"Aye, I see you two are hard at it," he commented, and withdrew.

Alison leapt to her feet, following him into the foyer, closing the door behind her. "Sean," she tended softly, and sidled up to him, a little hesitant in her announcement. "I thought I'd like to have Annabelle for my bridesmaid."

His eyes opened wide. "To be sure, and I'll marry the both of you, so I will."

She reached up and kissed his hoary cheek, uttered, "No you won't," and returned to the library. So, while they perused books, discussed society generally, Alison was left with the problem whether to ask Annabelle then, or first speak to Jane and Prissy. The trouble was, when Annabelle did leave it might be weeks before they met again. So, she thought, she would make sure it was not weeks. Then, if she delayed asking her now, she would feel guilty, knowing she had only asked, after conferring with the other two. No, she decided, 'I want her as my bridesmaid. It's *my* wedding.'

Tentatively she said, "Annabelle, we have not actually set a wedding date — it will be this year — however — ah — we'd like to have you as — my bridesmaid."

The girl swallowed, her eyes glistened. "Are you sure?"

"Very sure, Annabelle. When I suggested it to Sean — just now actually," she admitted, "he said he'd want to marry the both of us."

The thought made Annabelle wish she could have Sean for herself. Not really, although a man like him. It seemed there was no one of her own race she felt that way over. Perhaps she was being fussy. "Father's always pointing out men for me to marry," she confessed, then shrugged. "I want to make my own choice."

Annabelle was facing a problem many, many women were to face in the future. Her education was such, while she was happy to be a wife and mother, she did not want to be a doormat. She had to find a man, not only to love and be loved, but who would respect her for what she was.

Later that morning, when Sean was allowed to intrude — as Alison put it — the subject arose. It arose in jest when Alison said, "We've got to find a suitable man for Annabelle; someone with a bit of sense."

"To be sure, have not we all got sense?"

"No!" Alison argued. "Put it this way, you don't always use it."

Annabelle stared across the valley, where fingers of low cloud caressed the hills. Had not Alison been present she might have laid her hand on Sean's, extending the moment, because while Sean's action was purely brotherly, her inward response was one of yearning. Not really for Sean, because she had no intention of attempting to lure him away from Alison, but for someone like Sean. Why were they so few? In all her life she only knew two or three comparable: one being Ben, now well and truly married. She recalled, fully ten years ago, she had a crush on him, although he obviously had not committed her to memory, having not recognised her on the more recent day of the picnic, when Alison was unceremoniously tipped for the canoe, and had crept home without telling anyone.

Alison was actually jealous: jealous because obviously Sean liked Annabelle — who could not? — and he might just find her a better prospect than herself, unless *her* father also objected. Then he could have two reasons . . . Alison decided she was worrying unnecessarily. Besides, they had overcome most of the objections to her marrying Sean.

Other than Alison, Annabelle was not Sean's only admirer.

Whenever Jane was in Sean's company she now felt uneasy: a feeling she had not previously experienced until Alison's party. Prior to Danny her relationships with men were distant or reserved. Even now with her husband she was reserved, accepting she was duty bound to satisfy his needs. Fortunately those needs were not as frequent as she expected: not that she knew what to expect, having never actually discussed the subject with him.

Now regularly in Sean's company, and deliberately so, she did feel a latent stirring, not so naive to know it as a sexual attraction: admittedly a one-sided attraction. God forbid she ever let on how she felt about him. She made excuses to cross to Kowhai, although as often as not Sean was nowhere to be seen.

On one such occasion her mother questioned her presence. "My dear, it is not like you to run out of sugar?"

"I did not order enough," Jane lied.

Louise smiled. She also frowned, although unaware that her daughter had an ulterior motive for her more frequent visits. Perhaps she was genuinely seeking company, yet was too proud to admit it. After all, there were only the two of them and Douglas in Jane's homestead, the rest of the family being 'miles' away.

The visit was timed for afternoon tea. Jane in her eagerness arrived too early so would have to linger before the chances of Sean being present, although as likely Alison would be with him. "I suppose I had better get back," she reluctantly said, with a sigh and a furtive glance across the back yard, sighting only the cat slouched against a tree root, and a few hens pecking for scraps. Instead of going out the front door, she hoisted Douglas on to her hip, and went out the back door, passed the cottage and then headed to her own home, not seeing sight or sound of Sean, meeting only her husband at the boundary fence, expressing her disappointment with a snide remark.

CHAPTER NINE

February turned to March: March to April, and autumn edged aside summer, and with the rains came the mud, especially in the horse paddocks and fowl run. Excess stock sold off. Fruit and vegetables harvested, stewed and bottled before trees lost their leaves. A sense of waiting shrouded Kowhai: not so much in anticipation of a spring wedding, rather uncertainty.

Still nothing was said of Alison's inheritance, and the longer she was kept in abeyance the more morose she became: even Sean feeling the effect of her mood.

One incident began when Alison uttered contemptuously, "I hear Jessica is kicking up again."

"Alison, that is not a nice thing to say," her mother reprimanded, putting down her knitting, reaching towards the fire: an early cold snap encouraging the family to light it fully a month before they usually did. "I must say, dear, you are becoming very distasteful in your attitude. It's not like you at all."

"Am I, Mother? It would not be anything to do with me becoming a pariah, would it?" She began to rise from the chair, preferring the natural coldness of her room to the unnatural chill of the lounge.

Her father laid down the *Weekly News*, and warned, "I wonder Sean still wants to marry you . . ?"

"Well, he does. Have no joy in your thought."

"On a night like this, I would have thought he . . ."

"On a night like this, as you say, Father, he is helping Danny. Is there anything so wrong with that?" Just as she said it, a squall attacked the house: the wind howling along the veranda, a door slamming. "This will be him now." She knew it was not, although it was an excuse to leave the room.

Sean had stayed on at Kowhai after his mishap. As Alison had said earlier in the year, what was the point in him looking for other accommodation, or another job, for that matter, when they were to be married in a few months? She had hoped his job would be establishing the other valley as a farm. Now he did everything except, and on this foul night was assisting Danny to fix some machinery.

"So, they're set on it are they, Mother?" her father said to his wife.

Louise sighed, shaking her head. "Thomas, come rain, hail or shine, they are going to marry in September."

He had his thoughts: they may *have* to bring the date forward, since the couple all but slept together. One way of assuring their marriage: out of duty.

Louise considered more tastefully, "At least they shall know each other by then: more than some couples."

Thomas did not voice his thoughts knowing his wife would not entertain the idea for one moment. They certainly spent a lot of time alone, and he had seen them with his own eyes kissing fervently when they thought they were alone. He could not blame them for being passionate: Sean made a dashing figure, and Alison was naturally loving, although little of that loving was coming his way lately, all because he did not want her to make a mistake, allowing her heart to rule her head.

Since the church was the cause of division, Louise reminded him he could hardly condemn either of them, when he failed to practice his own religion. She got him to go to church once, maybe twice, a year. He in turn, called churchgoers hypocrites if they failed to practice what they preached: performed righteously on Sundays and spent the remainder of the week being as uncharitable and dishonest as they could: usually within the law, although hardly moral.

During that April Alison's problems took a back seat. A lady — exactly as Thomas condemned — who moaned and groaned her way through life, was so inhospitable her daughters preferred his own wife's company, learned she had something to moan about. Maude Caldwell was stricken with an advanced incurable illness, and her days were numbered.

"Oh, God," decried Alison, "I suppose we have to put up with her whinging until she dies."

And again her mother admonished her: first with a scowl, then reminding her of her recent behaviour.

Alison, who made the offer to her sister-in-law. "Prissy, if you want to stay with her, I'll look after Ben, and the children." Only after making the offer, did she realise it would get her out of the house, away from her father.

"Would you really, Ali?" She held her tight. "You're a Godsend. They've cabled Em. — She's in Australia," and added, "Sean is going to be so lucky."

Sean did not know how lucky he was. He did the morning milk, although in the afternoons Jane came across, and either milked them herself, or helped Sean.

"Just like old times," she said, after a few milkings. "I thought I might have forgotten how to do it."

"Something's you never forget, so you don't," Sean replied.

There was one difference for Jane: Sean's ability as compared with Danny's clumsiness. Jane *wanted* to cross the paddocks, drop Douglas in with her mother, and go off with Sean to fetch the cows and milk them.

If Sean observed her attitude toward him was more hospitable than for anyone else, he did not comment on it. He *did* observe it. They were sitting back-to-back on their stools milking cows, when Danny rose and deliberately placed his hand on Jane's shoulder for support. In an instant she had released a teat and placed her hand on top of his, then looked up at him appealingly. He grimaced playfully at her.

"Sorry, Sean I — I just think . . . It doesn't matter."

"It does matter. 'Tis good to get some things off your chest."

She shook her head. "This is something I have to live with."

Should he tell her, if she displayed the same attitude toward Danny as she did toward him maybe she could live with it? No, that did sound right in these circumstances. He knew Jane and Danny were a mismatch. He also knew, had things been different, he and Jane would have been a worse mismatch.

In her dying days Maude ran everyone ragged, particularly Priscilla. Jessica, in an advanced state of pregnancy, could not possibly attend her mother-in-law's needs. Nigel, her son, was too busy lining himself up for promotion, and that required him to work extraordinary hours.

At Kowhai, Louise learned of the situation, and since Priscilla was virtually on her own, she set out to relieve the younger woman of her burden. "Danny, run me to town," she commanded, on the spur of the moment.

And Danny was only too willing to oblige.

"Mother," Jane advised, "can't you wait until morning? Surely another day won't hurt Prissy."

"I don't know, dear. I would hate anything to happen to her, all because of that . . ."

"It's atrocious. Look at it. The roads will be treacherous." A sou-westerly squall swept through the gap, hurtled over the hills, and thrashed the valley, flooded the drive, and Jane could realistically imagine what condition the roads would be in.

"This will pass in a few minutes." Louise would not be dissuaded. Instinct insisted she travel to Waiuku that night: rain or no rain.

"Don't you attempt to come home tonight, Daniel Carsen," his wife warned. "Douglas and I can stay just as well here."

As soon as the rain eased, although another sinister cloudbank was gathering offshore, Louise had Danny drive her to Waiuku. Had he changed his mind, she would have driven herself.

"You be careful, Daniel Carson. Don't do anything stupid," his wife instructed. Why she should be so concerned for his safety was a mystery. Perhaps her mother's safety she was concerned about. It augured well to show feelings.

As they passed out of sight Jane crossed to the old cottage, rapped on the door, and called, "Sean Sullivan, isn't it time we went for the cows?"

"'Tis early, Jane. — Just a moment." Sean had been lying on his bed, listening dreamingly to the storm, and thinking as soon as it eased — like stopped altogether — he had better fetch the cows, without Jane. He did not know about Louise and Danny going into town, and was only half-awake when he let Jane in. He was also only half-dressed: in vest and trousers. Since it was Jane, he did not rush to put his shirt back on.

Jane had seen men stripped to the waist, yet now she stared admiringly at Sean. He certainly was not a weakling, she knew. There was something physically attractive about him. Those muscles and chest roused her passion. She had never been so attracted to a man, and certainly not to her husband.

"Turn your back, Madam, and I'll just change m' trousers."

Jane slowly lowered her stare, then did turn her back, saying over her shoulder, "I did not think you would be so bashful, Sean Sullivan." Envious of her sister, wondering if she had to turn her back and with a half a mind to face him. She wished at that moment she *were* Alison.

"'Tis not that I am bashful m' colleen. I just don't want to be giving you ideas." He said it without thinking, because he sensed she *did* have ideas.

"Sean, I am a married woman." She laughed, and at that moment she did not want to be, nor did she want Sean to be betrothed to her sister. She stepped from the cottage, the rain dampening her ardour.

They went off for the cows, milked them side-by-side, however the feeling persisted. It persisted until Jane wanted to reach out to touch Sean, and to embrace him, have him sweep her off her feet, and God forbid the thought, throw her amongst the hay bales, and make love to her. She broke into a sweat, quivered, closed her eyes, such desires totally out of character. Sean, although not oblivious of those desires, continued to jest, tease her with small talk: always joking, although working diligently, no need for her to have to shame him into doing the job properly.

In a desperate bid to end her plight, she suggested, "You clean up here Sean, and I'll take the cows out."

"To be sure they are out where they are supposed to be already."

"I — I just thought I'd put them in the next paddock over."

"You know best, m' girl."

"Won't be long."

What she meant was, 'Don't go up to the house without me.' She wanted to be away from him, believing the feeling must surely pass, yet she hastily slipped and slid between the meandering cows, with only one dog trotting beside her, the animal waiting for instructions. Jane heaved open the gate, sloshed through the entrance mud, and said to the beasts, "Get a move on. — Hurry, won't you." As for the cows, they had nothing to do, and all night to do it, so what was the rush. Jane sent the dog to chase them along. All the time she wanted to be in the dairy. However darkness was encroaching. 'Girl, you are behaving like your sister. That is just what she would get up to.'

A wrongful accusation, because love Sean as Alison did, she prodded him away any time he got a little too close.

Jane would never be married to Sean, so she had to make the most of her feelings when the opportunity arose, for surely it would not arise again. As the last cow skidded through the gate, dog on its heels, another savage rainstorm buffeted her. "I hope Mother is all right," she said to Sean on reaching the dairy, her concern genuine, although not what she wished to say.

"To be sure, she'll take the reins herself if your Danny baulks."

"No, Sean, Danny won't baulk at a storm." In that moment of truth, Jane relaxed, and the two dashed through the easing rain, Jane heading to the washhouse, and Sean to his quarters. "See you at tea in a few minutes," she called across to him as they parted, knowing it would take a lot longer for her to prepare tea.

Despite road conditions, when it would have been wiser for Louise to go to Waiuku by boat, except the tide was wrong, they arrived before dusk, more than a little mud-splattered the result of having to push the cart out of particularly deep mud. The rain had passed, and the late afternoon sun scythed across the emerald green land, valleys swathed in shade.

As they crossed the narrow wooden bridge at the north end of Waiuku, the Kentish Hotel dominating the opposite bank, Louise considered stopping to secure two rooms. Instead, due to her anxiety to see Priscilla, she urged Danny to proceed. A quarter of a mile further on Louise spotted Maude's house, standing close to the road, its typical square shape, front veranda, with a central door and a sash window each side.

"You see to our rooms, dear," Louise advised her son-in-law as they drew up. "There's Prissy. Come inside and have a cup of tea first."

Which left Danny still juggling whether to drive the short way into town and claim two rooms at the Kentish, or have a cup of tea? What if he stayed for tea, and other people took all the rooms, for surely on this wild night, travellers, having done their day's business, would not attempt to go to Pukekohe? "Should I not see about the rooms, Mother?"

"Plenty of time for that, dear." As she opened the gate and looked again at the veranda, it was not Priscilla who stood on it, instead Emily! "Oh — I didn't expect you. I-I thought . . ."

"Mrs Chester, what on earth are you doing out on a day like this?" Emily dashed forward to embrace and assist the lady she so much admired.

"To be sure, I wouldn't have come if I'd known . . ." Where did she get that phrase 'to be sure' from?

"We were, Mrs Chester. My husband is still there. I was lucky a boat was about to sail." She was fortunate the boat was also making Whatipu at the Manukau heads its first port of call.

And when Louise looked closer at the younger woman, there was no mistaking the fatigue in her face. "Now I am here . . ."

"Now you are here, Mrs Chester — ah, is that Danny I presume. He can jolly well take my sister back. — Is he going back tonight?"

"No . . ." Her daughter-in-law appeared. "Ah, Prissy, I thought I was seeing double." She was going to explain one moment one sister was on the porch, the next the other. However, important matters needed attending to. "So, how is your mother?"

Emily grimaced. Priscilla's red eyes conveyed the answer.

"Danny," Louise commanded, "when you go to get those rooms, these two ladies will be coming with you. — *Both* of them."

"Mother!" Priscilla exclaimed, protesting. Then referring to her own parent said, "Mother needs us both. She's . . ."

"Your children will need you even more, Priscilla. As for you, Emily dear, that rough crossing shows." In fact Emily had two rough crossings: the Tasman, in all its fury, and the Manukau: the waves smaller, as nauseating.

"I shan't stop for tea," Danny said. "I'll do as you say, and take the ladies to town."

The sisters looked at each other. Much as they knew they should stay with their mother, the thought of a few hours respite was tempting. They quickly packed, squeezed aboard the gig, and were driven to the hotel.

Only then did Louise make herself a cup of tea, and with it in hand, entered the lowly lit room of the dying woman. "Maude," she whispered.

Dreary eyes searched for recognition, her befuddled brain puzzling as to why Louise — she thought it was Louise — would be here. Her limp hand edged from the bedclothes, and Louise took it. How could a woman of such strength be reduced to such weakness? Far weaker than Louise expected: far less time left on this earth.

On learning both her daughters were out, just where or how long for, Louise did not say, Maude Caldwell still had the presence of mind to know Louise Chester would not be goaded into running after every whim. In reality, during the last hours she lacked the strength to make demands on anyone.

There was room at the inn. Emily commanded, "Prissy, you have Mrs Chester's, and I am sure Danny won't mind me sleeping in his bed." She said it with a touch of humour, although had no intention of luring Danny into her clutches.

Priscilla was too fatigued to catch on, and went directly to her mother-in-law's room, sagged on the bed, managed to wrestle with a few top buttons, unlace and kick off her shoes, then sleep fully clothed.

Emily ushered Danny into his room. "You won't mind me sleeping in your bed will you, Danny dear," she appealed. "I haven't any perfume on, so it won't smell."

Danny stood there, indifferent. Emily reached for his hand. "Danny, I am not going to seduce you. Now tell me, what has been happening at your place?" It was totally the wrong question to ask. And in hesitantly telling Emily he became more miserable. The last thing Emily wanted was to comfort him, so with a few words of matrimonial advice, she ushered him out the door, then slipped off her dress and shoes, lay on the bed, drew the quilt over her and fell sound asleep, undisturbed by the wind rattling a pail on the veranda.

Danny went to the public bar, and there on his own — not knowing a soul — despite living on the peninsula all his life, he drowned his sorrows. He had never been one to frequent such places, nr drink more than the occasional glass of beer.

A wet and blustery night.

Louise crept from the claustrophobic bedroom, scratched around in the kitchen for something to eat, yet felt little care for it, and settled in the lounge, hoping to hear Maude stir, although the periodic din of rain on the iron roof made that near impossible.

Something roused her sufficiently to go back to the bedroom. "Hello, I'm still here," she whispered.

For a moment the vacant eyes glimmered, Maude opening her mouth to speak. Her voice had gone, and as if the last straw, her last command unspoken, her head fell to one side.

Louise took her hand. "Goodbye, Maude. May God keep you." Tears came to her eyes. She brushed them away, yet more came.

Now what to do? Should she call the doctor? No point in dragging him out on a night like this. No use calling the girls. She could not call the girls anyway, since Maude did not have a telephone. And where *was* Danny? He was supposed to drop the girls off and come back. 'I bet,' she thought, 'I bet Emily's got him; giving him a piece of her mind.' Not for one moment did she think Emily would be waylaying Danny for any nefarious reason. She could well imagine her having coaxed something out of him, because he was not good at concealing his feelings. Why could not life be smooth? Why could not marriages be smooth? Like her own.

Any ruffles in hers were only differences of opinion, not ever-widening rents.

Louise waited, and waited, eventually rapped a neighbour's door, hoped they would have a phone and pleaded for them to fetch the doctor, having had second thoughts on that matter. She had to plead, because Maude's elderly neighbours had been at odds with her for — as long as Louise could remember, possibly because their house was slightly more pretentious than Maude's. Still believing the girls would return soon, or Danny, she did not ask the couple to phone the hotel. As it was, this was long before country inns provided showers in every room, let alone phones, and getting word to the girls would be difficult. She returned to the morbid house, soulless at the best of times.

First to arrive at the house, not the doctor, instead the son, Nigel. He stormed in with more bluster than the rain that came with him. "What's happened? — Why are y*ou* here? — The doctor says Mother has gone? — She can't have. — Where are my sisters?"

Louise was neither quick enough, nor had the inclination to answer. Instead she softly retaliated, "Why weren't *you* here?"

He stepped back, shook his head, as if he was not hearing right. "I have Jessica to attend to."

Louise agreed. "Yes, of course you have. Then Priscilla has Ben and the boys and baby . . ."

"She hasn't gone home has she? Now?"

"Nigel, your mother passed away peacefully a little while ago. I have telephoned the doctor. Your sist . . ."

"The doctor said she might last . . ."

"Last for weeks, Nigel. Unfortunately she did not." Louise inwardly changed the word to 'fortunately', because she was more concerned with Priscilla's and indeed Emily's, health, than their dying mother's. "I expect them back here shortly. They are both having a well earned rest . . ." She did not enlighten him just where, in case he went off to fetch them back immediately.

"Oh . . ." He was momentarily lost for words.

"I suggest, Nigel, you pay your last respects to your mother — before the doctor arrives, and then perhaps you would be good enough to inform your sisters." Perhaps they should know immediately after all, she reconsidered.

"Ah!"

"And Nigel, then you should attend funeral arrangements."

"I have . . ."

Louise shook her head in disbelief. "Are not you the man of the house?"

"Ah." Subdued, Nigel took off his wet hat, Louise taking it from him, and his coat, and hesitantly — as if he did not want to face death — entered his mother's room.

He was there only seconds, and when he emerged sullen-faced, Louise said. "Perhaps it would be best if *I* told your sisters."

The thought of going out into the bleak night was unpleasant. The doctor arrived, so Louise donned her coat and hat, and quietly made her exit: preferring to face the elements rather than be confined to a morgue. She had second thoughts as she stumbled along the rough, undefined and unlit road. At the north-end of town she encountered a commotion near the Kentish Hotel. Her mission was to advise the girls, so she swept by, through a hotel entrance and waited until someone finally attended her at reception. "I have a room booked for tonight. — Mrs Chester — I think one of my daughters . . ." The message was getting complicated.

"Oh." The lady looked flustered. "Oh, it's terrible. They say he's dead."

The only death that interested Louise was Maude's. She sorted out which was her room, and without any bags climbed the stairs, and actually tapped on the door before entering.

Priscilla stirred. "Where . . . Mother." She called both women 'mother', and Louise was not sure herself whom she was referring to.

She sat on the bed, felt Priscilla's brow, and broke the news.

The tears came: not a flood, just drops slithering down her cheeks.

"Your brother and the doctor are there now. — Where's Emily?"

"I don't know. I must have fallen asleep . . ."

"You stay here, I'll look in Danny's room." As expected, she found Emily asleep, woke her with a gentle shake, and before she had time to gather her senses, also told her that her mother had died, and in the same breath asked, "Where's Danny?"

Emily grimaced sleepily, sighed and answered, "I think he went out somewhere." Slowly her wits gathered. "Wasn't he going back to Mother's?"

"What I thought too, dear, but not a sign of him."

Reluctantly the three women went down stairs, located the gig, behind the hotel, and in the dead of night trundled back to Maude's place, half expecting Danny to be there, since he was nowhere to be seen at the hotel. No one there seemed to be interested where he was — they did not know of him — and were more concerned about the incident outside the hotel earlier in the evening, when some fellow had been run down.

The doctor had gone, and only Nigel was present, head in hands sitting in a well-worn armchair.

Not a soul in sight when Louise arrived home. She first went to her own room, took off her hat and coat, gazed solemnly out the window, watched distant sheep, gathered her thoughts. From Ben's old room looking down into a newly established glade she spied Jane, with Douglas running around. She went down to the kitchen took a large bottle of home-made lemon squash from the safe, poured three glasses, and went to her daughter.

"Hello, dear," she greeted.

Jane raised her hand shielding her eyes from the sun. "Hello, Mother," she answered softly. Louise offered the drinks. Jane gave Douglas a sip, then asked her mother, "I suppose it was one of those infernal motor cars that ran Danny down?"

Louise could have blamed an automobile. There were one or two in town. It would have been a lie. "No, my dear, it seems Danny just stepped in front of a cart." Then she suggested, "Would you like me to get Sean to run you into town, now I am home. — Where's your father, anyway?"

"He's taken some cheese to the wharf. I can't go. Sean can't go. We've got the cows . . ."

"*Damn* the cows!" Louise snapped, expelling her breath. "Jane, your husband is first. Sean can get there and back before milking. If not, I'll milk them myself. I'm quite capable of milking a few cows." She could have enlightened her daughter of a lot of things she was still capable of. When Jane hesitated, Louise ordered, "Now, Daughter, obey me — for once."

Jane swayed back breathing heavily, her mother's uncharacteristic language stunning her.

Sean obligingly took her to town in Louise's gig: the one he had restored. Jane could have taken herself there, although that would have left them without transport. Being with Sean, sitting beside him, brought on one those frequent urges. She was going to see her hospitalised husband, and all she wanted was to leap off the gig, drag Sean into a paddock, and, despite the circumstances, make mad passionate love to him on the grass, wet or not. She imagined his underpants were similar to those she had seen him in the other day, and she knew that her own drawers had an opening for convenience, so neither would have to undress. 'Fancy thinking a thing like that,' she deliberated. 'I must be sick. I'm not sick. I'm desperate — I think that's what they say.' Her brow, her whole body was wet with perspiration, and she could do nothing, except ride uncomfortably with the man her sister was going to marry, because she knew very well he would not have a bar of it.

They struck the same sticky spot as Danny and Louise had done a day or two earlier.

"Nothing for it, my girl," Sean surveyed, "I'll have to push."

Without a word, Jane also alighted, and at Sean's side helped to push the cart across the deep mud.

"Dear girl, you'll be going to the hospital looking like a mud-lark."

Jane responded with, "Dear boy, if I don't help I won't get there at all." Then she added, "Much as your company is most pleasant I don't fancy cuddling up in this thing all night." To emphasise her point she swung an arm about. "I don't see a good Samaritan about to assist us."

Sean first took her to the hotel, where she obtained a room, waited while she removed some of the mud from her hands and clothes, then dropped her at the hospital. Before he turned the hooded horse-drawn vehicle around, Jane clasped his arm. "Thank you, so much. You're such a brick." Not wanting him to go. "Are you sure you won't pop in for a few minutes?" There could be only one reason she should suggest that, she told herself. She did not imagine them taking afternoon tea in the staff dining room.

"Ah, no, I'd best be getting on my way. P'haps another time."

"God, I hope he's out in a few days." With that, Jane reached across and kissed Sean's cheek, the nearest she could ever hope to get to him.

About the same time, less than a mile from the hospital, a lawyer presented the last will and testament of the late Maude Caldwell. To Nigel, her pride and joy, she left the house and most of its contents. To Priscilla went her late father's savings: shares in some unprofitable company, worth over a hundred sovereigns at present value, and a few oddments: like a particular china plate, and crocheted tablecloths. To Emily went her poker bag, with a note she hoped with her gambling habits she could turn the sum into a fortune: all five shillings and four pence of it.

At that point the lawyer looked up, undecided whether to snigger or frown at Emily.

Priscilla took her sister's arm and sniggered, "You probably will too."

Emily just shrugged. She did not expect anything more. To be so humiliated in front of her brother angered her, and she inwardly vowed there and then to prove her mother right, no matter how sarcastic the inheritance was.

Nigel cast a critical eye around the room. "She's let it go back a bit."

Which prompted Emily to remark sourly, "You should be thankful for small mercies."

The following day Maude was interred beside her long-deceased husband.

Despite the solemn occasion for Emily and Priscilla, and despite Jane's emotional feelings after visiting her battered husband, when all three women met for dinner at the hotel, it was Emily who offered a little light relief. While Priscilla and Jane had no money for extravagances, Emily had a few sovereigns to spare: more than a few.

"I have not received my inheritance. However I'll lay out that five and four pence, and clean out a gentleman or two tonight." Then she added quickly, "At poker, of course."

"You won't be allowed in," warned Priscilla, hearing the noise from the public bar, while they dined in the adjacent room.

Emily chuckled. "Oh, won't I just! You watch them try to stop me."

"Let's finish our meal first," Jane insisted, warming slightly to the idea.

"I don't think I should," Priscilla pleaded, not fearful of any reprisal from Ben, rather because it was unladylike.

Emily read her mind. "Sister, with what Mother dished out to you, after everything you've done, you deserve to act up."

When three ladies swept into forbidden territory, heads turned, the barman aghast, all but dropping the glass he was filling, then sweeping round the bar to usher them out.

Emily brushed him aside, and announced contemptuously, "My late mother has just left me her poker bag. What fine gentleman is prepared to win it off me?" She did not enlighten them how much it was worth.

The disturbed smoke from numerous cigars and pipes hung in wisps around dumbfounded groups. The draught caused by the ladies' entry flared the fire, stars twinkling on the blackened brickwork. Flustered, the 'barman' was still intent on ridding the public bar of feminine intrusion.

Emily appealed with her hands and eyes at the men. "These two sisters of mine will ensure *I* win your money fairly." She was gazed at with disbelief, and indifferent males resumed their conversations, ignoring the challenge.

"I'll take you on," a rough-hewn character uttered, glancing at the proprietor: not the barman as Emily had assumed.

Emily scowled at him. "I said, fine gentlemen, not a scrag-end."

"Me money's as good as any . . ."

"No doubt. I rather think it would be better spent on your children," Emily admonished.

That drew laughter, out of which a group of three men edged their chairs closer together, to make room for another chair, in which Emily was invited to sit, the other two women standing each side of her. She was offered a cigarette, but refused, with the assertion, "I have not much to lose, so I had best keep a clear head."

Jane thought, 'If only Sean could see me now.' She frowned on realising she was thinking of Sean, not her husband, at a moment like this. From this very hotel Danny had staggered into the path of a horse and cart, being trod on then run over. Jane was not thinking of that consequence, besides the first poker hand had been dealt, and even she knew what Emily picked up had the makings of a winning hand. Jane kept a straight face, and hoped Priscilla could contain herself. Then, maybe she did not know a good hand from a bad one.

As Emily selected only one card to throw away, gambling she would be dealt another king to go with her three queens. Jane thought, 'What a shame Sean did not stay on, and perhaps somehow advise Emily.' When Emily snuck a look at her newly dealt card, placed it inscrutably with the others, Jane knew she would be hard to beat, caught one of the men looking at herself, although gave no sign of what she hoped.

One player slid a sixpence across to the centre of the kitty, the next withdrew, and Emily murmured, "Raise you," and her bared fingers with bright red nails pushed two sixpences into the kitty.

The fourth player tossed his hand in.

"I'll raise you," and the suited man, with a gold chain hanging from his waistcoat pocket, drew on his cigar before matching his words with deeds, putting two shillings into the kitty.

"See you," Emily said softly, raising her eyes to meet his, at the same time adding another four sixpences.

He arrogantly swept down three tens and two aces.

Emily nodded silently, and laid down individually her three queens and two kings, then drew the kitty into her pile, so substantially adding to her original five shillings and four pence.

Priscilla and Jane looked at each other, and Jane thought, 'Perhaps she has no need of Sean's advice after all.' Again she frowned. 'Why do I always think of Sean? Is it Danny doesn't play cards, or Ben for that matter? That must surely be the reason.' With a shrug she realised, 'I don't know whether Sean plays? I suppose he does.'

Priscilla already felt dizzy in the lantern-lit smoke-filled room. She was self-conscious, yet despite rubbing shoulders with a bearded patron she had the impression he was more concerned over the game than the woman beside him being in a public bar: a male only bar.

"Should be interesting," he opined, and Priscilla imagined him as being a professor of philosophy or something intelligent.

In the meantime Emily tossed in her second hand, and Jane noted thereafter, Emily only bet if she was fairly sure of winning. It re-enforced what she had learned about her during the evening's meal, when Emily had given her and Priscilla some sound business advice. Surely gambling was not a wise means of making money?

"Em!" Priscilla exclaimed, when her sister later brushed her hand so elegantly across the table, sweeping over five sovereigns into her now well-enhanced funds.

"Come on, Emily," Jane begged, "you've won enough."

Emily reached back and took Jane's arm. "They still have a few shillings left."

"Oh, Em," Priscilla lamented again. "You mean thing."

"Oh, Prissy," she mimicked, "do you think these fine gentlemen would let me off the hook?"

"Listen you two," snarled one loser, who had already opened his purse twice for more money, which Emily soon added to her collection, "you're cheating. You shouldn't be in here anyway."

"My sisters are learning a fool and his money are soon parted," Emily quoted, glanced up at the gathering about them, yet quickly returned her attention to the game.

Censured, Jane and Priscilla took umbrage at the accusation, and for that reason stayed put. They also thought they would have great difficulty in extricating themselves from the crowd without getting molested.

"I don't suppose anyone would care to get my sisters and I a drink would they?" Emily requested, holding up a half-sovereign. "What would you have, Girls, it is on me?"

Jane had warmed to the occasion, and wondered what whisky tasted like? Perhaps she should stick to a sherry. No, she would try spirits. She needed something to give her courage, because in the morning she would visit Danny again, then the three ladies would head home, and she could tell Sean all about Emily's escapades, *if* she beat Alison to him. That is also when she realised once Priscilla returned home, so Alison would also return to her home, and indeed, she (Jane) would have no excuse to linger at Kowhai. She sighed, 'Why do things have to be so complicated?'

Priscilla chose sherry, although wanted to finish it quickly and get to bed. She did not give any thought at all as to whether she would tell Ben of what they had been up to.

Time was running out. Not so much time, rather two players were getting very testy at being beaten at their own game by a woman, and beaten soundly. The third player was not so concerned about his loss. He frequently glanced at Emily's blouse with its tiered frills and choker, imagining what it concealed, and wondering how easily it could be dispensed with should he entice her to his room.

The landlord, so reluctant to allow the women entry, now smiled on his good fortune, the lingering crowd rushing him off his feet. When Emily finally poured her winnings into her purse she was richer by over twenty-five pounds, and that was a considerable sum. Smiling, widening her appealing eyes, she begged the landlord, "I do not suppose, Sir, you could provide three ravenous ladies with a late supper?"

"I'm sure, Madam, we could." Even if it meant dragging his wife out of bed to oblige, since she had effectively been recently banned by law from serving. A pretty woman behind the bar tended, according to some, to lure men to drinking more than they should. That aside, the publican's takings, thanks to the ladies' influence, were considerably higher than usual. The last of the losers was left counting his losses, in more ways than one: Emily politely declined a nightcap with him.

The sequel was, the ladies caught a steamer from Waiuku to Pollok, where Sean collected them. It was not half so exciting telling him about Emily's win, as it was being part of it: at least not for Jane. Emily sat herself beside Sean, while Jane and Priscilla sat in the back seat of the buggy.

"I was a-thinking I would have had three very sad ladies aboard, so I was?" Sean said, staggered by their jovialness.

"'Tis really a sad time for all of us," mimicked Emily. "Life is full of such sorrow, so sometimes we have to lighten it a little." She clutched Sean's arm, laid her head momentarily on his shoulder, and Jane was instantly jealous. Emily could do so, for she had no ulterior motive. Jane wished to do the same, not out of jest, rather desire. She looked the other way, sought something to distract them. There was only the deserted track, with cows grazing nonchalantly at the passing horse and cart.

They dropped Priscilla off, waited while Alison packed her things, then headed to Kowhai.

After her sister had gone, Priscilla happened to open her handbag, and deep in its recesses she made a discovery: five sovereigns. What puzzled her was how Emily had managed to put them there. She knew where the windfall had come from. Later, when Ben returned to their cottage she told him of where she had been and Emily's win, then of her inheritance. "Maybe, we should give them to Emily to look after."

"What, five sovereigns?"

"No, silly, the shares."

"You could do worse, Prissy, a lot worse." Ben had soft spot for Emily, and believed in her.

Sean heard a tinkle when he gathered up his coat, thrust his hand into the pocket, frowned, and drew out five sovereigns, and for the life of him, he could not recall when he last earned that amount of money, or that he would leave so much in his pocket.

Alison, on hearing of Emily's adventures, was envious that she was stuck with Ben and his children, while the others were obviously having a great time, when they were supposed to be in mourning. All the way back to Kowhai, she had sat silently, while Jane and Emily went on about it.

Emily did spend a few days at Kowhai, and contrary to custom, she did not go around in black. "Who's to know?" she told Louise. "Besides, I've only one black dress with me."

Louise accepted Emily's indifference to protocol, although was more concerned with what had taken place at the Kentish Hotel. "So I hope, my dear, you have not encouraged my daughters to take up gambling?"

Now much more at ease with the older lady, Emily assured, "I do not think so." She chuckled impishly. "I would never live it down if I have." Then she added, "I think the little distraction did Jane a world of good." She raised her eyebrows at Louise.

One event — a mere trifle — stood out for Emily during her stay. They were all gathered at the big homestead for lunch, including Jane and Sean. Later, reclining in various chairs in the spacious lounge, one of them prattling on about something — Emily could not remember who or what — she happened to look at Jane, most attractively attired, as if crossing the paddocks to Kowhai was worthy of dressing up for. Her gaze lingered. It moved from her dress to her face, her naturally irate appearance having been replaced by one of devotion: that devotion directed towards, as Emily observed, Sean. She shifted her focus to him, who, utterly nonchalant of both admirers, was staring with similar devotion at Alison. 'I see,' she murmured. 'There's trouble brewing there.' A general shift around occurred, and the moment passed, Emily thinking no more of it.

After Emily had left Kowhai Alison discovered five sovereigns in, of all places, a shoe, and wrapped in notepaper with the message: *For being such a brick.*

Jane did not discover her similar gift until three days later. Which annoyed her, because by then Emily had gone. She knew where it came from, and from that day forth would not hear a word spoken against her: especially since her own desires had been awoken in the presence of Sean, and she began to understand Emily's urges. Except Emily was able, even if not morally correct, to put them into practice. Jane knew she would have to subdue hers.

*   *   *   *   *   *

Thomas Chester could not bring himself to officially tell Alison and Sean the land they desired was theirs. He came across them lolling on the front lawn, and, squatting beside his daughter, he suggested, "Instead of wasting time, shouldn't you be looking over the bricks and timber we have been landed with."

"What for?" Alison asked curtly.

"To see what sort of house you can build with it." He made it sound if the couple themselves should have been thinking on those lines.

Even then Alison did not capture the significance of what he was saying, so responded negatively, "And where would we put the house, Father?"

Thomas re-lit his pipe, sucked in a few breaths to ensure it was going, and pointed with it across the paddocks. "See that knoll over there. I'd say there would be as good a place as any?"

Sean could not discern the knoll. Alison looked beyond the established farm, and asked tentatively, "You mean among the bush — near the drive?" She happened to know there was a slight rise within the bush-clad southern end of the valley.

"Mm, about there," her father confirmed.

Without a word Alison turned to her father, looked at him solemnly, her mouth quivering, then walked away, thrust her hands to her face, the two men hearing her sobs as she stumbled on the steps. Thomas shrugged. He could not win either way.

"'Tis very generous of you, Mr Chester," Sean accepted. "'Tis very generous." He also walked off, not so much away from Thomas Chester, instead going after his bride-to-be. He found her in the kitchen, face buried in her mother's breast.

Louise, also looking as if she had learned of another death, said to Sean, "I am very pleased for you both." Gently pushing her daughter from her, she advised, "You had best do what Father says, instead of bawling your eyes out."

Alison could not respond to the occasion. She had been deeply hurt having to wait so long for her inheritance — long for her — she only slowly regained her merry self. The couple assessed what size house they could build with the bricks and timber jettisoned when the *Reliance* ran aground.

Ben, who had opposed Danny's inclusion in the family's farm arrangements, now not only offered Sean his best wishes, he also drew up plans for their house.

"Why did father hold off for so long?" Alison asked her brother.

"Who knows? You know what he's like." He expelled his breath in frustration with his father. "He was being stubborn."

"He was hoping Sean and I would break up," Alison responded. She also sighed, laid her head on Ben's chest, and cried, "If he'd given it to us sooner, we could have cleared half of it by now." Her assertion was not quite true, but they could certainly have cleared a few acres.

"Never mind, Sis, we'll make up for lost time," her brother promised: a promise difficult to keep during the winter months.

"Thank you so much." Still with her head on his chest, she complimented, "Prissy's so lucky."

Ben thought otherwise: because from the time of their marriage he had worked tirelessly on his farm, helped Danny, and now was offering to help Sean. It seemed he would never have time to spend with his family. If he had known what the future held he would have more cause to be concerned over his long hours of work. He was not to know, so assumed in a year or two he would have more leisure.

Thomas and Tom had known each other for many years on more than just a nod-of-the-head basis. To further that friendship, Annabelle's father drove his daughter to Kowhai for dress fittings: the two men using it as an excuse to down tools and yarn on the veranda, while a dressmaker fussed over the girls within the house.

September sloshed through the mud: rains that poured prosperity into the earth, although made no allowances for the wayfarer. Often the only way to travel was by water, slide first through the mud to Pollok wharf, then use the serviceable sea to reach Waiuku, or wherever.

"I hope, Mother, it *does* clear up," Alison appealed.

"My dear, if we get any more rain the whole country will sink beneath the sea."

That brought a smile to Alison's lips, and Louise reached out to kiss her forehead. Gone was the frivolous daughter. Louise knew precisely when her character changed: about the time Sean was first washed up on their shores. Not Sean himself who converted Alison, rather events surrounding his coming, and, staying. Louise feared that had he not stayed, Alison might well have run off after him, and they would have lost her entirely. On reflecting on the weeks before the weddings of her three children, Louise thought only Ben's had been joyous. She knew why Jane remained morose: an attitude that had since seldom left her.

Priscilla's and Alison's wedding days had at least one thing in common — they had several things in common actually. The skies cleared and the sun shone days before the big event. Roads dried out before they could be smoothed, so wheel tracks were rifted and brittle, broke beneath steel wheels, and jolted those negotiating the tracks. Tom and Ben organised teams to level the worst of local roads, particularly Kowhai's notorious drive.

"So, how many of Tom's lot are actually coming?" Louise asked her daughter.

"I have not a clue, Mother."

"I must know how many to cater for?"

"Mother, we are having a hangi, it doesn't really matter. I can assure you there will be no shortage of food."

"Some guests will still want — you know."

"I can imagine Emily up to her elbows in pork." And Alison laughed at the thought of her dignified sister-in-law tucking in: probably sitting on the grass among Tom's family, while some guests no doubt would keep their distance.

Emily arrived two days before the wedding. Her first mission: to make a detour to see her sister, Priscilla. She had met and kissed Ben on the road amid howls of derision from fellow toilers, who at the time were smoothing the rutted roadway for guests. At Kanuka she was glad to have Priscilla on her own.

As her sister placed the kettle on the range, Emily fossicked in her handbag, drew out an envelope, and handed it to her. "Your first dividend," she said with a smirk.

"Oh, thank you. How much?"

"I re-invested it, and it worked out. I suppose I should have told . . ."

"Emily, you're a wonder. Is this all mine?"

"It is no one else's."

Still holding the money order for over twenty pounds — not a bad return on her original shares worth about a hundred and seventy pounds — Priscilla enfolded her sister in her arms. "You *are* wonderful. Do *we* need this?"

"I thought you might."

(By the end of the twentieth century twenty pounds would be the equivalent to about fifteen hundred dollars, such was the inflation, particularly during the last quarter of the century.)

After a cup of tea Priscilla gathered her two pre-school children, hitched up the buggy, and drove Emily down to Kowhai.

As she had done at Ben's wedding, Emily pitched in.

"So, your husband still sees us as being too primitive," Louise questioned.

Emily sighed, and admitted, "No, Mrs Chester, I honestly think he would have come. Unfortunately he is down to it."

"I'm sorry, Emily." She had never seen Emily look so concerned. Instinctively she reached out and clasped her arm in consolation. The more she learned of Emily's generous nature, the further her less proper activities diminished into the background.

"It is a combination of things, Mrs Chester. I rather think I am going to be a very young widow before too long."

"Surely not, dear."

"He *is* a good deal older than me. I cannot really complain," Emily said, as she rolled out some pastry. "I am gradually taking control of his business interests. And I tell you, Mrs Chester, I am glad I have a business head." She thought the lady probably believed she was only a good time girl. So to quell those beliefs, she told Louise, "I was able to get Prissy a good return on Mother's inheritance."

"And what of your own?"

Emily smiled. "Oh that. My dear Mother would turn in her grave if only she knew how much it has earned me . . ."

"Not if you keep giving it away." The lady shook her head. "They all found their gifts." When she saw Emily blush — or was it the heat of the kitchen colouring her cheeks — she asked, "Tell me, you would not know how Sean found five sovereigns in his pocket?"

"Sean? Was he the fellow who ran you to town — and looked after us so well?" She grinned impishly.

"It was indeed?"

A beautiful wedding: a colourful wedding. Because of the earlier opposition to her betrothal, Alison only expected a small celebration. Things got out of hand, and by the time Tom and his family turned out, all in their Sunday best, and Annabelle's brothers' mates who managed the hangi — it took several of them, although not all were strictly necessary — the wedding was as big as any to be held on the peninsula.

Thomas Chester was almost ashamed he had ever opposed the union in the first place, such was the adoration showered on the couple. The bride radiant: her locally grown bouquet almost as big as her. Annabelle nearly stole the show: setting a new style — not actually new, rather one that had been closeted for most of the last hundred years — a lower neckline allowing her olive skin to contrast with her vivid white dress. Her bouquet was as all-smothering as Alison's. The bride's niece, two-year-old Kathy, was one flower girl, and Annabelle's little sister, Lottie, of about the same age, was the other. Sean had both Ben and Danny attending him: Ben having to calm the groom with a whisky — just a shot — at his home before the show.

Jane was not put out at all when her sister opted for a friend as bridesmaid, rather than her. Alison never knew why. At the ceremony it was bad enough watching Sean marry her sister, let alone had she been part of the bridal party. When Douglas became restless during the service, Jane tugged his arm angrily, and the boy sidled over to his grandmother, took her hand and looked appealingly up at her, wondering why she had tears in her eyes.

Nor was the object of Jane's attention fully aware of her feelings. Being such a naturally friendly fellow, he took Jane's friendliness towards him as being reciprocal. Certainly he knew her relationship with her husband was far from bliss. It gave him no cause to think she actually lusted for him? Even if he had, he would not have responded, because from the moment Alison rescued him from the surf, he had not so much looked at another woman with anything more than courtesy.

The thrill of being a bridesmaid was mixed with awe for Annabelle. Her fear: she would be the only olive face in a sea of white — when white was white, and not tanned by the sun, or a mixture of two races. Had she dared to look around at the gathering, she would have seen her brothers and sisters, and parents, and her own grandmother. Not a matter of restricting the number of guests because Kowhai could take them all. Annabelle spared a thought for Sean: not a relation, nor friend in sight. When the matter was earlier raised, Annabelle had responded, 'We're your family, Sean.'

The bride herself gave no thoughts to anything other than she was marrying the man she loved, and, with the blessing of her parents. So immersed in those thoughts, she hardly heard a word said, almost missing her cue, 'I do.'

After the ceremony, she said to her husband, "When the vicar said that about anyone not approving of us being married, my heart stopped."

"To be sure, I was worried."

"It was really only Father who — anyway, he has long since conceded. I'm just so relieved, darling." She sighed. "It's a wonderful day. The hangi smells divine. I hope they think to give us some."

All too soon it was over, register signed, another kowhai planted, and the feast. True to form, Emily was to be seen amid Annabelle's relations, up to her elbows in pork and puha. Unlike some, she did not have to put on airs. While the celebration was at its height, Sean and his new bride were driven from the valley and down to the harbour edge. At least they had planned the day to coincide with a late afternoon tide. They travelled to Auckland, took a coastal steamer to Waiwera, staying at the spa hotel, bathing in its hot pools.

The week's honeymoon passed swiftly, and they returned to Kowhai until their home was completed: a job delayed by winter storms.

Blessed with a break in the weather, from dawn to dusk the three husbands and Alison clambered over the new house, soon having it fit for habitation, and although she had crossed the threshold many times, when it was deemed finished — although there were many little jobs to do — Sean gathered up his wife and carried her through the front entrance, amid cheers from the family, including Thomas and Louise who had come across to inspect what the couple had done with the jettisoned courthouse bricks and timber. Not Jane: she could not bear to watch the frivolity.

As for the family's cows, they never knew who would turn up to milk them: the task being done by any one of four or five valley inhabitants, although Jane managed the butter and cheese making.

Time — a few more years — slipped past.

It seemed to Louise her daughter Jane would have just the one child: a thought she did not like, believing one only offspring were spoiled. However Alison began to make up for her sister's lack: having a child every second year, and Louise was destined to have several grandchildren after all: all living close-by, and on reaching school-age attending the local school: the clan eventually contributing to a large percentage of its pupils.

Despite having children Alison managed to retain her trim figure, and whenever Sean entered the house after a day's work, she would be there for him to admire, after changing from her day clothes, into an evening dress: his favourite having a deep 'V' bodice, with a frilly lace insertion rising to her neck. Cut to retain her slim waist, it had another lacy 'V' from her hips, the otherwise plain pastel blue bell-shaped skirt frilled at its hem. Rather a shame there was only her husband to admire it. For Alison's part, although she had had little opportunity, she was clothes conscious, and always felt good when well dressed. When she was at Waiuku, she stopped by Harts drapery, if for nothing other than to admire materials she could neither afford to buy, nor would have the opportunity to wear garments made from such lovely cloth.

Her sister-in-law Emily, on the other hand, had many opportunities to wear glamorous clothes. She said to her ailing husband, "I'm going, even if you are not."

"And, my dear, what will people think, you traipsing about town, going to the theatre, or a recital unescorted." He expelled the rest of his cigar-tainted breath, and added, "They'll wonder whether you are indeed married."

"I will not be unescorted." She watched his face fume. "I shall not be on my own. It so happens, my dear, I *do* have lady friends. Even so, it is a pity you are going to miss this play. It is, after all, about the evils of men abusing their wives."

If Will Todd barely noticed his beautifully attired wife, then other people did: particularly men. There were many fashionably dressed ladies present on this occasion, yet Emily seemed to rise above the average. Her two-piece a riot of lace and frills from neck to waist and halfway down her arms. A tasselled stole, flower-decked hat and pointed parasol. Her petticoat-inflated apricot dress flowing as she glided down the stairs and into a cab, and was taken to the theatre.

Emily was very much part of women's movements, and Susie MacTier's novel, *The Hills Of Hauraki* adapted into a play was in the mood of that movement. Christina Beaminster had married a man who inherited his parents' pub. Against her will she has to serve in the bar, and to drown her humiliation, she takes to drink. Tragically, one day she confuses ammonia with brandy, and dies.

CHAPTER TEN

"You lads love wallowing in the water, so I have a little job for you — starting right now," Ben Chester told his sons.

George Chester was old enough now to understand his father's ways. 'Never put off till tomorrow what you can do today.' He looked down thoughtfully, wondering what *work* his father had for them. Certainly not play. He knew his father was something his mother called 'impulsive', doing or buying things on the spur of the moment. So, what had he suddenly decided to do, with their help?

What Ben had decided: was to reclaim the swamp he had bought five years previously from its destitute owners. Having cleared most of his inherited land, he only now turned his attention to this mire, although he had often mulled over how to actually do it. And why now? No particular reason, except summer rains had left the ground he intended to excavate soft. Also, his nephew Stanley was on hand, staying with the family over Christmas, so now was a good a time as any to accomplish the deed.

"With three willing hands, Son, we'll have a shot at draining the old swamp, eh," he announced, ruffling the boy's hair.

"Wow!" And George raced off to fetch James and their cousin, Stanley.

Jessica had condescended to allow her precious child to stay at Kanuka, although would never learn during the first few days he had tumbled from a horse — twice — fought with his host, lost his pocket money, not that there was anywhere much to spend it, and torn his best trousers, which according to his Aunt Priscilla he should not have bothered to bring. Sunday best was not necessary on the farm. Even so, he was thoroughly enjoying himself, much preferring the carefree country life to the fuddy-duddy atmosphere of his own home.

Earth moving machinery to cope with the task had not been invented, or if it had, it certainly was not available in such remote areas, and was in any case primitive. Therefore George, Stanley and

James, under the supervision of Ben, would manhandle the tons of earth to be moved. One section of the proposed channel would be several feet deep, and as wide. No easy task, having beaten the two previous owners. It would *not* beat Ben!

A stream did ooze from the lip of the swamp, and the boys thought it only necessary to widen it. "No, Son," Ben disagreed, when the boys suggested the easy way out. "We'll cut a separate channel."

Ben's father, Thomas, still insisted he was mad, after riding across and surveying the site for himself, then, having given his biased opinion, rode back home, not before Ben called after him, "After we've drained this, Dad, we'll have a go at yours, while we've got plenty of labour."

All he received in reply was a down-wave of his father's hand.

Ben dug, and the three lads shovelled. For periods, about thirty minute stretches, other local lads pitched in, found the going too tough, and sloped back home. Nevertheless, after the first day, commencing from the lower end of the channel, they had completed over thirty feet: admittedly starting from zero depth, and reaching only three feet.

What Ben did notice, and he had noticed it before, George, probably because he was a year or two older than James, bossed his brother about, and James seemed to accept it. At the time he wondered whether he should tell his older son to be less authoritative, or let the boys sort it out for themselves. Perhaps as they grew older the age difference would lessen and James would learn to hold his own.

"We'll have this done in no time," he said to the boys, as they downed tools — they had downed them several times during the day — and headed for the house. What Ben failed to observe, good progress was the result of keen competition between George and Stanley: neither prepared to allow the other to get the better of him. James, being younger, was not expected to achieve the same mark. The end result, only minutes after tea, all three boys admitted they were a bit tired, thought they would have a rest for awhile, and fell asleep the moment their heads hit their pillows.

Ben, up with the birds, expected his youthful labourers to be up also. No such luck. They mutinied: believing one day's work should be rewarded by one day's play. He soon learned shovelling was harder than digging, if he did not know already. Every spade dug, and not heaved aside in one movement, meant at least two shovel-loads. Funny how loose earth expands. After an exhausting day he could hardly compare his effort with the previous day, even taking in account he was gradually digging deeper.

"So, are you lads going to play today, or help me?" Ben appealed to the boys the next morning.

"As I said, Father," George proclaimed most authoritatively, "one day's work, one's day's play."

A hard slog, and Ben now doubted if he was doing the right thing by cutting a new channel. Probably the easiest route would have been best. Both Sean and Danny wandered across to have a look, although declared they had other work to do. 'Making the most of the fine weather,' they both offered as an excuse.

That evening, after the children had been tucked into bed, again only too happy to sleep off their weariness, Priscilla crossed to the lounge curtains and re-opened them, her husband frowning in puzzlement.

"What are you watching, dear?" Ben enquired.

"Just waiting."

He heaved himself from the armchair, obliged to go to his wife's side, and watch for whatever she was waiting for.

The eastern horizon glowed yellow-white, the rising full moon sliding behind layered clouds, breaking free, silently beginning its nightly ascension.

Priscilla gasped. "Isn't it lovely?"

To Ben, the moon was the moon.

"Look now," his wife exclaimed. "Look! It's shimmering on the harbour."

"Mm."

"Ben — you're not romantic at all. It doesn't always do so. It depends on where the moon rises?"

"It always rises in the east."

"Not always. Like the sun, it moves about." She rested her head against her husband's shoulder, looked up at him, and murmured dreamily, "Moon over the Manukau."

"Mm." Ben sort of agreed, with a sigh, wanting only to rest his weary body.

"Now it's shining on the swamp. Look, Ben!" She stood watching it, little realising that the scene would never be exactly the same again. If her husband did not enjoy such beauty, then she would.

The next day happened to be the last of 1912: a year during which one major event had captured world headlines: the sinking of the *Titanic* on her maiden voyage. Closer to home was the loss of Captain Scott and his Antarctic adventurers: their bodies to be discovered early in the New Year. These tragedies were not on the minds of the family when they decided to make a picnic of Ben's drainage efforts. And an explosive picnic it would be, because he was going to blast his way through a rocky outcrop.

"We'll see some progress today," he told the boys, "so don't go wandering off." Which meant, there was a fair bit of digging and shovelling to do before he would have the offending rocks ready to be blasted.

It was lunchtime — how time flies when you're working hard — before Ben had completed the cavities for the dynamite, so he suggested, "We'll knock off for a while, eh boys."

They had been waiting for him to suggest it for the last two hours.

Priscilla drew a jar of beer from the swamp, saying to her husband, "It does have some purpose."

"I don't intend to drain it all, Prissy," he advised her. "I thought it would be nice to leave a little — sort of lake."

"That would be nice," she agreed, wondering what purpose they could put a lake to, apart from it being a refuge for wildlife.

Knocking off for a while would have been better phrased for a 'few minutes', because no sooner had they settled, gobbled their picnic lunch, than Ben was back on his feet. "Now you go over there ..."

"Just wait 'til we've finished, dear," Priscilla objected, hurriedly repacking the basket, thinking it was not much of a picnic. It had taken ages to prepare, yet her husband had not settled long enough to enjoy a morsel of it. Men! They took their wives for granted: something she had been told over and over again, and today believed it to be true.

'Over there' was on the opposite side of the swamp to the distant farmhouse, and downstream.

So they waited, watched Ben fiddle with wires, turn to see that his family were all correctly assembled, then slam down the plunger. With a whoomph, earth, rocks and shrubs rose in slow motion as if a giant worm had burrowed through the ground. The odd missile hurtled clear. Two native pigeons lifted themselves from a treetop, clawed their way upward, then swooped to gain speed. A pair of tui took a more direct route from the disturbance, swishing past the family with agitated screeches.

"Oh, my! — What a bang!" Priscilla exclaimed, clasping her hand to her mouth.

The trembling earth resettled: dislodged boulders plunged from higher reaches, smashed their way through scrub and splashed into the swamp.

Ben surveyed the site. "Not too bad at all." He signalled the boys. "You lot, let's start shovelling." James, the youngest, brandished a stick to beat the older boys into work, had it twisted from his hand, and replaced with a shovel.

By mid-afternoon, the channel had been cleared, and Ben inserted more charges among the rocks, adding a few more, since the first blast was a little on the light side. He gathered his family in the earlier 'safe' place, glanced about, then set off the next charge.

For a second the valley remained silent. A thunderous explosion rent the air, birds fleeing from trees in confusion as the blast reverberated up the valley: a valley which shook, and continued to shake and rumble longer than expected. The ground yielded, heaved, wobbled like jelly, and subsided, sucking earth into fissures.

Ben stumbled to his family, grabbed Kathy, and plunged through the slide. He glimpsed the boys as the hillside above rent, and tumbled towards them. Sweating with panic, he tossed his daughter from danger, clambered back, despite falling stones, and snatched Stanley. There lay James, stunned by a rock, crumpled amid mud.

Mud!

Why mud? The soil was barely moist above the swamp. Now it oozed like potters' clay.

No sign of his wife or George. He whirled about, seeking them in one direction or another. They must be buried — alive. In those seconds he imagined life without them. Who would look after his two remaining children? Not Alison. She was married now. He would have to live at Kowhai. His mother would look after them, while he faced up to his folly, and live with a father who had so condemned his stupidity.

"Stay there!" he screamed at Kathy, who was wailing for her mother.

He staggered through the slide, sought an arm, a leg, anything protruding. In one foolish stroke he had killed his wife and son. God, how could he ever forgive himself? His two remaining children would forever detest him.

"Ben!"

His head flicked around. She was haunting him already: his wife.

"Ben"

No ghost: miraculously a living wife, dragging a living son across the mire.

Ben staggered towards them, stumbled, fell face down in his haste to claim them. He clutched his wife, drew his son close to him, as they fought their way to safety.

Head in his hands, Ben sagged on to the solid earth.

Priscilla expelled her breath in annoyance, fussed over the children. "It's all right now. We're all here, and none the worse for wear."

"Why the mud?" Ben protested. "Why the mud?"

"Never mind that. Let's just get away from here — as far away as we can." Anger was building within her.

"I just don't understand it. It was as solid as a rock."

"That maybe. However you did meddle with nature, and besides everyone said there was a hoodoo on the place ." She did not really believe that herself, but used it to enforce her opposition.

"It's not that."

"It was something unnatural." Seldom had Priscilla been angry with her husband. Now she glared at him, tight-lipped, enraged he should have put them to so much danger, all over a blasted swamp: the swamp he had just blasted.

"Here's your spade, Father," George offered.

"Thanks."

"There's my shovel," observed James, already shrugging off his stoning.

Ben gestured. "Look. Look to where the explosion was. It's all quite . . ."

"*Look out!*" Priscilla screamed. "*Run!*"

Like rabbits they scurried before a wave of debris-imbrued mud surging towards them. They could not see the cause of this new threat, only flee before it, fearing it would gather momentum and overwhelm them.

Above the home side of the swamp the hillside had slipped, thrusting a wall of ooze before it: a wave that swept over the ridge and spread like devouring lava across the valley below. One victim was Ben's tethered horse: the mud rising up its poring legs, rolling the animal over, filling its mouth with mud, torturing it to death.

Ben did not see his horse die.

Thomas Chester stood on the road high above the valley, holding back the gathering crowd least they unwisely rush into the valley and themselves become victims. The first explosion, which might not have been much to Ben, had shaken the countryside, rattled lunch tables, and lured locals to the road. Now they watched from afar Ben detonate the second of his charges: the land on which they were standing quivering. After the dust had subsided, from their position, they counted all present and correct: Ben and his family, although only miniatures on the rugged landscape.

"Look at that!" yelled an observer.

"The whole hill's going!"

"Run, Ben! — *Run!*"

"They're just standing there."

"They can't see it."

They grimaced in despair as the wave of mud, remnants of the swamp, swept over the ridge, and apparently engulfed the family where they stood.

"Danny, go for the doctor," Thomas ordered. "We'll mind Douglas."

Danny, already on his horse, spurred it into a gallop, and charged along the ridge, trying to remember where the nearest telephone was. Te Toro, he thought. Miles away.

"John," Thomas demanded of a neighbour, "you and your boys go down Cemetery Road, and get to them from that side."

"Right." No argument.

"Sean, you and Logan see what you can do from this side." He looked about, clasped Alison's arm. "Dear, you and your mother had better go down to their place, and — and — you know." He could not bring himself to suggest they prepare it for the bodies of his son and family, if they ever dug them out. He stayed where he was, and should any of the lost family emerge from the mire, he could direct rescuers to them. Hopefully at least one had been spared, he thought.

Logan, Sean and a third neighbour negotiated the steep grassy slopes into the valley, scattering sheep ambling away from the danger. They by-passed Ben's house and rejoined the main track beyond it, then had to detour round a separate slip. "That's about where Ben told me he should not have cleared it, so he did," Sean remarked, and edged his horse upward, above the devastated land.

Since they had taken a high route, they stayed aloft, and from their position looked down at where the swamp had been. "Ben sure kept his word," Logan observed, "He got rid of the swamp. Pity he didn't live to see it."

"So, what do you think? Why did it all come down? Surely not because of the explosion?" Comments from the third rider, who carefully coaxed his horse downward beside the ruined land, trusting it was safe enough.

They speculated on reasons for the collapse, including its notorious legends. Only later would the truth emerge.

"So, the land above the swamp fell into it," Sean determined, "and pushed the swamp over the ridge."

"Something like that."

"Ben and the rest of them were over there, so they were," Sean indicated, searching for any sign of life.

"I guess so."

Cautiously they crossed the broken land where the ground was most firm. Forced from its original setting, the swamp had swept like a wave over that ridge, momentarily engulfed anything before it, like Ben's horse, then passed on, until it re-settled in another depression: actually in a neighbour's property.

"They must have gone with it," Sean declared, since there was no sign of the family. Surely one of the members would have been cast aside. No, nothing!

"There's a few tools over there. Strange those weren't . . ."

"Maybe they got out."

"Let's just keep looking." Sean refused to believe they had all been engulfed.

Unbeknown to Ben, his first explosion had diverted an underground stream, saturating the already unstable land above the swamp. The second explosion had brought the lot crashing down, and now exposed, the stream threaded its way through the rubble. As the ooze had slithered toward them, Ben and his family scrambled across another small stream and clutching at anything they could, climbed above the dislodged swamp, and from safety watched it slide past. Then, rather than climb higher, Ben realised it would be easier for them to aim for Cemetery Rd.

Immersed in bush they scrambled across the natural landscape, eventually reaching the road, sagged on to the grass verge and recovered their breaths. Further along the same road, yet out of sight, rescuers entered another property, and groped their way towards the landslide.

Kathy began to whimper again, and Priscilla cradled her, saying to her husband. "You'll never live this day down, Benjamin Chester! — *Never!*"

The way she spoke, he knew she was uncharacteristically livid, and he bit his lip, sucking in a remorseful breath. Little did he realise then, how he would never live the day down, or how significant the event would be for future generations of Chesters.

"Where is everybody, I wonder?" Priscilla demanded, expelling her breath in frustration. "I would have thought everyone would be here."

"Maybe, it wasn't . . ." No, it must have shaken the district, Ben believed.

Heaving themselves reluctantly to their feet, they walked up the road, past the Pollok school and church, and before turning into their own driveway, spied the lone figure of Ben's father, still peering into the valley far below.

"Hey, are you looking for us?" Ben yelled.

His father turned, although his family were too far away to see, his eyes opened wide in disbelief. "My God, Son!" he called. "How did you get up here?"

"Walked," Ben advised, as his father mounted and rode towards the survivors.

"So, you're the only one here?" Ben remarked. "Bit of a mess, Dad, I'm afraid."

Thomas Chester raised his hand as if to hit his son. "You young *fool!*"

"Eh? I . . ."

Priscilla looked up at the older man. "We are all safe, Father. Almost unscathed."

"That maybe so, Priscilla. At this moment your mother and your sister are preparing your home for your bodies." He dismounted and clambered on to a bank to see if he could view the valley. "Sean, and John and all the boys, are down there somewhere, risking life and limb searching for you." Shaking his head. "You can't see them from here." Then he instructed. "You, Priscilla, get down to the house, tell my wife you're all unhurt. You and I, Boy, had better try and stop the search parties." Then he thought of Danny, looked about for Danny's son, Douglas, and gathered he had must have run home to tell his mother about it. "Danny's gone for the doctor." He shook his head again. "No doubt he's half way here by now. A waste of time. He has better things to do today of all days to come out on false alarms."

Having had his say, leaving his opinion firmly on his son's mind, he got on his horse, and galloped the short distance to his viewing place. Ben ran after him, realising those below might just recognise him standing beside his father, who had already begun shouting, and waving his arms frantically at a rescuer in the valley. It must have worked because the person waved back, and his call to other rescuers carried by the breeze, faintly reaching Thomas, who then pointed to Ben, now beside him.

He did not get the chance to further harangue his son, because Danny returned, having found a phone, as he thought, at Te Toro.

"You're sure Prissy doesn't need a doctor?" Thomas said to his son. "If not, we'd better stop him."

"He can't be far off."

Only Thomas had the presence of mind to calculate just where on the road the doctor would be, and whether it would be possible to stop him. No, he decided, the now not required doctor would have to arrive, then be turned away again. The good man would insist on checking over the family: particularly Priscilla, who Thomas believed was worse for her experiences than she admitted.

Eventually they all gathered at Kanuka, including the doctor, and once the sobs of relief had subsided, the 'funny' side of the whole episode emerged, not that there was much to be funny over. From the gathering's initial depressed mood emerged a pre-New Year's party atmosphere, Priscilla hastily making some scones, while the men drank what remained of Ben's meagre beer supply, then accepted cups of tea.

Although being told not to, the children went off to explore the landslide nearest to the house, muddying their clothes further, and adding to their numerous scratches.

Danny made the first move to leave, saying, "Ben, give us a warning before you next blow the place up." He chuckled: something seldom heard: something they would never hear again!

Despite the day's disruption, the family re-gathered at Kowhai to see the old year out, and the new in. A few of the relieved rescuers and their families were last minute additions to the party.

Louise Chester was puzzled that Jane did not come across early, either to help out, or to bring her baking contribution. However she kept her concern to herself, and concentrating on other preparations put the matter to the back of her mind . . .

. . . Until Jane's son Douglas turned up before dark, saying to his grandmother, "Daddy sent me over by myself." Adding sadly, as if he sensed something was wrong, "Mummy isn't home yet."

"Oh," Louise questioned. "Did she go out?" Yet where would she go? Only here, to Kowhai. The occasions her daughters Jane and Alison had called on each other could be counted on one hand.

"Daddy doesn't know."

Louise gave the lad a fizzy drink, a fistful of sweets and led him to billiard room, where the boy sat on a chair and watched the pretty balls whiz about the table.

Within the hour the party had gathered full momentum, brushing aside the day's calamity. Even Thomas had relented, offering his son a drink, as if Ben was incapable of fetching his own. There was reason to be jubilant. Sheep farmers were riding on a wave, few troughs to upset their incomes, and Ben's decision to stock sheep had paid off. The price of wool had doubled since the turn of the century, although items of expense had not weighed down the debit side of their balance sheets. Even Danny was in the good books: both with his farming, and apparently with his wife, Jane. Where were they anyway? Another passing thought by the family over their non-appearance.

As the evening progressed Ben became morose, and settled at one end of a couch, beer going flat, barely saying a word to anyone. The loss of his horse did weigh heavily on his mind. There was something else disturbing him, and he could not put a finger on it.

Twice he got up, walked on to the veranda, and stared into the dark night: listening. No sound, no signals came back to him. On both occasions he returned to the lounge. He also seemed oblivious to his sister's non-appearance.

Louise was banging away on the piano, and missed having her elder daughter singing beside her. Still, it was early. Plenty of time for them to arrive.

Hoping to catch Louise in the kitchen, Danny stood at the back entrance, as if not allowed further. Only Alison was there. "Ali," he called softly.

"Danny!" Her surprise gave way to a frown.

He fidgeted uncomfortably. "Jane isn't here, is she?"

Alison first shook her head, then confirmed it with, "No. — For goodness sake, come in. We've been wondering where you two have got to." He was still hesitant. Apprehension overtook her, and in her expectant condition she needed a seat. To relieve that fear, and Danny's disappointment, she said, "Douglas is here, somewhere." She noticed Danny had not dressed for the occasion, so he did not expect his wife to be at Kowhai.

Thomas Chester seemed unaware of his daughter's absence. As midnight approached he looked at the year in retrospect. Four events on their side of the world captured at least local headlines: Captain Scott's tragic Antarctic journey: the fall of the Liberal Government after William Ferguson Massey's no confidence vote: the Waihi miners' strike that even had their wives and children marching in support: and the death of the Father of Auckland, Sir John Logan Campbell, who with John Brown, were the first Europeans to step ashore at Auckland. They established Brown and Campbell, which traded in just about everything. Campbell lived to see the first few huts expand to the isthmus city he had dreamed of. The city responded by forming the longest funeral procession in its short history, and he was laid to rest on the hill he donated to that city.

Alison was not concerned about such events. She was waiting for someone to mention her sister, and only moments after mid-night,

Louise said to her, "A very funny thing dear, Jane and Danny not coming. Do you think they had a tiff?"

Alison shook her head. "Mother, I should have told you, but Danny has been — hours ago — looking for Jane."

Louise believed something must have occurred. Possibly they had not fought. Possibly her daughter had just up and left for some deep-seated reason, although hardly in the middle of baking. "First of all, Danny, we shall have to see if she has taken any clothes," she suggested next morning.

"I didn't think to look." What he should have done, and not to have, made him feel even more ridiculous. He was, as his mother had so often said, stupid.

Alison had come across early, sensing there was more to Jane's non-appearance at the party than they thought the night before, was realistic. "Danny would not know what clothes Jane had."

Even so, mother and sister of the missing woman went with Danny back to his place to determine if Jane had left home, or — they dared not to think of the alternatives. They found the humble house as Danny had indicated.

Ben and Sean arrived, then began a search of the farm on horseback. Thomas rode through the gap to the beach, on some pretext his daughter might have gone there, perhaps to spend a quiet time on her own. To go there for an hour or two was one thing, not to willingly stay overnight. He looked along the coast for her. He dreaded what he might find as his horse sank into the soggy sand, and his glances out to sea viewed ominous clouds on the horizon. He also rode cautiously along the cliff track, seeking a sign she had walked that way, and either fallen, or had been carried away in a landslide: the unstable land continually tumbling into the sea hundreds of feet below.

At Kanuka Priscilla was in the midst of organising her two sons and Stanley to look for their Aunt Jane, although she expected they would discover all sorts of red herrings, when in drove a raving Jessica and supercilious Nigel, unaware of the search, only intent on claiming their almost dead son. Stanley, far from being almost dead, grumbled miserably when dragged away from this new adventure.

Louise took it upon herself to travel to Auckland. A summer thunderstorm left in its wake shredded clouds, shrouding higher hills on the peninsula and Waitakere Ranges across the narrow entrance of the harbour. A late afternoon tide meant the lady did not arrive at Onehunga until darkness had closed in. Most passengers were ashore before the boat tied up, Louise waiting for the gangway, too unsteady in body and soul to jump across the concertinaing gap. She rescued her baggage from a rough hand, walked along the cargo-strewn wharf and, with a heavy heart, trod the slope to the road.

Pockets of light glimmered in the night: fantasising aqueous eddies. Between infrequent gas lamps darkness was deep and damp. Someone stumbled and cursed. A face appeared in a flame: the bearded sailor lighting his pipe, then scurrying into his warren. Those comparatively few steps for a lady who had walked so far in her life urged Louise to contemplate terminating her journey for the day at the Manukau Hotel sited at the tram terminus. She thought better of it, on the grounds of the stories that abounded about such places, and the fact in a half an hour she could be at Emily's. As it happened the tram was still there.

"Hurry along, Lady, if you're boarding," the conductor called.

Louise urged herself faster. She thought herself a fit woman, yet that night she lacked both energy and drive. The conductor took her bag, while she hauled herself aboard, murmured, "Thank you," and made her way through the smoke to the front of the tram, where there was no smoking. For all their haste at getting off the boat, her fellow boat passengers were now fellow passengers again. Only a passing thought, interrupting what was most on her mind, locating Jane.

She was apprehensive as the car swayed as it rattled along, lurched to a stop, and with a clang moved off again in surges. She saw little of the suburbs they whizzed through, because now rain slanted across the windows. Late as it was, they jostled their way through Newmarket trundling slowly across junctions where other lines joined the journey to Auckland. Despite the driver's caution, the tram pole flicked off the overhead wire, and they were momentarily stranded in the middle of an intersection. Then she was in a panic. Which stop was Emily's? She did not know in the dark. She would hate to miss it, and have to trudge half way up Manukau (Parnell) Road: its hill too steep for a lady suddenly feeling her age.

She sought the conductor. He was with the driver. Anyone would tell her. Would the elderly man take her approach the wrong way? Surely not. "Excuse me, please?" she dared to enquire.

"Yes, ma'am." He was polite enough.

"I need to get out at the — is it Saint Stephens Avenue?"

The man reached up and stabbed a button. "You almost missed it," he said, as the tram skidded to a halt, the few passengers flung forward.

"Thank you so much," were Louise's words as she gathered her belongings, almost slipped as she alighted, and found herself on the footpath opposite the road she sought. The shower intensified, and she clutched her coat, pressed herself against the window of the weatherboard building. At least, she thought, it was not cold. As soon as it eased she hurried across the road, fearful of the traffic, such as it was, although far more than she ever experienced in Waiuku, and sought Emily's house: the one with the welcoming light shining from the front porch, its door ajar. She dragged herself up the steps, was about to knock, when a magic hand opened the door wide.

"Mrs Chester. — Oh my dear thing. What a positively ghastly night to be out," Emily greeted. "Here, give me that." She reached for the suitcase. "I was sure you would have not come tonight, otherwise I would have sent a cab for you."

"Of course not, Emily. I should have got the morning boat." She sighed, shoulders sagging. Her anxiety, her reason to be there, overflowed. "I have to find her, Emily, I have to."

Emily's concern was for Louise. "Anyway, you are safe and sound." She reached out, this time to embrace and offer comfort to the older woman. "It is far too late to do anything tonight, so let us get you into a hot bath, and then make plans for tomorrow."

"Emily, I don't expect you . . ."

"I must, Mrs Chester. I can only assure you I have not seen sight or sound of Jane. I only wish I had."

Despite that anxiety, Louise was pampered when Emily's maid ran a steaming hot bath with sweet smelling salts for her to relax in. As Emily said, they could do nothing that night, so she may as well try and relax in the bath. She would feel much better for it.

Almost an hour later when Louise sought Emily, and found her, in an office-cum-study, head down laboriously writing in what appeared to be an accounts book. She felt she should not disturb her. Emily sensed her presence and turned.

"There you are."

"Don't let me disturb you."

She placed the pen in the inkwell, and said. "These? — Nothing. I can do them any time. It serves me right for taking on so much."

"Do you do the accounts?" Louise thought they would have accountants.

"Yes, Mrs Chester, I do a lot of them. I trust myself. My husband has had people put things across him. He may be good at making money: regrettably he is even better at losing it." She gave a little chuckle. "That reminds me. One of Prissy's little investments turned out well, so I shall give you something for her."

One thing Louise had learned, largely through her daughter-in-law, Emily may be a shrewd businesswoman, however she was honest, and Ben and Priscilla had no qualms about leaving investments in her hands. If some did not turn out well, then that was luck of the draw, not misappropriation.

Emily rose, ushered Louise from the room, and into a small tastefully furnished drawing room: sort of ladies' room Louise gathered by its decor. She rang a bell, and said, "Now, I am sure you must be starving."

It seemed to Louise her own personal comfort was more important than the fact she was here to search for a missing daughter. "I suppose I had better have something. It is so late."

"My dear, meals are had at any hour in this house. However you are right. You just stay here. Would you like a paper to read? I shall see what we have in the larder."

Louise accepted the paper, thumbed through to the news items, and although only printed in minute type, with barely a heading, her eyes focussed on the story of her own missing daughter. And when she read it, she let the paper fall to her lap, tears rising to her eyes, because the paper told her, between the lines, what she refused to believe, the mystery of Jane's disappearance was stranger than fiction.

Since Louise had been expected, all Emily had to do was re-heat the steak and kidney pie her cook had prepared. When she brought it into the drawing room, she paused, placed the tray on a chair, and crossed to the weeping woman. "My dear, dear, Mrs Chester. Please, please, we are going to leave no stone unturned until we find her." Emily seldom used her standing in the community to her advantage. However this was one occasion she would. She would do anything to help this distressed woman, if for no other reason than in return of the hospitality Louise had always shown to her.

Concentrate as she must, Louise found that the bath had made her sleepy. It could not be weariness overtaking her in response to her overdoing it? She stifled a yawn, one that Emily saw, and said, "Mrs Chester, you pop off to bed, and have a well-earned good night's sleep." She shook her head. "We cannot do anything until the morning, so you shall be much better for it."

This was not mother advising daughter, rather a daughter-in-law advising a mother, and Louise, having only pecked at her food, admitted defeat. "I'll have it for breakfast, Emily," she promised, because she was not one for wasting food.

"We shall see," Emily said, although had other ideas.

Louise was pampered further, and although she desperately wanted to lie in bed and think, nature switched off her conscience, and she slept soundly. Overslept.

Breakfast — not the re-heated pie — brought to her in bed, by Emily. Louise could not recall the last occasion she had had breakfast in bed. The search of her memory was brief, because Emily was making suggestions of what they could do. "If she is in town we can try the hotels for a start. I suppose you do not know how much money — of course not."

"Emily, she hasn't taken a thing, other than what she stood up in."

There was no satisfaction for either of them, that day, or the next, as they poked and prodded: poked into obscure hotels and boarding houses, prodded peoples' memories. A telegram advised them that Jane had been sighted at Frankton Junction, near Hamilton. The sighting turned out to be a similarly poised lady called June Craig, who was due to be married the following week.

As Emily had first thought, searching for Jane in the city was futile.

Of an evening, with Douglas staying with Alison, Danny sat with head in hands, his slow-witted mind trying to determine why Jane had left him and not taken Douglas. She seemed to love her son, despite forever reprimanding him over some trivial incident. He himself was still in awe of her, and the subject of love for each other was rarely referred to. Nor were worldly events: only brief remarks concerning the farm, price of wool, or cost of sheep drench. Few people called on them, and there were no local shops for Jane to have met anyone else: only the school and church, and recently, the cream stand at Pollok. Jane's only contact the cows now was making cheese or butter, or taking excess down to the wharf, for shipping to Onehunga. Danny's mind, like others, was fixed on the idea she had on the spur of the moment run off, and no other reason for her disappearance stayed long enough in their heads to warrant investigation.

The police called and re-called on Danny, and the longer his wife remained missing the more their enquiry changed from missing, to foul play. They spoke to Thomas, made remarks like, 'It's strange Mrs Carsen should up and leave like that,' and, 'Mr Carsen doesn't seem the sort to — ah — retaliate. Although you never know.' Thomas caught the change in direction of the enquiry and reminded them, 'For all the time that afternoon he was within sight of me.' Their response, 'We do not know for sure what time she — ah — left home.' And, 'We have only her son's word she was baking after lunch. He cannot give us a precise time.' Their assertion lacked reason.

Unfortunately the line of enquiry got back to Danny, and despite his innocence, some believed he had been provoked into killing his wife both frightened and disturbed him. He never openly denied the allegations, because he could not get his mind round them. Whatever he did wrong, was surely through his own stupidity, so she should scold him. It was all so confusing, and his misery indicated his suffering.

January passed. School started again, and the troops ensured Douglas, now back at home, was collected every morning.

In the meantime the shearing had to be done, including Danny's. The wool baled, and sent off, and despite his despondency he had to see to this himself, with no Jane to assist. There was culling and drafting, Danny keeping a lot of the season's lambs to increase his stock, yet now there seemed little reason to.

Ben, on the other side of the hill, did the same, and only after those tasks had been done, did he again turn his attention to what he and nature had contrived. With a heart almost as heavy as Danny's, and he could not fathom why he found it so, he began clearing away the debris, more or less smoothed some of the rough patches left by the landslide, then haphazardly flung grass seed over it, hoping grazing animals and time would un-ruffle the quilted land.

He had the problem of the remnants of his swamp strewn across his neighbour's property. 'No use to me,' the neighbour had told him on more than one occasion. To his father Ben said, "I'll have to buy the land off him?"

The returns that year were handsome for Ben, so, although he did tighten his belt a little, he also paid off his father — it was not much — and bought the land: or at least gave the neighbour a worthwhile down payment, with promise of the balance the following year. Of the landslide between his homestead and the lower paddocks, Ben shored it up, then cut a new track across it, although suspected winter rains would make it hazardous until it fully settled and re-grown, if ever. He never felt at ease walking across the broken land, often involuntarily shuddering.

Danny decided to build a sheep race at the top of his property beside the road. It was as good a place as any, although its site was purely so he could communicate with passing travellers, on the off-chance one might have news of his wife.

There was the rivalry between her son George and her brother's son, Stanley. Although attending different schools they were at the same standard. Always Stanley came out on top, or near it. George on the other hand was being groomed for farming, and brains took second place to brawn. This year he surpassed himself, topped his class, when compared with other peninsula schools, and received higher overall marks than Stanley. Jessica declared, 'The teacher marked Stanley's class hard.' It did not lessen Priscilla's pride in her son. Unlike her sister-in-law she did not push George. Whatever he achieved was through his own efforts, with only a helping hand and encouragement from his parents.

Another rivalry began at that time: between two seven-year-olds: Priscilla's daughter Kathy, and Douglas, who retracted into himself, and seemed to spend most of his time quietly drawing, or studying, seldom coming out to play. Kathy was his yardstick, and whatever she achieved, he also achieved, despite having no mother, and a father whose intelligence had never aspired to the heights his lost wife had aimed for.

At her tender age Kathy strolled up her driveway, crossed the road — her chances of being run down by anything were zero — and slithered down Danny's steep drive to play with Douglas. On this occasion the two children sat together against a tree scribbling on their slates then erasing it.

"That's my daddy on a horse," Douglas showed his cousin.

Kathy grimaced critically. "It doesn't look anything like a horse."

"Does."

"Its legs are too short. Here, I'll show you." She snatched at the slate.

Douglas hauled it away, and pushed his cousin.

"Ouch! That hurt. I was only trying to show you."

"I can do it."

Kathy pouted as she watched Douglas add strokes to each of the horse's *five* legs.

"You can't count anyway."

"Can too."

Again Kathy snatched at the slate. "Look, – one – two – three – four – five, see?"

"I'll rub one out." Unfortunately, sliding the eraser up the page, he lost the entire drawing.

Kathy laughed.

Douglas again hit her — hard: the girl grazing her hand as she tried to stop her fall. "Ouch!" She began to cry, punched Douglas in response, scrambled to her feet blubbering, then shouted back at him. "I hate you!" She stumbled on a few paces, turned and yelled, "I'm glad your mummy's dead!"

"I hate you too."

"She fell over a cliff so she wouldn't have to live with you. You horrid thing."

Douglas stood up, started to chase her, then stopped, rubbing his eyes with balled fists, sobbing at the hurt she had inflicted.

Kathy stood where she was, then returned to her cousin. "I'm sorry. I didn't mean to say that."

"I don't want to see you anymore."

"I'm sorry."

Both children crying: Douglas turning to face the tree, Kathy walking up the path, wiping her hand across her eyes, then studying it for graze marks. She was disappointed they hardly showed, so he couldn't have hurt her much. He was still a nasty little boy though, and she hated him . . .

. . . Until the next day.

Thomas employed a farm hand, who found himself working on any one of four properties, although mostly Kowhai. Thomas himself took more than a passing interest in foreign affairs: those concerning Europe: incident after incident between bordering nations, and alliances that indirectly brought New Zealand into the frame through its relationship with England.

On the home front, when his farmhand, Bruce, suggested, "I think I'll bring the ewes over this side."

Thomas mildly questioned his decision, with. "A bit early, isn't it?"

"I think we're in for an early winter, Sir. There's quite chill in the air over there." He was referring to the seaward facing slopes for Kowhai.

"As you like. I'd hate to run short of hay over winter though." He was referring to overgrazing the valley.

"We've a good lot in. You never know, it might be an early spring as well as early winter."

CHAPTER ELEVEN

Brother and sister both lived the high life. The high life for Nigel Caldwell at Waiuku was hardly comparable to the high life of Emily Todd's environment.

Nevertheless the rural community did have its garden parties, and regular occasions when Jessica could attire her children in the finest of clothes. Not that her two eldest, Stanley and Penelope, appreciated being made a fuss of. The youngest, Nathan, was a chip off the old block. As for Stanley, as often as he could he made his way, on occasions without his parents' knowledge, to Kanuka.

On one occasion his Aunt Priscilla asked, "Does your mother know you're here?"

Stanley looked down, rubbed his bare toe across the floor, and mumbled, "I s'pose so."

"Oh my," Priscilla sighed. At times like this she wished they did have a telephone, now that some of the Pollok community had finally been linked telegraphically to the outside world. At least she could let his parents know where the lad was.

His parents would soon learn. They learnt at the tea table, when Jessica called them for the evening meal. "Now where has that brother of yours got to, Penelope?"

She flicked her head as if a melody was dancing inside. "I expect he's where he said he'd be."

"I see." Even Jessica could interpret that message.

The father of the house, and they knew it, dropped heavily into his seat, and uttered, "I'm not going after him this time."

"I will," Penelope offered.

"You shall do nothing of the sort," Nigel ordered.

She pouted.

Her younger brother piped up. "You'd get lost, and a bogey man will eat you all up, and that would make me laugh."

Very casually Penny scooped a slice of butter, supposedly for her potatoes, flicked it across the table, smacking Nathan in the middle of his cheek, the missile falling on to his new jacket. The Caldwell's dressed for dinner.

Their mother raised her hands in horror, intent on whipping her daughter's face. Washing Nathan's face was easy enough: the thought of his jacket being stained exasperated her. "Now look what you've done; you foolish child!"

"He deserved it."

"Penelope, go to your room, this instant!" was her father's solitary command.

"I'm not hungry anyway," the miscreant child murmured, as she obediently rose from the table. In fact she was starving. She would sneak something later. If Stanley had been home he would have brought her something. Not Nathan; she could die before he lifted a finger to help her.

Alison, gave birth to her third child, whom the couple called Jennifer. They might have called her Jane, after her missing aunt, because for all intents and purposes, when Louise, who had not attended the birth, first sighted Jennifer she believed the child was Jane reincarnated. She held her tongue, other than saying, "She looks well enough," then quickly diverted the subject to her daughter. "How are you, dear?"

"Fine, Mother. I feel fine."

"So, no complications?"

"None at all, Mother."

"Good."

Alison frowned. So unlike her mother to be curt. Perhaps she was tired, having looked after her two older children during Alison's confinement. She did not see any resemblance between her new child and her lost sister. After all, she was the younger, and was not around at Jane's birth.

Louise excused herself, returned home, and sent Alison's two out to play, "Go and look for your grandfather," she instructed them. She felt the need to lie down, something she never did during the day. She shut her bedroom door, then lay on her bed, weary: very weary, as if the incidental troubles over many years had accumulated, and now burdened her. She knew those troubles were nothing, compared with what she had just seen.

When her husband returned to the homestead, Alison's two tagging along, he discovered the kitchen empty: no sign of an evening meal being prepared. "Come along, let's go and find grandma."

If she was not the lounge, she must still be at her daughter's. Something must be wrong over there. "You two stay here awhile. Play with the blocks, or something; your doll, Adrienne."

Thomas first went to his — and his wife's bedroom — to change, and discovered the prone woman, and his body went cold: apprehension gripping him.

She stirred at his entry.

"Louise?" And he sighed with only slight relief.

"I'm sorry." She shook her head, tears glistening in her eyes. "Thomas, can you manage. I — I just . . ."

"Of course we can. — But . . ?"

"Don't ask, dear, just don't." As mothers did, she softly issued him instructions where he would find what. They could live for weeks on what was always available in the pantry. There were leftovers, homemade biscuits and certainly pickled pork and jars of preserved fruit.

When next morning Louise was still listless, Thomas called the doctor, thankful they *did* now have a telephone, and although Louise believed her condition was not a physical disorder, she was glad to have him call, although only if he were coming out their way. For Louise, the doctor would make any necessary detour.

"There's nothing really wrong with me," she told him, then explained her feelings on sighting Jennifer.

His response. "I naturally do not believe in re-incarnation myself, yet if you say the resemblance is striking, then remember Alison and Jane were — are sis . . ."

"Yes, Doctor — *were*. I know it now."

"My dear, let us just pray it is still 'are', and the resemblance is as I say."

"Why Jennifer? Why not Adrienne? She certainly does not look like Jane."

"No, however she does take after her mother."

And Louise had to chuckle. Adrienne was certainly her mother over again.

Even so, Louise took an inordinately long time to recover from her shock, and found it very hard indeed to hold the newborn child. She was angry with herself for having such qualms about Jennifer, and hoped in time she could treat her with the same fondness as her other grandchildren.

Late that year Emily Todd, her husband, who looked even more like her father, and Jonathon crossed to Melbourne for the Cup. Emily, unknown to her family, while there, was keeping an eye out for Jane. Melbourne was considerably bigger than Auckland, and the chances of running into her were remote. If she were there, then she was bound to attend Flemington, and so were fifty thousand other people!

At least Emily, her gambling streak frequently favouring her, did back *Posinatus,* which indicated she also had knowledge of the sport. She coaxed her husband to place a bet on the horse.

Together they cheered *Posinatus* to victory, turned to congratulate each other, and William collapsed!

"Will! — Will!" Emily dropped to his side, while those around ignored the incident until the winner was confirmed. "Please get a doctor, someone," she pleaded.

"Doctor! — Is there a doctor about?" a voice cried.

Where would a doctor be at a time like this? Probably beating it to the bookie to collect his winnings. As for Jonathon, he gaped with the crowd. Emily glanced up at the stupefied faces, her glare meeting *Jane's!* "Oh, thank God . . ." The vision vanished.

On his eventual arrival, the doctor pronounced William Todd to be dead. His widow choked back tears, maintained a courageous disposition as William was removed from the racecourse, then she had the unenviable task of arranging the transport and burial of his body.

To complicate matters Auckland's waterfront was in the midst of a strike, delaying the unloading of Will's body. In fact fourteen unions between them had brought the city to a standstill, and apparently if newspaper subscribers wanted to know what was happing they had to go to the point of publication, since newsboys were also on strike. Emily was unconcerned over the issue for the time being.

To a shipping official she personally demanded, "Can no one row out to the blasted boat and get it? Or do have to do even that much for myself?"

"Madam, I can assure you everything has to be done as regard to your . . ."

"Don't give me such twaddle. Does my husband have to rise from the dead, walk across water, so I can bury him?"

The official swallowed. He did not know of Will Todd. As for his widow, he *did* have visions of her rowing out to the steamer, humping the man's body down the ship's ladder and rowing ashore with him, despite a British warship having its guns trained on the city. Such an occurrence would make him a laughing stock. "I shall have your late husband brought ashore first thing in the morning, madam."

"Any later, Sir, and he shall be late for his own funeral!" With that, she stormed from the office.

Emily achieved some measure of what 'Massey's Cossacks' (strike breaking mounted police) had not so far achieved, and Will Todd made it to his own funeral. Out of respect, Emily had him buried beside his first wife. Why? When questioned, she just shrugged. To Will, she had been a wife in name only. And she could not imagine, in some distant future she hoped, being buried beside him.

Nor did she mope about mourning his loss. To his son, she advised, "Your father's interests as you know, Jonathon, were wide and varied, and I am going to make sure no one thinks they can pull the wool over my eyes."

"Yes — ah — Mother." He still found it difficult to call her mother, and, although he considered himself old enough to handle his own affairs, he did agree Emily was the best person to manage their inheritance.

Emily discovered while she was untangling one complicated arrangement, another was tangling. Plus, several of the businesses were strike-bound. She did need help. Whom could she trust? A phone call to Kowhai resulted in her inviting herself to the valley: a few days respite was just what she needed.

Since Emily was not intending to indulge in any social life at Kowhai, she packed lightly, and journeyed, as most did, by tram to Onehunga, baggage and all, by boat across the Manukau to Pollok, there being met by Ben, who took her directly to the farm. As the horse trotted up the hill from the wharf, Emily breathed in deeply, sighed, laid her head momentarily on his shoulder, and admitted, "Ben, I *do* envy you living out here."

"Mm." He shrugged. "I sometimes envy you, in the city."

"Oh, why?"

He did not tell her exactly when he began to lose interest in farming, instead simply replied, "It's all work and no play — farming."

"Ben, how could you say that?" She gave a polite wave to a passing farmer taking empty cream cans back to his property, since he had his own separator, and only sold his cream. "Would you rather work all hours in an office, and never see daylight?"

"No, I suppose not."

"So, count your blessings."

Emily raised another subject: to do with farming, and it was as if, although her interests were city-based, she had knowledge of rural economies as well. "I did not realise until going through Will's documents that he ships out your wool."

"Our wool?"

"Not necessarily yours, but wool. He actually owns — or seems to own — a trading company: a sort of agency that handles meat and wool out of Auckland. It's a lucrative business too. I presume I own it now."

"I suppose he made more out of it than we do." Ben looked across at Emily, wondering if her fabulous clothes came from the profits her late husband made from being an agent. It seemed himself and his fellow farmers did all the work, while Will Todd and his lot merely arranged shipments — five minutes work according to farmers — and made a fortune.

"I don't think so, Ben. The margins he worked with were tight. I think it was the sheer bulk of what we export made it profitable." Emily knew she had touched a raw nerve, so diverted the subject again. "This despicable strike has thrown everything into chaos. I really feel sorry for you chaps. When did you ever hear of farmers going on strike? Surely no one works under more atrocious conditions than you?" She hoped she had made amends by asserting that truth.

"Not me so much, Em, but cow cockies have no respite. That's why I chose sheep. At least I don't have to get up at five o'clock every morning to milk the blasted things."

They trotted past the church and school, then down Kanuka's drive for Emily to at least say 'hello' to Priscilla, and remark how fast George and James were growing.

"Where would Kathy be?" she asked.

"Probably over with Douglas. You might find her at Kowhai if not." Priscilla was unconcerned over her young daughter's whereabouts. It wasn't neglect, rather trust: knowing she would be safe, wherever she was.

Ben drove Emily over the ridge to Kowhai, where he discovered both Kathy and Douglas in the kitchen with their grandmother. He deposited Emily there, and fetched his daughter home.

Emily immediately became immersed in Kowhai's charm. Relaxing in an armchair, cup of tea in her hand, she said to Thomas and Louise, "My darlings, I have not come here for a holiday — just a short rest. I need your help?" Emily was never one for beating about the bush.

Louise frowned. How could they possibly help her?

Thomas also frowned, looked across at the elegant woman, and also thought, how could he, a farmer, help whom he knew to be an astute businesswoman? Looking at her now, listening to her, he observed how she had changed over the years, and imagined, if need be she would still get herself tangled up in a canvas marquee, as she had done at Ben's wedding.

"I need someone I can trust." She took a sip of tea, breathed in and out, as if to relax further, then explained, "As fast as I sort out one of Will's messes, another crops up, and I am left wondering how much I have lost in the meantime."

"Emily, what do I know about companies?"

Emily pouted. "It is not so much what you know . . ." And for the life of her she did not know whether to call him Mr Chester, or Thomas, if they were to become partners. ". . . It is not what you know, rather what they *think* you know."

Louise shook her head. "Sounds like an old head on young shoulders to me."

Thomas did not bother to ask why the lady did not seek her own banker brother's help. "This must surely mean me coming to Auckland?"

"Of course; all expenses paid. In fact I would expect both of you to stay with me."

"And what about here?" Thomas reminded her.

"I am sure three able-bodied men can look after four farms."

"There is no dissuading you, is there, my dear," Louise opined. "So, it is over to you, Thomas?"

"I hope I can meet your expectations."

Emily rose from the chair, crossed to Thomas, and kissed his forehead, as gracious an action as his wife had seen. Any wonder she had many admirers. She did believe that even her husband at that moment was taken aback. Louise's thoughts were cut short when Emily turned to her, bent down, almost knelt, and kissed her on each cheek. "It is a weight off my shoulders already. And I am sure life for all of us will not be all work and no play."

No mention was made of remuneration, and Thomas genuinely thought his reward was helping out the family. Emily had other ideas. Those she would keep to herself, at least until the matter of payment for services rendered was raised.

Emily managed to acquire a new admirer during her short stay.

"She's certainly taken to you," Louise said, as a kitten again leapt on to Emily's lap.

"You are beautiful," Emily cooed, allowing the cat to muzzle her. "Beautiful. — Beautiful. — Beautiful."

"If you think so much of her, dear," Louise suggested, "you may as well take her home with you."

"Can I?"

"Of course. We've got enough cats around here, and I'm sure she is going to a good home."

Emily wondered whether her new cat would adopt the same principles as her Kit, which had died a year previously, and leap on to her bed each morning. Unlike Kit, this new kitten would not have to share her affection with her late husband.

Emily did question her own judgement in having Thomas come to her aid. As he had said, there were very capable professional people. Maybe she viewed the Chesters as family: much more so than her own brother, and she knew whatever Thomas did, for better or worse — which sounded like a marriage vow — his judgement would be honest.

Emily rested for a just three days, spending time at Kanuka, also with Alison, and crossing to Danny's place, preparing a meal for him and Douglas, not arriving back at Kowhai until late that night.

"He is a sad, sad man," was her only remark to Louise next morning.

They and the kitten crossed the Manukau, Emily having arranged for a motor cab to transport them and their luggage from Onehunga to her place.

"Every time I come across," Louise said, "the place has changed."

"Mm," Emily agreed. "And I am sure it will change a lot more during our life time."

The couple found Emily the perfect host, and, as good as businesswoman as they had first supposed.

"William did leave a lot of loose ends," Thomas confirmed.

"I thought I knew most of his affairs, however . . ." She shook her head. ". . . I have never heard of this company."

It was one of Will's many excursions into companies of dubious character.

They had no sooner arrived in the city, than Emily had to attend a formal function. The invitation to the opening of the Auckland Exhibition had been for Emily and Will. It was now for Emily and Thomas, with a space made available at the banquet for Louise. Emily was not without influence on such occasions. The opening went ahead despite the industrial trouble, with the Federation of Labour and the Farmers Union at the forefront of move to improve working conditions and wages.

The excuse from Louise, 'I haven't anything to wear,' was promptly answered by Emily sweeping her into Smith and Caughey's, and emerging with a gown Louise feared she would wear just once.

"I trust not," Emily argued.

Most women in mourning would have worn black. Such austerity by Emily would have been dishonest — to Will. If ladies of society were not yet accustomed to her ways, they would learn on that day. She wore a fabulous flowing outfit of lilac and mauve. The lilac rounded-neck silk blouse had pleats below her generous bust. A frilly jacket, with wide lapels and frilled half-sleeves, a broad band round her slender waist, and an urn-shaped mauve skirt: folds cascading to the hem. On her head, appropriately enough, a lilac coloured floral-topped merry widow hat.

Needless to say Louise's dress was not so flamboyant. She was humbly introduced to the city's mayor, James Parr, while Thomas greeted him with no more formality than a doorman: a manner that prompted the mayor to converse with the farmer, unaccustomed as he was to such indifference.

"I believe you are assisting Em — Mrs Todd with her . . ."

"Yes, to make sure none of you city slickers put one across her."

"Mr Chester, it is most unlikely anyone could ever, as you say, put one across Mrs Todd." Abruptly changing the subject, he enquired, "I believe you have quite a lot of land yourself?"

"I did have. My sons have most of it now. I have to watch them every minute, in case they go overboard, get themselves into debt, and all that nonsense."

"Surely . . ."

"You'd be a wise man to follow the same path with the city's finances."

And that was telling the man precisely what he thought, long before Auckland had any debt to worry about. No, Thomas and high society did not mix. It did not stop Louise having a thoroughly good time: being introduced to so many ladies, all except one or two names passing straight out of her head. She was also amazed how Emily could hold her own conversationally with both the women and men fully a generation older than herself.

A week or so later while reading a *Herald* Thomas said, "I see, Emily, Parnell is now part of Auckland."

"Yes. I don't know whether it is a good thing or not." She grimaced with indecision. "Perhaps we were too small to be on our own. No doubt time will tell." Due to other more personal issues, this was one debate Emily had not entered into.

As December came to its festive season, she suggested, "We should have a celebration here."

"Emily, you are supposed to be in mourning," Louise admonished, and at the same time relented. "I don't suppose we shall be missed too much at Kowhai."

"Kowhai can come to us," Emily decided.

"All of them? Can you imagine it?"

"No, I suppose not. Perhaps just my darling sister, and that husband of hers."

Louise said softly, "I think, Emily dearest, you are forgetting, New Year's eve . . ."

"Mrs Chester, I am *so* sorry." Emily sighed despondently, more distressed over the first anniversary of Jane's disappearance, than her own recent loss.

"Still, it — oh — Emily, why not? I'm sure Ben and Prissy would love to have Christmas here." Louise thought if they withheld celebrations this year because Jane's disappearance, would they continue to do it every year afterward? It would hardly be fair on the children. A toast to absent friends would be sufficient.

Louise, with the help of Emily's two servants, began preparing for a Christmas away from home. By now she was getting used to gas and electricity, and wondered whether when she returned to her own home would she lament not having either at her immediate service?

Thomas was sitting commandingly at Emily's desk, while she was sitting opposite him, like a modern day secretary. "My dear," Thomas began, "I think we had better sell off a lot of these bits and pieces of Will's . . ."

"I could not agree more."

"We might be selling a winner, then we might also be selling a loser. However, Emily, you will not lose out if you put that money into land around the perimeter of the city."

She nodded. "Any particular area, Thomas?" While she called his wife, 'Mrs,' she had finally settled on 'Thomas' for her husband: as a business partner.

He expressed his foresight. "You can pay higher prices for land on its edges, or look at a longer term — like about ten years . . ."

"I shall be an old . . ."

"You'll still be in the prime of life in *twenty* years from now, Emily, let alone ten."

"Thank you. You are so sweet." And even he could not help but be affected by her appreciative smile.

"You don't need any more money than you've got right now, so ten years out — or further — is a good strategy." He picked up a sheaf of hand-written papers: notes he had made about the state of Will Todd's affairs. "Sell off parcels of land when the price has peaked, Emily, and you can't go wrong."

"We shall drink to that," she said in her precise manner. And she did! Crossing to a small cabinet — the larger was in the lounge — and pouring both whiskeys. "Water?"

"Thanks."

Seven days before Christmas Emily gave her employees an interim wage rise of two shillings per week: equivalent to about a five percent increase.

Six days before Christmas a tree arrived, and that occupied Louise for some time — decorating it.

Three days before Christmas Emily's sister, Priscilla, Ben and their children rolled in.

After the sisters embraced, Priscilla said, "It is so good of you to have us, especially . . ."

"Especially nothing, Prissy." And she kissed her again. "Life is too short to mope about. Besides, Thomas and I have been too busy to think of the past. We have enough on our plate thinking of the future — including yours."

"Oh?"

"My darling, we have reinvested your money — or going to. You shall be quite rich in your old age."

"That long." Then she saddened. "Mind you, with one thing and another, I have felt ten years older just this last year."

"I know." She sighed. "It has not been a very good year. Still, darling, let us try and be happy." She did not add to her sister's burdens by telling her what Thomas had prophesised over the simmering European scene.

Emily's kitten, now officially named Jet, because it was black and Emily believed cats only learned short words. Anyway Jet spent most time under or on Emily's bed, emerging only for a meal, or to go outside, and now decided Priscilla's lap was as good as any.

There were people, who shall remain nameless, living in Waiuku, who were abhorred by the thought Emily had thrown open her husband's — late husband's — home to all and sundry. Priscilla was not sure if she was the 'all' or the 'sundry'? Her brother might have been a self-styled big shot in Waiuku. Emily, even by comparison of populations, was a much bigger shot in Auckland.

Leaving Thomas perusing financial papers, Ben perusing newspapers, grimacing at a full-page ad for Cadillac cars from Dexter and Crozier, or Canadian style all-wool ladies and children's bathing costumes, Emily took the ladies and her nephews and niece to town, and they shopped until they dropped. For a treat they lunched in an exquisite tearoom, with its dark panelled walls, electric fans hanging from the ceiling, live rubber plants, and dainty black-attired waitresses with their white pinnies and bonnets. Eleven-year-old George got a crush on one, who was no more than a few years older than himself, but looked so much more mature.

While the cat's away, the mice will play. It was not quite like that. Ben soon tired of reading the paper, while his father was as immersed as ever in Emily's affairs. To Thomas it was like a cryptic crossword, and each time he got the right answer he marked it off. Except this crossword did not have a set number of clues, and as fast as he got one right, another was added to the total to get right. Anyway, it was all beyond Ben, so he walked to Parnell, and sauntered down the shopping street. He was not intending to shop, not even to get something for his wife. She usually bought and wrapped her own present, and *he* was the one who got the surprise when she opened it.

"Hello," a softly spoken lady said, as if she knew him, although was not sure.

"Hello," Ben replied out of courtesy, tipping his hat.

"Ah — no — I suppose not." The lady seemed embarrassed as Ben shook his head. "I thought for a moment you were the man I sold my sheep to."

"Of course! How are you?" His whole countenance brightened, although he had not seen or heard of the lady since that day.

"I am very — ah — I'm sorry, I've forgotten your name."

"Not my face, obviously. Ben Chester, and I must admit I've forgotten yours." He would not have recognised her, since her appearance now was so different.

"You should not have. It is the same as your sister — remember — Alison Mackenzie."

"Of course." So, standing outside a shop they began a conversation, neither indicating they must get away. Ben for once in his life had nothing to do. Alison, he got the impression, wanted someone to talk to, someone she could relate to, not that he understood much about human relations and needs.

They went through their health, their respective families, why they were both in Parnell at the same time, until Alison suggested, "Perhaps I could treat you to morning tea?"

"I don't know about treating me."

"It would be a treat for me to take tea with you, Mr Chester. . ."

"Ben," he suggested.

She smiled, her cheeks flushing further. "Ben." She became inexplicably excited over the prospect of taking tea with Ben, and could not recall another man, other than her late husband, having such an effect on her.

By now he had recalled many of his earlier thoughts of her.

Alison looked at her watch. "Actually, it's closer to lunch time, ah — if we could change the order."

"I guess I could. It must be the city — it makes me hungry." It could have been he ate more here, because he did not have much else to occupy his mind.

As they sat themselves in the tearoom — about the only one in Parnell, and lucky to have customers — Ben wondered, then asked why she had not remarried.

"Ben," she replied, reaching out with her now gloveless hand and touching his: a gesture that sent a thrill through his body, and he thought of Priscilla, wondering why his wife's touch did not thrill him. Perhaps it was familiarity. He missed part of her answer. ". . . My chances. What with the children I just haven't really wanted to. They are older now, so . . ." She grimaced. ". . . Maybe, one day."

While his wife was having a rather noisy lunch with her family, Ben was having what turned out to be an intimate lunch with a lady he had done business with ten years earlier. In truth, the lady who thought it intimate. Ben did not know the meaning of the word. Nor was he up in etiquette; not that he was an embarrassment, just out of his league. Difficult enough for him to drink tea out of a china cup, let alone determine which knife was for what, especially when the waitress — about the same age as the one his son was googoo over — changed the eating utensils, because he had opted for fish, which was apparently eaten with a different knife than steak.

Nor did he conceal his ignorance. "I'm afraid I'm just as likely to have my dessert off the same plate as my main course — if Priscilla's not looking." He had to be honest and defend his wife, although he knew some people did not use two plates when one would suffice.

"Ben, don't for one moment think I'm accustomed to this either. It is awfully nice, thank you." She could not think of more pleasant company. A rough-hewn farmer maybe, although a most courteous one, and she felt envious of his wife. She hoped the lady appreciated the fine gentleman he was.

All too soon it was over, Alison insisting it was her treat, and time to part. Would another ten years go by before they met again? She hoped not. "Thank you for a most pleasant lunch, Ben." As she put on her gloves, tears came to her eyes. "I have never forgotten you — your name maybe — although not what you did for me then."

"It was just business."

"It was — decency; a man not taking advantage of a vulnerable woman."

Ben felt uncomfortable. He had the urge to repeat his invitation of all those years before for her to come to Kowhai. Now the situation was different. It was certainly different at his place.

Alison had the urge to suggest when he was next in town they could again have lunch. She now knew his ventures into the city were few and far between, and anything could happen between now, and whenever he next came to town.

Outside the tearoom they lingered, each not wishing to have the last word, until Ben finally said, "I'm sure we'll meet again."

She smiled. "Till then, Ben. Goodbye."

He nodded, replaced his hat, and slowly walked back up the street. He had the inclination to turn and look back at her, but dismissed that as being silly. Alison had the same inclination.

A long, thoughtful afternoon for Ben. At almost five o'clock the peace was broken by an eruption of activity as his family and Emily returned, and scattered their bagged, not yet wrapped, presents all over the place.

Perhaps the saddest thought for Emily that Christmas was not mourning the loss of her husband, rather regretting she had no children of her own to fuss over. As usual she disguised her disappointment and made the most of fussing over her sister's children.

Kathy received an exquisitely painted china doll with four sets of clothes to dress her. George and James got fishing rods. And they all received clothes. Emily bought her sister an expensive tea set: for special occasions. It would be rarely used in her household. As for getting Emily something? What do you get for a woman who has everything? They pooled their resources and presented her with a set of miniature paintings of local scenes.

Next day, Friday as it happened, was Boxing Day, and being brilliantly fine, they trouped to the Ellerslie races: they and almost *forty thousand* other Aucklanders, about a third of the city's population. They passed through the new Greenlane entrance, could barely hear the Garrison Band playing beneath the trees, or admire the resplendent flower gardens, and arrived in time to place bets on the second race: the Great Northern Foal Stakes.

By now the queues at the world's first automatic totalisator, installed earlier that year, were long. However Ben waited his turn, and watched fascinated as the attendant accepted his bet, and placed a ticket into the machine pulled on one of thirty pump handles, and by a complicated system if weights and pulleys, the ticket was printed, and the bet recorded so the odds on each horse were tallied up. Ben had five bets to make for himself, Emily and his father, and began to wonder if the race would be run before he had placed the last bet, and expected to be told to get a move on from the man behind him.

Making his way into the crowded stand Emily edged closer to Louise to make room for him.

Several minutes later the favourite Hyettus set the pace for the six-furlong event. For someone supposedly in mourning Emily yelled as loud as anyone as *Recontre* challenged the leader, to win by two lengths from Troy, with *Hyettus* another three lengths back.

"Not bad, Ben," she said. "A win and a third."

"You certainly know your horses, Emily," Louise congratulated.

Louise herself was content to watch the passing parade: if not the horses, then the fashionable ladies and gentlemen who charmed the course with their presence. Where she was sitting they *were* ladies and gentlemen. Elsewhere there were many lesser mortals, who in truth did not have the money to spend on horses. Most men wore suits and hats, and the women's dresses that scraped the earth, and the only difference between rich and poor was the cut and state of repair of their clothes, until they spoke, then their education was obvious. She also enjoyed listening to the Auckland Mounted Rifles Band playing in front of the grandstand, although often the music was lost amid the chatter of race-goers.

They took lunch at the kiosk, and were lucky to find a seat: Ben and Thomas standing, and juggling cups and sandwiches and savouries.

Early in the afternoon they all waited expectantly for the feature race: The Auckland Cup: one of the great races of the Southern Hemisphere. Thomas had been cautious and put his money on the favourite, while Emily and Ben had a bet on the favourite and a lesser horse. *Jolie Folie* led them out, and at the cutting it was two-and-a-half lengths clear.

"It can't keep that pace up," Thomas told Emily.

"I hope it doesn't," she responded.

As they thundered past the stands for the first time, kicking up dust from the dry turf, *Jolie Folie* was still clear. The noise ear-splitting. Not the horses, the spectators urging their bets on. Round the back again, and still that horse led, and finally they turned for home on the clockwise track, with the crowd on their feet barracking the bunching horses. They galloped past the tiring *Jolie Folie,* and barely emerging from the bunch the favourite *Sir Solo* came home, just three-quarters of a length clear in a time of three minutes, twenty-nine and two-fifths seconds for the two-mile event.

"So, we get something back for our money," Thomas said.

Emily with a hint of sarcasm suggested, "Hardly worth fighting the hordes to collect."

Ben looked at her askance. He had often looked at her that day. Indeed over the last few days. And, ironically, he felt a little sorry for her. He was certainly enjoying his stay in Auckland, although thought Emily might be putting up a good front on their behalf. He did wonder how long she would remain a widow? For surely there must be many men who would love to share their life with such a beautiful and worldly woman.

CHAPTER TWELVE

Someone had been assassinated In Europe. Few on the Awhitu Peninsula observed the precise details. After all, lambing was near, and if some silly ass decided to pop off a couple of dignitaries in a faraway place, then they did not deserve to get a hearing. And what was to it New Zealand, anyway?

"No — Ben — no!" Thomas Chester contradicted his son. "This *is* important. It's not that Arch-Duke Ferdinand and his wife have been shot. It is another atrocity creating a cauldron in Europe."

"It's still nothing to do with us," Ben dismissed.

"It is, if it brings England into it."

"Let's know if I've got to buy a rifle." About as much as Ben knew about warfare.

Countries whose sovereigns were related, whose statesmen were comrades, whose bordering populations mingled, now turned gladiators. And Europe was the chosen arena. The populous lands surrounding this pit would be drained of manpower before this bloody encounter ended. And all for nothing!

As well the Chesters celebrated the previous Christmas, because there was nothing to celebrate the next one. Ironically, it *was* celebrated, not only in New Zealand, but in the very spheres of warfare, when soldiers laid down their arms, no doubt to the annoyance of the war conveners, and being Christians they celebrated the occasion, to the extent of in places crossing to opposing lines. Next day they obediently took up their arms again and slaughtered each other. They did not hate the people they were fighting. In fact they had less to fight over than schoolboys. Their minds were propagandised with the glory of battle, so they obeyed whatever was asked of them without question or reason. Like sheep following one another they were driven over the brink and plunged into pitch battle. Such human sacrifice would soon rid the world of men who in future years could have served their countries on much more useful grounds.

In New Zealand the call went up for food. Volunteers were sufficient to fill battle lines, and farmers must produce more food to fill their stomachs, and wool to keep the allied army warm. Not all that was produced reached its destination: much going down with torpedoed ships.

Eight months elapsed before the European conflagration penetrated New Zealand. The flames did not reach that far, although the smoke did: smoke in the manner of letters sent home by troops pinned down on the cliffs of what would be known as Anzac Cove, Gallipoli: a torn strip hanging off the Turkish mainland. Daily bulletins informed relatives of the fate of their loved ones. They could only imagine what it was like. Reality was far worse.

"So, you have enlisted, Bruce," acknowledged Thomas Chester.

"Yes, Sir."

"You realise of course your work here is just as important as on the front."

The young man toyed the earth with his shoe, looking down at the land that had been so good to him. Much as he loved working it, he now believed he must fight for it. How could he explain those feelings to someone so opposed to warfare? "Sir, beg your pardon for my impudence, you could come out of retirement, and — be a farmer again . . ."

"I did not think I had ever retired. However, go on."

"Sorry, Sir. You can't be expected to go to war." He did have more to say, but thought he had said enough.

"Yes, young man, I can still put in a good day's work here, however the day you return, you come back here."

"I will, Sir." Then it depended how long he was away for. Too long, and he imagined that his shoes would be filled by one of Ben's boys.

So Bruce, and other local boys, was given a send-off. All over the peninsula during the next months — and years — young men left the safety of farming for the perils of war.

Ben Chester noticed his son enjoying a moment's play with a dog, flinging a stick across the yard for the dog to fetch and lay at his feet. He was unsure whether to disturb him then, or wait until later. In fact he wasn't at all sure if he should ask this — what was on his mind — of his son.

"That's enough, Tag," George said, and withheld the stick, the dog looking plaintively up at him in anticipation, its tail wagging vigorously. "No more." And he put the stick behind his back, the dog immediately scampering round to retrieve it.

"Son," Ben called.

"Yes, Father."

"Son." He had started, so he might as well go on, although looked for an interruption, by the way of his wife or another child arriving on the scene. "You're a bright lad . . ."

"Thank you, Father."

"Yes, I suppose you realise how much extra burden this blasted war has put on farmers." ('Just get on with it,' he chided himself.) "Take my clip. It might all end up in the bottom of the ocean."

"That would be terrible, Father."

Ben raised his eyebrows. "Let's hope it doesn't." He thought, 'It might also end up on soldiers' backs, and be buried with them before it has been worn in, let alone worn out.' He said, "Even so, the more we produce, the more that will reach England."

"Mm." George was now sitting on the back step, looking down at the circle he was drawing in the dust.

"Son, I'm asking you to do a bit — sort of play your part . . ."

"Go to war?"

"Of course *not!*" He knew in some countries children as young as his son, were armed with rifles, fighting for their own innocent lives. "No, what I am asking, you spend your weekends at Kowhai, helping your grandfather . . ."

"Um, Father." The boy breathed a sigh of relief. "I thought you were going to send me off to boarding school, or something as horrid. You see, Father, I was just thinking how I'd tell you — I've already asked grandpa if he'd like me to help him."

Ben swallowed. "I see." What more could he say, except, "I'm jolly proud of you, lad."

"And Stanley is going to help me help grandpa."

Ben swallowed again. He could not imagine Stanley obeying orders from George, yet he could imagine Nigel's wayward son — in as much as he had no commercial interests — obeying orders from Thomas.

So, it was done. Why had he procrastinated in the first place? He should have known his son better. That evening he mentioned it to his wife. "I suppose you know of George's offer to my father?"

"Yes, dear, and of Stanley." Priscilla gave an amused pout. "It should be quite interesting. I can imagine what my brother is thinking right now. Stanley says he will ride up after school on Fridays."

"All worked out between them, eh."

"Something like that, dear."

And so it was throughout the land: the oldest and youngest generations manning the farms, while many of the middle generation went to war, a lot never to return.

Thomas had the opportunity to buy the land north of Danny's. That would mean going into debt, and he was not going to do that, certainly not at his time of life, even though circumstances were positive, farms profitable. Danny had also been interested in the land. He had other ideas. The property passed into undisclosed hands, and a man as old as Thomas, and a young lad, too young to fight, managed the rugged farm. Their efforts in vain, or the new owner had overburdened himself, and the property was again put up for sale, although there seemed no interest in it.

Before then came another bombshell: the reason why Danny had not been interested in the land. As solemn as always, he entered the back door of Kowhai, not because he was not permitted through the front door, rather he knew he was most likely to catch his mother-in-law either in the kitchen or washhouse. "Mrs Chester," he said almost enquiringly, although before she could say anything, he murmured, "I — I have enlisted."

She shook her head, as if not hearing right. "No, Danny!" Still shaking her head. "You can't." He nodded, so she questioned, "Without even discussing it with us? We need you here."

He also shook his head, and explained in his slow stumbling manner, "There is talk of con — conscrip — tion . . ."

"I know, but that is . . ."

"One day — Mrs Chester — one of us will have to go. And, I've got the least — ah. — I'd like to have a go at them."

"Who is to look after your place?"

"Excuse my — ah — I — I reckon with George and Stanley helping, and James — you could manage." The tears of gratitude were glistening in Louise's eyes. "Mrs Chester — would — would it be too much to ask if Douglas . . ."

Louise's head was shaking, not in refusal, rather in acceptance. "Of course Douglas can live here, if — only if — Danny, it is what you *have* to do." She knew there was more to his decision than going to war. For all their ups and downs, he had deeply loved her daughter Jane. And once again, as so often even after more than two years, Jane came to mind. The pain of her loss, although still there, was not as great now. Louise laid her hand on Danny's arm, and whispered. "You are a good man, Danny, a very good man."

He also had tears in his eyes, turned as if embarrassed, and said as he went out the door, "I'd better get back," as if his life was still dominated by Jane's demands.

"You'll not stay for a cuppa?"

He shook his head, and plodded down the steps, Louise following, watching him mount his horse, and clatter round the side of the house: the last time he would ride away like that, she supposed for a long time. She sighed, and thought of Jane. Her daughter had apparently vanished off the face of the earth. Louise found it hard to believe Jane was so despondent over her marriage she had taken her own life by walking into the sea: yet there was no other plausible explanation to her disappearance. So now Danny, who some thought had murdered his wife and disposed of her body, was going to war. Danny was no fighting man: couldn't even kill a chicken for dinner, was prepared to make such a sacrifice for the family he had married into. Louise nodded her head, and murmured, 'You're a good man, Danny.'

"Damn, Danny!" Ben snorted. "He makes me feel a coward."

"Don't be silly, Ben," his wife argued. "Nothing of the sort. We know he's doing it for you and Sean. He thinks if conscription comes in, then with only two of you managing four farms — count your father out — there's no option other than for you two to stay."

"All the same."

Priscilla laid her hand on her husband's. "Danny's a dear. Don't argue with him over it, please. Remember, he no longer has a wife, and only one child."

Danny was his son's hero. The boy believed soldiers were brave men who rode great horses, or charged on foot, firing without fear, shooting down the enemy right, left and centre. He ran around the house with a stick, shooting objects. Kathy played war with him once or twice, then grew sick of it. Time would come when he would learn the truth — especially about this war.

Ben brooded again. As so often Jane's disappearance played on his mind. She was his sister after all, and although he had little affection for her, or even talked to her often, as far as he could see her behaviour before her disappearance was no different than usual. So, that she would abandon her home and walk into the sea, having just made a batch of scones, was as ludicrous to him as it was to his mother. If he had accepted her ill-humour, and treated her as he did his other sister Alison, then he might not feel so bad about her loss now.

In Auckland Jonathon Todd had been brushed aside by some redhead, and in a fit of despair joined up.

The soldiers loved Emily: although not for the reason Jessica Caldwell and the likes of her preferred to think. For the first time in twenty years the Parnell mansion was filled. It was a haven. The drawing room became the billiard saloon, the morning room for cards, the lounge for entertaining friends, the bedrooms out of bounds for women, except the three ladies running the establishment. The tennis court was cleared, and the sea was only a stone's throw away. They could gamble to their hearts content, yet no one left the house richer or poorer in that sense. Emily had hotels where the stakes were cash.

On the farms Thomas, Sean and Ben, with the help of the boys tended the sheep, and cattle. They worked just that much harder, and hoped this war would be over quickly.

The instigators and profiteers of this conflict would ensure it was not over quickly.

Another deep depression was clawing its way across the Tasman Sea. Its preceding nor-wester overshot Kowhai and hit the valley floor mid-way across. Although only rustling leaves at Kowhai, it whipped tall poplars at Kauri, Sean's home. Sean, ever watchful over his flock, gave thought to moving them from seaward pastures, where wind and sand now stung their eyes, matted their wool. They were nonchalant of a refreshing sea breeze on a summer's day, yet, as far as they were able, dreaded winter storms: the third in as many weeks.

At its zenith sun and clouds wrangled, afternoon darkening, wind strengthening. The first shower splattered dusty yards, drummed on iron roofs, and mothers hoped their children would get home from school before the rain set in.

In Auckland streets dust swirled around pedestrians, coated them as they alighted from trams. Trees shed leaves; clothes were snatched from lines. Emily watched white horses charge across the harbour, gallop into Hobson Bay: no waterfront drive to hinder them. She paused to see a troop ship slug it out with rising seas as it rounded North Head and headed into the Pacific. "Poor things," she murmured, "They will be as sick as dogs." A lingering thought, since duty took her away from gazing longer out of the window.

Concerned for his sheep, Sean took two dogs with him, and on horseback climbed up the valley wall towards the sea. From high the boulder-strewn beach and sea seemed flat, only white-crested waves and swirls portraying its fury. Sean held on as the wind buffeted him, unnerved his horse: the animal reluctant to tread the bracken-tangled tracks. He had already driven most sheep to leeward slopes. The last few were on the bluff. "C'mon boy," he coaxed his horse, edging it along a track. Even though in places the sandstone cliff was unstable, Sean had no fear. In a minute or two he knew he would be back on more solid ground . . .

. . . Its great limbs shivered, groaned, sagged, its claws scoured the cliff, raked tons of sand, rock and shrubs across the path, swept sheep, dogs and horse from the ledge, catapulted the shepherd through thrashing branches, and flung him aside to tumble down the cliff, coming to rest precariously on a ledge. He did not see his companions perish, or the tree splintering as it crashed on to sea-assaulted rocks. Or his horse struggle to rise, drag its broken body a few yards, then collapse in a bloody heap, waves washing its wounds, soon to consume the carcass. Sean's eyes closed; feeling ebbing from his contorted body, pain dulling, awareness deserting him. A scurrying shower: prelude of that to come, bathed him.

Alison noticed their sheep wandering over the hill without drive or direction, and paused in her work to seek Sean. She was not sure if they were the same flock her husband was retrieving. The scene was not out of the ordinary. The sheep were not precise in their actions, unlike cows that wandered towards the milking yard at about four o'clock, regardless of the weather. She continued with her tasks: baking scones for her school-aged children — two were at school now — to devour when they arrived home, and that should be at any moment. She grew apprehensive: a chill clasping her body, and shut the kitchen window. Not that sort of chill she was experiencing. Instead the same feeling she had known, now she remembered, when the storm of 1907 wrecked the *Reliance* and brought Sean into her life. Her present concern: her children. 'Come on,' she urged. 'Where are you?'

She hurried to the front porch, and sighed. There they were, ambling down the valley drive, dragging their school bags, nonchalant of the rain thrashing them. She would have to dry another lot of clothes now. "Will you come out of that rain," she called. "Hurry!"

By the time she had scolded them for dawdling, stripped them of saturated clothes — they had not taken raincoats to school, then lovingly fed them, given them hot cups of cocoa, almost another hour had passed. Her only consolation, it was Friday, and she had the weekend to dry everything. Only then did she return her concern to Sean, and again the sinking apprehension chilled her.

With no phone she could not contact anyone without leaving the house. They thought one telephone between the four farms was sufficient to connect them with the world beyond their haven. If only they had devised some sort of communication system between them, Sean and Thomas and Danny, and Ben. Danny was not there now, and Ben was over the hill, so only Thomas, her not-so-young father, could she contact.

As the night closed in, having fed the children again, she begged them, "Daddy hasn't come home. Now Mummy has to go across to Kowhai. Will you promise to sit here, right here, and not touch anything, while Mummy goes to get Daddy."

"Daddy never goes away."

"No. I think the storm — maybe your grandpa needs a hand and Daddy's there." God, she was getting herself deeper every moment. "Please be good. If Daddy comes home, tell him where Mummy is." Would they remember all that? Would they burn the house down? Those were her concerns. No thoughts of strangers lurking, because such a situation was as remote as the stars.

"Promise," agreed her elder daughter, and with her brother, sat rigidly in the couch. Fortunately Jennifer, their brat of a younger sister, was asleep, and Alison prayed she would stay that way. An express train squall thundered across the valley, slammed against the house, hammered the roof. The minute it eased, Alison mounted her horse, taking care not to strain herself, and with Kowhai's flickering lanterns as beacons, she rode through the night, the moon briefly shining between scurrying clouds: enough for her to determine the path thirty yards ahead, and ensure there was nothing across it. Over the bridge, up the last stretch of drive, and she edged from the horse, then plodded up the stairs and banged like a tormented traveller on the door, before thrusting it open.

"Mother! — Father. — Have you seen Sean?" She paused, undecided whether to go to the kitchen or lounge. "Mother! — Father! — Where are you?"

"In here, dear," her mother called from the cosiness of the lounge.

Alison staggered into the room. "Sean, have you seen him?"

Her mother shook her head, while Thomas turned in his chair. "Not for hours, Alison."

"He went out to . . . Oh, Father, something's happened to him. I know." She trembled, her lips quivering. She knew whatever had happened had occurred hours ago. That was the most dreadful part.

Louise sighed, saying to herself, 'Not again.' She recalled how Danny had entered — not burst in like her daughter — when Jane went missing.

"Mother, I know something has happened. I knew it this afternoon — just like when Sean was ship-wrecked."

Thomas advised, "Yes dear, first of all we'll have to round up the troops." He thought for a moment, even noticed Alison dripping over the carpet. "Get the boys, Louise," he ordered. "George can go for his father. Stanley can come with me."

"I'm coming with you too, Father."

"But your children," Louise reminded her, although suspected there was another reason why her daughter should not again venture into the foul night.

"Could you — please, Mother. I must go."

"Of course, dear, if you're sure . . ."

"I'm fine, Mother. Truly."

Louise shook her head with doubt. It would also mean leaving Douglas alone, even though he said he would not mind. Douglas had spent a lot of time on his own over the years, young as he was, and Louise knew he would just sit quietly, or maybe play with his toys, for hours on end if necessary. She did not expect to be away long.

Going out into a stormy night might have deterred some youngsters, however for both Stanley and George it was an adventure. Thomas and Stanley saddled two horses, fortunately stabled for the night, rode past the dairy, caught up to Alison, and they crossed the squelching lower paddocks, then negotiated the south side of the gap, and on to Sean's property, horses sinking into the soggy grass-covered dunes. Constant wind and frequent squalls threatened them.

Meanwhile, young George fetched his horse from a nearby paddock, and with only reins, he rode bare-back out of the valley, caught the full force of the storm on the ridge road, treaded carefully lest he end up in a ditch, or worse, trotted down Kanuka's drive, and informed his father.

For all riders a half-moon infrequently shone through scudding clouds, and gave them some light.

"He's got to be across this side, I would say," Thomas yelled: the words whipped from his mouth, so Stanley only caught half the sentence.

"Do you want me to go over there?" Stanley suggested, risking falling off as he pointed to another area of the rugged landscape.

'Best left as scrub,' Thomas now thought, and answered, "No, Boy, we'd best keep together." They should have taken different paths, yet for the moment Thomas wanted to keep the boy close to hand, although Alison went off on her own, believing herself to be within hailing distance.

Briefly the moon illuminated the slippery path, and the sea that threw back effervescence at the silver-edged clouds. Great waves tumbled over each other in their haste to reach the beach, only their spent force now surging into the gap. The tide, having done its destructive work, had receded.

Thomas had little time to admire the awesome scene. Fused light reflected on the havoc wrought by the landslide, only the shattered tree left lying among discarded boulders, animals and earth all devoured. Not devoured yet was a bundle curled on a ledge below. Without a word he and Stanley dismounted, tethered their horses in patch of scrub, then slid and slithered their way down to Sean. Stanley believed his uncle dead. Thomas was not so hasty in his judgement. He had once before, only fifty yards or so from this spot, attended the same prostrate person, the same closed eyes, tortured body.

"Get your aunt," he ordered Stanley.

His coat offered some protection, his hands care. And he cursed himself for not coming better prepared. He might have known if Sean was missing, he would be lying injured somewhere.

Stanley climbed back up the cliff: a hazard he had previously negotiated with George as being fun. Now it terrified him, yet too proud to renege, and at the top he called out for his aunt. Alison fetched the rope from her father's horse, looked down at the two men and murmured a short prayer, flung the rope down to the ledge, and before descending, begged of Stanley. "Could you ride back to Kowhai on your own . . ?"

"Of course, Aunt."

"Someone — Ben — must arrive there soon. And you'll need to bring back the stretcher. Your uncle knows where it is." She held his arm. "Please ride carefully. Walk if necessary. A few minutes, Stanley, can't make much difference — now."

It might well make a difference for all she knew. Something she would have to live with, rather than risk Stanley's life through haste. Only after seeing the boy safely passed the cliff ledge, did she cautiously climb down the face, thankful her rough and tumble childhood days enabled her to make such a descent. She was amazed her father had made it without the rope.

"How is he, Father?" she pleaded softly.

"Not too good, I fear," he replied, not withholding the worst from his daughter.

"I've sent Stanley back to Kowhai."

"Good lad that. He'll make it." He kept his hand on the crumpled husband of the daughter beside him. "I think we'll just have to stay here until help arrives, dear."

"You don't think we should try and get him back up?"

"No. I don't know how bad he is. He's got a few broken bones, but just what else . . ." Thomas hoped his son-in-law's back was not broken, or something equally as paralysing. He only gave a brief thought whatever Sean's injuries were, it would leave them shorthanded, hopefully not for too long.

Together they crouched on the wind-swept ledge, the full fury of a squall thrashing them. Wind and rain they could take, their only concern the cliff above stayed there. Thomas did not seek Sean's horse or dogs, assuming they had either gone home, or were down there: among the rubble below the cliff; what was left of it.

That same squall saturated Stanley. He was saturated already, yet did not deter from his mission, and found only Douglas at Kowhai obediently sitting in an armchair. Now shivering, he took another lantern, recalled that George had once shown him the stretcher used to get Sean from the shipwreck to the house. He then had to remember where it was, and with only the lantern, almost oblivious of driving rain, he crossed to the barn to search for it. He heard his Uncle Ben call out, and yelled into the night. "We've found him, Uncle. Grandpa wants the stretcher."

"That bad eh, Boy," Ben said. Now what? Who to send where? There was little point in phoning for a doctor. No chance either, when Ben went indoors and picked up the phone, wound the handle to get the exchange, and assumed the lines were down anyway. "Stanley, you've done enough for one night," he advised. "Get out of those wet things, and have a bath to warm up. Then stay here." A chore for him, because it meant he would have to heat water in the copper, and ladle it into the bath. Nevertheless he obeyed, discovering the water in the copper was already warm.

Ben sent his son to Kauri to tell Louise of the accident.

Ben rode alone towards the cliff face having a fair idea where Sean was. He recalled the previous occasion they had carried Sean back from the water's edge. Bad enough that day, but this night was far worse. It seemed an age ago to Ben. So much had happened during those intervening years. He did not give time much thought as he rode the same route his father and sister had taken over two hours earlier. The weather did not look like abating. On the contrary, as he threaded their way on to Sean's property, the full force of the storm lashed and blinded him: the driving rain having long since penetrated his clothes, so he dismounted and walked the horse carefully along the cliff track.

They crouched beside the unconscious Sean Sullivan, and despite the possibility of aggravating his injuries edged him on to the stretcher, then holding the ropes — Ben having dropped a second down the cliff — with one hand, the stretcher with the other, Ben and Alison in front they clawed their way to the cliff top. There was no way down: only a sheer drop of sixty or seventy feet on to the rocks. Reaching the track was their first object; negotiating the bluff the next, all the time being bullied by the unrelenting storm. Alison moved to the back with her father. They took it in stages, slipping and sliding, resting, going back to fetch the faithful horses, which could not possibly be enjoying the conditions any more than the rescuers.

George had dutifully crossed to Kauri to tell his grandmother what had happened. Louise had already heated water for a bath, then further warmed him with a hot drink and range-made toast, and despite his age tucked him securely into his aunt's bed, with a loving and deeply thankful kiss on his forehead, letting him sleep, something that came quickly to young George Chester.

Louise stayed where she was at Kauri. Ben and Alison stayed at Kowhai, with Thomas, whom they sent off to bed, as they did to Stanley and Douglas. Only Priscilla, on the other side of the ridge, remained unaware of the tragedy, and had to bear the situation. She also had a copper full of water for Ben when he returned. She eventually fell asleep in an armchair: the storm less forceful in their sheltered location. She dreaded what it might be doing to other parts of the property, and the peninsula.

Later that winter's night the rain set in steadily, and if Sean could be thankful for small mercies; at least his inert body was securely tucked in dry sheets, and his wife kept a constant vigil, should he awaken.

Dawn flickered above the hills in the wake of the passing rain. It took a long time to develop: slow, insecure, torn between blue sky and black. Water swept over Kowhai's drive a foot deep, threatened to take the bridge, and leave them completely isolated. As it was, the only way into the valley, or out, was via Danny's precarious drive.

They had made Sean comfortable, and there was no point in taking further risks, so Ben did not ride for the doctor until dawn. If by chance he found a working telephone on the way, so much the better. As on the last occasion he had gone for a doctor, he had to go all the way to Waiuku. Priscilla had to wait until Stanley was despatched to Kanuka. Thomas belatedly rounded up the cows, and dragged George out of Alison's place at the same time. Some tasks did not wait while the family sorted out priorities. And all the while frequent sou-westerly squalls lashed the land.

This time Ben had to wait for the doctor, and when he did return home, the practitioner sighed. "What, Ben?"

"Sorry. It's Sean, Doc. I reckon he's in a bad way."

So the doctor was informed, and his verdict. "We'll have to bring him to hospital this time."

That meant a twelve mile rough journey overland, or if the tides were favourable — which they were not — five miles on the back of a cart, then by boat. First the doctor had to assess his injuries, and since ambulances were not used out this way, a cart it would be.

Alison looked appealingly from Sean's bedside up at her mother. As she had nursed him back to health after the shipwreck, so she wished to again. There was significant difference between then and now, and both women knew it. Not only in the extent of his injuries, which were more than a broken leg as last time, Alison now had a family to care for as well.

Louise Chester shook her head. "I can't, dear. I can't, much as I'd love to."

"You are looking after Douglas?" she questioned, although herself knew that was no argument either.

"Douglas is one," Louise reminded her, and need not add he was also older than Alison's three.

Nor would Sean be hospitalised at Waiuku. Instead, once the doctor had assessed his injuries, he was transported by cart out of the valley, down to the Pollok wharf, placed aboard a steamer, and with other passengers, conveyed round the headlands into bays across the harbour to Onehunga. From there he had the distinction — not a very noble one — of being the first of the family to be taken to Auckland hospital in a motorised ambulance.

Alison went with him, to stay at his side for a few days, booking herself into a nearby boarding house.

So, another valley home was abandoned: temporarily this time. Adrienne and Patrick moved across to Kowhai, and three-year-old Jennifer stayed with Priscilla, literally getting under her feet.

Perhaps the hero on this occasion, and more particularly its aftermath, was George Chester: fourteen, and taking on a man's work. On those frosty winter mornings he rose long before dawn, fetched the cows, milked them, then went to school. 'I'm doing it for Aunt Ali,' he would tell himself. Or, 'I'm doing it for grandma.' He did not think he was doing it for his own parents, because a ridge separated Kowhai from Kanuka, his parents' farm, and that ridge made the difference.

CHAPTER THIRTEEN

With help Thomas worked his farm and Sean's by day, and if some jobs were not done, so be it. Ben worked his own farm, and Danny's, and, as if guilty over being about the only able-bodied male of fighting age locally, ensured when Danny returned his farm would be in good working order. When would Danny return? Ben had taken some notice of what his father maintained about the war, when he thought, 'Those war mongering sods will kill every man in the world for their own profit.' They would not quite do that, although they would certainly leave many countries, including New Zealand, grievously short of manpower. And worse was to come, although Ben did not know it then, nor did anyone else for that matter.

His sister Alison did not think too much of the war when she was at Sean's side. Her thoughts were dominated by how would she and Sean cope now. She might have been thankful they lived on an almost debt-free property: the land given to them by her father, the house courtesy of the storm that brought Sean into her life. They still had to farm it. It was almost debt-free, although she did not know how much 'almost' amounted to.

Sean, as he limply held his wife's hand, thought only how he had so let his family down. From the day he was first washed up on that shore he had been nothing but trouble for them. The intervening several years of good times were momentarily dismissed from his thoughts, and he saw himself only as a burden.

Alison's frequent reasoning, "Sean, dearest, it was an accident," was no consolation.

Although his back was not broken physically, it was broken spiritually. That he believed his active farming days were over severely depressed him. Despite his wife's reassurances, even now with her at his side, he could only think of the worst. Everything he had ever done was strenuous: being a seaman, fisherman, smithy; even a mechanic tinkering with automobiles. All entailed stooping, reaching for hawsers, steadying frenzied horses — and he had a vision of his horse falling on to the rocks, trying to regain its feet, then sagging back on to those wave-swept rocks — or himself sliding beneath cars. Mentally he was not cut out for any soft job. He was not cut out for such jobs educationally either. Not for one moment could he imagine — in his present state of mind — his wife's family rallying round indefinitely. Even if they wanted to, the war prevented it. Although being reassured by Alison they were coping at Kowhai, he could not fully believe her. She was just saying that to make it easier for him.

She sighed, sitting at his side, smiled — or tried to smile — down at him.

Then along came something to make her smile. Actually someone! — Emily breezing into the ward, carrying a box looking suspiciously like chocolates: presumably for Sean, since she was heading directly his bed.

Emily took one look at Sean, and uttered, "Oh my!" Then glanced down at her offering and said to Alison, "I suppose, dear, you and I will have to eat them."

Sean smiled, ever so weakly, and both ladies swore a tear slipped from his eye.

"So, he has been in the wars again?"

"I'm afraid so, Em — badly this time."

"I know." Emily shook her head. She laid her hand on Alison's wrist. "Now don't you worry about a thing." She again looked at Sean. "And don't *you* worry about things either," shaking her head. "You may think so now, however it is not the end of the world."

Alison knew Emily had enough on her plate, without concerning herself with their plight. She could just have easily said so and they would have agreed.

"So, he has a bed for the night, what about you, Ali?"

She knew what was coming, although admitted. "I — I stayed here last night. But I've got a place around the corner — quite near."

"That *is* silly of you. Because, darling, I live . . ." She tossed her hand toward the window. ". . . A stone's throw away."

"I know, Em — but . . ."

"No buts — unless of course you would prefer not . . ." She raised an eyebrow enquiringly.

"Em, you know I would be ever so grateful."

"You shall to earn your keep," she advised most businesslike, although Alison knew 'earning her keep' would be pitching in and helping with running her place. That she would willingly do. After all, she was used to eighteen-hour days. "I think you had better come with me, now."

Alison looked at Sean, then Emily, and back to Sean. His response was a tired nod of his head. "Would that be all right, darling? I'll . . ."

"Of course it will be all right," Emily insisted. "Even *he* can see you are dead beat." So Alison was hustled out of the hospital, into Emily's car. She immediately suggested, "I'll have to teach you to drive." Before receiving an answer asked, "What happened to the poor chap?"

"I — I thought you must know."

"Your mother, darling, simply telephoned me to say he had been in an accident, and you were both at the hospital."

So, during the short drive to where Alison had taken a room she spilled out the story.

Emily's, "That is terrible," was said as if she was indifferent. "I am sure — in fact, we shall make sure — he is in good hands." Then, without further ado on that matter, she said, "I did mean it when I said you would have to pitch in . . ."

"Em, I'll do anything." The tears flowed: in despair, and in gratitude; despair at her plight, and gratitude over Emily's compassion. The last thing she wanted to do was board in a strange house, and find her way about the city on her own. Ten years earlier it would have been an adventure. Now, in her present state, the idea horrified her. "I'm ever so grateful, Em. You're sure you're not too busy. What with . . ."

"Oh do not go on so. We shall have a cuppa when we get home, then see what needs to be done."

Alison profusely apologised to the landlady, and as the woman began to object, Emily thrust some money into her hand. "Perhaps that will make up for the inconvenience."

"Oh! — Ah. — There's really no need."

"It's the least we can do, Madam."

When Alison walked in Emily's door, heads turned, and sensing their thoughts, Emily said, "Now listen here you chaps. This is Alison — my sister-in-law. Her husband — yes *husband* — has been badly injured in a farm accident, so we are all going to take care of her, aren't we?"

Even in her depressed state Alison had to smile wanly as pouts replaced smiles on the soldiers' faces. Frankly, she could not imagine any of them admiring her now, not like a few years ago when she was young and vivacious. It *did* seem an age ago, yet it was only a few years. Nor could she imagine herself ever being frivolous again. Here was Emily, several years older than her, come to think of it, acting with commanding authority: as if these men had swapped a military general for a civil one.

They had their cup of tea at the kitchen table, which gave Emily time to think where she would put Alison. It was to be in one of the maid's quarters, this one in the attic, too high for her aging regular maids to climb day in and day out. Alison did not object, yet she did have one concern: a concern she would not foster on to Emily: she was expecting again. Still, she could see no reason why she should not climb the stairs; she would make sure she did not do them too often. Thankful at least she was fit, and trusted anything Emily subjected her to, would not be injurious to her or her baby, as yet she believed not noticeable. She was unaware her mother already knew the truth.

So, back in the kitchen, Alison's first task was to peel potatoes — dozens of them.

Nor did she know it then; this was to be her home for five months. It was not intended for one moment she should remain in Auckland, although in reality worked out easier, despite what her mother had earlier said, for her to stay and aid Sean's recovery, as well as help Emily, than to occupy her own home. Her children remained fostered out — at least with loving relations.

When Priscilla received the news her sister-in-law was staying on in Auckland, and with Emily, she announced to Ben, "Emily to the rescue."

"Now what has she done?" he demanded, although in a jovial tone: a manner Priscilla seldom heard these days, and if it took Emily to make him see the funny side of their situation, so be it.

She waved Alison's letter at him as she flipped some eggs in the frying pan, since Ben did not like them sunny side up. "My dear sister gathered Alison from the hospital and had her peeling potatoes. So many, she says, she had no time to think of how bad things were here."

"As long as you don't mind having Jennifer?"

"She's company for Kathy, Ben, since her brothers have abandoned this place for your father's."

"Yes, it looks a bit like that." Ben expelled his breath. At times he could do with extra help on his own farm, however to ask either of his sons to oblige was becoming difficult: almost as if he was estranged from them. Nor was it this beastly war that caused the separation, rather events before then: events concerning the blowing up of his swamp, even if unintentional. It had put a feeling of insecurity or something, Ben was not sure, over his land, whereas Kowhai was stable, as if it had been there for always, and nothing would disturb its security.

"You must say Em is doing more than her bit for the war, and for us," Priscilla reminded him. "More than I can say for Jessica. *That* woman drives me to distraction, the way she flounces around. She does five minutes work for the cause and tells the world about it." Priscilla uncharacteristically slapped the fish slice on the range, lifted the pan, and asked her husband, "Is that enough, or will I do you some more?"

"That's plenty, Prissy." It was really enough, although he knew half a world away many people would not see one egg and a slice of bacon from one week — maybe month — to the next. His purpose was focussed on trying to get the maximum production from the land, although they never went without their food. Was that selfish? Ben did not think so, now his attention *had* been drawn indirectly to other peoples' plight. He then wondered how Emily managed food-wise in Auckland. "Do you think we should send something to her?" he suddenly asked.

"Who?"

"To Em. Eggs and stuff. Ham. What do you think?"

"Would it get there?"

"That's a point." Having fed her husband, Priscilla placed two strips of bacon, an egg and two small preserved tomatoes in the pan. "We know we could get it safely to Onehunga. "I'll write to Em. Better still, I'll telephone her." Not a simple matter of using Kowhai's phone, because the distance between Pollok and Auckland necessitated a toll call, and that cost money: more than a letter. Under the circumstances it would be a lot easier to telephone her, or leave a message for Emily to return the call, since the chances were she would not be sitting beside the instrument waiting for it to ring.

Without turning, she advised her husband, "You know Alison is expecting again — according to your mother?"

"Ah." He had his thoughts. 'Fancy getting herself that way at a time like this.' Not thinking of Sean's injuries, instead during a war.

"She is, and there's nothing you can do about it, Ben. I was going to suggest we have her other two, to give your mum . . ."

"I don't fancy Jennifer running about here any longer than necessary. She is just like her Aunt J . . ." And he stopped short. That is who she was exactly like in temperament. On the matter of his lost sister, Ben could not speak. Nor could he even now, years after her disappearance, think fondly of her.

"I won't. It might not come to that, dear. We'll see how your mother copes."

Ben, knew his mother would cope very well, or pretend to. After all, the war could not go on forever.

Although Alison could not tend her hospitalised husband she soon learned that while Emily's soldiers had largely recovered from their physical wounds, some remained mentally effected by the war. She was walking past the open door of a bedroom one evening, after 'lights out' when she detected a whimper from within the room. She paused, uncertain just what to do, then entered, and listened. Again she heard the whimper, and thought it came from a lower bunk.

She crossed to it, was unable to lean over it due to the bunk above, so sat on the edge. "What's wrong?" she whispered.

The soldier sucked in a breath, as if startled, or concerned because his distress had been heard, by a lady.

"Can I give you anything?" Alison asked quietly, hoping not to waken those sharing the room, unless they were already awake, but remained silent. The hall light cast only a reflected glow on to the bunk, however this was sufficient for Alison to observe the soldier's tear-streaked face. She fetched into her pocket, withdrew a hanky and wiped away his tears. "Is that better?" she next asked, knowing what little she had done was ineffective. She rested her hand on his left shoulder. He raised himself slightly and reached for her, but Alison leaned back to avoid the embrace, although rested her other hand on his right shoulder to restrain yet not push him away.

By now she had assembled what she thought she knew of him, if he was the person she was thinking of, and acted accordingly. During his short time at war he, like many others, had encountered horrific events. He had witnessed children dying when caught in the crossfire between opposing armies. She wasn't sure of the details, but the tragedy had etched itself nightmarishly in his mind.

"Lie back," she advised, and gently edged him down. "I'll stay here."

He stared up at her with glistening eyes. Was she misinterpreting the message in them: that he wanted her to hold him tight? Perhaps a comforting smile would satisfy him? His head rolled slightly to one side, and Alison took his hand with both of hers, sandwiching it. Again he seemed to choke on his sorrow, then settled. Alison silently stayed with him for several more minutes, despite her own fatigue, and when he seemed to be asleep she leaned over and tenderly kissed his forehead, feeling him stir slightly beneath her lips. He may or may not have heard her whispered, "Goodnight."

She did not notice the room darken due to someone briefly standing in the doorway, observing her tenderness, and not for one moment thinking Alison was being anything more than a caring nurse. Emily tip-toed away and walked up the stairs to her own room.

Alison slowly edged from the bunk and as she walked up the stairs she heard the click of a bedroom door above.

Next morning when several soldiers had gathered round the dining room table for breakfast she wasn't sure who was that man, if indeed he was among that lot.

Nothing was said of the incident, not even by Emily, who had on occasions offered similar comfort to a member of her flock.

*　　*　　*　　*　　*　　*

In the black of the night, for they say the night is blackest before dawn, an alarm clock rang — persistently. George rolled over in his bed fumbling for it, while irritated James muttered, "Turn the silly thing off."

"I'm trying to."

To which James then objected, "You set it too early."

George managed to switch it off, then retorted, "It's the same time as yesterday." He swung out of his bed and stood up, rubbing his eyes.

James sat on the edge of his bed, chill immediately shivering him. Both were aware of rain beating on the roof, although James had to say, "It's raining — again."

"I'm not deaf."

Obviously neither boy enjoyed the moment: unlike rising on a crisp spring or summer morning.

George fumbled in the dark for the matches, then lit a candle in a holder. "I was dreaming."

"What about?"

"Not saying," George refused, the vivid dream of moments ago already fading.

They dressed and with George carrying the candle went downstairs to the kitchen. Early as they were, Louise was already there, with a kettle boiling and thick slices of buttered toast for the boys. She poured the boiling water into two mugs and stirred the cocoa.

Undaunted by the time or the weather she cheerily greeted, "Good morning, Boys."

To which James again stated the obvious, "It's raining again."

"I'm sure you boys are used to it." As they sat at the table she assured them, "I know, my dears, it is hard on you, but you are really doing a wonderful job. We are so proud of you."

George grunted. "I just want to sleep in once in a while."

Louise clutched his shoulders and kissed his hair. "I have just written to your Uncle Danny in France or somewhere — they don't tell us exactly — and told him what a wonderful job you are all doing." She poured hot water into a billy and put a lid on it. "Your granddad will be down soon to help."

Taking their mugs and toast with them the boys went to the washhouse and put on their oilskins. From there they trudged across the puddle back yard down to the dairy where cows, apparently totally nonchalant of the weather, were nudging the post and rail fence, more concerned over emptying their udders. George lit hurricane lamp and hung it on a rafter, then poured some of the water from the billy into a bowl. James fetched the first of the cows, nudging them into the bails and tying their legs. They bathed the cows' teats, George recalling his dream when it was not a cow's teats he was he was handling but — it could not possibly be Penny's because at twelve she was flat-chested, but fifteen-year-old Ngaire, wasn't.

As if conscious of his brother's thoughts James raised the subject. "Who did you dream about — Penny? She's sweet on you."

George snorted in disgust. "I don't dream of Penny. She's only a baby."

"She's my age, and I'm not a baby."

"At least it's winter, and there aren't many to milk."

"What about Ngaire? Do you dream about her?"

"We really don't have to get up so early."

"I've seen the way she looks at you." James moved a pail aside,
    untied the
cow's leg, and gave it a slap on the rump. The cow backed out,
mooing. The next cow was waiting.

They were unaware of the rising glow in the eastern sky, and
were milking the last two cows when Thomas, later rather than
sooner, arrived on the scene. "You've got them done quickly
today."

"Not much to milk," advised George, half-expecting to be told
they had been too impatient with the cows.

Instead Thomas commented, "Less for me to separate. You two
go on up; I'll finish off here."

By now Kowhai's kitchen was a hive of activity. Louise being
assisted by Ngaire, and a fetching Maori she was. There were also
four other children, the three youngest sitting at the table eating
porridge, while an eight-year-old girl stirred another pot of
porridge.

As George and James entered James nudged his brother
playfully, looking at Ngaire. He sniggered, causing Ngaire to turn,
although because of the chatter did not catch James' remark, "I bet
you dream of her."

"Don't!" Nevertheless George was blushing.

Unaware of the situation, or maybe aware but not showing it,
Louise said, "Sit yourselves down, Boys." She set plates of porridge
before them.

Intending to return to the dairy later, Thomas now hitched two
horses to the dray, and was still adjusting the harnesses when the
first of the children ran bare-foot down the back steps with his
leather schoolbag and scrambled aboard the tray, followed by all
but the youngest, who stood on the back porch snuggled up to
Louise, who waved them off. "Drive carefully, George. The roads
will be slippery after last night's rain."

"He always drives carefully, Mrs Chester," Ngaire complimented,
who was last to climb on to the cart.

James and George slung nose-bags on to the tray and climbed on
to the driver's seat, and with a flick of the reins urged the horses

onward, scattering chooks intent on snapping up any grain that might have fallen from the nosebags.

Following as far as the bridge the dogs returned to the yard, one snapping at a chook.

On the Awhitu Rd, Kathy was waiting at her gate. "You're late," she informed them curtly, and scrambled on to the cart, shoving a child aside so she could sit next to Ngaire.

Rounding a corner they were stopped in their tracks — by a landslide.

"We could just about get passed," James examined.

"You'll have to all get off," George decided, receiving groans of disapproval.

"We'll all get muddy."

"Too bad."

George alone on the cart, with James holding a rein carefully negotiated the slide, and once across it allowed the children to reboard, dollops of mud smearing the tray.

"We'll be really late for school now," Kathy next warned.

To which James responded, "Too bad."

"It's not our fault there was a slip," George explained.

They were still some distance away from the Pollok School when the bell rang. Even so George did not hurry the horses. He turned the horses into a paddock beside the school. All except James leapt off and hurried inside, hoping to sneak in while the teacher's back was turned, while Gorge and James unhitched the horses, tethered them to a post and rail fence, gave them their nose bags, and casually entered the schoolroom.

They made no effort to conceal their lateness, knowing the schoolmaster's temperament.

"So, what is you excuse for being late this time?" Smithers demanded.

"There was a slip across the road," James said, with a chorus of agreements from those from the cart.

"There was a slip, who?"

"A slip, Sir," George responded.

"I was addressing your brother."

"I was telling you why we are late — Sir."

"You should have left home earlier. Sit down."

That roused further protests.

"Be quiet."

As George sat next to James he muttered, not very quietly, "The old grump."

"Quiet, Chester. Extra homework for you tonight."

He abruptly turned his attention to the blackboard on an easel, aware that the children were making faces at him. Whipping around again he confronted inscrutable looks.

By afternoon in the stuffy room, despite it being winter, James began to nod off. Smithers, with a smirk, crept up on the twelve-year-old and rapped him on the knuckles, bringing James instantly to reality. He lifted him by the scruff of the neck and marched him to the front of the class.

"Stand there." From his desk he extracted a leather strap. "Hold out your hand." James obeyed. The strap whipped his hand and he winced. "Now the other one." This he struck harder. James drew in his hand in pain, whimpering. "That will teach you for being lazy."

Kathy was out of her seat and confronted Smithers. "You're mean. I'm going to tell my father."

"Sit down and be quiet, otherwise you'll get the same."

"Sit down, Kathy," George advised, and Ngaire tugged her dress, careful not to draw attention to herself, because she knew Smithers believed she should earning her keep rather than being at school.

After school that day Kathy put her small arm about James, walking with him to the cart. "I'm going to tell Father. I hate Mr Smithers. Why can't we have Miss Jenkins back? She was so nice."

"It doesn't matter, Kathy," James pleaded. "You'll only make him more angry.

At Kowhai nothing was said of the punishment while five children sat at the library table and did their homework, with hot drinks and biscuits in front of them.

Ngaire sat next to her eight-year-old brother, Tane, observing he had printed the letter 'h' around the wrong way. "No, Tane, you do an 'h' like this," and she corrected the letter.

"I'll never know nothin'."

"You will — if you try." She squeezed his arm.

"When Daddy comes home from war will we live together again?"

"I suppose," she lied, knowing that neither of their parents would return: both being dead.

A girl of Tane's age sitting opposite him blurted, "Your daddy's not coming home. Teddy said they all got killed."

"That's not true," Ngaire stated emphatically, scowling at the girl. "Some got killed. Some got captured, and others are still fighting "

"I miss Daddy awful."

"So do I, Tane, and Mummy."

The boy began to whimper and Ngaire held him closer.

Louise entered the room and witnessed the compassion. "Ngaire, dear, when they are in bed tonight why don't you read them a story?"

"Yes, please," begged another child.

"But, Mrs Chester, I have work to do."

"Oh, I think your work can wait another day," Louise assured.

George at the time was with his grandfather milking the cows. After tea that night he sat alone in the library to do his homework by lamplight.

The following morning Kathy was not standing at her gate, rather in front of her father Ben on a horse. Ben rode to James' side, Kathy slid off and clambered on to the cart.

"So what's this about that teacher yesterday?" Obviously Ben was aware of Smithers' reputation even before the previous day's incident.

"It was nothing, Dad, I fell asleep."

Ben nodded, then spurred his horse on ahead, pausing to ensure George with his load of children made it through the partially cleared slip.

To his sister James admonished, "You shouldn't have said anything."

"I should so too. You're my brother, and he was mean."

Ben did not race far ahead of the cart, nevertheless was at the school in time to confront Smithers, who happened to be on verge of hurrying indoors, before the cart children arrived. "Mr Smithers, just the man I want to see."

"Mr Chester — isn't it?" Smithers confirmed, although knew very well who Ben was.

"As you well know. I understand my son nodded off in class."

"I believe he did at that."

By now the children had arrived, and Kathy was out of that cart and at her father's side in a flash. Ben put his arm about her.

"Listen, Mr Smithers, my sons have been up before dawn to milk their granddad's cows."

"That is no excuse." He was going to say more, except he caught Kathy's defiant stare, and was actually a little contrite.

"We'll see about that. I'll tell you what, Mr Smithers, I'll take my children and their cousins out of this school. I'm sure my mother would set up a Dame school at Kowhai."

"You can't do that."

"Can't I just. With them gone, there would hardly be any children left to teach, and you would be out of a job. Think about that."

To which Kathy implored, "Oh please let Granny teach us."

And Smithers, with attempted superciliousness, accepted, "I shall, Mr Chester, I shall."

With that he hurried indoors to quieten the babbling school.

Ben went to his lingering son and assured, "You won't be strapped again, Son, at least not for that."

James scuffed the ground with his bare foot.

Came Saturday, and with the sun barely above the hills a gig trundled along Kowhai's drive. The horse may have realised it only had a few yards to go before being relieved of its forced labour. It was driven by a slim red-haired girl who looked not to have a care in the world. However this was deceptive, as Penny Caldwell cared very much about the world. She waved vigorously at George, ploughing a paddock next to the drive. She drove into the back yard and 'Whoa'd' the horse, which did not need a second instruction and stopped dead.

In the yard Thomas was loading boxes and cartons on to the cart. Nearby two children were collecting vegetables and placing them in the boxes. Another two children, one standing on a box because of her size, were hanging washing. Louise, in a baking ingredients-smeared apron appeared on the back porch.

High spiritedly, Penny called, "Hello, Gran." She leapt from the gig and rushed into Louise's arms. "I've come to help."

In mock sternness Louise asked, "Penny, do your parents know where you are?" She also wondered how Jessica would react to the 'loss' of the family gig.

"Um — probably. If they don't, they'll soon work it out."

"Oh, dear, you do get me into awful trouble with them."

"Oh, poof to them. Don't they know there's a war on, and work to be done."

"I think they do, dear."

James, the same age as Penny, had wandered from the barn and was looking at the sweating horse.

Louise called to him. "Dear, your irrepressible cousin has just driven that horse like the wind. See to it would you, please."

"What does irre-something mean?" Penny asked.

"Ir-re-pres-sible. It means, my girl, there's nothing stopping you."

"Anyway, she hasn't come to work," James said, "she has come to see George."

"I've seen him. He's ploughing a field. So there." She poked her tongue out at James, kicked off her shoes and slung them into the gig, then ran to the garden, picked up a box of cabbages and carried it to the cart. There were already several boxes of winter produce aboard. "Granddad, can I take it down to the wharf?"

"I don't know, dear. The roads are slippery."

"I know. I've just driven from Waiuk, and it's miles and miles."

"You're a courageous girl, Penny. All the same I think someone should go with you."

Louise by now had approached the cart, and with a sigh looked at Thomas, then at Penny, "If she insists, Thomas, I shall go with her. James could do with a rest."

So shortly after, with Penny at the reins she and Louise trundled the cart from the yard. By now George was closer to the driveway, and Penny, despite having already claimed to have seen George, clambered from the cart, ran up to him and gave him a hug, saying, "We're taking all that to the boat."

For Louise, although having made the journey to the wharf many times, on this Saturday morning she was able to relax, having complete confidence in the driving skill of the young girl beside her.

The hazy Manukau Harbour was in sight when Penny wanted to confirm, "Is this all really for Aunt Emily?"

"Oh yes, dear. Aunt Emily has a lot of recuperating soldiers to feed."

Penny thought about that for a few seconds, frowning. "What does re-cu-something mean?"

"It means they have been injured in war, and are out of hospital but need to be looked after. And that is what Aunt Emily does."

That further puzzled Penny, because she had heard something about her father's sister. "Mother says Aunt Emily is a naughty lady, that's why the soldiers are there."

Louise swallowed. Not only was she irrepressible, but she knew a little too much about life than was good for her . . .

. . . Particularly when Penny blurted, "She has lovers."

There was no denying that, however Louise put it in context. "Darling, in the past your Aunt Emily was favoured by men, but I'm sure the soldiers she is caring for are not, as you say, lovers."

"Anyway, Aunt Adda is there."

Louise was not quite sure what her younger daughter had to do with the situation, particularly in her very expectant condition.

"I don't mind about Aunt Emily. I love her to bits." Then she lamented, "But I don't see her very often."

"So you should love her, Penny. She is a fine lady, and doing so much for those poor soldiers, giving up her home as she has done." She did not remind Penny that some people were less modest about their war effort, including Penny's own mother. No, she had no real objection to either Penny's or her brother Stanley's regular appearances at Kowhai.

Later that day George and Penny were sitting on a post and rail fence. Not particularly doing anything other staring across the yard. They were allowed moments like this; idle, but hardly disorderly. Penny broke the reverie.

"Georgie," she asked cheekily, "do you have a sweetheart?"

"What's a sweetheart." He knew exactly.

"Oh, silly, a girl you love."

"Gee, I don't love any girl." He was astute enough to detect Penny's hint of disappointment. "I mean, I think you're corker, but . . ."

"Can I be your sweetheart?" She slipped from the railing, and either as a diversion or an enticement, mentioned, "I think I was supposed to be going home today. Let's milk the cows, then it will be too late for me to go home." She chuckled and ran bare-foot towards the dairy.

Needless to say, not without a contentious phone call to her parents, Penny stayed overnight. After all she had as many clothes at Kowhai as she had at home: probably the result of bringing extra clothes with her and conveniently leaving them behind.

As it happened next morning Ngaire and Louise were in the kitchen baking, when George ambled in and said, "What's next to do, Gran?"

"My dear, I think it's time you went out and played."

"I'm too old to play." He looked at Ngaire as if embarrassed.

"I mean, kick and ball around with your brother."

"I thought you meant, play with my blocks, or something babyish." That allowed Ngaire a chuckle. "Anyway, James has gone home."

"George," Louise recited, "all work and no play makes Jack a dull boy." She shot a smile at Ngaire.

"My name's George, not Jack."

Over her shoulder Ngaire interpreted, "It's a saying, silly. All work and no play makes George a dull boy."

"I'm dull am I?"

"Get away with you — both of you. George, take Ngaire fishing, if you must work."

Ngaire's eyes brightened. Not only was she being relieved of work, not that she minded doing it, but she would be with George.

To which George replied, "Fishing's not work."

"It is — if you bring home tonight's meal."

Ngaire was already untying her apron.

From the rocks Ngaire watched George bait a hook, then whirl the line and sling it some distance into the turbulent ocean. He then baited a hook for Ngaire, and tossed her line to the north of his. "All you do is hold the line until you feel a nibble, then give it a tug." However this was not like fishing from a harbour wharf — which Ngaire had done — and the line constantly was 'nibbled' at. She could not differentiate between a movement and a bite. George apparently could, for within minutes he was hauling in his line.

"That's one," he bragged.

"You are so clever," Ngaire complimented, and moved slightly closer to him, watching him remove the hook and drop the fish into a sack. It had not been the first time she had been to the gap, but this day was much more exciting. She had had those urges before, and wanted so much to release them. She knew next to nothing about herself and certainly had never been told right from wrong. She did know George was handsome and likeable. She had known boys who were handsome and not likeable at all, so she presumed she was right to feel this way about George, although younger than her, certainly not a child.

She also knew, because Penny had told her, she was not the only girl who admired George.

"George, Penny's too young to be your sweetheart."

George's attention at that moment was on his line and watching terns take off from the beach and dive into the sea, then return usually empty-handed — or in their case empty beaked — to the beach.

Nevertheless their presence indicated that his only catch so far was not a fluke. He barely heard Ngaire's comment, until she repeated it.

"What are you going on about?"

"Penny said she was your sweetheart."

"Penny sometimes has a head full of cotton wool; that's what my dad says."

Rather than be disappointed by his response, Ngaire considered it to be an opening for her; having no rival.

At that point in her endeavours her line jerked.

"You've got one. — Quick. Give it a tug," George instructed.

Ngaire soon learned the difference between the line's agitation on the ocean floor and a snapper frantically trying to free itself.

"It's too hard for me to get in," Ngaire called.

George disengaged himself from his line, and crossed to Ngaire, and she almost forgot why he was standing so close, her feelings for him rising to adoration. "It's a beauty," George assessed before the several-pound snapper broke the surface

"Much bigger than mine."

All too soon, for Ngaire, the excitement was over, and with two fish in the bag the pair separated and continued to fish. Her next question was less intimidating — for George. "Why don't you and James live with your parents? Don't you like them?"

"Of course we do. It's just with three men gone from here, there's lots of work to do."

"Three?"

"Yep. Granddad had a farm hand, and he went to war. Then my Uncle Danny went, and my Uncle Sean fell down the cliffs — just along there.

"How did he do that?"

"He was rounding up sheep, just over there," he indicated, pointing to the cliff face across the gap, "when the cliff fell down — or something."

"Oh gee." Ngaire thought George might need comforting after disclosing that.

"Anyway, I'd better get back," he decided.

"Your grandma said you were to catch tonight's tea."

"We have — with your big one — and I've got another."

Not totally rejected Ngaire confessed, "I like being here with you — away from everyone." By now George was winding in his line so made out that he had not heard her. "If I was a boy, I'd like to kiss a girl here."

"What?"

"Don't you want to kiss me?"

"You're too old."

"Not!"

"You're a lot older than me." By then his attention was fully on his line; another snapper hooked, bigger than his first one, but smaller than Ngaire's.

"Only a year — and a bit. So don't then. I don't care." She began to wind in her line. "I've got to get back too."

Whatever Ngaire may have wished with George, that night, after the youngest children had been put to bed, and George and James had also gone to bed, having to be up again early, Ngaire and Penny sat on the lounge floor before Louise. She was spinning wool, and both girls, although unsuccessful at winning George's heart, were spellbound by Louise's deftness.

On another occasion when Penny trotted into Kowhai, the horse trotted obediently to Penny's commands — she and Ngaire were planting a variety of crops for the coming summer.

As if she had been riding on a cloud and swooped into the valley out of the blue Penny said, "Gran said that you haven't any parents. Are you an orphan? Ngaire stood up and silently wiped her eyes. Penny asked a little contritely, "Have I said something to make you sad?" The Maori girl bent down and continued planting. "Sorry."

"They both died."

"Oh, that's horrid."

"My dad went to war, and my mum." She sniffed back her sorry. "I don't know why she died. They didn't tell me."

"That's sad. I don't think I'd even cry if my parents died."

"Don't you like them?"

"Not much," Penny admitted. "Not at all, really."

"You would if you didn't have any."

"I love Grandma and Grandpa. They are not my real ones though. I haven't any real ones."

Penny's enquiry open Ngaire's door a little. "Me and my brother were in an orphanage for awhile, then we were sent here. I don't know why." She paused. "I think it's because they know my family or somethin'. Anyway, we're both happy here, and I don't mind how hard I work."

Both girls stood and looked along their not exactly straight rows.

"Nor do I — here," Penny agreed. "We've just about finished. Granddad will be pleased." Looking at her mud-smeared smock she exclaimed, "Oh, my smock is all dirty. Never mind, it will wash easily."

Thomas was across the field talking to George. Penny shouted, "Granddad, we've just about finished here; what's next to do?"

Thomas gave the girls a wave, continued talking to George for another minute then strolled across to the girls. "You have done well, Girls." He did not criticise their rows for not being perfectly straight. "The ground is so soggy they won't need watering."

"We're just wondering what to do next?" Penny offered.

"I think it is time for you to rest. I'm sure there's a drink and something nice to eat at the house."

That was a cue for the girls to follow him to the homestead. Looking over her shoulder Penny saw George directing the horse and plough across the field and wondered if his rows were straighter than their planting. She also had something else concerning George in mind.

George had been at it for awhile, so his mind began wandering. Having sighted Penny and Ngaire earlier he now imagined Ngaire without her pinny coming up to him with a home-made lemonade drink, and their hands touching. He further imagined her lingering, and both of them looking about to see if they were alone, and Ngaire again asking for a kiss. During the intervening time between going fishing and now his views on Ngaire had changed slightly.

His reverie was shattered when a familiar voice shouted, "Georgie, I've got you a drink." Penny walked briskly up to him with the drink in one hand and biscuits clutched in the other. "Gran says you have to stop for awhile."

"Eh?"

"You have to stop. You can talk to me if you want."

George wiped his brow and accepted the drink and slightly crushed biscuits.

"So what will we talk about? Gran says when I come back next weekend you will have a baby calf. Won't that be exciting."

On the driveway Ngaire was walking head down to avoid puddles. She had in her hands a glass of lemonade and biscuits for George. She looked up to see where George was, sighted Penny with him, and worst of all he taking a swig from a glass. Biting her lip, she turned and retraced her steps. She did not see George raise his hand and wave beckoningly to her.

Minutes earlier Ngaire had decided to change from her soiled dress and put on a fresh one. She did have a reason for this, and since she often did the washing she did not think it a burden to anyone else if she wore two dresses in one day. What she did not count on while changing was; in the kitchen Louise poured out an extra drink for Penny to take to George, so when Ngaire arrived, and Louise had herself left the kitchen, Ngaire also poured out a drink for George, and with some biscuits, took them to him.

She returned despondently to the kitchen, where Louise was now gathering ingredients for baking. "He didn't want it," she murmured.

"Oh, I thought he would be thirsty."

"Penny had already given him one."

Louise nodded knowingly. "You may as well drink it yourself."

"But that would not be fair; me having two drinks and the others only one."

Louise smiled at her maternally. "Dear, drink it quickly, and no one will ever know."

But Ngaire could not see the fairness in that, so said, "I'll put it in the safe for later. George might be thirsty again."

"If you must, dear."

Biting her lip, Ngaire said, "Anyway, he doesn't like me, because I'm a Maori."

That utterance caused a sharp reaction from Louise. "Whatever put that nonsense into your head?"

"I don't know. But it's true."

Louise clasped Ngaire's arm, "It is not true at all. I'm sure George likes you very much. You are a lovely girl." She drew Ngaire closer. "But he is only fourteen, and his mind is fixed on working on this farm, not on girls."

"I suppose."

"So I'll hear no more nonsense." She sat Ngaire into a chair. "You are a very lovely girl. You have been so good helping to teach the younger children, and reading them stories. Maybe you will become a teacher. Think of that." She nodded emphatically. "We will give you all the help you need."

"You have been very good to me and Tane."

"And I will tell you something else, dear. You are lucky, because, unless this war goes on much longer, when you want to get married there will be plenty of boys your age to choose from."

"I suppose?"

"But it will not be — even now — for girls just a few years older than you."

"Why?

"Because with so many young men killed in this beastly war there will be a shortage of them. I am afraid there will be many girls now who will never have the chance to marry. Isn't that sad?"

Only days later there occurred a surprise which took Ngaire's mind off George. The new mail boy rode up to the house on horseback, knocked on the front door and came face-to-face with Ngaire. The surprise was finding her again after their youthful friendship had been cut short by her moving into an orphanage. Now here she was.

CHAPTER FOURTEEN

All was not that rosy in the valley. Thomas who had to accept that situation. The problem was a looming one: what to do with Sean's property — eventually? For Thomas to buy back his daughter's place, having only given it to her a few years before seemed absurd. Admittedly what he had given was un-cleared land. What they had now was an almost fully developed farm. Besides, he accepted Alison and Sean and their family had to have money to live on. As the months of his hospitalisation extended it became obvious he could never return to the land. Unlike Kowhai, where young George believed he was running things, Sean did not have a son old enough to accept such responsibility. Thomas, untrusting of the future, and of bankers, was not prepared to mortgage Kowhai to re-purchase Kauri, his daughter's place. (He still referred to the property as belonging to Alison, rather than Sean, his son-in-law.)

Emily took the opportunity, despite the war, despite everything else, to make use of Alison as a companion. With the change in fashions, women wore looser dresses, so Alison's condition was not readily noticeable. Emily had wheedled it out of her within days. That being the case, she trotted her off to the theatre, or to concerts.

"I did enjoy that," Alison commented. "Thank you so much for making me go."

"I am certainly not going to stay home and mope," Emily stated. "We are doing our bit, so a little entertainment is a good thing."

While out with Alison she made a discovery: not like when she suspected her late husband was lurking behind a curtain in Miss Harkness' millinery, rather something very much above board. They were passing a hotel just off Queen St, and although Emily knew of it, and had always admired its ornate facade, on this occasion she spied, for it was not a bold announcement, a window notice advertising that the hotel was for sale. The *Ambassador* was its name, and Emily considered it certainly outwardly lived up to that name. Observant as she was, she also noted that the sign at been there for at least several weeks. In that case she would mull it over. She had recently sold off two of her less appealing assets, so had money to re-invest.

On that day other matters pushed the hotel into the background, and it was not until a week or two later she reviewed the idea of owning the Ambassador, and skilfully showing reluctance to the sellers set the wheels in motion to purchase it, if the price was within her budget.

There were nights when that entertainment kept them at home. Emily bought a piano, and around it the soldiers, since there was usually one who could play, had sing-songs, Alison and Emily's maids joining in. Alison still felt guilty: enjoying herself when the world, including *her* world, was in such a state. She felt further guilt when, instead of visiting Sean every day, she reduced it to every second day.

Emily was not confined to domestic matters. On the contrary, with Alison being as capable as running the household as she, she turned her attention back to her many businesses, ensuring they kept running smoothly. Nor was that easy, when shiploads of produce went to the bottom and she had the ensuing debacle over payments. She was also grateful that she had assets that did not require attention, such as land. Although Europe might be the centre of the conflagration, many other nations were not involved, and from those nations Emily purchased cloth for her wholesale and distributing firm: Fairprice Fabrics. As they say, the show must go on, and some of those fabrics no doubt did end up on stage, while most were turned into everyday garments. In fact, during those troubled times her businesses expanded, although her profits found their way into numerous pockets, as she distributed her wealth among family and friends, particularly those in need.

During those months Alison also gained knowledge of some of Emily's business affairs, and instead of being morose, looked on the brighter side, occasionally. She even filled in at Fairprice Fabrics for a day or two each week: an occupation that might one day come in handy.

On her first day at Fairprice Fabrics Emily introduced her to another lady. "Alison, this is Mrs Alison Mackenzie. She has been with me for over a year, so she will show you the ropes."

The introduced ladies smiled at each other, neither knowing of the other's connection to another member of the Chester clan, Ben. With one thing and another Alison was acquiring more of a taste of city life, as she had done spasmodically on the earlier occasions she had stayed with Emily With one thing and another Alison was acquiring more of a taste of city life, as she had done spasmodically on the earlier occasions she had stayed with Emily, and meeting the pleasant-natured Alison Mackenzie was another favourable connection with the city.

The two hotels Emily had sold at a reasonable price were little more than drinking establishments. Emily went ahead with her purchase of the six-storey Ambassador, little knowing what an important feature it would be in her future life, and indeed many of her yet to be born relations.

She went to town with Alison, and paused as they walked up the street opposite her new acquisition. "So, what do you think of it?" Emily indicated.

"Over there. That hotel?"

"It's mine."

"It is beautiful. Oh, Emily, it has so much character."

"Mm. That is what I thought, darling; a much more admirable building, than those other two awful places."

Alison agreed, yet did not voice her agreement, in case she offended her host.

"So let's have a look at it. I don't think they know they know I've bought it."

They crossed the road and entered the hotel, a concierge greeting them.

"Good morning, Ladies."

"Good morning," Emily responded as politely. "Can we take tea?"

"Most certainly, Ladies."

They were shown to the sumptuous lounge.

Alison gazed wondrously at the ornate décor, including large kentia palms which added to, for Alison, its exotic atmosphere. "It is very you, Emily."

"I thought so."

Alison also noticed the concierge talking quietly to another staff member who glanced in their direction. "You've been recognised," she informed Emily.

"Are you sure, my dear? They could think that you are the new owner."

"I hardly think so." Even so, she was mildly pleased that Emily held herself in the same regard as herself.

Needless to say the service was excellent and Alison did wonder if all patrons received the same attention.

Emily hoped once it was known that she now owned the hotel it would make for a smooth changeover.

*　　*　　*　　*　　*　　*

At any other time the arrival of twins would have been heralded with ecstasy. For Alison, it was a tragedy. Although she knew beforehand, she still wept after their delivery.

Only after their birth did they tell Sean. "The luck of the Irish," was his response, then sank into another depression. He knew they would blame his religion for his wife's babies: now five of them, all under seven. That she was expecting before his accident did not enter into it. There was no chance of it happening again, he thought, not while he was in this condition.

A fine looking lady, herself childless, clasped Alison's hand, and spoke with pride and hope. "Ali, they are so, so beautiful." She was going to say, 'I wish they were mine,' however did not want to put the idea into the despairing mother's head. "They are going to grow into fine boys. You keep a stiff upper lip, my darling."

The fatigued mother looked solemnly into the eyes of a woman she had grown to love and admire so dearly. Her fatigue was not so much physical, rather mental, and that could have a dire effect on her recovery.

Emily said to her there and then, "My darling, I could say to you and Sean, forget all your troubles and let me take care of you. Would that be fair on you, Ali?" She clasped her hand tighter, leaned over and again kissed Alison's cheek. "Come on, Girl, you've always been a fighter, so fight now."

Alison nodded, and uttered a weak, "Yes." She rolled her head to one side. "Em," she murmured, "I feel so tired. Just let me sleep." She let go her sister-in-law's hand. "I'm sorry."

"You do not have to be. You should be as proud of yourself, as I am of you."

And Alison in her depressed state could not see why Emily should be proud of her, when it was she who had carried the burden, especially over the last few weeks, of looking after her.

Emily leaned over and for the third time kissed Alison's cheek, hoping to convey her love, and, the family's. "You sleep. I shall sit here quietly beside you."

She did not remind Alison of the thousand and one things to do at her home, because, although true, it would not help Alison to have that confirmed, even if she knew it.

After spending just ten minutes at the sleeping mother's side, she took herself off to Auckland Hospital where the staff knew better than to disallow Emily out of visiting hours.

She did not beat about the bush with Sean, and without enquiring of his health, advised him, "Now listen here, old chap, how about bucking up, doing something for yourself, so you can help your wife. You may think you have troubles, however Alison's are a sight worse."

Sean could not imagine how he could either help his wife from a hospital bed, or how her troubles could be worse than his, when he could not even walk!

Alison lay wearily, her thoughts drifting beyond the room, beyond the country, lingering with Henry. She wished he were with her now, because he would have, as Emily, offered hope, encouragement, and yes, love. She would write to him, and let him know of the twins. He had been a comfort to her, yet she did not want him to think she could return his love, rather be the friend to him she had promised.

Louise with help manhandled three boxes of produce from ship to shore, on to a tram, and off again at Parnell, again with the help of the conductor and two passengers, while an impatient motorist blasted his horn at being delayed. She left them beside a shop, and walked the short distance to Emily's. Here she rested, while Emily on her own cranked her Chevrolet Classic 15 into action and drove quickly back to the intersection did a precarious 'U' turn and pulled up beside the boxes. She loaded them into the car, and swung into her street, another motorist braking to avoid her.

Louise rested long enough to have a cup of tea, then visited Alison, sternly advising her daughter, "My girl, you can dismiss thoughts of selling the farm. Have you no faith in God — or of Sean making a full recovery?"

Alison limply shook her head. "You know, Mother, Sean will never walk again." She stared at the blankets, believing this to be the lowest point in her life.

"So the doctors have said. Then what do they know of miracles, of human endeavour. I'll wager they won't stop him from trying to walk. Alison, you and he have to do his have faith in yourselves. I'll say here and now, dear, your husband *will* be walking before those new sons of yours." Then she realised she had not yet seen them, and promptly ensured she did.

While she was in town, she also called on Sean. Where she learned the truth: Sean had debts on the farm, and those debts were with Nigel Caldwell. Enough for her to retract her assurance to her daughter about not letting it go. She could not imagine that avaricious man — and being family — allowing such circumstances hinder his intentions of acquiring Sean's farm. Nor could she imagine him acquiring it for his own son, Stanley. If that was the case, then, since Stanley had long since been enfolded into the Chester clan, it would be like keeping it in the family.

Louise now knew why her husband was in such a foul mood over the property. He was aware to expand, Sean had gone to Nigel. He probably did so out of generosity, believing he was doing the banker a good turn, sort of keeping the business within the family. He should not have been so considerate.

Louise's baking was interrupted by the phone; her daughter back with Emily while her twin sons spent another week or two in the nursing home. "Mother, Em's had terrible news," Alison audibly cried. "Jonathon's been killed in action."

While Louise could not weep for Jonathon, tears came to her eyes at the thought of Emily who had done so much, now having to cope with that. He was not her own flesh and blood, however after his father's death she had drawn closer to him.

"Em was only saying the other day, she just wished Jonathon would return, to take up running the . . . Mother, I just feel so sorry for her. I've never seen her cry before . . ." Her voice faltered. ". . . She's always been the shoulder for us to cry on."

"So, you take care of her for a change, Alison." Being aware of the cost for Alison to make the toll call, she abruptly changed the subject. "Is everything all right, otherwise?"

"I suppose so." Said without conviction.

"If that husband doesn't buck up his . . ."

"Mother, he *is* trying to walk."

"You make sure he keeps trying."

Alison could not agree with her mother's hard line. She was sure Sean would walk if he could. Not for one moment did she believe, no matter how bad his injuries, he would deliberately exaggerate them.

Her turn to comfort Emily, even take interest in the running of her affairs, in as much as answering trivial questions, making decisions on Emily's behalf, hoping they were the right decisions. At least she knew her sister-in-law would not scold her for a wrong choice. During those months Alison acquired a taste of the commercial world, to the extent she liked making such decisions as much as the domestic decisions she made in her own home. She fancied herself as having a business head!

Alison returned home with her babies, and there was a general shift around within Kowhai. She wanted only to go back to her own place, although agreed, after an argument with her mother, it was not practical. Twice a week she made the journey back to Auckland to visit her husband, and once a week she personally delivered supplies to Emily.

The new steamer *Waiuku* berthed at Onehunga, and she had to see to getting the produce — carried free of charge — from ship to shore, and to save expense, she carried the boxes one at a time up to the tram stop — Adrienne being too young to help — placed them aboard a tram, and at the stop within a hundred yards of Emily's piled them all on the footpath, waited with them, while Adrienne fetched Emily and her soldiers to complete the journey, had barely time for a cup of tea, then hurried on foot to the hospital, since matrons tended to be strict over visiting times, even in Alison's case.

Although Sean was delighted to see his daughter, he did have other things on his mind, and the presence of Adrienne meant telling his wife would be difficult. So, after a few minutes, all the while wrangling with the problem, he simply said, "Adrienne, my pet, why don't you say hello to Mr Barker over there."

"I don't know him."

"He doesn't have any visitors, pet, so you visit him."

"S'pose so."

"That's a good girl," her mother agreed, puzzled over Sean's insistence. And when she was gone, she began to tell Sean more of what was happening at home, until he stopped her.

"My dear woman, will you let me speak."

"Eh?"

"I want to speak to you privately."

"What about?"

"Listen, before she comes back."

"Is it *that* important she cannot hear also?"

"My love, just listen to me."

"I am. You haven't said anything yet."

"I'm trying to. Now listen." He finally silenced his wife, just as he noticed his daughter about to leave the other patient's bedside. "Mr Nigel has been to see me . . ."

"*What!*"

"Shsh, Woman! Don't tell the world. Mr Nigel has made me an offer."

"For what?"

"The farm, of course."

"We're not leaving!" The matter was final as far as Alison was concerned.

Sean shook his head, just as Adrienne bounced back.

"Mr Barker does have visitors — a granddaughter — just like me, so there."

"I must have been asleep when she came," Sean said.

"Fibber, Father. You wanted me to go away so you could tell each other secrets, I know."

"That is true. What your father had to tell me is not really for little girl's ears."

Adrienne looked down at the bedclothes. "Is it to do with me? Am I going to be sent away?"

Alison was appalled. "Most definitely not! Whatever put that idea into your head?"

"Because you can't afford to keep me."

"Darling, your father and I have to discuss something — it is just between me and daddy."

"Daddy and I," her daughter corrected. "So, you want me to go and visit someone else?"

Alison's attention was diverted to her daughter's correcting of her grammar, and she could only put it down to her own mother's influence.

"I does not matter, pet," Sean intervened, oblivious to his wife's thoughts.

"It *does* matter," Alison insisted.

With a reluctant, "All right then," Adrienne sauntered off.

Immediately Alison challenged her husband. "Sean, we are managing. And soon everyone will be back home, and . . ."

"Don't be silly, woman. We can't expect to depend on others, so we can't. Nor can we afford to pay anyone."

His wife looked down at the sheets, and appealed to him solemnly, "We cannot just leave. What will we do? Where will we go? I have lived there all my life."

He rested his hand on hers. "I know. I know all that. I only wish . . ."

"Sean, let's just try for a little longer. Please darling, for my sake, for the children. They could not possibly leave their cousins, not now." She could have told them how well they were all working together. She did admit they were only children, behaving like responsible adults, having missed some of their childhood years. She knew it was certainly the case for George and Stanley: both performing ably about the farm, with little opportunity to explore their young lives. Their case was repeated all over New Zealand, and she knew in many other parts of the world. It was such a beastly affair, this blasted war.

Their problems were not much to do with the war, rather with her husband, as the result of an accident. Alison asked repeatedly, 'Why was he on that cliff track at that precise moment?' A few paces either side of it and he would have missed the fall, and been fit and able to run the farm, and they would not have to move. She knew herself what he said was right. They would have to sell up. The very thought of it was so heart-breaking.

Without telling Sean, she wrote to her soldier friend Henry, telling him of her plight, and knowing he could not advise her in time, she expected a return letter, or a postcard, within a month or two?

The war had a way still to run. After all, there were still lambs to go to the slaughter. 1916 turned to 1917, and the very farms Alison was talking about were struggling. They just did not have the manpower — decades later it would have truly been termed people power — to manage them properly, and properties fell into decline. Ben let go most of the lambs, and many ewes that culling found a little long in the tooth. It meant output would be down in the future, although it also meant a lot less work. Likewise with the calves, and many favourite old cows, despite his sons' youthful insistence that they could manage. Now mid-summer, easier to get up in the mornings — easier all round. What about another winter, even if all the children were a year older than the last? It would not be fair. He dismissed the argument they could just as easily round up and milk twenty cows as ten. Ben kept two for their own needs. Why wasn't his sister Jane here to make cheese and butter?

During a rare quiet moment Alison escaped from the house, wearing beneath her dress woollen swimming togs. Intentionally she strolled down to the waterfall, and for several minutes sat at the pool's edge contemplating her life. 'It hasn't turned out at all as I hoped,' she thought. 'But you, stream, are still here,' she murmured, looking at the disturbed waters: recent rains having increased the stream's flow. She slipped her dress over her head, kicked off her shoes, and cautiously eased herself into the chilly waters and gasped, 'It's supposed to be summer.' She held her arms close to her chest protecting herself against the cold, then courageously lowered herself deeper into the pool. 'Brrrr.'

She looked at the cascade, and waded towards it until the tumbling waters immersed her. 'Shall I, or shan't I?' She imagined Annabelle watching from above and goading her on. 'I wonder if she still goes swimming? I must ask her when I see her. — If I see her again.' She looked about, clambered up to the ledge, and edged her way behind the fall, and after a moment's hesitation dived through it, remembering to keep her legs straight. Rising to the surface she smiled at her achievement, and said almost aloud, 'If I can do that, I can do anything.' Satisfied with the single plunge, and shivering with cold, she vacated the pool.

That was a moment of respite. There followed a moment of truth. Simple truth. Alison was too proud to admit it to her parents. She furtively mixed some glue on the kitchen range, went into the barn, rummaged around the bench for a strip of leather, and, recalling one of her brother's many lessons, cut out new soles, then fastened them to a pair of shoes worn through to the inner sole. Breathing deeply with sorrow, and shame that she had been reduced to such secrecy, she stuck the new soles over the worn, then using a shoe last tacked them on, admired her handiwork, and as furtively returned to the house. She could have given them to her father to mend, because there was no shame in having shoes wear out. Yet she could not now even admit to that!

Thomas took time off to visit Sean, and although there was talk of a railway to connect Waiuku with Pukekohe, and therefore Auckland, he, for the time being, still had to be driven by gig to Pollok, board the steamer, then take a tram to Newmarket, then walk across the Auckland Domain to the hospital. Nor did he appreciate the walk: the lawns now too manicured for him, with little sign of the exhibition he had earlier attended. His attention was focussed on visiting Sean, not admiring exotic flowers.

"How are you, old boy?" he greeted. "You look better than I expected." That gave the patient little room to answer.

"Fine, so I am. — Except for my legs."

"Yes, perhaps in time. You might be fine here, but we're having it rough on the farms." And that left Sean with no room to answer either.

"I wish so much, Sir, I could help."

"You can't, that's that!" Thomas was rather direct. His next question was to the point also. "I understand Caldwell has been to see you?"

"Yes Sir, Mr Nigel has been — just to see how I was getting on."

Thomas Chester sneered. "I'm surprised at his concern. What did he offer you?"

"Offer?"

"How much is he going to pay for your place?"

There was no sidestepping Thomas, and Sean should have known it. "A — a fair price — I suppose, under . . ."

"Under the circumstances. *His* circumstances, I'll wager?"

Sean nodded.

"The man's a rogue. If I had the cash, I'd buy you out myself. It grieves me to think you are so anxious to sell."

"I can understand, Sir. But my wife and I have to support ourselves. The price is lower than I hoped for," he admitted. "Who else is there to buy it?" Unfortunately Sean did not look very far in that respect: his thoughts remaining within the bounds of the valley, and immediate neighbours.

"And, Boy, when you have sold up, paid Caldwell his dues, how much will be left for you and my daughter?"

"Quite a lot."

"Enough to support you, while . . ?"

"Hopefully."

"As I thought. Nothing, or next to nothing." Thomas could have lambasted Sean into the perils of going into debt: so much apparent debt to jeopardise his property. That could come later, when he and his family were out on the street. Instead, he was resigned to say, "What is done, is done," and advise him. "Perhaps one day we will have the opportunity to buy it back."

Little did he know then how circumstances would change within the family.

Having said his piece, and learned the truth, he did not spend much more time with Sean just for appearances sake. He strutted from the hospital, was in no mood to visit Emily — which was a pity — and caught a tram back to Onehunga, then ambled round the developing, yet in places derelict, town — like the rusting iron and steel works — stayed overnight at the Manukau Hotel, and caught the boat back to Pollok with the morning tide.

MOON OVER THE MANUKAU

Family Tree 1916

Thomas and Louise Chester

    Jane, b 1876 – m Danny Carsen

        Douglas, b 1905

    Ben, b 1878 – m Priscilla Caldwell

        George, b 1902
        James, b 1904
        Kathy, b 1906

    Alison, b 1882 – m Sean Sullivan

        Adrienne, b 1909
        Patrick, b 1911
        Jennifer, b 1913
        Athol and Egan, b 1916

Maude Caldwell (widow), d 1905

    Nigel, b 1877 – m Jessica

        Stanley, b 1902
        Penny, b 1904
        Nathan, b 1908

    Emily, b 1878 – m William Todd

Priscilla, b 1880 – m Ben Chester

CHAPTER FIFTEEN

". . . And, Nigel Caldwell, if you think for one moment we are going to share that confounded valley with the Chesters, you can dismiss the thought from your head."

"No, Jessica, my dear. I am a banker, not a farmer," he pleaded.

"Of that I am glad. It has taken *me* fifteen years to establish us in this town . . ."

"Yes, my love . . ."

"And, I'm here to stay."

Which surprised even Nigel, believing she might wish to live in a more grandiose location. He held up his hand to halt her further admonishment. "I only intend to put a manger on it, in the meantime, and wait for better times to sell it."

"That *is* a better prospect," she relented. "You *are* a wise man."

He was glad of that. He thought himself very clever, even if his wife often had her doubts.

"I suppose it would be quite nice to go up there for a holiday, come to think of it."

"I'm sure it would," he agreed, only to keep the peace, although his wife's term of a holiday would hardly embrace conditions he knew existed at Sean's place. A thought he would have to get out of his head. It was *his* place now, or would soon be, once matters had been finalised. While the purchase of Kauri was never far from his mind, he was involved in many other transactions on behalf of *his* bank: fussing over details, and making his assistant manager wonder what he was doing there, having little authority passed down to him.

Alas, the most unfortunate thing happened to Nigel Caldwell that same week. He caught a cold, and was confined to bed. What with one thing and another his overtaxed body had little resistance, so there he stayed. His belief he was the bank was quickly dispelled when an efficient young replacement was sent form Auckland: the local assistant being by-passed for temporary promotion.

Penny burst in on her father on the Saturday. "Mr Goldstone wants to see the farm. I'm going to show him." Not, 'Can I show him?' rather, 'I'm *going* to'.

"If you must," Nigel accepted, too sore in the head to care.

His wife must have been somewhere else, because she never got to hear of the excursion during its brief planning stages. So thirteen-year-old Penelope borrowed her father's phaeton, and minutes later trotted out of town with Mr Goldstone as a bewildered passenger.

"You will positively love the valley," she assured him. "My brother works there. It is a matter of having to, these days."

"I thought there would be no need of that. You seem quite comfortably off."

"We are, Mr Goldstone. At least, I think so. But that is not the point," she explained most authoritatively. "What with all the men overseas . . ." And she wondered why he was not there also? ". . . Someone has to keep the world in food and clothing, and every little bit helps, you know. I mean, it's not much use having stacks of money, if there's nothing to spend it on, is there?" Not part of her explanation as to why Stanley worked on a farm.

Mr Goldstone by now had decided this girl was certainly not a chip of either old block: her mother or father. All the way she told him of who lived where, and what they did: stories about people a girl of her age should not know. What also amazed him how unfazed she was handling the phaeton: the road remaining little more than a track. He admitted, only inwardly, if she showed no sign of fear as they wound round hills, steep drops at times on both sides, then his nerves were taut. So much so, he could not fully appreciate the scenery. Finally, they turned off the rugged ridge road, and dropped over the brink into the valley, Penelope handling the phaeton masterfully until she safely reached the floor, where her brother was repairing a fence.

"Hi, Stan!" she hailed. "I've brought a man to see our place." Turning to Mr Goldstone, she advised, "This is my brother — look at him — a farmhand."

Stanley took his eye off the staple he was hammering, and paused with his hammer raised. "I'll scrag you, Penny, I promise I will."

She laughed in her high-spirited manner, and with a sweep of her hand, announced, "All this is really Kowhai, the Chesters' place, even the part my dad wants." That was telling the young banker precisely what she thought of her father's activities. "He doesn't know a thing about farming. But my brother does, don't you, Stan?"

"What?"

"You know a lot about farming?"

"A bit."

"Is grandma Chester home?" Louise was not the girl's grandmother, although Penny liked to think so.

"Yeah, I'd say so."

"Come on then, Mr Goldstone, we shall go and see Granny first. She's wonderful." She flicked her head towards Stanley. "I'll see you later." Nudging the horse into action, she said to Goldstone, "Maybe my father will let Stanley manage his farm, and I could come up and cook for him, and work on the farm as well."

"My dear, I hardly think two children could run a farm."

"Do you want to make a bet?" she challenged him, as she also challenged her schoolteacher, and a few other superiors to boot. "Stanley just about runs a farm now," she advised Goldstone. She did not add that Stanley, with George and Thomas, and young farmhands combined, ran the farm. He would soon learn that without being told.

That she was still a child was evident when she threw herself into Louise Chester's arms, knowing no matter what the relationship between her father and the Chesters was, she was as welcome as ever. She even put the suggestion to Louise she could also help on the farm. The sight also pleased Joseph Goldstone, because the girl did have some child-like traits left.

"Miss Penelope, your father would accuse me of abducting you."

"What does that mean?"

"Kidnapping you, dear."

"That sounds awfully exciting. Oh, *please* do." How she would love to be live here all the time, especially now they owned some of the valley. "I'd work hard, truly I would."

"I'm sure you would too, dear. Perhaps, one day." And Louise was actually thinking on the same lines as Penny. Just possibly her father would allow — in the future of course — Stanley and this girl to manage Kauri. At least it would be some consolation, rather than have a complete stranger move into their valley. She repeated, "Yes, Penelope, I am sure you would."

"Aw, don't call me that, Grandma, it's priggish."

"I should call you 'Halfpenny', because you are not worth your name when you talk about running away from home."

She pouted. "You see! I'll do just like Aunt Emily did. And look at her now?"

"Yes dear. Your Aunt Emily has gained a lot — however also lost a lot into the bargain," Louise said, probably — hopefully — over the child's head. On second thoughts, she recalled this bright child already knew of Emily's lesser righteous activities.

Penny skipped out the door, and changing roles, invaded Adrienne's domain, playing with some kittens, a streak of child left in her; more than a streak actually, although she would not admit it.

On the other hand Penny was growing up: a woman beginning to stir inside her earlier than many girls of her age. Her cousin George was the first recipient of her affection towards boys. While Goldstone was discussing the farm sale with Alison, Penny, after playing with the kittens, more by coincidence than design, happened to be alone with George: near the barn cum stable.

"Geor-gie," she said to bait him. "Away from school and work, who's your sweetheart?"

"School isn't a sweetheart, I reckon."

"What I meant, have you a sweetheart at school?" she probed, trying to untangle her earlier question.

"Heck no."

"You mean, you don't even think about girls?"

"Hardly." He screwed up his face at her. "What are you talking about?"

Penny shrugged. She looked down at the ground she was drawing in with her bare toe. "Doesn't matter."

"Come on, Pen," George prompted. "You don't think about boys, do you?"

She shrugged, then admitted, "Sometimes."

"Do you, really?" Then he recalled that this conversation with Penny was familiar; not the first she had challenged him with it.

"Why shouldn't I?" She walked away from him, stooped down and stroked one of Kowhai's dogs, which immediately decided it was an invitation to frolic.

George was bewildered, because he had always considered Penny as being Stanley's kid sister, apart from his cousin. He screwed his face again, not even considering she might like him to kiss her. The dog skipped from Penny to him, then back to his cousin: any romantic thoughts from either child dissipating.

Living back at Kowhai while her husband endeavoured to regain his feet in hospital, Alison was naturally present at negotiations between her father and a third party, whether that be a banker or prospective buyer. "I'm sorry, Father, but we have to sell out, and get whatever we can . . ."

"Humph! Do you know what the best price is nowadays?" He turned to Goldstone. "I'm sure you could provide us with real estate values?"

The young man swallowed. "Yes, er . . ."

"You might stammer!"

"I'm afraid it is not easy to sell farms at the moment, and — ah — Mr Caldwell's . . ."

"Well, he wouldn't pay a penny more than he had to for a start." Thomas faced Goldstone. "Mrs Sullivan's brother and I were planning to buy the property, as soon as we have sufficient to pay cash." He watched the financier's mouth open. "I'll have none of your mortgage proposals in this house, young man. That is what got them in this mess in the first place." Before Goldstone could defend that accusation, Thomas added, "Next thing we'd know you or that Caldwell fellow would be tuning us out as well."

"I'm sure it would not be like that, Sir."

"Humph!" Thomas scoffed at the reassurance. "No, I suppose you personally wouldn't. You're only a lad. Not a director like Caldwell."

In reality Joseph Goldstone could buy Nigel Caldwell out twice over, if he had a mind to. Goldstone's attention was not on his own inherited wealth, instead on Thomas Chester's belief that Caldwell was a bank director, rather than a district manager. Perhaps a mistake, or perhaps, just perhaps, Caldwell had promoted himself in the eyes of his family.

In the meantime Thomas was still decrying Caldwell. "If that fellow saw a bit of daylight occasionally, he would not catch a cold every time it rained."

Alison restrained him. "Now, Father, please don't upset yourself. We can't afford to have you ill."

That undermined Thomas' position, and he resented her inference, truth or not. "Oh well, Child, sell your inheritance, and see what you'll get. I think you'll discover, only too late, that it sells for a fraction of its real worth. — Just enough to pay back the bank!"

Goldstone disagreed. "I'm sure Mr and Mrs Sullivan will receive a fair price."

"Not from Caldwell they won't!" And Thomas would not let up.

"Father, please." Alison became sympathetic towards Goldstone, who was only doing his job.

Goldstone kept his cool, and was able to gain a respite when Louise entered with tea for the trio, spoke to him cordially, yet left him with the impression she also disapproved of the forced sale. That day he gained some knowledge: beginning with the slip of a girl who drove him to the farm, and ending with the same girl driving him — horse and gig style — back to his hotel. In between, he discovered a hard working family who, through circumstances beyond their control, were experiencing difficulties. He did see both sides of the argument: Thomas Chester's interpretation of banking methods, and Nigel Caldwell's manner of doing business. At the end of the day he rather hoped Caldwell would be confined to his bed until he himself could get a better deal for the Sullivan's, for what was being offered was little more than robbery. Goldstone, decided, Caldwell must be a fool to try and put one across Thomas Chester.

The Chester's having had more than their share of bad luck. Now it was the turn of the Caldwell's. Contrary to what he displayed Nigel was not *the* bank. When the distressing cold developed into a general breakdown of his health, Joseph Goldstone remained much longer in charge at Waiuku.

Louise played her part to. To the family doctor, who also attended the Caldwell's she mentioned, "Perhaps, Doctor, Nigel needs a holiday — away from the place?"

The good doctor nodded, exchanging glances with Louise. "I couldn't agree more, my dear Louise."

Nigel Caldwell, his wife and one child, Nathan, were packed off to Waiheke Island: a delightful spot in the Hauraki Gulf, and a place not easy to return from, given he would have to catch a steamer to Auckland, travel by tram to Onehunga, and then, providing the tides were right, get another boat to Waiuku. Nigel was too ill to make the effort, when he did eventually learn of proceedings concerning the Sullivan's.

Alison, this time in Auckland alone, visiting her husband, related the woeful tale, adding, "A Mr Goldstone is in charge now. And he believes he can get a better deal for us than Nigel's offer."

"Ah, that would be a far better thing, if he could." Sean had his own news, and although the sale of the farm was important, for the moment his news was even more promising. "Your mother was right, my sweet. 'Tis well I listened to her, and not to the doctors, totherwise I fear I would have aput m'self out of me misery, so I did."

"What do you mean?" She knew perfectly well what he meant by 'putting himself out of his misery,' although as far as the doctors were concerned.

"They say I'll walk again, m' dear. Shan't be able to lift or do anything heavy, but at least walk, so I will."

"I knew it! — I knew it!" Tears dripped down her cheeks, and she briefly hoped they could keep the farm after all. Then she thought of the alternative. "Perhaps you can take up auctioneering, or something like that. At least we could still live somewhere not too far away from the farm."

"P'haps I could at that."

"We could swap jobs. I'll wear the pants, and you wear the apron." For a moment the burden had lifted from her shoulders, and she was the girl he first knew: not a mother of five young children, with all the responsibilities of looking after them, and the disruptions she knew caused by her frequent visits to Sean. If only he could come home, then half of her troubles would be over. So engrossed in her own thoughts, she barely heard his reply to her suggestion.

"You won't after you've tasted me cooking."

With hope of some sort of future for them, she left Sean, and as if his news made the difference, she decided not to stay overnight at Emily's instead to return to Kowhai. Fortunately being summer, she could take a boat on the late afternoon tide, and be met at Pollok. Even that meant an extra strain on the family: someone having to drop whatever they were doing and go and meet the boat. During the boat journey an idea came to mind. 'What I said to Sean, about wearing the pants? I don't intend to supersede him as head of the house, however I can be the breadwinner.' Also, her experience with Emily, little as it was. 'Could I develop that experience into somehow running a business?' The big drawback was having five young children under her wing. Whether they lived on the farm or in town, they would still be under her wing. 'I can't imagine him doing domestic things, especially those revolving round changing nappies.' By the time the boat reached Pollok she had rejected then resurrected the idea several times.

"Fancy you turning up," Alison greeted with obvious surprise, and could have added, 'Like a bad penny,' A pun Penelope had already tired of. Strange, the daughter of the very man who had tried to swindle them out of the farm should come to meet her. As she treated this girl's brother, she also treated Penny: not a word of animosity, because she knew the girl also was a rebel, at least to her own parents.

Then, as Alison tossed her bag on the rack beneath the gig's seat, from behind hands reached up and clasped across her eyes. "Guess who?"

"Oh, darling," Recognising the voice, "you did give me a fright." She turned and gave her daughter a big hug. Then, not so much as an afterthought, when she climbed up beside Penny she also gave her a hug: as affectionate as that to her daughter, at the same time wondering just how much love the girl ever got from her parents. Then, sitting between the two girls, she put an arm about each.

Penelope had seen the mother and daughter hug and was a little put out. She could not remember when her mother had last held her that way. She had been held all right, while she got spanked. Although she may have deserved the punishment, surely there had been times when she deserved to be hugged? Then, in a moment all put aside when she also received a cuddle, and had they not been in such an awkward position she would have dearly loved to have laid her head on Alison's breast and been held even tighter. Which led her to wishing, 'Perhaps I could stay at Kowhai for always?' and sighed sadly. 'I suppose that is too much to expect. There's so many there now,' she lamented. For her it was wonderful just to spend time there while her own parents and that brat of a younger brother were away.

Now huddled together, each girl with an arm around Alison, in the gathering dark they sang their way to Kowhai. For Penelope one of the most memorable experiences of her life: the clip-clop of the hastened horse, their own voices, and during very temporary silences, the song of tui in trees overhanging the road, and various farm animals uttering last calls before all settled down for the night.

As well Alison did not stay overnight at Emily's. Next morning, being Saturday, Joseph Goldstone rode out to Kowhai alone, since his escort on the first occasion, Penelope, was already there. He actually missed her company: so young yet mature in manner. Naturally Thomas Chester was present at the kill, greeting the banker formally, while his daughter spoke pleasantly enough, yet was reserved. "Mrs Sullivan, I have better news for you," he announced, hoping to quell Thomas Chester's fears. "We have a potential buyer for your property, prepared to pay more for it . . ."

"How much more, Goldstone?" Thomas Chester demanded.

"Father, please allow Mr Goldstone to say . . ."

"Don't be hood-winked, my girl."

"I think, Father, this should really be between Mr Goldstone and myself." She glared at her father, indicating he should leave them alone.

With that Thomas heaved himself from the armchair, muttered under his breath, "You're a fool, Girl," and strode out of the room. His wife in the kitchen heard him still muttering as he went out the back door.

Goldstone made another attempt to advise Alison of the deal. "I think the offer we have, Mrs Sullivan is a lot . . ."

At the moment Jennifer burst in whinging, "Penny hit me."

Alison expelled her breath, cradled her daughter's head for a few seconds, and suggested, "Maybe you did something wrong, darling."

"I didn't! — She's a *bloody bitch!*"

Joseph Goldstone could not believe his ears.

Alison could, and the back of her hand whipped the child's mouth. "Don't you ever — *ever* —— speak like that again!"

If she had more to say, then it would have to wait. Jennifer wrenched free, howling louder, rushed from the room, seeking comfort from her grandmother, who was about to enter with tea.

Louise quietly put down the tray, Jennifer still clutching at her dress, grabbed the child's hand, and not too severely took her from the room, all the while Jennifer whimpering. Because she had her face buried in her grandmother's voluminous dress she did not realise where she was being taken to, and certainly not why. Louise lifted her over the wash basin, holding her firmly with one hand, while the other deftly turned on the tap, snatched up the soap, and thrust it into the girl's mouth, Jennifer's screech lifting off the roof.

Goldstone was explaining, "A Mr Conway from the East Coast apparently has at some time or other visited this area . . ."

"*My God!* — What has Mother done?" Both Goldstone and Alison whipped their heads round to the door, as if they expected Jennifer to be there, so loud was her scream. The sound had actually travelled from the bathroom, along the veranda and through three rooms. Alison did not think for one moment her mother had murdered the child, so she quietly rose, crossed the lounge and shut the door. "I'm sorry for this disturbance, Mr Goldstone. I'm afraid my daughter is a little troublesome at times."

"I suppose we all are."

"I certainly was, although I hope not . . ." Alison could not recall speaking to her parents like that, however she did not continue with the subject. ". . . You were saying a — ah — Mr Conway . . ."

"Yes, Morton Conway. He has made an offer. I believe a fair one under the circumstances."

"I'm sure it is, Mr Goldstone, if you say so. Il'll have to talk again with my husband," she advised him, her voice bearing the weight of the decade — less than a decade — between her single days and the present.

"Of course, Mrs Sullivan."

She sighed sadly. "I'm sure my father would disagree, not that it is his business, so I shan't tell him." Later when Goldstone left, Alison slipped from the house, and knowing at that time of the day the dairy would be deserted, she entered, sat on the stool both she and her sister had used so often to milk the cows, and wept: a little ashamed she, a grown woman, should be so despondent, nevertheless unable to hold back her sorrow

If she thought she was alone, she was not. Several minutes may have passed when Jennifer slunk from a corner, her own eyes still red from sobbing, came up to her mother, laid her hand on her head, and offered, "I'm — very — sorry — Mummy."

Alison, without looking up, reached for the hand, took it to her lips and kissed it. "It's all over now, darling." And it was. Alison's meaning referred mainly to the loss of the farm, rather than her daughter's earlier behaviour, although she wondered where the child had picked up such an expression.

                    *   *   *   *   *   *

Before the sale became unconditional Morton Conway, being an independent man, and not solely reliant on bank managers, or agents, travelled up from the East Coast, hired a horse at Waiuku, and rode out to view his acquisition.

Alison, having shaken off her flock, actually showed Conway her farm, and like Goldstone, he viewed the woman as deeply distressed, obviously torn between two needs: the need to sell, and her family, thus breaking up the farm. While his daughters might enjoy the company, he certainly would not, and rather than be a continual thorn in the side of the Chesters he decided to put a manager on to the property — if he could find one.

To Ben Chester, he suggested, "Do you think, Mr Chester, your family could continue to run the place — for a wage — until I get someone . . ."

"We've been doing it long enough, so I guess we can."

"That would be good of you."

Morton Conway rode alone from the valley, almost feeling he had wronged the Chesters by intruding into their lives. Having bought the property he was now definitely in two minds whether he wanted to live on it.

The sale went ahead.

If the Chesters thought things would settle down, they were in for another shock.

Alison now felt alienated from the farm, and in a way from her family. It was as when she first knew she wanted to marry Sean, and although no one had a word to say against him, nor did they have a word in favour of her marrying him. So this time she kept her own counsel, minding her own business until the deed was done. And that is exactly what Alison intended to do: mind her own business. "Mother, you won't have us under your feet much longer," she said softly, while both were baking.

"What do you mean?" Louise challenged sharply, resting the rolling pin on the table.

Alison hesitated, however, having started, she had to continue. "We are moving into town."

A moment's stunned silence. "Alison. — When? — Why?" Louise did not shout, yet her voice was firm.

"Because, I have bought a shop."

"You've *what?*" That raised Louise's voice a few notches.

With a shrug, placing a tray of freshly baked biscuits on the table, she told her mother, "I have bought a drapery shop. Harts — you know the place."

"You don't know . . ?"

"I'll have to learn won't I," she retorted, feeling she had wronged her mother. In truth she believed she had learned enough of the drapery business while working at Fairprice Fabrics to at least have an idea of what she was letting herself in for.

Louise taken aback, not so much over the news, rather the manner with which it was dealt; a *fait accompli* attitude, without consultation, without even a mention of her plans. While Alison might walk into that shop and by material without telling her mother, to actually walk in and buy the shop itself was a different matter entirely. "So, who advised you on this?"

"I think I am quite capable of such things," she stated firmly. "After the fuss Father caused over the farm, do you think, Mother, I would allow *him* to go off at me buying something as simple as a shop?"

"I see. You might have told me, your mother."

"And you would have told Father."

"Not necessarily, Alison." She shook her head, sorry her own daughter could not confide in her. "I don't have to tell him everything."

"I'm sorry then." She sighed with a shrug. "Anyway, it's done, and we can move in any time we like. It has its own accommodation." Alison did not tell her the accommodation would be a bit of a squeeze, yet she was sure they could make out.

It might have been acceptable to Thomas Chester for Jane to manage the dairy both before and after her marriage, and it might have been acceptable for Emily to take over her late husband's enterprises. It was not acceptable for his younger daughter, Alison, to buy a shop!

"You cannot run a shop and be a wife and mother," he informed her.

"I ran a farm and was also a wife and mother," Alison reminded him curtly, hoping to end the argument.

"Two different things . . ."

"Tell me how, Father?"

"How can you expect to serve customers and prepare meals for your husband — when he comes home — and children?"

"*That,* Father is something I shall have to learn to do." She did not suggest Sean might learn to cook, in a role reversal, until he was able to resume work — whatever that work might be. Nor did she suggest Adrienne was already taking on domestic responsibilities without having to be told to.

"You must learn the hard way, mustn't you?" Thomas grunted.

It was more than a challenge for Alison. She had to re-stock the shop, rapidly learn about the business — a far cry from farming — attend the needs of her family, and only once a week — on Sundays — visit Sean. Of course, that meant having someone in to mind her children: none old enough to act as mother for the day. One thing was certain, her family soon learned if they did not do things for themselves, then no one else would do them. Indeed they became a hard working unselfish family, although not without some disagreements, most often centred on Jennifer.

Alison lost the immediate help of her mother's invaluable presence when having to deal with the many domestic and child-rearing matters confronting her, although she gained the help of the fledgling Plunket Society: undoubtedly a boon for most mothers as it spread its assistance throughout the land, giving small children a better chance of survival, and, a healthier survival. That did not mean life was easy. The washhouse with its copper, rinsing tubs and wringer — a slight advantage over a mangle — was as much in use as the shop's small kitchen. Here three people were a crowd, where Kowhai could provide working space for six or eight.

Only Adrienne at going on eight was old enough to be of any help. Alison knew it was unfair on the girl to work her so hard, and vowed, when her daughter's turn came, she would ensure she returned the assistance. Many a wet Saturday afternoon or Sunday saw two wooden clothes horses in the shop festooned with nappies and numerous clothes in an almost vain attempt to get them dry. Again, unlike Kowhai, there was no space in the kitchen above the range for such hangings. The minute yard behind the shop hardly had space for hanging out so much washing when it was fine, and when windy she had to watch that the sheets did not brush against mouldy walls. Alison battled on, although the cheerful front she put on for her customers was just that: a façade. Adrienne, who shared the double bed with her, *was* asleep when she finally laid her to rest at night: sometimes so exhausted she cried for relief.

At least she was closer to the harbour. The timing was critical, since the Manukau reached to the heart of Waiuku only when the tide was full — it could be out as far as five miles — and Alison, having had her family up and breakfasted at an early hour, could catch the boat at the last minute, bay-hop down the estuary, or occasionally sail directly across it, should the boat not be the regular passenger service, then travel by tram to Newmarket, change to another tram, that took her up Khyber Pass Rd: the hospital so close yet so far, down Symonds St to Grafton Bridge — the huge, arched structure now part of the city's traffic system — and walk across it to the hospital. If the tide was not right she would return by tram to Newmarket, or on occasions walk there from the hospital, catch a train to Pukekohe, and young Penelope, despite her parent's protests, would be at the station to meet her. The arrangements took as much thought as thinking what she would tell Sean about the week just gone.

Nor did she sit idly on her various means of transport. She would either darn a few socks, write up her accounts for the week, or learn a little more of the trade she had bought herself into. The time she spent travelling was seldom enough to accomplish all three activities, especially if some neighbour insisted on chatting to her when she was only intent on learning. She did not mind talking while darning.

The summer staged its season. It made a curtain call at Easter, and bowed out.

The war seemed no nearer to an end.

Alison had her own battlefield: battalions of customers one minute, an empty shop the next: more so the latter than the former. It did worry her while she was serving one customer, others drifted out. Most probably returned, since she was the only drapery in town: in days long before supermarkets carried everything: generations before. Alison came up with an idea: one to cause customers to linger while she attended another's needs. She had Ben make her stand, and in a quite large vacant space where customers waited patiently, or impatiently, she placed articles on it for those people to notice, to toy with, and to buy, possibly on the spur of the moment. She did not patent the idea, just thought it clever marketing: although that word was not exactly known much about either.

Penny Caldwell, as she often did, dropped in one day.

"Good afternoon, young lady, can I help you?"

"Certainly, Mrs Sullivan." 'Mrs' in the shop: 'Aunt' out of it. "I would like five yards of blue ribbon — this wide," holding her fingers apart at concertinaing distances.

"Certainly, dear." Alas, part way through the service, a violent background disturbance arrested Alison's attention, and she was compelled to investigate.

Penny did not mind in the slightest. She swung round the counter, and ignoring Jennifer's screams, accurately measured her requirements. She was also interrupted — by a customer: a person unaware of the situation, only conscious of the turmoil behind the shop. Penny smiled, and offered very politely, "May I help you, Madam?"

"Yes, dear, I would like some silk thread to match this."

The girl ran her eyes down the display, selected a draw of pinks, and proceeded to match the colour. "I think we should look at this in the light," she advised, and crossed to the doorway to compare colours. "Yes, I think so. It is closer than this one, don't you think? You can never quite match them, can you?" she stated most authoritatively.

Anyone knew the price of silk thread, so the first Alison heard of the transaction was the winding of the till handle, and by the time she arrived the satisfied customer was only a silhouette in the doorway. "Dear, why didn't you tell me?" she lamented, because the loss of a sale, no matter how small, was important.

"I did not have to. I served her myself, and quite correctly, if I may say so."

"Darling, you good girl." Again Alison had tears in her eyes: tears this time of appreciation. A minor relief after what she had discovered out the back. Jennifer had smashed — deliberately smashed — Adrienne's doll.

Still sobbing her heart out Adrienne came into the shop, and clutched her mother's skirt.

"I know, darling, it was horrid and mean of her," Alison agreed, hugging the weeping child tighter.

"She broke my doll," the girl told Penny.

"That's naughty."

Penny decided she was too old now for her dolls, although she debated which one to give Adrienne, and felt a bit mean giving her the one she liked least.

"That is very kind of you, darling," Alison accepted. "Isn't it, Adrienne?"

The younger girl clutched the doll to her chest.

"Say thank you," her mother ordered tenderly.

"Thank you, Penny, so much."

And Penny felt even guiltier over only giving away her least-liked doll.

Penny Caldwell found herself with an after-school job. Not every day, just Thursdays and Fridays. She would have done it voluntarily, however Alison insisted on paying her a few pence — a generous two shillings actually — because the girl's help was such a relief.

Of course a certain person did not know of her daughter's after school antics. When she did learn, after Penny had run out of excuses for being late home, the woman exploded. "No Caldwell daughter has ever had to go out to work, and you are not going to be the first." She did not give Penelope the chance to appeal. "A schoolgirl — a mere child — slaving behind a counter." The lady was off to fetch her husband.

Penny went to her room, and set about doing her homework, as if her mother's words had gone in one ear and out the other.

At the dinner table Penny was again harangued. "I can imagine what everyone is saying. 'I saw Penelope Caldwell working. Fancy her mother sending her out to work — at her age. Or, she has to work for her own pocket money . . ?'"

To which Penelope interrupted, "You won't cut off my allowance, will you?"

"Are you listening to me?"

"Yes." She was not really. She was wondering how she could filch some extra peas off Nathan's plate. She happened to like veges, unlike some children.

"Now, I do not want to hear of you working in that shop again, understand?"

"No, Mother." Penelope by now had calculated work was a chore: something you *had* to do. Helping her aunt was fun: something she loved to do, like playing — playing shop. So, she would not work behind the counter, she would play behind it.

Promptly next day, Penelope returned to *play*: Alison not knowing of the previous night's altercation between the girl and her parents, and Penny was not going to jeopardise her 'play'.

Her father conceded first, although took a particularly dim view of the situation. Bad enough losing an opportunity to establish a financial interest in the valley, however to now have a second member of his family siding with the Chesters was a catastrophe. He could barely hold up his head, believing everyone in town must think it was a great joke. He would bide his time, and when the opportunity again arose he would pounce, and land right beside the Chesters, on one property or another.

During the war years George Chester had progressed from being a sheepo, ensuring pens were full for the shearers, to a fleeco, who gathered up the shorn wool, then to a slow shearer, known as a drummer, and now in his mid-teens was as good as any local ringer, although admittedly the competition was not high with so many experienced shearers overseas. Still seventy sheep a day hand-shorn wasn't too bad. Shearing was very much a family affair, with James and little sister Kathy working in or outside the shed, and irrepressible Penny at every opportunity pitching in. The classing was left to Ben, while Priscilla and Louise kept their extended family plied with food and drinks.

CHAPTER SIXTEEN

Annabelle, Alison's bridesmaid, had deferred getting married. She had met fine men over the years, yet for one reason or another, could not fall in love with them. To the extent, she often asked herself, 'Is there something wrong with me?' She knew there was nothing physically wrong with her, yet something in her make-up made it difficult for her to communicate with men. Every so often she thought back to Sean. She knew very well what her feelings for him were at the time, so remained ever envious of Alison: not spitefully so.

Then, along came a rather nice man, whom she decided, rather than desired, was right for her, or near enough. With less Maori blood than herself, he combined the best features of the two races. Besides, he was kind and gentle, something Annabelle did want in a husband. So, they got married. For a while they lived with her family, then moved into their own rooms in Pukekohe, both getting market garden work. And life became routine.

Very routine, because, although their relationship was not passionate, not that it should have had anything to do with it, Annabelle remained childless. By 1915 that factor became more important, when her husband was duty bound to enlist, so went to war. For Annabelle, life was lonely, because she was a rarity: a wife but not a mother, particularly in her family's eyes. Her father wanted to know what was wrong with her, although her elderly grandmother was more understanding, advising her son, 'Some women have babies, others don't. So there's no use you going on about it, Boy.'

Either way, Annabelle felt alienated, and drifted from her family, from her market garden work, and although she knew she could be better employed, drifted into domestic positions, eventually moving to Waiuku. For a woman of her intelligence, it was hardly satisfying. She now found herself a cause for undesirable attention, and so low did she feel on occasions very nearly accepted that attention out of sheer loneliness.

She had gone to her family's place, stayed overnight, visited a friend closer to Pollok wharf, and caught a late Sunday afternoon boat from there to Waiuku, sat among cargo, with a sigh, and as they crossed a particular bay, recalled the occasion when she and Alison had swum there.

"Annabelle?" a soft voice called her.

She looked up, squinted as the low sun partially blinded her, silhouetting the speaker, the voice was familiar.

"Annabelle, it's me, Alison."

"Ali!" She leapt up. "Ali, fancy you being on board. I was just . . ."

And away they went, chatting endlessly during the short journey, both spilling out their stories and their present troubles.

"So, how long then have you been living at Waiuku?" Alison wanted to know.

"Only a week or two."

"That's why I haven't seen you." She sighed with relief, hating to think they had been living for months in the same town without knowing it: hardly likely in Alison's case, because being a shopkeeper, most local ladies at least entered her life.

For Annabelle, also a relief. At least she had someone whom she could talk to, although they were now worlds apart. It need not be so. Annabelle would gladly spend Sunday's minding Alison's children, if she were asked. Alison would love to have a friend minding her children, except it would be imposing on her. Eventually their thoughts fused, and Annabelle regularly looked after Alison's children. Not always, for she sometimes had her own life to lead, so Alison had to resort to having friends and family help out.

Annabelle began to learn a little of Alison's drapery business, with the view of improving her position. She knew very well there was little chance of Alison needing her as an assistant, although she could get a position in a bigger town, or in Auckland. She thought of that as a possible new career, while thoughts of her husband returning and maybe having a family diminished.

They diminished totally when she got the dreaded information:
the same notice so many wives and families throughout New
Zealand received. What saddened her more, her husband had died
knowing he had no son to carry on his name. She felt she had let
him down, and for a long time could not face her father, lest he rub
salt into her wounds. Alison was sympathetic, and they took up
their friendship from where it had left off years earlier, although
under vastly different circumstances. A scene was about to change,
when Annabelle for some obscure reason, thought she was in the
way, even not wanted, so again sought new horizons, although
promised to keep in touch with Alison.

Alison was looking forward to the day when Jennifer started
school. Her mood swings, temper, moroseness were nothing
strange to Alison. She had seen it all before: with her lost sister. Her
elder daughter Adrienne was an angel: most of the time, when she
wasn't getting up to mischief with Patrick. Impish mischief: nothing
to be concerned about. Jennifer however could not be her child.
She had to be Jane's. 'How could I have produced another Jane?'
she berated herself. 'How could I?'

*　　*　　*　　*　　*　　*

Priscilla collapsed on the couch.

She turned a blind eye to the mess around her. The day had
been wet, so the children had been confined to barracks. That
meant her husband would have to lift his big feet to dodge the
strewn toys. She closed her eyes, and slipped into a dream: a dream
the war had ended, and the men were returning to their farms,
Danny coming home. Victory did not appear in her dream. As if
there had been no victory, no conquest. If one two or European
countries lost their thrones, her dream visualised that as being the
price of war. The important thing, they were coming home.

Home!

"I'm home!"

"Mm."

"I'm home. — Famished." Ben Chester looked down at his wife. "Have you been asleep?"

"Mm. Oh, Ben dear. — I was dreaming."

"I've been dreaming of a good meal for hours."

"I suppose you have. How can you possibly see out there at this time of night?"

"I've developed owls' eyes," he said. "Can't you get them to clean up?"

"I was just too pleased they all went to bed."

"All? How many are here?"

"Just four: two of ours and the twins."

Ben did not have to ask how she coped. After all, four was relatively few. However having two extra, on top of everything else, was a handful. A lot harder, he supposed, than rounding up a herd of cattle in the dark. At least a moon had played on the rugged scene between passing showers.

It had been a strange season all round: a spring void of splendour, only the awakening of the trees identifying it from winter. Although the days were drawing out, they were as cold, and certainly as wet, as winter. Perhaps also because not a solitary bleat had been heard from any of the Chester farms. Only Morton Conway's property had a few lambs, and they were generally kept at the far end, their cries unheard at Kanuka, Ben's place. Conway was not there, and the promised manager never eventuated, so the Chester clan cared for the lost farm as well as their own three.

Having seen his wife in a state of exhaustion, Ben returned to the kitchen, opened the range door, and there, as he expected, was a plate of hot food: the meat a little dry on the edges, although good enough for him, and he wolfed it down. His wife cleared a few toys away, then came to the kitchen, shifting the simmering kettle so it would boil, and made a pot of tea.

Sitting at the table opposite her husband, she rested her elbows on it, then rubbed her eyes. "I'm still half asleep."

"You had better go to bed then."

"I think I shall, dear." Looking at the unwashed dishes, she said. "This lot can wait 'til morning." With that, she walked round the table, clasped her husband's shoulder, kissed his cheek, and apologised, "I'm sorry, dear. I'm just so tired."

"I suppose you are," was all Ben could say, because he did not really understand how mental fatigue could be as exhausting as his physical fatigue. Not uncommon now for Alison's twins to stay at Kanuka when she went to Auckland to visit Sean. Alison would sometimes take her elder daughter with her, leaving her son Patrick and Jennifer with Annabelle (before she left Waiuku), or other friends. Annabelle and the friends described Jennifer being as good as gold, and Alison only wished she would be the same at home. Obviously what she could get away with at home she could not get away with elsewhere.

So, this weekend Priscilla had the Sullivan twins, her own daughter, Kathy, and her lost sister's son, Douglas. As she undressed for bed she reflected, with a sigh, 'Douglas *is* a loner. Funny he and Kathy should get on so well. — Not too well, I hope? I suppose at their age they would hardly be up to anything.' She sighed. 'You never know with introverted boys. Perhaps I'm judging him by others. I just wish he would be more open.'

Priscilla may have retired early, the mother whose twins she was looking after, was wide-awake. This had been the first time since selling the property and buying the shop she, when in the city, had stayed with Emily. The reason she was wide awake, was because Emily was haranguing her.

"Why on earth, Ali, did you not tell me?"

"About what?"

"Having to sell the farm."

"Em, you had enough to think about."

"Oh, such as?" She shook her head in frustration. "I shall tell you what I was thinking. I was thinking about my nephew's future at that very same time." She took a sip of her milk drink: a remedy she insisted made her sleep well at night. Alison did not see her put anything, like brandy, into the drink, so it must be pure.

Alison tried to figure out whom she was talking about, although Emily identified the nephew. "Do you think for one moment that stingy brother of mine is going to give anything to Stanley? Not on your life. The boy has been ostracised."

"I — I suppose he has."

"So, how is he going to make out? He is wrapped in farming. Where will he ever get the money to buy one? Tell me that?"

"I don't think any of us have thought about that, Em." Which was true; no one gave a thought of the future. They all just got through each day as it came. In those seconds Alison considered that while the Chester boys would inherit something, Stanley, after all his work, would be left out in the cold, probably to fend for himself. On the other hand she could not imagine her parents would allow that to happen.

"Ali, you know the farm next to Danny's went up for sale — it must have been about the same time as your place."

"Yes, that is what made it hard to sell ours. I was surprised Mr Conway chose our place."

"He did *not* have a choice. Someone told me about the other place. No one told me about you, did they?"

Alison shrugged.

"Not even you, Ali. — Why? — Why?"

Apart from not burdening Emily with her problems, Alison knew very well why they did not even mention the sale to her. For the very reason Emily had said.

"Conway did *not* have a choice, dear, because I bought the other place."

"You? — B-But."

"I have never set foot on it. I have a manager on it . . ."

"We knew he was a manager, but . . ."

"He does not even know who owns it." Emily shook her head. "Ali, I did not want anyone to get a whiff of what I had done; especially not Stanley."

"He is too young."

"Certainly, Ali, too young now, although with his experience, he will not be in a few years." Then she cautioned Alison. "Now, you know. Promise me not to let the cat out of the bag."

"That is very good of you, Em. So where do Sean and I fit in?"

"Silly. I would have bought your place off you."

"That would have been too much to ask."

"No, Ali. I might not have done it so much for your sake, rather than trick my brother." She shook her head, blonde tresses escaping her french roll. "I have since heard all about that too. I am just so sorry, Ali, I was not in the know."

Alison sighed. On one hand it would have been wonderful to remain on the farm, assuming Emily would have kept them on as managers, although that would have been impossible. Now, at least, she was independent — apart from having neighbours and relations help out at times like this. Those difficult times would soon be over also. Sean had regained sufficient use of his legs to at least walk with the help of crutches, and the next step for him was at long last to be able to leave the hospital. However, that would bring problems at home. Alison had become so much her own boss, running both the household and the shop, she wondered just how Sean would fit back in, as customary head of the house.

Then Emily suggested, "I could buy the farm off this Conway chap?"

Alison shook her head. "That is very kind of you, Em. However what is done is done." She added with a wry smile. "In fact I am quite happy running the shop. I did not think I'd ever want to live anywhere else except on a farm, but I don't mind being in town at all now, honestly."

"Oh well," Emily accepted. "The offer is always there, if you change your mind."

Alison reached out and took the other's arm. "You are an angel."

Emily blinked: blinked back sudden emotion. "I do not think some people would agree with you calling me that."

"You are, Em, honestly." And Alison meant it. She was angry anyone could think otherwise of Emily. To her Emily had a heart of gold, and if she just happened to like men, well that was her business. It never did anyone else any harm, so why should they be critical. She thought for some, it was perhaps a case of sour grapes, or an expression like that, and wishing a handsome man would whisk them off their feet. Why, she herself had thought the same, and recently. Some very fine looking gentlemen had passed by her door this last year, and despite everything, she did keep up her appearances. She knew when people learned she had five children, they were surprised, because she did not show it — outwardly. She certainly did inwardly, when all five were harassing her at one time.

There were lighter moments during this dark time.

"We're off to the circus on Saturday," young George Chester advised his grandmother with an air of finality.

"Oh, and pray who is taking you?" She knew he could well take himself, yet sensed her entire tribe of grandchildren and co were part of this walkout.

George bowed his head, toyed with the tablecloth. "Gran, it's like this. I'm taking Stanley, and Stanley's taking Douglas, and . . ."

"I see. All the way down the line." Louise nodded with a knowing smile. She would gladly take them all to the circus, although sensed they wanted to go on their own. For one day — or was it two — the big top would be at Waiuku, and every child up and down the peninsula, and for miles around wished to see it. War, or no war, the show must go on. For these youthful farmers a welcome respite to their daily tasks. They had long since discovered it was one thing to have to attend school five days a week, and quite another to work seven days a week, and, without holidays.

So, early that Saturday, the team piled on to a cart, wound their way out of the valley, and joined the well-spaced procession already on the move. George had the reins, Stanley beside him, with James, Kathy, Douglas and the orphans, Ngaire and Tane on the tray. They did not hurry, just plodded along, with all the time in the world to get there.

Down Mill Hill, and from crest to crest every fifty yards or so was a horse and cart, or just a horse and rider — or two, or three: some sturdy animals allowing three children on their backs. For those who had no transport, only a matter of waiting at their gate, to be scooped up by the first not too full cart. And even if no one brought them home again, six or eight or even ten miles was not too far to walk.

Black, brown, piebald, draught wound their way to the circus.
The Chesters still had room on their cart when they detoured to
collect Penelope. No show would be complete without Penny
Caldwell. And there waiting for them at the entrance of the
paddock were Adrienne, Patrick and Jennifer, all resplendent in new
clothes: courtesy of their mother's occupation.

Their problem now was: how to get in without paying?
They had their admission money, and a penny or two to spend.
If they could somehow wriggle — and squirm — under the tent,
They'd get in for free, and have twice the money to spend.
While some of them — not all were party to the plan —
Sneaked about looking for a likely spot,
Another — Penny Caldwell — the richest of the lot —
Slunk past the pre-occupied doorman,
And found herself a ringside spot.
She glanced about for her cousins,
Alas, they had been discovered,
And with shame cast upon them, paid up,
Then plonked themselves solemnly beside Penelope.
"I'll shout the sweets," she said, "If you want."

That offer was the remnants of the girl within Penny. Her cousin
George happened to be sitting on one side of her — she almost
ignored whoever was on the other — brought out those womanly
feelings. She had matured in some ways, and George had also in
others: mainly because of the life the war had forced on to him.
Several times during the excitement, Penny clutched George's arm,
and uttered exclamations, such as: "Wow, George, that was great!
— This is fun!" Then more to the point, "I'm glad I'm here with you,
George!" George however was too engrossed in the action within
the rings to take anything from Penny's actions out of them. Ngaire
was two or three places away from George, and besides, she had
transferred her interest to the post boy, not that she saw much of
him.

Penny sighed, and decided since George wasn't taking her bait,
she would have to get to like one of the local lads. Anyway, with

George stuck on the farm miles away, she hardly ever saw him. Not as much as she'd like to.

So much for the circus: its clowns, trapeze, lions and tigers, horses and donkeys, a monkey or two. For the children it was the ultimate in entertainment, although Penelope bragged that she had been to a picture house, although did not get in for free. Her words were actually a last ditch stand that day to impress George. He was too busy rounding up the tribe to take notice of her comment. Not that he had complete control over them. The children generally made their own entertainment, and their own mischief . . .

. . . Like on the way home when they, including George, discovered someone else's fruit to be tastier than their own. At that time of year it was decidedly green.

"Gid-ou-ovit!" raged the owner.

"C'mon, let's scram."

On to the cart and away.

A shot rang out, the pellets missing by miles, although scaring the pants off them. They were soon out of verbal and firing range. Alas, the excitement of the circus must have upset Douglas. That night he was a very sick boy. Louise Chester wheedled the truth out of George, and young man or not, he and the rest of them at Kowhai were commanded to open their mouths, and reluctantly swallow a spoonful of castor oil.

*   *   *   *   *   *

The clip was worse than expected. Ben baled only two thirds of that baled the previous year. His only hope now there would be a price rise. His luck had run dry, this year, 1918, the national export being 62% of the previous year, and prices remained firm. Nor was there anything from the mutton or lamb side of the business, because none and been disposed of: Ben keeping the few lambs. Dairying now only provided for the family's needs.

To add to the misery of low returns, two gales thrashed the land with the waning summer, and a third was to come during the winter. If the wind and rain were not bad enough, frosts descended, blanketing Auckland and particularly the sheltered pastoral valleys. The year was rapidly becoming the worst in the city's history. And there was worse to come. In the valley a slip rendered the old valley road impassable. They did not have time to clear it, and by the time they did, they had forgotten what had been a short-cut to Pollok. Besides, the rest of the road had sprouted weeds.

Mans own wrath was nearing its end: largely because the human resources of the contestants were almost depleted. The soldiers were not the naive and eager warriors of four years before. In fact their ego had died long ago, as they had done.

The European summer opened with Germany making bold strikes, once again threatening Paris, and being repelled with their goal just over the horizon. The British were on the advance in Turkey's stinking heat: this alone killing many men: the heat and disease. Originally neutral, Greece now joined the British against Bulgaria. The enemy's neighbour Romania fell by the wayside. Hungary was collapsing, its energy spent. The Russian front was no more, although earlier Austria had been crippled by revolutionary armies. Now the Italians struck at Austria across the Alps, while Germany braced itself for an offensive from forces accumulating in France. One wonders now how they managed to sort themselves out sufficiently to fight.

The tide had ebbed. Germany could not draw it in, although America could turn it — by manpower alone. Not by strategy or magnificent manoeuvres. They were sweeping across Europe, gathering up Allied forces, and engulfing the enemy in victorious waves. Their numbers alone encouraged the Allies to rise once more and join the great offensive.

Thomas Chester followed every action, although only received weekly reports, since they did not get a daily paper, and wireless was still in the future. "Well, dear," he announced to his wife, "I think the end is near. Those Americans came just in time."

"Are they much better than our men?" she questioned, hating to think any soldier was superior to an Anzac — giving the Australians their due.

"No, my dear, no better. This is a battle of numbers now."

"I see. I hope you are right."

"See what Danny says on his last whiz-back." He picked up the post card type mail and re-read the scrawl.

Where (sic) sixty miles from last time. Wow, that was close. My mate Claud copped it yestaday. We can shout at them. Cherio, Danny.

Thomas again plotted his son-in-law's progress on a large map of Europe he monitored, although the locations were more by guess than fact, then he allowed the subject to drop, reading other aspects of the *Weekly News*.

This year three of the four farms resounded to the bleat of infant lambs, and baas of responding ewes: almost four hundred lambs contributing to the orchestration of spring. All seemed well on the farms.

All was reasonably well with Alison in her drapery. Sean was home, able to hobble about. The one aspect that concerned him; he was no longer in charge of his own house. Much as his wife tried to make him part of the family again, it was to their mother the children went; to their mother salesmen called upon, and he often heard her laughter as she joked with them. He feared one day a traveller would sweep her off her feet, and she might just run off, leaving husband and family to fend for themselves. He never broached the subject, and therefore never understood Alison, although independent of him, was very much wedded to both her shop and her family. She revelled in it. From the carefree girl *he* has swept off her feet, to the mature mother and businesswoman.

Germany faced at Allies alone, and although her armies resisted the colossal forces, her heart collapsed, and it was all but over.

The world was about to rejoice!

New Zealand died — seven thousand deaths!

Died of an unseen cause: an influenza epidemic spreading across the country, indiscriminately choosing its victims, not sparing those who sought to escape. It mattered not whether one lived with the 'flu or fled from it. Auckland caught it first, apparently from some homecoming soldiers aboard the *Niagara*, which had not been quarantined. It concussed the already stunned nation: casualties comparable to the preceding four years of war. Beauty queen on Saturday; dead by Wednesday.

Jennifer went down, as did others in the district.

It did not do much for Thomas' religious opinions. Surely they had suffered enough to be spared a reprisal: as if because they had physically escaped the war, this swift, sneering death must torture them.

A telegram boy on horseback arrived at Kowhai, and Thomas braced himself for written word of Jennifer's death, thinking strange that Alison should have advised them like this. It was not from his daughter.

> *We regret that Private Daniel Carsen has died from*
> *injuries received while serving in France.*

Thomas gazed at the form, his eyes focussing on the name 'Carsen.' He shook his head, looked at the boy, wondering why he was just standing there, then realised he needed to be paid. He fossicked round for the fee, even tipping the messenger.

"Louise," he called.

As usual, in the kitchen, his wife frowned. She was 'Mother', not Louise. "Yes, dear," she replied hesitantly.

Thomas entered, and the first thing she noticed was the telegram. "Danny," he murmured, tears rolling down his weathered cheeks. His wife looked at the paper then her husband's tears, and need not be told anything further.

They would have to tell Douglas the one thing, the one person who kept him hopeful would never return. They would also have to tell Danny's mother. Louise decided to do this herself, hitched a horse up to her gig that very hour, drove slowly along the farm drive, poplars glistening in the sun, rain drops sparkling like crystals. Any other time she would have appreciated the beauty. Now, she gave it only a passing glance, then edged her horse cautiously out of the valley. She did think of calling in on Ben: half-expecting him to have heard the news directly from her husband by telephone, and be waiting at his gate to at least escort his mother. No, there was no sign of her son.

Louise was going to need a lot of courage and strength that day.

Mrs Carsen never learned of her son's death. She had succumbed to the epidemic only the day before, and a friend had everything in hand. So Louise could do no more than turn her horse and gig round and plod back towards her own place. She thought Danny had died so they could live in comfort. She had time to dwell on what the war had been fought over. And it all seemed so trivial.

There was now someone waiting at the top of Ben's drive, and as Louise slowly approached, she recognised her husband, and her frown deepened.

"We are needed down there," he said, nodding his wet face toward his son's home.

Louise looked at him blankly, her heart missing a beat, dizziness threatening to topple her, before she knew why they were needed. She moved aside to allow Thomas to take the reins.

It had rained heavily during the night: a downpour from the heat of early summer. Morning had broken fine: pleasant enough for Kathy and a young friend to go jauntily down Kanuka's valley, with its steep walls, its replenished creek tumbling over rocks.

"Oh, here are the lambs. Haven't they grown," Kathy pointed.

"Aren't they pretty?"

"Look over there. We've had a landslide. Daddy will be so annoyed. We had a big one there once. But I was too young to remember."

"Let's have a look. There may be some gold."

"Don't be silly. There's no gold around here."

"Might be."

Their discovery would lead to gold: although not what they imagined.

Kathy's friend peered intently at the fallen land and scrub. She peered even more intently, before screaming. "Kathy — Kathy! — Ugh! — Come here, quickly!"

Kathy Chester scrambled across the rugged ground.

"Don't touch it. Come away," begged the discoverer.

Kathy bent down, and looked at the skeletal hand. "What's that on the finger?"

"Don't touch it. — Come away."

They both fled, as if the ghost of that hand was chasing them: its bony fingers reaching for their necks.

"Daddy! — Daddy!" Kathy screamed, long before reaching their house, "Daddy? — Where are you, Daddy?"

Her mother rushed to the door, as Kathy ran first one way, then the other. "He's around the side. — Why?"

"Mummy, we've found a skeleton."

"A *what?*" Priscilla ran after the girls, mud splashing up her dress.

Ben's response, "What sort of skeleton?" For all he knew it might have been of a sheep.

"A body. — A person, Daddy."

Ben bit his lip. Still, it might be that of an ancient Maori, lost many years ago. Yet how come he had never discovered it? Then he learned about the new slip, and apprehension gripped him. He knew, felt within, that an ancient skeleton had not suddenly reappeared. He and his wife followed the girls back down the valley.

"There it is," Kathy pointed.

Ben stopped, looked around for his wife, reached for her hand, and together they approached the scattered remains.

"Go back to the house, Girls," Priscilla ordered. "*Now!*" She did not want her daughter to see her father vanquished. Ben had never been the same man since that day his canal draining efforts had brought much of the valley wall crashing down. She watched her husband reach down and take the ring from an outstretched finger, take a handkerchief from his pocket, and almost reverently clean it, locate the inscription, then look up at the sky, his mouth quivering.

"Who?" she pleaded.

Ben's eyes lowered from the sky, to the steep hills he had transformed, to the earth at his feet. He looked at his wife, and she saw in his glistening eyes life mirrored: triumph and tragedy, victory and defeat. She saw the young man who had swept her off her feet to propose, then conquer the land given to him by his father. She saw the land rent, and then the war where Danny had gone, never to return, as they had only that morning learned. She saw Sean's limp form, his long recovery. There had been three of them, and Ben's father. Now there was only one — one able to work — and he at that moment, defeated.

As he raised his hand to his ashen face, Priscilla again asked, "Who?"

He sobbed one word, "Jane!"

Introduction to:

Book Two

NEAP TIDE

CHAPTER ONE

September, 1924

A gale squeezed through the gap, levelled hillside grass, surged over crests, bowed poplars and slammed into valley buildings. Nature unleashed: mightier than any of man's creations: like the motor lorry precariously winding around those sodden hills.

Thomas Chester had set his sights on that lorry from the moment it appeared at the top of the south valley. He scoffed at whoever was fool enough to be travelling in such atrocious conditions. The storm had not arrived out of the blue, rather had been building for two days, so they were not caught out. Thomas kept his spyglass on the vehicle as it trundled along the ridge road, disappeared behind mounds, reappeared, lurched alarmingly, miraculously kept on track. "That's the trouble with people today — they can never wait five minutes."

Said half-aloud, although his wife — having a rare lie in this morning reading a book — heard the remark, and raised her eyes at her husband standing at the window. "I don't recall bad weather stopping you doing anything," she opined.

"I only did what was necessary," he reminded her gruffly. "I did not go driving round the countryside."

From the bedroom his view cleared the trees, so curiosity made him follow the lorry to see how far it got. What he next saw displeased him. He could see the tarpaulin-covered shapes on the tray looked like furniture, and now glimpsed the occupants. The vehicle stopped at the top of the track into the valley, and Thomas muttered, "Yes, Conway, you're at the right place — fool!" Turning to his wife, he advised, "The Conways have decided to come." He had received a letter from Conway only the week before indicating they would be moving into the valley, to finally take possession of their farm.

"Today?" Louise questioned.

"Yes — today." Expelling his breath Thomas strode from the room, while his wife flung the blankets from her, gathered up her clothes to take down to the bathroom.

From the landing Thomas roared, "George! — James! — Are you down there?"

From the drawing-cum-billiard room, his younger grandson muttered, "Now what does he want?" He thought on a day such as this, having milked the cows, they could relax.

Thomas took another look out of the bedroom window, returned to the landing, and leaned over the railing. "You two laggards, get your gear on — now!" . . .

. . . Another squall thrashed through the gap, sideswiping them as they rode along the drive. They exchanged abuse, not at each other, instead at this Conway character, who had only two or three times since his purchase of their aunt's place during the Great War set foot on the property, yet had chosen this day to settle.

"I can feel the old man's eyes drilling a hole in . . ." James' words trailed off as he sighted the object of their mercy dash. Objects, plural, of their mercy dash. Several years before Morton Conway had visited, towing his two young daughters. They were not being towed now — they were attempting to shove the motor lorry from the ditch he had slewed into.

Amazing the change of attitude at the sight of such beauty. "G'dday folks!" George hailed, tipping his hat, water spilling down his face, causing one of the girls to clasp her hand to her mouth to hide her laughter. Undaunted George offered, "In trouble?" He slipped from his horse. "Right then, we'll have you out in a jiffy."

"Oh, please help us, Sir," the same girl now pleaded, splaying her hands.

George noticed her wide, blue eyes. "Our pleasure," he assured, while James muttered something like:

"That's not what you were saying . . ."

"Yes, we're experts at this sort of . . ." George attempted to assure the girls.

"I don't recall you dragging anything like this out of a ditch." Carts they had retrieved from ditches, but not laden motor lorries.

"Did you make a comment, James?"

"No — no, Brother. I was just suggesting you tell the young ladies to step aside."

"Are you two going to push, or just stand there gawking?" That comment came from Morton Conway, still perched lopsidedly in the cab.

"We're just — ah . . ."

"They are working out how to do it, Father," explained the only daughter who had so far spoken. Not that the boys knew, because they had changed positions, and being identical, even similarly attired, neither knew who was who. They did not know one 'who' let alone two by name.

"You just steer it, Sir," George advised, and put his shoulder to the back of the lorry. James added his strength. Push and shove as they might, the vehicle barely budged.

Splashing through the mud, choosing the ditch side, one of the girls braced herself against the tray, and in between heaves, gasped to George alongside her, "I'm Alice."

"Nice to know you," he grunted back. "I'm Saint George." Flicking his head towards his brother he indicated, "He's brother, James — the dragon." It got him a laugh. Again, those incredibly appealing eyes charmed him.

The second girl braced herself next to James, although omitted to introduce herself. Their combined effort did the trick. United we stand — divided we fall: and Alice fell flat on her face.

George shamed Raleigh: scooping her from the muddy ditch, Alice momentarily clasping her arms round his neck before he stood her upright in the middle of the track. "Oh, what a mess I'm in," she spluttered, then smiled. "Thank you, kind Sir." Despite her condition her heart fluttered ever so slightly.

"Don't thank him, Lady," James scoffed. "He thought you were blocking the ditch."

"I'm sure he gave no such . . ."

"I s'pose it's your best dress too," George lamented, not that he could see much of what she was wearing beneath her sou-wester.

She looked down at herself and repeated, "I am in a mess. I'm afraid it was, but never . . ."

"Fibber," blurted her sister. "Your best dress is on the . . . Father! — Father!"

"Blimey!"

While youth had been play-acting, the lorry was freewheeling down the treacherous drive.

"Giddy up!" James yelled after him.

"Stop him!" Alice screamed. "Stop him!"

"Oh, he'll stop alright," assured James.

C.J